WOLFEBLOOD

A MEDIEVAL ROMANCE

BY KATHRYN LE VEQUE

PART OF THE DE WOLFE PACK
GENERATIONS SERIES

Print Edition

Text by Kathryn Le Veque
Cover by Kim Killion

KATHRYN LE VEQUE
NOVELS

WWW.KATHRYNLEVEQUE.COM

ARE YOU SIGNED UP FOR KATHRYN'S BLOG?

You'll get the latest news and information on exclusive giveaways, exclusive excerpts, coming releases, sales, free books, cover reveals and more.

Kathryn's blog followers get it all first. No spam, no junk.

Get the latest info from the reigning Queen of English Medieval Romance!

Sign Up Here

De Wolfe Motto: *Fortis in arduis*

Strength in times of trouble

What happens when a high-bred, proper lady meets up with a knight who kills with his bare hands and has no problem breaking wind in front of mixed company?

Chaos and hilarity ensues!

- Enemies to Lovers
- Forced marriage
- Feuding Families
- And more!

Gareth "Gar" de Wolfe, son of Troy and Rhoswyn (DarkWolfe), is a savage among knights. A knight's knight with the killer de Wolfe instinct, he is a rabid supporter of the king and much decorated in battle. He's rough around the edges, sleeps with his dogs, sups with his soldiers, half Scots and half English, and all man. There is no warrior more admired on the Scottish borders than Gar de Wolfe.

Enter Lady Matilda "Mattie" de Reyne.

There is no more refined lady in all of England than Mattie. She is what all ladies aspire to be—proper, full of manners and grace, speaks five languages, reads, writes poetry, and paints like a master. The list goes on. She comes from a family of refined people, her brothers included, and long ago, a betrothal was made between her father and Troy de Wolfe to join their children in matrimony. The pair have only met once, when they were younger, so to say that Mattie is in for a rude awakening when she finally meets her betrothed on the eve of their wedding is an understatement.

In fact, she refuses to marry him.

All Gar knows is that he has a task to complete—an order to fulfill—with the marriage and he's bloody well going to do it. All Mattie knows is that she wants nothing to do with the big, burly knight who smells like sewage. But Mattie doesn't know that Gar, beneath the dirt and savagery, is a man with a kind, soft, mortal heart, something he keeps carefully hidden.

It'll take the right woman to bring it out.

Join Gar and Mattie on the romance of a lifetime as the refined lady tries to help the savage knight find the true man within himself. From the brutality of the wars with the Scots to the political winds of England's politics, WolfeBlood is an epic Historical Romance.

AUTHOR'S NOTE

Get ready for a sexy, bloody tale!

I think I estimated, at one point, that William de Wolfe had over forty grandsons (and counting). In the case of Scott and Troy, having married super young and then lost their wives, they married again and had more children, so there are more families and more generations of de Wolfe grandchildren. I've written stories for Scott's eldest (with Athena de Norville), Troy's eldest (with Helene de Norville), all four of Patrick's sons, James' eldest (with Rose Hage), Edward's eldest (with Cassiopeia de Norville), but not Thomas'—not yet. He was so much younger than his brothers that by the time his boys mature into storytelling material, there are going to be de Wolfe great-grandsons to write stories about.

Literally, the never-ending series!

This is such a personal series for me because it was my first big one. Back in the day when I first wrote *The Wolfe*—the story that all of the others have sprung from—there was no such thing as a series. "The Wolfe" was a stand-alone and there had never been any intention on my part to write a series, but when Indie publishing began to take off in 2012, readers were the ones who began to form the market for series. They loved *The Wolfe* and wanted more, so that's when I wrote *Nighthawk*, Patrick's book. Honestly, at that point, all I knew was that William and Jordan had only had Scott, Troy, and Patrick—no other de Wolfe cubs were ever named in *The Wolfe*, so I came up with James (after my own son), Edward (named for William's father, Edward de Wolfe), and Thomas (named after Jordan's father). I added Katheryn, Evelyn, and Penelope just so they'd have a few daughters. And the de Wolfe progeny were formed.

De Wolfe Pack Generations has been a great opportunity to show the exponential progression of the de Wolfe family. In this particular book, we have Gareth "Gar" de Wolfe, the eldest child of Troy and Rhoswyn from *Darkwolfe*. Troy's eldest with Helene is Andreas, and he had his story told in *Wolfeblade*. Now, we've got Andreas' younger brother in Gar. Half English, half Scots, and all de Wolfe. Remember that Gar's mother, Rhoswyn, was a warrior in her own right, so Gar has it in his blood on both sides.

Let's just say he's a knight's knight, a warrior to the bone.

The House of de Bourne is briefly mentioned in this story. You'll remember them from *The Dark Spawn*—Ares, Atlas, and Anteaus (Anteaus is now part of the Blackchurch Series). Keep in mind that *The Dark Spawn* happened seventy-something years before this story is set, so the Ares de Bourne mentioned in this tale is a grandson of the original. Not the same guy. Eventually, I will have a series revolving around the original Ares, Atlas, and Anteaus, slated to start in 2028. I'm excited to get to it because I absolutely adored the brothers in *The Dark Spawn*.

Let me talk briefly about the setting for this novel. In *Wolfeblade*, I used The Hermitage castle in the Liddesdale Valley, a very famous fortress with a unique design. I've mentioned before that Wolfe's Lair, the crown of the de Wolfe castles, also has a similar design. Now, we have *Gleann na Fola* Castle, which essentially means "Valley of Blood" in Gaelic. It is located to the southwest of The Hermitage, set within the ancient Forest of Nichol, right on the Scots border in a desolate area that has been called "The Debatable Lands" for centuries. But there is a valley there—easy access to any invading army from the south to gain traction into Scotland—and that's what Gleann na Fola is guarding. It's remote, but strategic, and in my world, the same designer who built The Hermitage built Gleann na Fola in essentially the same design, as a guardhouse against invasion. It's an enormous, well-fortified castle that protects the Gleann na Fola Valley—i.e., the Valley of Blood—because of its easy access from the borders. (Not so.) Fun fact: the Liddesdale Valley, where The Hermitage rests, is called the bloodiest valley in Britain. Gleann na Fola is to the south, same area, and given basically the same name. That should tell you what kind of battles they've had there.

Nasty ones.

Now… a final word… it's well established in the canon of the de Wolfe Pack that William de Wolfe died in 1296 A.D. That is the year in which our story is set. I will state, clearly, that he does not die in this novel. I'm not prepared to do that. But it is the year he passes away, and perhaps this novel—chronologically speaking—is the last time he makes an appearance, so enjoy it. It's William at his finest and he will always be my favorite hero.

The usual pronunciation guide:
Ean—Basically, Ian. EE-in
Gleann na Fola—Glenna-foal-uh

And that's it!

Now, we begin. Welcome to *WolfeBlood*. It's a heck of a love story and a worthy addition to the de Wolfe Pack series.

Happy Reading!

Kathryn

PREFACE

The Mystery of the Patchwork Pants

Victoria and Albert Museum
South Kensington
London—Present Day

"WHY ARE WE here again?"

It was a bright spring day in London, cold in the shadows and shade, but warm if one was standing in the sun. Given that it was a Saturday, people seemed to be out in force on the streets, dressed in jumpers and boots, but also sleeveless tops for the women in the hope that they could feel some of that sun on their shoulders when they weren't under the canopy of the occasional tree.

"We're here because I have to do some research in their textiles section." A young woman with blonde hair, pulled back into a messy bun, spoke. "I'm doing it because it's part of my thesis in my Industrial Revolution module."

"But why textiles?"

"Because no one else will be talking about them," the blonde said. "I want something unique in my paper, something pertinent. Honestly, Heather, I told you that. You need to listen when I speak."

Heather, the brunette with the braids and a dark blue beret on her head, grinned. "You need to see the Leman collection," she said. "Besides, I know that textiles were transformed during the Industrial Revolution from smaller businesses to big factories. See? I *do* listen, Katie O'Fallon, you big know-it-all. But after we see that, can we please get some lunch? I'm freaking starving."

"Sure," Katie said, sounding disgruntled. "But not until I get what I need. Just keep your shirt on."

Heather giggled. "That might be kind of hard if the security guards are hot."

"Shut it, you tramp."

Heather put her hand over her mouth, stifling the snorts, as she and Katie made their way into the stone building that was the Victoria and Albert Museum. They were two American students in London, both of them from different parts of the United States, but they'd met at the Richmond American College in London, both of them pursuing economics degrees. Katie was a year ahead of Heather, focused on Industrial Revolution economics and historical factors, in which she intended to immerse herself at the museum.

She was here to see the Leman collection.

Entering the building, they headed to the main ticket desk. The lobby was a spectacular, two-storied space with Greek Revival pillars set within the Victorian ambiance. After getting their tickets, Katie and Heather headed off toward the Medieval and Renaissance section, winding their way into the textile exhibits. It was crowded today, given that it was a weekend, and the museum was full of families. The voices of children echoed off the walls and every so often, a museum attendant was positioned, standing vigilant watch over the collections.

"There," Katie said, pointing ahead with her museum guide in hand. "The Leman Album is up there."

Heather was trailing behind her, reading from the museum's guide. "'The Leman Album is an early eighteenth-century album of ninety-seven astonishingly vibrant designs on paper for woven silk fabric, many on fold-out pages and in colors that look as fresh as the day they were produced,'" she said, verbatim. "'Created between 1706 and 1716, the designs are Europe's earliest surviving dated patterns for woven silk, produced by Huguenot master weaver and designer James Leman, a prominent member of the Spitalfields silk industry in London's East End.'"

Katie already knew that. She'd studied Leman and his fabrics. The textile exhibits opened up before them, cases of various types of textiles on display for the discerning eye. Because textiles were probably fairly boring to children, this was a quiet part of the museum. There weren't many people around peering into the hermetically sealed glass cases.

Katie was particularly interested in seeing some of those vibrant fabrics, but in order to get to them, she had to pass by other cases. She almost didn't notice them until she happened to glance at a case coming up on her right.

The Mystery of the Patchwork Pants.

Curious, she paused.

Inside the case was a badly degraded pair of pants, linen, stitched in pieces of patchwork. The shape was clear enough, as there were legs with frayed and torn edges, stains all over the material, and a waistline that had ties on it. In short, they were very Medieval-appearing breeches. Fascinated, Katie read the information card on the front of the display.

Breeches from the late 13th or early 14th century, high-quality linen, Flanders or Germanic origins. Silk stitching. Inscription on waistband:
"Queenie"
Generously on loan from the Earl of Warenton

"What are you looking at?" Heather asked.

Katie was still looking at the pants. "Those," she said. "It's amazing to think that those belonged to someone. Like, a man eight hundred years ago wore those, you know?"

Heather was looking at the pants, too. She went to the opposite side of the case, studying them. Then, she shrugged.

"Why would a family keep those things?" she said. "They're all torn up and stained and dirty."

"I can see that," Katie said. "Look at the description—on loan from the Earl of Warenton, whoever that is. But it's clearly a family heirloom."

"It is."

Both Katie and Heather looked over to see a woman a few feet away, by one of the other cases. She was petite, with a slender face, glasses, and her red hair cut in a severe bob. When she saw that she had their attention, she smiled.

"Sorry," she said. "I heard you talking about those breeches."

Katie pointed to the case. "You know about these?"

The woman nodded and came over to the case. "They're actually pretty famous around here," she said. "They have quite a story."

"Really?" Katie said, interested. "Where can I find it?"

The woman shrugged. "You can probably find it online somewhere," she said. "Or ask one of the docents here. Luckily, I happen to be one."

"That's great," Katie said. "I was on my way to the Leman display, but these caught my attention. They look like something a Viking would wear."

The woman chuckled. "You're not far off," she said. "Long ago, they belonged to a knight."

Katie looked at the pants. "Makes sense," she said. "Only the nobility could afford the imported linen like it says on the description card. My name is Katherine O'Fallon, by the way. This is my friend, Heather Atkinson. We attend Richmond American."

The docent shook Katie's outstretched hand. "Mary Bolthouse," she said. "Lovely to meet you."

"You too," Katie said. "So what's the story behind these?"

"Well," Mary said, turning her attention to the pants, "they're a family heirloom belonging to the Earl of Warenton, something they've kept stored away for centuries. Family lore says that they were made by a lady for one of the DeWolfe knights, who wore them into every battle. He never wore anything else."

"DeWolfe?"

"That's the Warenton family name."

"Oh," Katie said. "But this inscription? Who is Queenie?"

Mary chuckled. "Possibly a wife," she said. "As the family tells it, the lady who made these breeches didn't like her husband going off to war all the time, so she stitched her name in the pants to remind him to always come home to her. Kind of like marking her territory, I suppose."

"And you know who owned them?"

Mary nodded. "One Sir Gareth," she said. "He was one of the many DeWolfe knights. It was a huge family that dominated the north in the thirteenth through the seventeenth centuries, until Oliver Cromwell started blighting everything. DeWolfe held the north against Cromwell, but at great cost. When Cromwell became Lord Protector and essentially ruled England like a dictator, he was very unfriendly toward the House of de Wolfe. They survived him, but it was a difficult fight. The Earl of Warenton is one of our oldest earldoms."

Katie's gaze was lingering on the pants. "Interesting," she said quietly. "So these pants belonged to an authentic knight?"

"One of the very best in Sir Gareth, so we're told."

"And the pants were made by his wife?"

"A very accomplished woman who clearly wanted to remind her man whom he belonged to."

Katie grinned. "It makes me wonder why those pants in particular," she said. "I know Medieval people didn't have huge wardrobes, but why those pants? And why the patchwork?"

Mary shook her head. "We'll probably never know," she said. "We call this display *The Mystery of the Patchwork Pants* because there's surely more to the story, but it's something lost to time. All we know is that Warenton held on to them, so they meant something to the family, but they don't even really know why. We just know they are precious to the family's history, but more importantly for us, the linen is in excellent shape. They're a stunning example of Medieval garment construction, which is why they're on display here."

Katie studied the pants a few seconds more. "Amazing," she finally said. "Thank you for your time, Mary. I hate to cut this short, but we're going to head over to the Leman display. I've got a project due and need to check it out."

Mary pointed in the direction of the Leman exhibit. "That's one of my areas of expertise," she said. "Shall I go with you and answer questions?"

"I'd love it."

The three women headed off toward the Leman cases and Mary was already rattling off what she knew about James Leman. Katie was listening, but her mind was still lingering back with the stained, torn pants made from patches of linen.

Queenie.

She must have been quite a lady, indeed.

PROLOGUE

Year of Our Lord 1287
Hensingham Castle, Cumbria
Seat of the House of de Reyne

"DID YOU SEE them?"

"Who?"

"*The boys!*"

The excited hiss came from a young girl no more than nine or ten years of age. She was standing with a gaggle of other young girls, all of them dressed in their finest, all of them tittering with delight over the young beaux who had entered their realm. Hensingham Castle sat slightly inland from the Cumbrian coast, a windswept property that faced the sea, glorious with salt upon the wind and seabirds and the general vibrancy that came when one was near an ancient coastline. There was something timeless about it, but also something damp and fishy.

Such locales were often a paradox.

Hensingham's granite stones had long been beaten by the gales that swept in off the Irish Sea, but it was still standing, strong and tall against the elements. On this day, as the wind blew and the birds rode the drafts overhead, Hensingham was the setting for a marriage a long time in coming, one that had drawn fine houses and allies from all over the north of England. The sister of the current Lord Hensingham was marrying a de Grey in what was considered rather a victory for the aunt, who had reached the ungodly age of thirty years having never been married. But, in a bolt from heaven, a widowed de Grey brother seem to think an older wife was what he needed to manage his brood of six children, so the match, and the marriage, was swiftly made.

It had barely been a month since everything had been settled.

The young girls chirping about the boys were wards of Lady Hensingham, the chatelaine of Hensingham Castle. There were four young ladies, not including her daughter, Matilda. Matilda Eleanor Joan Julia Catherine Fernanda de Reyne, or Mattie as she had been known since birth, was smaller and less imposing than her long name implied, but she was learning to find her voice. At nearly ten years of age, she had been a rather quiet child, but her pack of young woman had forced her to learn to stand up for herself or be forgotten.

Mattie wasn't the forgotten type.

In fact, at her age, she was already quite the beauty.

Most de Reyne women were. They had a reputation for dark brown locks and sea-blue eyes, with skin as fair as an infant's cheek and a smile that could stop wars. That was the rumor, anyway, more than likely started by another de Reyne somewhere back in the lineage, but in Mattie's case, it happened to be true. She had the de Reyne dark hair, long and wavy, but her eyes were the color of copper. Bright gold and brown. Coupled with her sharp mind and aptitude for languages and singing, it was a striking combination that already had more than one father inquiring about her hand for their sons.

Not surprisingly, Mattie's father was rather choosy and that distinction hadn't sat well with one of his visiting allies.

There was a de Vries son that wasn't going to be pledged to the eldest de Reyne daughter and Oswald de Vries had been sure to tell his son, in a fit of rage, that he wasn't good enough for Mattie de Reyne. Nay, Percy de Vries would *not* be part of the de Reyne family anytime soon. Unfortunately for Mattie, she knew nothing of it, so as she and her friends admired the many handsome young men who had come for the wedding, she was being stalked by one of them.

And she wasn't aware.

"Look!" one of her companions called out, pointing. "The de Wolfe brothers from Berwick. See how tall and handsome they are!"

The girls began to squeal at the sight. The wedding feast was in full swing and although the hall was full of revelers, the children in attendance were essentially told to stay out of the hall. Lady Hensingham had tables set up for them just outside the door, with gaily colored canopies over head, that would keep them away from the drunkards and the bawdy songs. The young girls were standing around the corner from his area, so they could see quite plainly when the de Wolfe, de Reyne, de Royans, and de Winter offspring began to gather around. So far, there were no fewer than twenty sons and daughters from various houses, all of them between the ages of around eight years of age to fifteen or sixteen. The boys outnumbered the girls, and they were those of the group in their teen years, and they very much resented having to sit at the children's tables at a wedding.

Patrick de Wolfe's sons seemed to be the most vocal.

Evidently, the eldest one, Markus, was in the hall because he was over the threshold of being considered a man, leaving the younger three brothers and their two sisters outside. Paired with their cousins, Ronan de Wolfe, son of Blayth, and Gareth "Gar" de Wolfe, son of Troy, they made for some young lady eye-candy.

"I am going to marry Cassius de Wolfe," one young woman sighed. She was fair and lovely, from the Summerlin family of Norfolk. "Do you not think he is handsome?"

She was pointing to the tall lad with the dark, curly hair. The young ladies with her nodded emphatically. "So handsome," a lass with the surname of de Allington said dreamily. "So are his brothers. Magnus and Titus are remarkably handsome. I've heard their grandfather is a Dane king!"

That was impressive and the tittering young women agreed that, surely, that must be why they were so handsome. But Mattie was fixed on one of the cousins.

"I like the blond boy," she said, gesturing. "I believe he is called Ronan. Do you think he will sit with me at sup?"

That question had every young woman's heart swelling with hope. Romance was heavy on their minds as Mattie's older brother suddenly appeared.

"Break up your little hen gathering," Maksim de Reyne said, walking right through the middle of their crowd. "Stop hiding and come and sit."

Mattie frowned at her bossy brother. "I am going to tell Mama on you, Max," she scolded. "You cannot tell us what to do."

"I can and I will."

"Says *who*?"

"Me!"

She put her hands on her hips and scowled. "No one will listen to you!"

"Is that so?"

"'Tis!"

Maksim made a threatening move in their direction and they screamed and scattered. That had all of the young men they'd been secretly spying on looking over to see what the fuss was. Maksim was waving his hands, herding the well-dressed young women toward the tables, but Mattie had run off in another direction. There was a big yew tree near the entry to the boxlike keep of Hensingham, and she'd rushed over to collect a switch from one of the branches. Weapon in hand, she charged back toward the tables where Maksim was forcing the young women to sit and be still.

Mattie came up behind him and whacked him across the buttocks.

The young men at the tables thought it was great fun to watch Mattie chase her brother around. Maksim tried to get away from her at first, but soon enough, he took a stand and faced her, reaching out to grab the switch when she came close. He was easily able to disarm her and she cried in pain as he yanked the wood through her hands. She had a splinter, so she said, and as she inspected it, Maksim felt bad enough that he went to see what he'd done. As soon as he lowered his head, looking at her hand, she rammed two fingers right up both nostrils.

Maksim howled in pain and the laughter exploded.

Mattie had her switch back now and she lashed her brother on the backside as he tried to recover from nearly having his brains punctured through his sinus cavity. But just as she ran past one of the tables, pursuing Maksim, one of the older boys sitting alone stuck out a foot and tripped her.

Down she went, onto her face.

Percy de Vries had been that lad. He'd been stalking Mattie all afternoon, watching her, waiting for his chance to exact his revenge. When she started running recklessly after her brother, he saw his opportunity. He smiled smugly as Mattie pushed herself up and realized she had a bloodied nose. She put her hand to her face, in obvious pain, as Percy stood up.

"Now you're not so pretty, are you?" he said. "No one will want you now, you little snipe. I hope you stay ugly forever!"

A shadow fell across Percy's path. Startled, he looked up to see the three very big de Wolfe brothers glaring at him, flanked by their equally big and mean-looking cousins. One of the cousins reached down to help Mattie to her feet as Cassius, Titus, Ronan, and Magnus de Wolfe ganged up on the unfortunate Percy.

"So you like to hurt girls, do you?" Cassius said. At nearly seventeen, he was a man grown and very nearly a fully fledged knight, making him positively terrifying. "Why don't you bully someone your own size, Percy? Here—I'll make it easy for you. Knock me off my feet if you can."

Percy was a few years younger than Cassius and not nearly as big and muscular. He looked at Titus, younger than Cassius but taller, and then Magnus, who was shorter than his brothers but built like a bull. They were around fifteen years of age and thirteen years of age, respectively, but they were absolutely enormous for their ages. Beside them, their cousin, Ronan, was a little younger than Magnus, and hadn't hit his growth spurt yet, but the young man had his fists balled.

He was ready to brawl.

As Percy began to realize that he'd something very wrong by picking on a girl, Maksim came out of nowhere and slugged him squarely in the face. As he went down, the de Wolfe brothers gathered around, and Percy was in a world of hurt as Maksim pounced. The fists were flying, and Percy was wailing, but over at another table, Mattie wasn't paying any attention to it.

She was paying attention to something else entirely.

Gar de Wolfe had been the young man who had picked her up out of the dirt and chivalrously helped her to sit down at one of the tables. She was bleeding down the front of her lovely silk garment and Gar had ripped the sleeve of his tunic to come up with soft wool to stem the blood. He was being quite kind and gentle with her, a youth who had probably seen somewhere between fourteen and fifteen years, but he had a sweet, deep voice already and his big hands were quite careful. He held the wool to her nose, encouraging her to tilt her head back to stop the blood flow, as her anxious friends gathered around.

"You'll heal," he told her kindly. "I've seen this kind of thing before and it will heal quickly. You'll be chasing your brother again in no time at all."

Head tilted back, tears streaming on to her temples, Mattie was trying desperately not to sob. "Who is that boy?" she said. "Why was he so mean to me?"

Gar looked over his shoulder at the young man who was becoming a battered mess thanks to Maksim and the de Wolfe brothers.

"I do not know," he said. "But I heard what he said. Do not listen to him. You are not ugly."

That seemed to stop Mattie's tears like magic and she lowered her chin a little, just so she could look at this sweet young man.

"You… you do not think my nose is broken, do you?" she said as she touched the bridge of her nose.

He shook his head, daring to take the cloth away to see if her nose was still bleeding. "It is not broken," he said. "But you took a good fall. You should find your mother and tell her what happened. She can make a compress for you to keep the swelling down."

Mattie smiled at him, feeling better with his kindness. The fact that he was easy on the eyes seemed to be the best medicine of all. He was a big lad with nearly black hair, rather ruddy skin, as if he spent most of his days in the sun, and eyes of the palest green she'd ever seen. They only time she'd ever seen a color that bright was when lightning bolted across the sky or the flame in the hearth was blinding. There was something mesmerizing about his eyes.

Kind eyes, she thought.

He was kind.

"I will send one of my friends to fetch her," she said, tearing her eyes off him long enough to send one of the hovering girls running for Lady Hensingham. "You have been very kind, my lord. You did not have to help me."

Somewhere over in the pile of young men, Percy emitted a cry for mercy that was quickly silenced. Gar grinned at the sound of it.

"Of course I did," he said. "You were set upon by a foul beast, who is now more than likely wishing he'd not been so dastardly. We do not take kindly to men who mistreat women."

"That is very chivalrous."

He shrugged. "It is the right thing to do," he said. "Women

are weaker creatures. They must be protected."

He was regurgitating what he'd been taught, but he sounded as if he meant it. Meanwhile, over in the skirmish, two of the de Wolfe brothers were hauling Percy to his feet and shoving him onto the nearest bench. He couldn't stay upright, however, and toppled onto the ground.

The de Wolfe boys simply stood there and looked at him.

Maksim, however, didn't care about his victim. He came over to his sister, rubbing at his bloodied knuckles, and looked at her with concern.

"Did he hurt you badly?" he asked.

Mattie shook her head. "Not too badly," she said. "Who *is* he, Max?"

Maksim wasn't convinced that she didn't have one foot in the grave. He peered down at her, looking at her eyes, which were already starting to darken underneath with the starting of a bruise. He sighed sharply, with displeasure.

"That's Percy de Vries," he said. "I heard Papa speaking with his father earlier today when he asked if you were betrothed to anyone. Papa said you were too young and Lord de Vries seemed to take that personally."

Mattie peered around her brother, at the body still on the ground as the de Wolfe men kicked at him. One of them was even kicking dirt on him, trying to bury him like a dog burying a bone.

"He… he is angry with me for being young?" she said, confused. "But Mama says that I almost a woman. Why would Papa say such a thing?"

Maksim scowled. "Because he does not want you to marry Percy de Vries," he said, stating the obvious. "You do not want any part of that family. They are mean and stupid, and I should think what Percy just did to you would be proof of that."

Mattie wasn't quite sure what to say after that. She looked at Gar, who simply nodded. "'Tis true," he said. "Everyone knows that the de Vries family behave like lowborn."

"But they are nobles."

"They live like pigs," Gar said. "The only reason they're here is because they have a big army, or so my father says."

"Who is your father?"

"Troy de Wolfe."

Maksim pointed at Gar. "*That* is the kind of betrothed you want," he told his sister. "A de Wolfe is the most sought-out husband in the north. You do not want a de Vries, Mattie, trust me."

Mattie peered around her brother again in time to see the de Wolfe men heaving Percy onto the end of the table. The young man was so beaten that he couldn't sit up, so they simply laid him on the table. Gingerly, Mattie touched her nose, realizing that it was beginning to throb. The events of the day had already taken a toll on her and the day wasn't even over yet. Her focus returned to Gar.

"You have been very kind, my lord," she said with appreciation. "I do not think I want to wait for my mother to attend me. I will retreat to the keep, if you will excuse me."

Gar stood up as Maksim helped his sister to her feet. "I'll take you," Maksim said, grasping her by the arm. "Can you walk well enough?"

Mattie could have been honest with him. She felt well enough, but she could also see Gar out of the corner of her eye and she wasn't quite yet willing to part with him. He'd touched her with his chivalry, which wasn't difficult at her age. She spent her time being harassed by Maksim when he wasn't defending her, so a gentle and kind young man had her little heart fluttering.

"I… I think if both you and Gar help me, I shall make it," she said. "I feel a little faint."

That brought Gar. He took her left arm, as Maksim had her right, and they began to walk her very slowly back toward the keep. All the while, Mattie feigned weakness and, at one point, even pretended to stumble so Gar would hold her arm more tightly. It worked, because he did.

Smiling to herself, she let Gar and Maksim take her all the way to the keep steps.

At that point, Gar had to let her go. She thanked him again and Maksim helped her inside, all the way to her bed, where she wearily lay down. Maksim wandered off to find a servant to help her remove her shoes and make her comfortable, so Mattie had plenty of time to lie there, staring at the ceiling and dreaming warm, little dreams about Gar de Wolfe.

That is the kind of betrothed you want.

If her father was already thinking about marriage for her, then perhaps he needed to know.

Better lock down Gar before someone else did.

Margaret de Reyne was horrified when she saw her daughter and heard the story of Percy de Vries and his deliberate actions. She went so far as to send for her husband so he could see the de Vries lad's handiwork. Reece de Reyne was predictably upset about it, his anger focused on the de Vries son, until Mattie tactically informed him about Gar de Wolfe's kindness toward her. Surely her injuries would have been much worse had Gar not protected her. Mattie leaned heavily into Gar's actions, going so far as to mention he'd make some woman a wonderful husband someday.

Perhaps even her.

Mattie was young, that was true, but she wasn't too young for a betrothal. Even Reese knew that. It hadn't really been on his mind until de Vries brought it up, but now… now, Mattie had him thinking about it. A de Wolfe husband for his daughter? He couldn't ask for finer. Gar de Wolfe was Troy de Wolfe's eldest son with his second wife, the daughter of a clan chief. He had Scots in him, but he was all English. He was a young man with a big future ahead of him.

Why *not* Gar for his Mattie?

Troy de Wolfe wasn't in attendance because Gar had come with Patrick de Wolfe, Troy's younger brother. As soon as Reece returned to the great hall, he started in on Patrick about a betrothal between Gar and Mattie, linking two longtime allies with an unbreakable familial bond. Gar wasn't Patrick's son, and he thought he was a little young to be betrothed, but he agreed that the alliance would be beneficial. That was all the ammunition Reece needed to approach Troy, a man considered by most to be someone of little humor and abrasive in manner.

Troy, surprisingly, didn't think his son was too young for a betrothal, especially when Reese sweetened the deal with a landed title for Gar that had come through Mattie's mother and a dowry in the thousands.

Before the year was out, Mattie got her wish.

Gar de Wolfe had become her betrothed, which was something she would remember when she came of age and saw Gar again for the first time in twelve years right before their wedding.

Be careful what you wish for.

In this case, it happened to be true.

CHAPTER ONE

Year of Our Lord 1296
Gleann na Fola Castle (Valley of Blood)
"The Debatable Lands," Scottish Borders

THE HEAVENS HAD opened up.

Surely, the torrents of rain were indicative of an angry God because there had been nothing but chaos since the storm had rolled in three days ago, right as the battle in the Valley of Blood commenced. The first blow from a sword coincided with the first crash of thunder and then, after that, bedlam reigned.

It was madness.

It was also a blood feud, meant for vengeance. About six months prior, two knights from a castle known as The Keld, seat of the House of de Bourne, had been traveling north on business for their lord when they were captured by men from Clan Maxwell. The Maxwells of Westerkirk were notoriously unfriendly, and suspicious, and they executed the men as spies, which brought the wrath of Ares de Bourne. He was not only the Lord of The Keld, but he was also the Sheriff of Westmorland, and he amassed an army of two thousand and crossed the border on his quest to obliterate the Maxwell of Westerkirk.

Unfortunately for the House of de Wolfe, a few of their properties were in the path of that massive army and the fact that they were allied with de Bourne meant they sided with the man in this feud. That made it difficult because Gar's grandfather was Red Keith Kerr, allied with some of the Maxwell clans. But this specific clan seemed to be quite rebellious and even their own clansmen weren't particularly fond of them, so three days ago, about fifteen hundred Scots and nearly four thousand English collided in the aptly named Valley of Blood for a great battle.

The bloodiest valley in Scotland.

That was what they called that particular vale and Gar de Wolfe, in command of Gleann na Fola Castle, which literally meant Valley of Blood in Gaelic, guarded the southern gateway to it. It was located in the desolate area called the Debatable Lands simply because no one was really sure if it truly belonged to the Scots or if it truly belonged to the English. Even so, one thing was for certain—everyone agreed that it was guarded by a man the Scots called *Cù fola*.

Blood Wolfe.

That name was never more evident than it was at this very moment. Three days of battle, blood, and brutality had left the entire army covered with mud and filth and blood, all of them pouring back into the bailey of Gleann na Fola like a tide of walking dead. The injured were being dragged, carried, or carted back to the castle while the quartermasters organized areas for the wounded and the unwounded, which was no small feat considering how many there were of both.

Everyone needed a place to settle down.

Fortunately, Gar had two quartermasters who were perfection when it came to their craft. One of them, an old soldier who had served his grandfather at Castle Questing on the England side of the border, was even his majordomo. Without a chatelaine at this godforsaken castle, it was up to men to do the jobs that women normally did. But Gleann na Fola, a remote and windswept castle, was no place for any woman.

It was hardly a place for men.

But here they were, fighting a war that would hopefully prevent the entire border from blowing up. Wildfires of vengeance and rage could explode quickly, so the hope was that in beating down the Maxwell clan who had recklessly killed two English knights, revenge would be satisfied and there would be no retaliation.

One could hope, anyway.

And no one was hoping harder than Gar. He was covered in blood and dirt, entering his castle like the lord and master that he was, looking every inch the powerful, barbaric, battle-born knight. He was surrounded by family members—his younger brother, Reed, his older brother, Andreas, and his older cousins, William "Will" de Wolfe and Thomas "Tor" de Wolfe. Even his father was with him, riding in behind him astride a destrier that had been cut up in the battle. The horse needed tending. But he could hear Troy de Wolfe bellowing to the men behind him, telling them to secure the gatehouse once the army was through, and he let his father give the orders considering that, technically, Gleann na Fola was his father's property. It had been for the past four years and in all that time, Gar had been the only commander of what was perhaps the most volatile castle on the Scottish borders.

Truth be told, Gar was used to the madness.

"Well done, Gar," Andreas said, slapping him on the shoulder as he came up behind him. "You have Poppy's talent at commanding battles."

"Poppy" was what the greatest knight of his generation was called by his grandchildren. William de Wolfe, the legendary Wolfe of the Border, the Earl of Warenton, was that knight. The third son of the Earl of Wolverhampton, William had earned a name for himself when he'd served Northwood Castle many decades ago. He'd been captain of the Earl of Teviot's army, the largest army on the border at the time, and William had been flawless in action and decisions, so flawless that the king himself took note. William had married a Scotswoman and had ten children, so his grandchildren at this point numbered into the sixties.

De Wolfe had spawned a very large family.

"I fostered at Northwood, as you well know," Gar said, eyeing the brother who was around sixteen years older than he was. "Their training methods were established by Poppy, so of course I think like him. We all do."

Andreas grunted in agreement. "Indeed, we do," he said. "But this battle seemed particularly… bad."

Gar came to a halt. They were standing in the inner ward at this point, a small circle of real estate that surrounded the enormous keep of Gleann na Fola. There were concentric circles around the fortress, each one of them with moats and walls and berms, all designed for maximum protection. Since the battle had been to the north, the castle itself hadn't been touched, but the army that was now filtering into the outer ward looked beaten to death. Therefore, Andreas' comment had merit.

It *had* been particularly bad.

"The Scots were mindless in their fighting," he said. "Did

you notice that? Reckless and indiscriminate. I saw more than one English soldier fall and beg for mercy only to be murdered before I could get to them. That smacks of madness, Dray."

Andreas happened to hold an equally enormous outpost along the border, so he knew what Gar was talking about. "I know," he muttered. "There has to be something more than simply the murder of two English knights. We've been told they were executed as spies, but it doesn't seem to me that spies would drive that kind of barbaric response in battle."

"As if there's something deeper behind it."

"Exactly."

"I wonder if de Bourne stopped to ask the Maxwell before they attacked them."

Andreas shrugged. "Ares de Bourne is a man of diplomacy," he said. "He doesn't have a hotheaded reputation, so I would assume he at least communicated with them before this bloodbath."

"Gar!"

A shout came from behind them and both Gar and Andreas turned to see their younger brother, Reed, approaching. Reed looked much more like the Scots side of the family with his stocky build and auburn hair, but he was all English. Next to him walked Linus de Grey, a big knight with a shorn head and the House of de Grey lineage behind him. Like Reed, he served Gar at Gleann na Fola, and the three of them were a formidable trio. While Will and Tor seemed to be involved with Troy and his injured horse, Reed came to stand alongside Gar and Andreas, but unlike his brothers, who both possessed a calmer and more deliberate personality, Reed was very much puffed up like the conquering hero as he surveyed the returning army.

He slapped Gar on the side of the face, affectionately.

"Well done, *bràthair*," he said. "You ended this decisively by cutting off the head of the beast. Several heads, actually. The Valley of Blood is earning its name this day."

Gar eyed his brother. Reed was savoring the victory while the more seasoned knights like Gar were feeling less euphoric about it.

"There is nothing to gloat about," Gar said. "This is not over. If you think so, then you are delusional."

Reed frowned as water was thrown onto his triumphant fire. "Why do you say such things?" he said. "You are gloomy, Gar. *Too* gloomy. Stop being so dour and enjoy this day. You have earned it!"

"Leave your brother alone."

The words came from Troy as he appeared, flanked by Will and Tor. As he spoke he was looking at Reed, who scowled at his father.

"But Papa," he said, jabbing a finger at Gar. "He is being a doomsayer again. He is diminishing this victory!"

Troy cocked an eyebrow. "He is diminishing nothing," he said. "Unless you want me to turn your mother loose on you, behave yourself, Reed."

"But—!"

Troy cut him off. "This is one of your first battles as a fully fledged knight and I understand your excitement, but you are acting like an idiot," he said. Then, he looked at Will, the heir to the entire de Wolfe empire. "Get this whelp out of my sight before I do something he regrets."

Will fought off a grin as he reached out and grabbed Reed by the arm. "Come along," he said. "Our father is going to do something horrible to you and then tell your mother that it happened in battle."

They could all hear Reed protesting as Will dragged him away. Troy shook his head at his son. "How did I raise such a fool?" he muttered to no one in particular. "I have perfect knights in Andreas and Gar and Corey, but something happened to Reed."

He was speaking of the son who was born between Gar and Reed, a fine knight who had remained behind at Monteviot Castle, Troy's seat, to guard the garrison when the army went to assist Gar. But the comment made everyone grin.

"Reed is an excellent knight, Uncle Troy," Tor said. "He just has to learn to settle down."

Troy grunted in disagreement at his tall, blond nephew. "I should live so long," he said as Tor snorted. But his focus turned to Gar. "Poppy arrived while you were out hacking off Scot heads, Gar. He is inside, somewhere, so we should go and greet him."

The humor vanished from Gar's face. "Poppy is here?" he said. "Why did no one tell me?"

"Because I asked them not to," Troy said. "You have an army to command. You do not need the distraction of your grandfather's presence. But now that we are back, I suggest you let Tor and Linus and Will settle the men whilst you and I attend your grandfather."

Gar was already heading for the enormous portcullis that led into the heart of the castle, leaving his cousins and knight behind as his father had suggested. The structure of Gleann na Fola had several major towers, including a massive central tower where the great hall was located on the first floor above ground level. That made for a lot of slippery stairs and a good many torches to light the way in a stone castle that was as cold in summer as it was in winter. Not much about Gleann na Fola

Castle was warm, including the name. It was the biggest, most forbidding castle in the entire de Wolfe collection.

And Gar was damn proud of it.

The great hall could easily hold hundreds of men at any given time and on this day, it was lit up with an enormous fire in the hearth on the west side of the room and two massive wheel-shaped chandeliers over head that were burning thick, yellow tallow candles. The floor leaned slightly because of the sheer weight of the stones and wood upon the joists, but it was secure enough. Nothing could take the place down. As the men entered the hall from one of three spiral stairwells that led up to it, they could see someone sitting at the dais.

They moved in that direction.

As Gar drew near, he could see his grandfather clearly. William de Wolfe was sitting in the middle of the table, in a seat of honor, and Gar thought that was the most appropriate seat in the entire castle for him. He sat like a god, tall and proud, with the familiar patch over his left eye, something he'd lost in battle many years ago. William was extremely advanced in age, but there was no mistaking how sharp he still was. The man had the same mind he'd had in his youth even if his big, old body had shown signs of slowing down years ago. When he saw his son and grandson approaching, his remaining good eye twinkled and he slowly rose to his feet.

"You have both returned safely," he said with satisfaction. "I am pleased."

Gar was already moving around the table to embrace his grandfather. "We did," he said, putting his arms around the man. "It was not a simple thing. The Scots are very angry this time."

William squeezed his grandson before releasing him. "They

are always angry," he said, shrugging. "I have been dealing with that anger for many years. It never gets any better."

Gar grinned. "Yet you married a Scot," he said. "Does that not give you any consideration when facing their rage?"

"It does," William said. "It seems to make them angrier because I took one of their women."

Gar broke into soft laughter, motioning for his grandfather to sit down. "Please," he said. "You have come a long way, Poppy. To what do we owe this visit?"

William lowered himself wearily. "I will admit that I do not travel as well as I used to," he said. "Your grandmother insists I use her cushioned carriage."

"Did you?"

"I may be prideful, but I am not stupid. Of course I did."

Gar chuckled. "There is no shame in being comfortable," he said. "You have earned that much."

"I've earned far more than that."

"So why did you come? To ensure we did not ignite the rest of the border with this skirmish?"

William's humor faded. "Something like that," he muttered. "You know it is particularly brittle right now. Phillip of France has pledged to aid the Scots in their war with Edward and I received news several days ago that the King of Germany has failed to support Edward against the Scots, so something like this, as small as it seems, can have larger consequences."

Gar knew that. He was well aware that the English king was locked in a battle against the Scots, which was usually a constant state during any particular reign, but over the past several years it seemed to have grown worse. Unfortunately for Edward, he had a lot of enemies more than willing to aid the Scots, making the situation particularly volatile.

"This was a private battle, Poppy," Gar assured him. "It was the House of de Bourne against the Maxwell of Westerkirk and it has been settled."

"How?"

"We destroyed the clan."

William's brow furrowed. "What of the women and children?"

Gar glanced at his father. "They were taken away."

"Taken where?"

"That is for Ares de Bourne to decide."

William grunted unhappily. "God," he muttered. "How many of them?"

"One hundred and sixty-seven."

That brought a reaction. "*One hundred and sixty-seven* women and children?" he said incredulously. "You let de Bourne take them all away?"

"It is not as bad as it sounds, Papa," Troy said, supporting his son. "Gar only let de Bourne take them with the agreement that they would be taken to abbeys in Northern England for safekeeping. They are not being executed."

William eyed his son. "And how can you guarantee this?"

"I sent my own men with them," Gar said. "The women and children are being guarded by my own men, who will ensure they reach Rieveulx Abbey, Fountain Abbey, and Whitby. I was not barbaric, I assure you, but we could not leave them behind. Especially the male children. You *know* that, Poppy."

William did. It wasn't an ideal situation, but he understood. "Very well," he said. "It is not as if you had control of the situation, but at least you insisted on the humanity of it. The last thing we need is for one hundred and sixty-seven women and children to be murdered at the command of an English lord. That would turn the north into a wildfire."

"I did the best I could."

"Then it is enough."

Gar was relieved he wasn't going to get more of a scolding from his legendary grandfather. It had been a difficult enough situation and, as he'd said, he had done the best he could given the situation. He smiled at the man, trying to bring some of the warmth back into the conversation now that the business had been discussed.

"Thank you," he said, noting the remains of a meal in front of his grandfather. "Have you recently eaten?"

William shook his head. "Nay, not recently."

That had Gar sending a servant running for food and drink. Meanwhile, Gar began to peel off his gloves and remove his weapons while his father and grandfather began speaking on some gathering that William and his wife, Jordan, had hosted a couple of months earlier. Something about a betrothal feast for one of William's youngest son's children. Gar wasn't paying much attention to it until William returned his attention to him.

"Speaking of betrothals," he said. "That is another reason why I've come."

Gar glanced at him as he went to remove a dagger strapped to his leg. "That is an odd subject to bring up now," he said. "What betrothal?"

"*Your* betrothal."

Gar paused, mid-movement. "My betrothal?"

"You have one. Or did you forget?"

"I have not forgotten."

"Good," William said. "Because Reece de Reyne has written to me about the betrothal and has asked that we move forward with it."

Gar frowned. "Why would he write to you?" he said. "Why not my father?"

"Because I am the one who will make all things possible."

Gar glanced at his father, who simply looked away. He knew that Troy wasn't hugely enthusiastic about a marriage to Gar at this time simply because he was fairly young for such a thing. He was a young, powerful, and extremely intelligent knight who was just starting to build his reputation. He'd been a fully fledged knight since seventeen years of age simply because there was no reason to not grant the man his spurs.

Gar was already something of a legend.

Somewhere back in the family lines, Gar had inherited the same height that his Uncle Patrick had, though it wasn't as pronounced. Still, he was almost a head taller than his father, and taller than his grandfather, and he had an enormous, muscular build. He'd looked like this when he turned eighteen years of age and he swung a sword better than more seasoned men, with impeccable decision making in the heat of battle. That made Gar de Wolfe something every knight strove to be—infallible, but with heart.

He most definitely had heart.

He also had no shortage of female admirers. There were rumors about him on the borders, how the dark and swarthy grandson of the Wolfe was as handsome as a god with his sun-kissed skin, black hair, and pale green eyes. He wasn't a rake, either. There had been more than one inquiry from hopeful fathers on his marital status, but they were turned away disappointed to learn that Gar was already betrothed to a daughter of the House of de Reyne. A fine match, most said. A fine match to a perfect warrior. But there was one thing those fathers, and daughters, didn't know that would make them glad for no betrothal if they did.

Bluntly, Gar lived like a pig.

The man had no sense of hygiene, cleanliness, or anything along those lines. If it was natural, he accepted it, no matter what it was. That came from living with men, and training with men, and in all honesty, women scared him. He knew nothing about them and he couldn't control them like he could control men, so anything out of his scope of expertise had him intimidated.

And William knew this.

God help him, he knew. His wife knew. Gar's mother knew. The women in the family knew that Gar was wildly handsome and, in truth, quite gentle toward the opposite sex when he wanted to be, but he had no idea that the way he lived or kept himself was offensive. He was an idiot when it came to sensing a woman's thoughts or needs. If they said the sky was blue, he would think they meant it was red because all things were red and brutal and harsh in his world. The world of a knight living in a border castle that was always on the alert. Always fighting for its life. Gar wasn't used to not being in battle mode, every hour of every day, so to relax with his family was difficult for him. To relax and be pleasant around a woman he had just met was even worse.

Mattie de Reyne had no idea what she would be getting in him.

William wasn't sure how he was going to break it to Gar.

Clean up, lad. Your betrothed is expecting you.

But Gar had to know.

"*Now?*" Gar finally said, breaking into William's train of thought. "De Reyne is bringing that up now?"

"Now."

Gar frowned. "But why?"

William shrugged. "Because the lady is of an age where she should be married," he said. "There is nothing unusual about that, Gar."

No, there wasn't, but Gar wasn't ready for it. It was written all over his face. "We have only been betrothed eight or nine years and—"

"Nine. Closer to ten, actually."

"*—and* some betrothals go on for many more years," Gar said, finishing strongly because he didn't like being interrupted. "Men must become established."

"You are established."

William seemed to have an answer for everything, which was driving Gar to desperation. "Poppy, I do not wish to bring a wife to this place," he said, gesturing to the hall, to Gleann na Fola in general. "This is no place for a woman, especially not now. It is too rough. Too volatile."

He had a point, but William wasn't going to let him off so easily. "Mayhap that is true," he said. "But you said yourself that the battle with the Maxwell is finished. Did you not just tell me that?"

Gar had. He silently cursed himself for giving his grandfather ammunition in this argument, but that didn't matter.

He didn't want a woman here.

"I did," he said. "But you know as well as I do that sometimes, battles do not remain finished. Sometimes they flare up. I cannot be worrying about a new wife when I have to worry about the Scots."

William nodded thoughtfully. "I thought you might say that," he said. "Therefore, I am sending you five hundred more men in addition to another five hundred that are part of your de Reyne dowry. I will also send Atreus de Norville to you. You will be well fortified with men and knights and can, therefore, afford the time to focus on your new wife."

"I don't want to focus on my new wife."

"You have no choice."

Gar didn't know what to say. The man had everything figured out. Trying very hard not to have a tantrum, he looked at his father, who had thus far remained silent throughout the exchange.

"Well?" he said to Troy. "Do you have anything to say about this? Do you agree with him?"

Troy grunted and scratched his head. "Lad," he said after a moment. "All of the refusals in the world will not change this. When you marry a member of the House of de Reyne, that means we will be linked to the Lords of Hensingham by marriage and then by blood when you have children. That is an extremely valuable alliance and I, for one, see the strength in it. It is a noble calling."

Gar could see that he'd get no support from his father. "And you agree that I should bring her back here, to this dangerous outpost?"

Troy sighed. "She will be your wife and she will go where you go," he said. "Women have survived at dangerous castles before. And before you say another word, know this—your mother told me to tell you that if you voice any further objections, then *she* will come here and you will be very, very sorry. Are you willing to risk the wrath of your mother?"

Gar wasn't. There were a lot of things he could deal with and do so ably, but an angry mother wasn't one of them. Rhoswyn Kerr de Reyne had been the only child of Red Keith

Kerr and he had raised his daughter like a warrior. As his grandfather once told him, Rhoswyn and Troy got into a battle years ago and Rhoswyn defeated him, which led to a marriage. Rhoswyn was as tough as nails, so under no circumstances did Gar want to tangle with her.

Heavily, he sighed.

"Truly, Papa?" he said with displeasure in his tone. "I must *truly* marry this girl?"

"You must."

"But I do not even remember her," he said, trying not to sound as if he were whining about it. "She was a little girl I was kind too those years ago and nothing more."

"You made enough of an impression on her that her father asked for a betrothal."

Gar rolled his eyes. "So my reward for saving a… a child is that I have the privilege of being married to her?" he said. "That is ridiculous. It was ridiculous from the start, but you saw an alliance in it, so I have been forced to accept it."

Troy cocked an eyebrow. "I was forced into a marriage with your mother for the sake of an alliance and I am a better man for it," he pointed out. "Poppy and Matha have the most chaotic romance of all because long ago, she belonged to Poppy's liege. At least you do not love a woman who belongs to someone else."

"I do not *love* anyone."

"Enough, Gar," William said softly, stopping the argument. "The subject is not up for discussion. You are going to travel to Hensingham Castle, where Lady Matilda de Reyne is waiting for you. You will spend some time there, coming to know the woman you are to marry, and then you shall wed. That is what her father wanted."

Even Troy looked at his father curiously. "They do not want a wedding right away?"

William shook his head. "Nay," he said. "His missive said that he wishes for his daughter to come to know her betrothed before the marriage is to take place. To be fair, I have heard of something like this before, but usually when the brides are quite young. Lady Matilda has recently seen her nineteenth birthday, so she is not a child. She is a grown woman."

Troy shook his head. "I think that is a very bad idea."

"Why?"

Troy grunted, exasperated. "Although a period of acquaintance can be beneficial if the couple comes to like one another, it can also be a terrible thing if they cannot stand the sight of each other, knowing they still must wed."

William glanced at Gar. "And you afraid that will happen?"

Troy looked at his son, who was sitting moodily in his seat, clearly pondering how he could get himself out of this predicament. "If they do not get along and the lady wants out, and Gar agrees, the betrothal can be broken," he said. "I do not think you want to see that happen."

"So you feel a swift marriage is for the best?"

"I do."

Gar abruptly stood up. "You two decide what you want," he said. "I have an army to see to. I haven't slept in three days and I've hardly eaten, so do what you must and let me know what you decide since I do not have any choice in this matter."

He stomped off, heading back across the hall to the spiral stairs that would take him back down to the ward. He was battered and bloodied and irritable, so neither Troy or William blamed him. It had been a brutal campaign and he'd come home to something he'd been avoiding, and ignoring, for years.

"If I were you, I would send Rhoswyn here to ensure this place is cleaned up to the point where a woman could actually live here and not die of a disease," William said quietly. "Gar is not a cultured man or one who cares about appearance. I fear Lady Matilda's reaction when he brings her back here."

Troy couldn't disagree with him. "So we pretend Gar isn't as slovenly as he is?" he said. "I do not think that is fair to the lady."

"It is more than fair," William said. "The lady does not need to face such barbaric conditions when Gar brings her home. We do not want to frighten her."

Troy sighed heavily. "Once Gar leaves for Hensingham, I suppose I could send my wife over here, but she's not the best of chatelaines. You know this, Papa."

William's mouth twitched with a smile. "She's hell in battle, however," he said. "She is a worthy woman."

Troy looked at his father and, seeing the smirk, broke out into a grin. They both knew that Rhoswyn had not grown up being taught usual womanly duties, including how to tend a keep, and it had been Troy who had been forced to take on that role for some time after they were married.

He wasn't about to do it again.

"Mayhap there is someone else who can help other than Rhos," Troy said. "Andreas' wife is closer by proximity, anyway. She has managed to keep The Hermitage quite habitable."

"True."

The servants chose that moment to appear with the food Gar had requested. He wasn't there to eat it, but that didn't mean that Troy and William didn't make a feast out of it. Even if Gar lived in a pigsty, the man always had excellent food and drink. Troy and William took advantage of that because they were quite certain this wasn't the last battle they were going to have with Gar about his betrothal.

They had to keep up their strength.

They were going to need it.

CHAPTER TWO

Three weeks later
Hensingham Castle, Cumbrian Coast

"HIS PARTY IS nearly here!"

Mattie heard those fateful words, uttered by her cousin, and family's ward, a young woman by the name of Agnes de Witt. She was the only ward at this time because Lady Hensingham, Mattie's mother, had made the decision that she simply didn't want to deal with a gaggle of young girls at this time in her life. She didn't have the patience any longer. But the truth was that Agnes was enough to make anyone want to forgo the company of multiple young women because she was loud, opinionated, excitable, sweet, and silly. She was a handful at the best of times and she'd whipped Mattie into a frenzy for the past several days because they knew Gar de Wolfe was on the approach.

Now, he was here.

Mattie thought she was going to faint.

"They are?" she gasped, running for the lancet window of her bower and straining to see the road that led to the gatehouse of Hensingham. "Where? I do not see them."

At Mattie's feet, her dog, Winchester, jumped excitedly. Winnie, as he was called, was a long-legged dog with a big head, quite smart. He'd latched on to Mattie as a puppy a few years ago and never left her side. She gave the dog a pat on the head as Agnes pointed from the window.

"They will appear soon," Agnes said confidently. Then, she yanked Mattie away from the window and forced her to stand before her. "Let me look at you. We must make sure you are as beautiful as you can possibly be."

Mattie prepared for inspection for the third time that day. With a grin, she sighed impatiently as Agnes scrutinized her and Winchester ran circles around them both, sensing the excitement in the air. She was forced to turn a circle in front of Agnes, who found a spot on the yellow silk surcoat that looked as if it might be trying to unravel. Agnes inspected the jewelry, her hands, and her hair, which had a circlet of gold around the crown with a semiprecious stone hanging from the front so that it draped over her forehead.

In a word, she looked stunning.

She smelled good, too. Agnes had made sure to rub her arms and neck with perfumed oil, smelling of roses. It was a heady scent. Not one part of Mattie wasn't polished, primped, or presentable. She'd been working on her clothing for weeks, preparing for the moment when she would meet the man she was betrothed to. The boy she'd met only once, but a boy who had made a lasting impression. Mattie had been waiting for nine long years and now that the moment was upon her, she could hardly contain herself.

It was what she'd been praying for.

"Tell me about him again," Agnes said, using a horsehair

brush to sweep away what she perceived to be dirt on the hem of Mattie's surcoat. "Tell me how handsome and brave he is."

Mattie smiled as she remembered the young man in her mind, somehow creating an almost godlike vision of him. "Very handsome and very brave," she said. "Papa tells me of Gar's adventures when he hears of them. I know that he is a garrison commander on the Scottish border and that he commands a thousand men. Imagine that! A thousand-man army!"

"A thousand men," Agnes sighed. "He must be very powerful."

"He is," Mattie said. "He is a de Wolfe, after all. His father is the second son of William de Wolfe, the great Wolfe of the Border. Of course you know who that is. You have heard of the Earl of Warenton."

"I have." Agnes nodded. "Is Gar his father's eldest son?"

"Nay," Mattie said. "He has an older brother, from his father's first wife. She was killed and his father married a Scotswoman, and Gar is the firstborn of that marriage."

Agnes flopped onto Mattie's bed, her elbows bent up and her chin in her hands, as Winchester jumped on the bed and lay next to her. "Is he rich, then?" she asked.

Mattie shrugged. "I do not know," she said. "I think so. Everyone knows that the House of de Wolfe is the largest and richest in the north. Papa told me that Gar will inherit wealth from his mother's father because she is his heiress."

Agnes pondered a rich husband with de Wolfe ties. "Think of the home you will have," she said. "Think of the magnificent castle you will be chatelaine over. It will be the biggest, most beautiful castle in all of England and you must have many feasts. You must show them what a great wife Gar de Wolfe has."

Mattie found her way over to the polished bronze mirror that had a surprisingly true reflection. It was about as tall as she was, five feet in length or so, and she admired the beautiful garment she was wearing. The neckline was a little daring and it nipped in at her waist, accentuating her figure. The sleeves were long and belled, giving her an elegant appearance. But the more she looked at herself, the more the doubts began to come.

"I hope I will be a great wife," she said wistfully. "I do so want to be a good wife to Gar. I want to be helpful and obedient. I want to learn of the things that are important to him."

"What about the things that are important to you?" Agnes asked.

Mattie considered that question. "I'm sure that what is important to me will be important to him, also," she said. "I am certain we are of the same mind. We both want a fine home, and children, and the respect of our vassals. Aggie, I have spent the past nine years dreaming of this marriage and I feel as if I already know it. I feel as if I am already in it and I am Gar's and he is mine. We will be *perfect*."

Agnes smiled dreamily. "Of course you will," she said. "You have planned and prepared for it. You are ready to become Lady de Wolfe."

"I am," Mattie said, grinning. "I am ready and willing. But he must hurry up and arrive!"

Agnes scrambled off the bed and ran to the window as Winchester leaped off the bed after her. "Shall I run down the road and take a stick to his horse to make him move faster?"

Mattie giggled as she went to the window, pushing her eager dog aside. "Aye," she insisted. "Gar will be the most handsome knight of the entire escort. You will know him by his dark hair and green eyes. I remember those eyes. They were magnificent."

"Gar was magnificent."

"He was," Mattie said. "I can hardly…"

A knock on the door startled them away from the window and when the panel swung open, Mattie's mother was standing in the opening. Julia de Reyne took one look at her daughter and motioned to her furiously.

"Quickly, Matilda," she said. "He is approaching the gatehouse!"

Mattie bolted, but Agnes had made the unfortunate mistake of standing in her path as she tried to run to the door too.

"Get out of the way!" she roared at Agnes. "*Move!*"

She shoved, Agnes went sideways, and Mattie beat a mad pace to the open door where her mother was. She blew past her mother, stepping on the woman's toe, and Julia growled at her smarting foot.

"Slowly, Matilda!" she called after her daughter. "Careful down those stairs. They are treacherous!"

Agnes, having recovered from being pushed aside, finally made it through the door, following Mattie's trail. The dog was right behind her, barking excitedly. Unfortunately for Mattie, she was going a little too slowly because of her mother's admonition and Agnes was going too fast to keep her balance, so she slipped on the steep spiral stairs and crashed into Mattie from behind, and the two of them went sliding down the rest of the stairs until they hit the bottom. Winchester, thinking it was all great fun, jumped on them and barked. By the time Julia reached them, Mattie was slapping Agnes on the arms, scolding her for having crashed into her, and pushing her jubilant dog away.

Snorting at the ridiculous young women and one excited

dog, Julia pulled her daughter to her feet and encouraged her to continue to the keep entry, leaving Agnes to collect her dignity. Winchester remained with Lady Hensingham, sadly, as his mistress ran outside. For certainly, the entire world awaited Gar de Wolfe, who was a cross between God and Adonis in the eyes of Mattie. He was knightly perfection and she was ready to worship on the altar of his greatness. As she'd told Agnes, the man was positively perfect. She hadn't seen him in nine years, but she didn't need to. She simply knew.

God's Bones, but she was wrong.

Very wrong.

CHAPTER THREE

"ARE YOU GOING to say something to him?"

"Say what?"

"That he must look better than a pig who has been sleeping in his trough?"

The words were hissed between Andreas and Troy, with Andreas asking his father if he was going to do something about his slovenly brother. A brother who was about to meet his intended, but he smelled like a compost heap.

Even the men, who weren't hugely given to extreme hygiene, found it offensive.

Troy sighed heavily.

"I have," he muttered. "You have. His mother has. Poppy has. Even Matha has and she went so far as to force him into a tub of water, but he would only take his tunic off because he did not want to undress completely in front of his grandmother. Matha took a brush and soap and scrubbed him so hard that she made him bleed in places, but he got out of the tub and continued to wear those damp breeches until they smelled to high heaven. He's wearing them even now. That is what you smell—mildew."

Andreas knew that. He knew all of it. But he still could not believe his brother had no real sense of cleanliness or proper grooming when it came to not only visiting an ally's home, but meeting the man's daughter, who happened to be his betrothed.

It was an appalling situation.

"I am going to try one last time," Andreas said. "Gar may be the most handsome out of all of us, but he is also the filthy boar of the family."

Troy shook his head. "He does not care."

Andreas pursed his lips angrily and reined his horse around, heading for the rear of the escort where Gar was located. He didn't want to be in the front because he was still protesting the match in general and didn't want to appear eager by being in the lead as they arrived at Hensingham Castle. Andreas found his brother in the very rear of the escort, astride his distinctive black-and-white warhorse, aptly named *Taches*, which was a French word meaning spots. Taches, which sounded much like the word *dash* when spoken, was a very intelligent horse who was hell in battle.

Gar adored the beast.

"Hensingham is just over the rise," Andreas said as he drew near. "I came to tell you that there is a stream to the south. We can stop if you wish to wash your face and clean up a little."

Gar eyed his brother. It was the same tune he'd been hearing from the man since they'd departed Gleann na Fola weeks ago and, much as when Andreas had mentioned washing the first time, Gar simply ignored him. He'd been doing it the entire journey.

Andreas still hadn't gotten the message.

"Nay, thank you," Gar said. "I am definitely smelling the sea. I'd forgotten how much I love that smell. We do not get it where we live."

He was changing the subject from his stench to the fortress before them, but Andreas wasn't going to let him. "Speaking of smell," Andreas said, reining his horse alongside his brother's. "You stink."

"That is only your opinion."

Andreas rolled his eyes. "Christ, Gar," he said. "It is everyone's opinion. Our grandparents, our father, your mother, the farmers in the fields and the priests in the churches. *Everyone* thinks you smell because you do. Lad, you cannot meet your bride like this. The woman will be horrified."

Gar grunted, refusing to look at his brother. "That is her misfortune," he said. "I am what I am."

"That is all you have to say about this?"

"What more would you have me say?"

Andreas cast him a long look. "Gar, I know you are not this stupid," he said. "Are you deliberately doing this? So she will take one look at you and beg her father to break the betrothal?"

Gar still refused to look at him. "Think what you will."

"I can and I do," Andreas said as if a revelation had just occurred to him. "Now this is starting to make sense. You are trying to break the betrothal yourself by presenting a picture of the worst husband a woman could have."

Gar shrugged. "I am a knight," he said. "I serve at a border castle. It is the most brutal life imaginable. It is no place for a woman, so if she cannot accept me for who I am, then it would be best that we not marry."

He meant it, every word. Andreas felt foolish for not figuring this all out at the start. "It will not work," he said. "Papa is not going to break this betrothal and if you keep this up, he will not break it simply to teach you a lesson. You cannot bend him to your will, Gar. You *know* this."

Gar still didn't respond. He simply spurred Taches forward, carving a path through the center of the escort until he reached his father. As he drew near, he heard Troy grunt.

"God," he muttered. "I can smell you coming."

Gar reined his horse alongside his father. "I do not understand why everyone is making my personal choices out to be such a monumental issue," he said. "You sent Dray to speak to me about it again? And he accuses me of deliberately avoiding washing myself so the de Reyne daughter will take one look at me and demand her father break the betrothal? I find that incredibly insulting."

Troy looked at him. His big, handsome son with Rhoswyn, their firstborn. He'd been so proud of Gar and, truth be told, still was. Nothing could change that. But he was being pushed to his limit by a stubborn man and, quite frankly, he was at the end of his patience.

It was time for this game to end.

"Do you know what I find incredibly insulting?" he said. "That you would think so little of the de Wolfe name that you would deliberately shame your family with your actions."

Gar looked at his father, frowning. "How am I shaming the de Wolfe name?"

Troy sighed heavily. "I am not going to explain this to you yet one more time," he said. "You know the issue, yet you refuse to amend your actions or your appearance. You know that the moment we go through the gates of Hensingham, I will be embarrassed. Dray will be embarrassed. Poppy, the greatest knight of his generation, will be shamed by your actions, a man who has done nothing to deserve it. All because you do not want to do as you are told."

"But, Papa, I—"

Troy cut him off. "Shut your lips," he growled. "I do not want to hear your excuses or your reasons, because they mean nothing to me. You have always been my most obedient son, Gar, the man I could depend the most on. But when it truly comes to something important, like a marriage to create a strong alliance, you would rather ruin this for all of us than do your duty. If you truly feel like our relationship will be the same after this event, then you must continue. But know that I, for one, will never look at you the same way again."

With that, he spurred his horse forward, away from the escort and over the rise as the great fortress of Hensingham Castle came into view. He left behind him a son who was genuinely hurt by his words, mostly because nothing he'd said was untrue. That was the truth of it. Gar had resisted, even pitched a tantrum, but he'd been unsuccessful at getting his way. He *was* unsuccessful. An entire de Wolfe family harassing him hadn't done what a few short sentences from his father had done. Troy finally put it in terms he could understand.

Shame.

Nay, he didn't wish to shame his family. No matter how much he didn't want this marriage, he didn't want to ruin his relationship with his father more. It had come to that. Perhaps it was time to finally put aside his monumental pride and do his duty. As much as he hated to admit it.

The escort continued the rest of the way to Hensingham's gatehouse in silence.

When the party drew close, Gar could see his father in the gatehouse speaking to a tall, gray-haired man. His father was off his horse, standing alongside the man who seemed genuinely glad to see him. They were having a rather animated conversation from what Gar could see, but he rode straight up to the men, dismounted his horse, and focused on the man who was speaking to his father.

He didn't even wait to be introduced.

"My lord," he said, interrupting their conversation. "I am Gar de Wolfe. Are you Lord Hensingham?"

The man appeared both pleased and slightly taken aback by Gar's seemingly forceful manner. "I am," he said. "I am Reece de Reyne. Do you not remember me, Gar?"

Gar smiled weakly. "I was young those years ago, my lord," he said. "I apologize that I did not recognize you on sight. But I am hoping you can assist me before we proceed further."

By this time, Troy was looking at him with great curiosity. He was afraid that Gar had another end game in mind, but Reece didn't know that. He nodded to Gar's question.

"If I can," he said. "What is it you require?"

Gar pointed to himself. "I have just come from a series of battles on the Scots border that has seen my garrison in the center of it," he said. "When you sent word to my father about executing the marital contract, I had very little time to do much more than get on my horse and come. As you can see, and possibly smell, I've not had the opportunity to bathe or clean up as I had hoped. We simply came as soon as you summoned us. I am ashamed that you should see me in such condition, but such is the life of a fighting man. I do not wish to risk offending your daughter, so I am hoping you can provide me with a place to wash so that I might be presentable."

As Troy fought off a smile, one of both relief and approval, Reece was more than willing to help Gar in his time of need.

"It would be my pleasure," he said. "I have heard about the trouble you are facing on the border. I am glad to see that you have survived without injury."

Gar nodded. "It was not for the lack of trying on the part of the Scots," he said. "The entire de Wolfe family on the western end of the border has been caught up in it. I was only able to come to Hensingham because my uncles and brothers and cousins are manning my post until such time as I can return, but as you can imagine, the fight has been… intense. I am afraid I am still in battle mindset most of the time."

There was appreciation in Reece's eyes as he sized up Gar, whom he only remembered as a younger man from several years ago. The Gar he knew then had grown up and out and was a tall, muscular specimen of a knight. He would be one hell of a son-in-law, one a man could be proud of.

He put a hand on Gar's shoulder.

"You needn't apologize," he said. "I understand completely. My son, Maksim, is around here somewhere. Let me summon him and he can help you in your moment of need. I am afraid, however, that my wife and daughter are quite aware of your arrival and…"

He was too late. Women were suddenly appearing at the gatehouse and Gar found himself looking at an older, handsome woman with smooth skin and impeccable clothing. She smiled at him and he acknowledged her with a bob of his head, startled by her appearance, but he was even more startled by what was standing next to her.

Who was standing next to her.

His breath caught in his throat.

A petite young woman with long, wavy brown hair was clad in a dark yellow silk that was studded with tiny pearls. The neckline of the garment was slightly off the shoulders, exposing an exquisite neck and décolletage. She was wearing jewels, but tastefully so, and her face… Gar got to her face and he had to do a double take. It was the girl from those years ago—he recognized her eyes. Like liquid copper. They were a color he'd never seen before, but those eyes were now set in a face that had matured over the past few years into something refined and magnificent. She had wide cheekbones, an upturned nose, and kissable lips that were a faint shade of pink. The entire picture was something he'd never expected and, quite honestly, more beautiful than anything he'd ever seen in his life. Before he could speak, however, Reece piped up.

"Julia, my dear," he said to the older woman. "Please take Mattie to the great hall. We will join you there."

He was practically manhandling the woman, trying to force her to turn around, but she wasn't cooperating. In fact, she batted his hands away.

"No need," she said. "We are here now. We knew Lord Braemoor and his son were arriving and wished to greet him as soon as he entered the gatehouse. My lord, we are honored to receive you."

She was speaking to Troy, who held the title Lord Braemoor. "Lady Hensingham," Troy said, dipping his head in greeting. "The honor is ours. We are looking forward to this visit and this union."

All eyes shifted to Gar, standing filthy and slovenly next to his father. Gar felt the horror of the women as they looked upon them and, for the first time since the journey to Hensingham started, he felt somewhat embarrassed by the state he'd let himself enter. But he was saved from speaking when Maksim suddenly appeared. The eldest, and only, de Reyne son took one look at Gar and went to him, putting his arms around him in a decidedly brotherly gesture.

"Gar!" Maksim exclaimed. "You wild beast, it is good to see you. Welcome to Hensingham!"

Gar hadn't seen Maksim in at least a couple of years, not since they'd run into one another in London while Gar had been there on business for his grandfather. Both he and Andreas had been in London and Andreas had taken him to an underground guild called Gomorrah. It was a place lodged in the vaults of a ruined church on the outskirts of London, one that was known for its entertainment and fine food. But it was very exclusive, because one could have any kind of entertainment one wished for, up to and including sexual pleasure, so it wasn't spoken of in the open. Therefore, Gar didn't acknowledge that it was where he'd last seen Maksim. Or *whom* he'd seem Maksim with.

He didn't think the man's mother would approve.

"Maks," Gar said, smiling. "It is quite agreeable to see you. How have you been?"

Maksim was slapping him on the shoulders. "Well, lad, well," he said. But then, he began to get a whiff of Gar and how badly he smelled and his face screwed up in distaste. "God's Bones, Gar. You smell like a bloody compost heap. Are there no baths in Northumberland?"

Gar cleared his throat uncomfortably, knowing that his betrothed was hearing the conversation. "I have been in the midst of battles for the past few weeks," he said. "When we received your father's missive, I did not have time to change my clothing. I simply came."

"Now that he is here, it would be good of you to help him clean up so that he will not offend the women," Reece said, lifting his eyebrows as his son looked at him so he could silently hint that Maksim's assistance was desperately needed. "Take him to the knights' quarters and find the man some soap and water. I am certain that Mattie will not mind waiting."

No one even looked at Mattie to get her opinion or permission. They all knew what she was thinking. If she had a nose that worked, she could smell Gar the way everyone else could. She'd have to be dead not to. Therefore, Maksim grabbed Gar and practically yanked the man through the gatehouse, heading for the knights' quarters on the southern end of the long, rectangular bailey. The moment they began to move, however, Winchester the dog, who had followed his mistress outside, seemed to think that it was a battle and he, too, went into battle mode.

The long-legged mutt charged.

As Gar was half pulled, half escorted into the bailey, Winchester ran up behind him and, with a growl, grabbed part of Gar's boot. He didn't pierce Gar's skin, but he had hold of the man's boot and was furiously trying to tug at it. Gar looked at the dog with annoyance as Maksim tried to shoo the dog away. Winchester, however, wouldn't be deterred.

"Matilda?" Maksim called to his sister. "Come and retrieve your vermin-ridden canine!"

Mattie came through the gatehouse, rushing in her dog's direction. "Winnie!" she demanded. "Winnie, *stop*!"

That only seemed to make Winchester tug harder. Gar didn't want to see his boots torn up by a rabid mongrel, so he shook his leg, trying to dislodge the animal. He managed to release its hold, but that made it more angry, and it rushed Gar gain. Gar stuck out the same boot and shoved the dog away by the chest. He didn't think the kick was too hard, but the dog went rolling away, much to the distress of Mattie.

"Winnie!" she gasped, moving to pick her dog up from the

dirt. "Are you well? Did he hurt you?"

The dog's answer was to run at Gar again as the man tried to walk off, snarling all the way. He lunged at Gar and managed to get a piece of his breeches, which were the same breeches Gar had been wearing for weeks. The same ones his grandmother had bathed him in. They were made from canvas, a strong material, but it wasn't impervious to naughty dogs. Winchester lunged, grabbed a fold right on the seat of the breeches, and yanked. A great ripping sound followed, and Gar's entire right butt cheek was suddenly revealed to anyone standing behind him.

Mattie happened to be one of them.

Startled, Gar tried to get the torn segment of his breeches out of the dog's mouth, but Winchester was on a tear. He snarled and yanked, ripping the breeches further as both Gar and Maksim tried to beat him off. Mattie, catching a glimpse of Gar's bare buttocks, quickly turned away and covered her eyes as her brother tried to control the dog.

"Matilda!" Maksim roared. "Come and take your dog!"

Mattie still had her hands over her eyes. "I cannot!" she said. "I… Maks, you'll have to get him away. I cannot look!"

The rip was becoming worse. The more Maksim tried to grab the dog, the more Winchester ran away, thinking it was a game. All the while, he had the fabric in his mouth and ended up running a circle around Gar's legs, ripping enough of the fabric to expose the man's entire backside and then some. Gar was left trying to preserve his modesty and fight off the dog that no one could seem to catch. Soldiers in the bailey, watching the spectacle, were roaring with laughter as Mattie stood there with her eyes covered as Gar's dignity was exposed for all to see. Trying to escape Maksim, Winchester managed to crash into the back of Gar's knees, and he went down on top of the dog.

Maksim leaped in to grab him.

"Matilda!" Maksim yelled again, holding Winchester by the scruff of the neck. "Get your dog before I throw him in the sea!"

Maksim had only ever called her by her full name and he was the only one in the family who did, but hearing him shout it in that angry tone was indicative of his frustration. Mattie dared to uncover her eyes and, realizing that Gar was now sitting on his exposed buttocks, she rushed over to collect Winchester, pulling the dog away as he tried to rush at Gar again.

"I am very sorry, my lord," she said, unable to look at Gar as he sat on the ground in torn breeches. "I do not know what has come over him. He is usually much better behaved."

"Nay, he is not," Maksim said, rage in his voice. "Get that beast out of my sight or I will put him on the fire and roast him!"

Properly rebuked, and just a little fearful that her brother would do as he'd threatened, Mattie picked up Winchester, who wasn't exactly a small dog, and rushed off. She was joined by Agnes, who had been watching the entire situation unfold. She didn't move to help tame the dog, mostly because she'd gotten a naughty peek at a man's bare arse and she'd liked it. She was hoping the dog would tear more of his breeches.

Unfortunately, she did not get her wish.

Gar sat on the ground, watching the two young women and the dog run back toward the keep. Truly, he wasn't angry as Maksim was. He figured it was some measure of Godly punishment for smelling like something a dog might want to fight. It was his fault, he was certain. As he sat there, watching the lovely vision in yellow silk run away, a hand suddenly appeared in his face.

"Come on, lad," Maksim said. "Let me help you up."

Gar looked up at Maksim, shaking his head in disbelief. "Did that dog truly just tear my breeches and expose my arse to the woman I am supposed to marry?" he asked.

Maksim was trying very hard not to laugh. "He did."

"I hate that dog."

"He hates you."

"I am going to kill it the next time I see it."

Maksim shook his head. "You'd better not," he said. "Mattie loves that dog. It would not be a good way to start off your marriage."

Gar sighed heavily. Without further ado, he accepted Maksim's hand and stood up, trying to keep his backside covered as he did so. He could see the soldiers standing around, still grinning at what had just happened, and he also saw that his father and escort had chosen that moment to come through the gatehouse. He could see their curious expressions, their wondering why he'd just got up off the ground, with torn breeches no less. Rolling his eyes, Gar turned away.

"You'd better take me somewhere to bathe and recover my dignity," he said. "And I'll need new breeches."

Maksim was still biting his lip to keep from smiling. "I can find you some," he said. "But well done, you."

"Well done *what*?"

"You took that humiliation like a man."

"Is that what your sister thinks?" Gar said with sarcasm. "Did I impress her somehow?"

Maksim shrugged. "She's probably grateful that you simply didn't kill her dog," he said. "I cannot understand what got into Winchester. He does not usually attack like that."

"Clearly, there is something about me that the dog took offense with."

Maksim was in agreement. "The smell."

"The only answer."

Maksim let his grin break through. They continued on to the knights' quarters, which was an outbuilding lodged against the exterior curtain wall, built from the same gray granite that comprised most of Hensingham. The ceiling was low, however, and they had to duck in when they arrived, but there was a manservant immediately upon entering. The small, older man took care of the knights of Hensingham, Maksim included, and when Maksim explained what he wanted, the servant went running for the necessary items.

"In here," Maksim said, directing Gar into a chamber that was small and dark, crowded with a bed frame. "You can use this chamber for your stay. I'll have someone bring your things."

Gar let go of the piece of torn breeches he'd been holding up to cover what he could of his backside. "You have my thanks," he said. "If you see my father, please tell him where you have taken me."

"I will," Maksim said. "Now, I go on the hunt for something for you to wear. Is there anything in your saddlebags I can retrieve?"

Gar didn't want to tell him the truth, that he'd brought nothing more to wear because he wanted his new bride to see just what a slovenly beast she was going to marry.

"Not really," he said. "As I said, we received word from your father and simply came. I did not have time to pack much. But my father might have something for me."

Maksim nodded, his gaze lingering on Gar for a moment.

"The battles on the border," he said quietly. "Were they terrible?"

Gar nodded without hesitation. "Bad enough," he said. "The Scots are angry and that is never pleasant."

"What happened?"

"A clan murdered a pair of English knights and the liege of those knights wanted revenge," he said. "At least, that was the catalyst. But the truth is that any skirmish on the Scots border is never a simple thing. Anything can set it off."

Maksim nodded. "So I've heard," he said. "But we do not get any action where we are. I think the last danger we faced was during my grandfather's time. Hensingham is peaceful, here in the wilds of Cumbria."

Gar peered from a small window, into the bailey beyond. "The castle seems to be in good condition."

"You intend to take my sister into the brittle borders?"

"If she is my wife, she will live with me and that is where I live."

Maksim sighed faintly. "Matilda has never been around that kind of thing."

"Then she will have to become accustomed to it."

But Maksim shook his head. "You do not understand," he said, looking the man up and down. "The last time you saw one another, she was a child and you were barely a man. Things change. People grow up."

"What do you mean?"

Maksim was looking at the man before him who looked like he lived in the mud. "I mean that she has grown into a fine lady, Gar," he said. "She is not a warrior's daughter. She did not grow up around battle. She grew up learning to paint and to sing and to dance. She can speak four languages. She is intelligent and cultured. To take her to a warring castle would be like taking a white dove and shoving it in with the chickens. It will be as alien to her as living on the moon."

Gar looked at him, then. "If you have any objections to this marriage, then I wish you would tell your father," he said. "I have tried my best to break this betrothal, but my father and grandfather are set. They will not break it. Mayhap your father can."

Maksim's brow furrowed. "You do not want to marry my sister?"

"I do not think I am a good prospect for anyone to marry."

At least he had avoided insulting Mattie, but Maksim wasn't stupid. He could see that Gar didn't seem to have any interest in the marriage. With that realization, he grunted unhappily and rubbed at his forehead.

"She has been looking forward to this for ten years," he said. "You must not tell her that you do not wish to marry her, Gar. It will break her heart and if you break her heart, I will break *you*. Do you understand me?"

Gar looked at him, seeing the protective brother, and his hard stance softened a little. "I have sisters also," he said. "I understand your instincts when it comes to your sister. I can assure you that I will not deliberately hurt her feelings. But I am a terrible match for her, Maksim. I spend my days fighting Scots and my nights seeing to the defense of my castle. We live on alert every moment of every day. I do not have feasts or dances and I have no need for a wife who speaks four languages and is adept at painting. Do you not see? This is not the marriage she was hoping for."

"Nor were you," Maksim finished quietly.

Gar sighed heavily. "It has nothing to do with your sister," he said. "She is just a woman I do not know. I have no feelings toward her one way or the other. But I have a life, and a vocation, and a wife does not fit into either right now."

Maksim understood, but still, given that the subject in question was his sister, he struggled not to be offended by Gar's attitude. He looked at Gar again, from head to toe, seeing the filth and the dirt and the disheveled appearance. He gestured toward him.

"Is this truly your natural state?" he said. "Or was this part of some plan to offend my sister so terribly that she would beg my father to break the betrothal? Because no man is this filthy, Gar. Not even a warlord on the Scots border."

Gar looked down at himself. "I do not have a wife telling me what to wear or to clean myself," he said. "I am what you see, Maksim. I am sorry if that is disappointing."

Maksim simply shook his head as if disheartened by the entire situation. "As I said before," he said, "she has been looking forward to this for ten years. If you are to discourage her, do not be cruel about it. She does not deserve it."

The manservant chose that moment to return, followed by men bearing a big copper tub and still more men bearing buckets of steaming water. As Maksim quit the knights' quarters, Gar finished stripping off his clothing and the tub was filled up. He climbed into the bath, hissing because the water was so hot, and the manservant pulled out a cake of white soap that smelled of pine needles along with a horsehair brush and went to work.

And Gar let him.

CHAPTER FOUR

WINCHESTER WAS TIED up.

It wasn't usual that Mattie tied her dog up, but unfortunately, he had earned it. He kept looking at her with sad doggy eyes, whining because he was restrained, but Mattie ignored him. He'd done something so terrible that she couldn't even look at him, horrified in a way that she had never been horrified before. She could still see her dog hanging on to Gar's breeches, tearing the whole back side into shreds and exposing the poor man's taut buttocks to the world.

She wasn't sure she would ever be over that.

Lady Hensingham was equally appalled even though she hadn't witnessed the event. Agnes had told Lady Hensingham, quite gleefully, and Lady Hensingham was suitably mortified. Unfortunately, she couldn't see to the man who had been offended in her bailey because she was busy with the man's father. As chatelaine, she had to focus on the most important person in her home—and that happened to be Troy.

It would be up to Mattie to apologize for her dog's behavior.

That was the message that Agnes had given Mattie and the woman had been beside herself with embarrassment and indecision. Gar had gone off to the knights' quarters with her brother and Mattie wasn't entirely sure that he wasn't going to lambast her for her disobedient dog. Not that she didn't deserve it, but the last thing she wanted was for Gar de Wolfe, her betrothed, to be angry with her.

She simply didn't know what to do.

Her first and only decision at that point was to tie the dog up so he couldn't wreak further havoc, but after that, she contemplated the course of action to take. As Mattie paced around in her chamber, wringing her hands with worry, her gaze fell upon her sewing kit. She came to a halt, looking at the kit and realizing that she could repair the torn breeches if Gar would allow it.

There was only one way to find out.

Rushing into her mother's chamber across the landing, she went to a big chest against the wall and began to rifle through it, looking for scraps of fabric that could be used to repair Gar's breeches. Agnes lent a hand and the two of them found several large pieces of sturdy linen that might be of service. Gathering those scraps, and her sewing kit, Mattie made a dash for the stairs but Agnes was right behind her. Perhaps a little too eager to see bare buttocks again, or so Mattie suspected. Agnes tended to be a little man-crazy at times. Forcing Agnes to remain behind was probably more difficult that trying to keep Winchester off Gar, but eventually, she triumphed. Agnes returned to her chamber to sulk alongside the dog as Mattie made her way out of the keep and over to the knights' quarters.

Truthfully, she never came to this part of the bailey because this was where the men were lodged, both knights and soldiers. It wasn't that she wasn't allowed here, but it simply wasn't a good idea for a woman to be in this particular area because of all the men. Still, she had a job to do, a peace offering as it were, and she was determined to go forward with it. Carrying the fabric, and the big sewing kit, she walked up to the door of the knights' quarters.

Then, she paused.

She couldn't very well go inside. Well, not really. She shouldn't. It was a men-only establishment. As she stood there, indecisive, she began to hear water splashing. Each chamber in the knights' quarters had small windows for ventilation, and they were just above her head. She couldn't see in, but she could hear more splashing and some grunting going on. At some point, someone cursed softly and demanded his skin not be scrubbed off his body.

Taking a deep breath, Mattie summoned her courage.

"My lord?" she called up to the window. "Sir Gar? Is that you?"

She was met with silence. Then, she heard more splashing and she called out again.

"Sir Gar?" she said. "This is Matilda. Mattie. Is that you?"

"It is."

Suddenly, there was a face in the small window and a deep, bone-rattling voice had replied. In fact, it had startled her. With a gasp, she jumped back a little, looking up to the window and seeing a nose and eyes.

She recognized the pale green eyes.

"I… I am sorry to disturb you," she said, suddenly nervous. "I came to apologize for my dog and to offer to repair your breeches. I have brought a sewing kit."

She lifted it slightly, showing it to him, and his gaze moved to the rather elaborate box. But there was awkwardness in the air, something not missed by either of them. A good deed was turning into an odd moment as Mattie wondered if he was even going to accept her apology.

She held her breath.

"Your apology is appreciated," he finally said. "But you do not have to make amends. It was just a dog, doing what dogs do."

Relieved that he was at least in a forgiving mood, Mattie shook her head. "But he is *my* dog," she said. "If you will give me your breeches, I will be able to repair them quickly."

His eyes disappeared from the window and she thought he'd stepped away, but she could still see his head moving a little. That black, glossy hair was catching the light. She wasn't sure what he was doing, so she thought that, perhaps, he might not have faith in her tailoring abilities.

"I promise that I do excellent work," she said, trying not to sound as if she were pleading. "You needn't worry."

He finally looked at her again. "I do not doubt you," he said. "I was simply looking at the breeches to see if they are even worth salvaging. I am afraid you would be wasting your time. I think they are beyond repair."

"May I at least try?"

He sighed. "Lady, they are the most foul pair of breeches you have ever seen in your life," he said. "I will be truthful and say that I do not want you touching them. I would be ashamed."

Mattie wasn't quite sure what to say to that, but she knew that, somehow, she felt hurt by his refusal. "Very well," she said reluctantly. "I will again apologize for my dog. I have tied him up in my chamber. He shan't bother you again."

With that, she lowered her gaze and turned away, but he stopped her. "Please do not think I am not grateful," he said. "I am very grateful that you should want to repair what was damaged, but I am not being dramatic when I say those breeches are horrific. I would not want your lovely hands touching them."

Lovely hands. It sounded suspiciously like a compliment and Mattie could feel her cheeks flushing. It was the first nice thing he'd ever said to her. She came to a halt and turned to him.

"May… may I ask you a question, my lord?" she said.

"Of course."

"Do you even remember me from those years ago?"

He nodded. "Of course I do," he said. "You were being set upon by Percy de Vries. A nasty man."

"Still?"

"He's dead," Gar said frankly. "Killed by one of his own men, I heard. Not surprising considering the entire House of de Vries is full of questionable men."

She looked a little surprised. "I hadn't heard of his death," she admitted. "After your visit those years ago, I never saw any de Vries ever again. My father said that they had become our mortal enemies because we had insulted them."

"How?"

"Lord de Vries wanted a betrothal between me and his son," Mattie said. "My father refused because he wanted you instead."

Gar hadn't known that. He'd been removed from the betrothal negotiations and, being firmly against the betrothal itself, he'd never thought to ask how it came about. Now, the entire situation was starting to make a little sense.

"Ah," he said. "Your father was hunting for a Wolfe."

Mattie shook her head. "I would not know," she said. "Like you, I was simply told about it. I was not involved in it."

Gar's gaze lingered on her for a moment. "You did not ask

your father to pursue me?"

"Never, my lord."

He had no reason not to believe her, but he was starting to think that she truly didn't realize how undesirable the situation was for them both. She was young and perhaps the least bit naïve.

"You *do* realize I am a good deal older than you," he said.

"I am aware."

He frowned. "And that does not trouble you?"

"Should it?"

"Do you not wish to marry someone your own age?" he said. "Someone who, mayhap, shares your same background?"

"What background would that be?"

Gar scratched his head. "That of a fine education and refined manners," he said. "Someone who is more civilized. A scholar or a courtier, in fact."

Mattie looked at him. She could still only see his eyes and nose, but in this brief conversation, she was starting to see more than that. She was starting to see his reluctance. Without a word, she went to sit on an upturned tree stump, one used by the knights to sit outside of their quarters on nights with pleasant weather. She was still within sight of Gar as she planted herself on it and opened up the sewing kit.

"You have been speaking to my brother," she finally said.

Gar watched her pull out what looked like big patches of linen. "A little," he admitted. "My lady, we know nothing about one another. I hope you do not fault me for a conversation with your brother about you. I would not be angry if you wished to speak to my father or brothers for what they could tell you about me."

Mattie laid the large pieces of linen in her lap and pulled out a big bone needle and some thread. "And what else did my brother tell you about me?"

Gar was careful in his answer because she seemed displeased. "Nothing terrible if that's what you mean," he said. "He said that you have been looking forward to this marriage for the last ten years."

Mattie threaded her needle. "From the way you say that, I take it that you have not been looking forward to it?"

Gar didn't want to dig himself into a hole. He really didn't. He didn't want to be married, but that didn't mean he wanted to hurt her feelings. Even without Maksim's threat, he still would not have wished to hurt her.

"Men do not usually look forward to things like that," he said. "They have other things on their mind."

"Like what?"

Gar shrugged. "It is men who control England," he said. "Men who keep it safe from the Scots and the Welsh and the French. We worry about making it safe so that ladies like you can live in peace and own wild dogs who tear people's clothing."

Mattie glanced up from what she was doing, which happened to be stitching together those big pieces of linen. "Is that what you do?" she said. "Protect women like me?"

"Aye."

"But I am nowhere near the Scots border."

"You are closer than you think."

"They never make it over here."

"That is because men like me are keeping them on their side of the border."

She paused in her stitching, looking up at him. "Fair point," she said. Then, she returned her focus to her sewing. "Tell me, my lord—if I were to ask your father or brother about you, what would they tell me?"

Gar could see that she was making something with those linen squares, but he couldn't tell what it was. "That I am devoted to my men, to my family, and to my cause," he said. "What else should they tell you?"

"I would hope they would tell me what kind of man you are."

"I just told you."

She continued to busily sew. "You told me of attributes," she said. "Is that all you are? Devoted to your men, your family, and your cause?"

"What else should I be?"

She shrugged as she added another piece of linen. "A well-rounded man is many things," she said. "Do you like to laugh? Do you enjoy singing? Do you enjoy telling stories of valor? Do you enjoy reading?"

"Reading?" he repeated, frowning. "I do not have time. I have a clerk that reads and writes for me."

"But you *can* read and write?"

"Of course I can."

"Then what are your likes, my lord?" she asked. "Do you have any diversions you are fond of?"

She couldn't see his expression as he watched her lowered head. "You ask many questions."

"It is my right. We are betrothed."

Gar didn't reply. Mattie continued sewing as he continued standing there, watching her through the tiny window. But he didn't want to do that any longer.

He needed to get out there and face her.

Unfortunately, he didn't have anything to wear. His breeches were in tatters and the tunic he'd been wearing, and the accompanying protection, was in a pile on the floor. The same servant who had washed him was shaking it all out, preparing to clean it, but Gar wasn't watching the man go about his duties.

He was more interested in what the man was wearing.

He had an idea.

Out in the sun, Mattie continued sewing the pieces of linen together, wondering where Gar had gone. He'd fallen silent. When she dared to look up at the small window, she couldn't see his eyes any longer. She was wondering if she'd offended him with her attempt to come to know him and thought about calling out to him again, but decided against it. He was still in there, somewhere, but clearly no longer wished to speak to her. As she debated what to do about it, the door to the knights' quarters suddenly opened. Mattie looked up in time to see an enormous man come through the door, shoeless, with breeches that were far too small for him and a tunic that hardly fit. He looked like a sausage that had burst its casing.

She erupted into laughter.

Gar knew he looked ridiculous, but her laughter was doing something to his ego. He frowned at her.

"I know how foolish this looks," he said. "But I have no other clothing and it is not suitable for me to continue to talk to you through a window. With a conversation like this, we must speak face to face."

Mattie had her hand over her face as she struggled to stop the giggles. Just when she thought she had herself under control, she looked at him and the laughter started all over again.

"You look as if you have stolen a child's clothing," she said.

Gar wasn't happy with her insult, true though it was. "I told you that I do not have any clothing of my own right now," he said. "Your brother was supposed to find me something to wear, so until he does, this is all I have."

Mattie was laughing so hard that she was crying. "Do not let anyone else see you like that," she said. "They will think you've gone simple in the head."

Increasingly annoyed, but strangely charmed by her laughter, Gar folded his arms over his chest and ended up tearing the seam on the tunic. The sleeve came away from the torso portion with a loud ripping sound. Mattie screamed with laughter as he tried to keep his dignity by pretending it didn't matter to him, but the truth was that the breeches were far too small and he risked tearing those, too. Better say what he needed to say and say it quickly before the entire garment came apart.

"I am glad you find my embarrassment so hilarious," he said sarcastically. "Lady, I've come a long way and I would appreciate it if you stopped laughing at me."

Mattie took a deep breath, struggling to regain her composure, but it started right up again when she looked at him, so she quickly focused on the sewing in her lap. Furiously, she resumed working on it.

"My apologies," she said, stitching quickly. "I will not laugh again."

He cocked a dark eyebrow. "Somehow, I do not think you can hold to that vow," he said. "I think you find me foolish, which brings me back to the point I was making before. Wouldn't you rather marry someone who is better suited to you?"

Mattie remained focused on her sewing. "Since you have asked me again, am I to understand that *you* wish to marry someone who is better suited to you?"

"This is not about me," he said. "I do not want you to make a mistake and regret it for the rest of your life. It would make both of us miserable."

"Just what is that you think makes us so unsuitable for one another?"

He wondered if he just shouldn't come out with it. Perhaps he'd danced around the subject long enough.

It was time for truth.

"My lady, let me tell you about my home," he said. "If we marry, I will take you there and that is where we shall live. My garrison is in a remote area of the Scots border called Gleann na Fola Castle. It is a fortress built for defense, not comfort. The walls are tall, the chambers small, the windows smaller, and it is rather compact. That means the stables and men are crowded into the lower bailey and the kitchen is in the lower level of the keep. The level above that is the great hall. Above that are more chambers, living chambers, but because space is at a premium, those chambers are often full of stores so the Scots cannot steal them. It is freezing in the wintertime and cold in the summertime, and there are no women there at all. It is all men. I have a thousand-man standing army, so it is crowded. It smells of men and animals and I am used to it that way, so have no illusions that it is a fine palace. It would be hell for someone like you. You would hate it the moment you arrived."

Mattie didn't reply right away. She kept her head down, sewing with purpose. She was clearly making something, but it still wasn't clear to Gar what, exactly, she was making. He was more focused on her, on her lowered head, watching her delicate hands fly with the needle, noting the myriad colors in her hair as the sun glistened off it. She truly was an exquisite creature, but even so, he sensed a steely strength in her. She wasn't a flighty female. That much was clear.

This was a woman of substance.

Already, he knew that.

"And you think I would be unhappy in such a place?" she said after a moment.

Gar nodded. "I do," he said. "I truly do."

She continued to sew, pondering his honesty. At least, he thought so. But he was wrong. Something else had been building up in that pretty head and it was about to come flying out at him.

"How kind of you to be concerned only with me," she said, but she didn't mean it. "But how manipulative. Do you think I am stupid, Sir Gar? Do you think I cannot see that you are trying to convince me that you are only concerned with my happiness so that I can break this betrothal that you clearly want nothing to do with?"

For such a small woman, she was intimidating when she was angry. Gar wasn't hard pressed to admit that. "My lady, I am simply being honest with what you are facing," he said evenly. "You and I were children when we met ten years ago. The situation has changed dramatically. I'm no longer that young man who saved you from de Vries and you are no longer the young woman who needed saving. We are two different souls, lady. Can you not see that?"

Her sewing was growing faster, her movements jerky. At one point, she reached into the sewing kit and pulled forth a pair of shears, cutting some material into strips, which she proceeded to sew onto one end of whatever she was making. She didn't reply to him, but continued working on her project until, finally, she seemed to be finished. The patches of linen she'd brought with her were now all sewn together and when she stood up abruptly from the stump she'd been sitting on, she held up what it was.

A pair of quickly stitched-together breeches.

"Here," she said, thrusting them at him. "Since my dog ruined your clothing, you can wear these until you find something more suitable. Burn them when you no longer have a use for them, because I certainly do not want anything to remind you of me."

He caught the breeches, which were practically thrown at him. Clutching them against his abdomen, he looked down at the garment in shock.

"You *made* a pair of breeches?" he said, astonished. "Right now? As we were speaking?"

She was closing up the sewing kit. "It is not as difficult as you make it sound," she said. "I just sewed the linen together. They are big pieces, so it was simple enough. There are two sleeves for your legs and the breeches will tie up at the top so you can secure it around your waist. I know it is not very elegant, but as you have pointed out, you are not an elegant man. But mayhap you can get some use out of them."

Gar didn't know what to say. As he looked at the breeches, a creeping sense of guilt washed over him. Had he been so cruel to this woman who was trying so hard to make amends with him for what her dog had done? Was he being so stubborn about this marriage that he was overlooking the fact that, perhaps, they weren't so terribly different?

He simply didn't know.

"My lady," he finally said. "I am… humbled. You did not have to do this."

Mattie closed the top of the sewing kit and faced him. "Aye,

I did," she said. "Your breeches were ruined because of my dog and since you would not let me repair them, I used what I'd brought for the repair to fashion you a new pair. But this conversation has been enlightening. I see now that you only came here out of obligation, but with no real intention of going through with the marriage. And you may deny it all you wish, but you have been trying to manipulate me into breaking the betrothal because you are too much of a coward to do it yourself. Given that I am the only one between us with a sense of decency, I will do as you wish. I will ask my father to break the betrothal. Is there anything else I can do for you to make your life easier, my lord?"

God, but the woman could be vicious when she wanted to. Vicious and utterly, completely in the right. Gar was a knight's knight, a man who commanded thousands, a man who could keep the raging Scots at bay, but at this moment, he felt completely belittled and beaten down by a woman half his size.

But he absolutely deserved it.

"My lady, I am sorry if you feel slighted," he said, genuinely meaning what he said. "It was not my intention to offend you. You are a beautiful woman, very accomplished, and any man would feel extremely fortunate to have you."

"Anyone but you," she said pointedly. Bending down, she picked up the sewing kit, preparing to take her leave, but her gaze lingered on him. The hurt, the disappointment in her expression, was obvious. "Just so you are aware, from the moment our betrothal was final, I have been completely faithful to you. There have been many men who tried to woo me, but I sent every one of them away. Every single one. You see, I was betrothed to the great Gar de Wolfe, son of Lord Braemoor, and a knight with an astonishing reputation even at a young age. I was so proud of that, so I considered it a privilege to be completely faithful to you. I can see now that my loyalty was wasted. You did not ask for it, but I gave it because it was the right thing to do. My apologies that you were betrothed to a woman who worshipped the very thought of you. My apologies if that was not what you wanted. I do hope you find a woman worthy of you, someday."

With that, she turned on her heel and headed back across the bailey, leaving Gar standing there feeling like a monster. A horrible, vicious monster. It didn't take an epiphany to quickly come to the conclusion that the only person between them who wasn't worthy in this situation was him. That articulate, kind, magnificent woman was far too good for him. She'd been open and generous, and he'd been a scoundrel. He'd just done what Maksim had told him not to do.

He'd broken her heart.

Devastated by what he'd just done, he took his patchwork breeches and headed back into the knights' quarters.

He had some thinking to do.

CHAPTER FIVE

"I DON'T KNOW what to say," Troy said. "Did she give a reason as to *why* she wants to break the betrothal?"

In the great hall of Hensingham, Troy found himself facing off against a fairly upset Reece. The man had just come from the keep where his daughter had told him that she no longer wished to marry Gar. The sun was setting and torches were being lit all over the bailey as servants lit the fat yellow tapers in the big chandeliers of the great hall, lowering them with a rope to be ignited before hauling them back up again so they loomed over the tables below. Troy and Andreas had been in the hall, enjoying some wine and sweet dough balls that Lady Hensingham had sent out from the kitchens, when Reece joined them. The man was overwrought that his obedient daughter had suddenly had a change of heart.

Or so he thought.

But Troy suspected otherwise.

"Something about not wanting to be married to a warlord," Reece said, agitated. "But she knew what he was. She has always known. Why does it bother her so now?"

Troy looked at Andreas, who gave his father a long look

before turning away. That left Troy trying to come up with something to soothe an agitated father and not explode at Gar at the same time.

"They've not seen each other in years," Troy said. "Mayhap when she saw him, he did not fit her ideal of a husband. Time changes people. She remembers that young man and Gar is no longer a young man. He has grown up. He is one of the more powerful warlords on the border."

"Pah," Reece said angrily. "She is being positively foolish and I'll not stand for it. My wife is with her now, trying to talk some sense into her. This *shall* be resolved, Lord Braemoor. Everyone becomes nervous before a wedding… don't they?"

"They do," Troy said. "I was. So was Andreas. In fact, let me leave you with Andreas and I shall seek out Gar to see if he might have said something to upset the lady."

He was already standing up, not giving Reece an opportunity to stop him. He knew why the young woman had suddenly changed her mind and he was going to seek the cause. He didn't know why Gar would have had the opportunity to speak with the young woman, especially without a chaperone, so whatever happened must have been clandestine on Gar's part.

The man wanted out of the marriage so badly that he'd done something questionable.

Truthfully, Troy was angry because Gar's behavior earlier had led him to believe that Gar had perhaps changed his mind. He'd asked for a bath and that had lured Troy into a false sense of hope. He trusted his son's word, but he didn't trust it now.

Things were about to get ugly.

He knew that Maksim de Reyne had taken Gar to the knights' quarters. He'd known that from the start, when they'd arrived and Maksim had led Gar away, so he could only assume that Gar was still there. His possessions had also been taken there, since men didn't usually stay in the residence of their host unless there were no single women present. Therefore, his destination was the knights' quarters—and if Gar wasn't there, he'd hunt him down like prey.

He was going to get to the bottom of this.

As he stormed toward the door, Gar was just coming out. He was wearing a clean tunic, his boots, and pale patchwork breeches that Troy had never seen before. Truthfully, he'd never seen the man in breeches that weren't leather, finely tanned, and shockingly expensive, and that included the pair he'd worn into the ground that more than likely had to be removed with a chisel today before he bathed. As Gar exited, Troy noticed that Maksim was right behind him, but Troy was focused on Gar.

He thrust a finger at him.

"*You,*" he growled. "I must have a word with you."

Gar came to a halt, looking at his father with something close to fear in his eyes. Not quite, but almost. Without delay, he threw up his hands.

"I know," he said. "Papa, I know why you are here. I was just discussing it with Maksim. I—"

Troy marched right up on Gar and grabbed him by the front of his tunic. Gar was bigger than his father, and heavier, but Troy's rage fed his strength and he ended up yanking Gar over to the exact area where his son and Mattie had indulged in their earlier conversation. As Maksim stood back, eyebrows lifted, wondering if he should try to help Gar, Troy let go of his son and got in his face.

"What have you done?" he spat. "You told de Reyne's daughter something, didn't you? Somehow, you had a conversation with her and now she is telling her father that she no longer wishes to marry you."

Troy, out of all the sons of William de Wolfe, with the exception of the youngest son, Thomas, was quickest to temper. He was well known for raging first, being rational second. It was a trait that Gar and his siblings were terrified of growing up and, truthfully, he was still terrified of it. When Troy was angry, the safest thing to do was run away. But Gar couldn't run away.

He was stuck.

"She came here to apologize for the damage her dog had done," he said, trying not to speak quickly out of sheer panic. "She offered to repair my breeches."

Troy frowned. "What damage?" he said. "What dog?"

Gar gestured in Maksim's direction. "Maks saw it," he said. "When he was bringing me to the knights' quarters so I could bathe, the lady's dog attacked me from behind and tore my breeches to pieces."

Maksim forced himself to step forward in support of Gar's statement. "It is true, my lord," he said. "My sister's dog tore Gar's breeches and she came to apologize and offer remediation."

Troy stepped back from Gar, looking between the two knights. "So she *did* come here," he said as his focus settled on Gar. "And you had a conversation with her."

Gar nodded quickly. "I did," he said. "I told her she did not have to repair the breeches, as they were beyond hope, so she made these for me."

He was indicating the patchwork breeches he was wearing. Big pieces of linen had been stitched together. The breeches weren't exactly fitted, but bigger and baggier. Troy peered at them, seeing that they were stitched with yellow silk thread. They were well made. The least bit puzzled, he shook his head.

"She did that?" he said, somewhat calmer. "That was quite generous of her."

"I know," Gar said. "I told her so."

"Then why is she telling her father that she does not wish to marry you?"

Gar hesitated. "I told her about life on the border," he said. "We had a conversation about it."

"*And?*"

Gar took a deep breath. "Papa, you should know that the lady is quite refined," he said. "She speaks several languages. She is very accomplished in all things that young ladies should be accomplished in and having a husband like me is an insult to such a woman. I am a knight. That is all I am. She deserves better."

Although Troy was calmer at the moment, there was no guarantee he was going to remain that way. "And you told her that?"

"Nay," Gar said honestly. "But I did tell her that I do not believe we are well suited. She would be miserable, Papa."

"You do not know that."

"Living at Gleann na Fola would be taking her away from everything fine and civilized and plunging her into hell."

Troy lifted an eyebrow. "And because you are so magnanimous, you have made this decision for her?" he said, a hint of anger coming back into his tone. "Are you telling me that you are only thinking of her in this matter? Because if you are, you are lying to my face, Gar. You know it and I know it."

Gar sighed heavily, looking at Maksim for a moment to see if he had the man's support in this matter. All he could see was a torn expression on Maksim's face.

"Just now, Maksim and I were having this same conversation," he said, his voice quieter. "I told him what the lady and I spoke of. I told him the situation for what it is. He is concerned for his sister, also. Papa, believe me—this isn't just about me. It is what's best for the lady, too."

Troy had heard enough. This time, he grabbed Gar by the arm and pulled him away from Maksim so he could have a private conversation with him.

"Now," he muttered. "I want you to listen to me and listen well. You had no right to speak to that girl about your betrothal, in any fashion. You knew this was a delicate situation and instead of respecting my wishes, you tried to go around me and ruin this."

"Papa, that's not—"

Troy cut him off. "Do you know what is going to happen if this young woman successfully breaks this betrothal because of what you've done?" he said, his eyes glittering dangerously. "Allow me to inform you of your future, Gareth. Not only will you lose your command at Gleann na Fola, but you will not be permitted to serve in any of the de Wolfe properties nor any properties of her allies. I will send you south, to London, where you can serve in the royal vaults. You can deal with royal prisoners for the rest of your life, away from command, away from battlefields, and away from me. If you do not think, for one moment, that I can do this, then test me. You've already pushed me to my limit. Push me over the edge and see what will happen."

Gar stared at his father. Truthfully, he was shocked and trying not to show it, but he couldn't quite manage it.

"You go too far," he said, frowning. "I do not take well to threats."

"And I do not take well to disobedient knights," Troy shot

back. "Because that is what you are—a disobedient knight. And disobedient knights cannot be trusted. You are afraid a marriage will ruin your life? Refuse this marriage and I can guarantee you that your life will be ruined forever because I will make sure it happens. And if you think I will soften over the years, think again. You know me well enough to know that I hold a grudge. And I do not go back on my word."

He was right, in both instances. Troy de Wolfe had been known to hold grudges for decades and Gar had never once seen his father go back on his word. Realizing he was at an end of his pursuit to get out of this marriage, he did the only thing he could do.

He surrendered.

"As you wish," he said, though he was grossly unhappy. "If you want me to repair whatever damage you think I've done, I shall. Since you believe my happiness is not important, but only your own wishes when it comes to using your children like pawns, I will accept that. *Your* happiness and *your* wants are the only things that matter. But know this—as you once said our relationship will never be the same, know that it is true for me, as well. Our relationship *will* never be the same. I hope you can live with that."

With that, he turned and walked away, heading over to Maksim and asking the man where his sister might be found. Maksim wasn't entirely sure, but he told Gar to head over to the castle garden, which was on the north side of the keep, and wait there. Maksim was going to try to convince his sister to at least speak with Gar.

If he could.

But Maksim made it clear he'd only help Gar this one time. If Gar didn't repair the damage, then their friendship would be over, too.

Troy heard everything. He watched Gar and Maksim head toward the keep and, for the first time in this entire situation, found himself questioning his decision. Was he thinking of his happiness over his son's? It wasn't happiness as much as it was simply duty. This *was* a duty. Marriage was a duty. It had been for him, too, but he'd been fortunate enough to fall in love with his wife. Perhaps Gar would find love with Lady Matilda; perhaps not. The hope was that he would at least grow fond of her.

Or not.

But in the end, Troy and his father would get what they wanted.

An alliance.

That was the only thing that mattered… wasn't it?

☙

"JUST COME DOWN to the garden, Matilda. It is not that difficult."

So Maksim said. But it *was* that difficult.

Mattie was in her bower, with Agnes and the destructive dog, sewing on a cloak that was to be part of her wedding trousseau. Only now, she wasn't going to be married, so it was just a beautiful cloak that had exquisite embroidery around it. A pretty cloak for a pretty girl.

That's all it was.

Marriage plans were in tatters.

"I do not need to go to the garden," she said, focusing on her sewing, which she excelled at. "Sir Gar made it clear that I would be miserable in this marriage and so would he. He said everything he needed to say and so did I."

She was unbending. Maksim could see that. Agnes was sitting on the end of the bed with the dog lying across her lap, looking at Mattie with some sadness. That was all Maksim needed to push forward with his request.

"Aggie," he said quietly. "Get out. And take the beast with you."

"Nay, Agnes," Mattie said evenly, still focused on her sewing. "You will not leave."

Maksim stepped into the chamber, fixed on Agnes, and pointed at the door. "Go," he said. "I will not tell you again."

Fearfully, Agnes leaped up and rushed out with Winchester on her heels. When the girl and the dog were gone, Maksim shut the door and faced his sister.

"I do not know what was said, exactly, between you and Gar, but he has given me a good idea," he said. "I will tell him what I told you, Matilda—if he broke your heart, I would break him. Is that what happened? *Did* he break your heart?"

Mattie wouldn't look at him. "Of course not," she said. "How could he? I do not love him."

Maksim knew that was a lie, mostly. "Nay, you do not love him, but you were very much looking forward to being married," he said. "He hurt your pride."

She faltered in her sewing, as if what he'd said hit the mark. But she quickly resumed. "I do not know why you are here," she said. "I did what Gar wanted. I asked Papa to break the betrothal. Why does Gar wish to speak with me about it now?"

Maksim planted himself on a three-legged stool, facing his sister. "Because it is costing him everything," he said quietly. "Matilda, I am going to tell you something about Gar de Wolfe that you should probably know."

"What?"

"You can never do any better for a husband."

She paused and looked at him, frowning. "What do you mean by that?"

"Exactly what I said," he said. "You will never do any better than Gar. Shall I tell you a little about him, things you do not know? To begin with, he was fully knighted at seventeen years of age. That is three years earlier than most knights, including me."

"I already know that," Mattie said. "Do not forget that I have been betrothed to him for ten years. There is not much about him I do not know. What I did not know is that the man is a coward."

Maksim's eyebrows flew up. "Gar?" he repeated, aghast. "A coward?"

"Aye," she said firmly. "A coward. He would not ask Papa to break the betrothal personally, so he sent me to do it."

"Did he ask you to?"

She paused before answering. "Nay, not directly," she said. "But that is what he wanted me to do."

"If he did not ask you to do it in words you can understand, then how do you know?" Maksim said. "Or did you assume it before having all of the facts and ran to Papa with your assumption?"

She scowled. "You will not blame me for this," she said. "That is exactly what Gar wanted and that is what he got."

Maksim scratched his neck in a frustrated gesture before continuing. "Let me tell you something about him you do not know," he said. "I saw Gar not long ago when we were both in London and I spent two days with the man and his brother, Andreas, who is here. It was Andreas who told me why they were in London."

"Why do I care?"

"Because you should know that Gar has been the garrison commander for his family's property at Gleann na Fola Castle for the past few years," he said. "Gar has singlehandedly kept that portion of the border from erupting, no matter what has happened elsewhere. He has been a wise and intuitive commander. He has made alliances with some of the local clans, making sure they have a mutually beneficial relationship. When one clan had an outbreak of sickness, Gar gathered physics and medicines and escorted all of it to the clan, through hostile territory. In the dead of winter. All because it was the right thing to do."

By this time, Mattie had stopped sewing and was looking at him with a torn expression on her face. "That is… admirable," she said. "But I do not know why you—"

"Because I want you to know about this man," Maksim said, cutting her off. "You seem to think he's a fool of a man, a simple knight, and breaking this betrothal is an easy enough thing. Aye, you know about his service record. You know he has been heavily trained. You know he has both Scots and English blood in him. Did you also know that Edward, the king, has asked for his service, but his father will not give permission?"

"Why not?"

"Because he knows Gar's worth," Maksim said. "He knows that the man is most valuable where he is, not riding escort for a monarch. I will agree that Gar is a knight who serves in some of the most remote lands of England. Mayhap he does not have manners or social graces. I have seen that for myself."

Mattie pursed her lips wryly. "That is what he said."

"He did?"

She nodded. "Aye," she said. "He said it is a working fortress with no great feasts or social gatherings."

"He is right," Maksim said. "Gar lives in a world of warfare, Mattie. That's all he knows. In a sense, I applaud him for telling you that so there are no illusions of the man. When you marry him, you'll not go to live in a fine palace, but a place of war. You've never had to do that."

Mattie thought on that for a moment before setting her sewing needle down and sighing softly. "Then why do you want me to talk to him again?" she said. "It seems as if the decision has already been made."

Maksim waggled his eyebrows, silently suggesting what was to come. "Because he is in trouble for being honest with you," he said. "Papa is furious that you want to break the betrothal and so is Troy. He told Gar that if he could not repair what he had damaged by telling you the truth, Gar would be stripped of his garrison and everything else he held dear. He would be sent away, never to serve the de Wolfe family again."

Mattie looked at him seriously. "Gar is going to lose everything for being honest about the situation?"

Maksim nodded. "That sums it up," he said. "I know that Gar might not be the refined lord you were hoping for, but that is because he's never had anyone—a woman—guide him. Matilda, when you marry Gar, you will be marrying a man who will be loyal to you for life. He will defend you to the death. He will never be abusive or cruel. You cannot say that about many men, but one can say that about Gar. Mayhap the reality of who he has become ten years after you first met him is not ideal, but he is still a good man. I would stake my life on it."

Mattie's defenses when it came to Gar were beginning to crumble. "And you think I should marry him?"

"Again, I do not think you can find a better husband."

Mattie sighed again, this time long and slow. It was clear that she was debating what to do, but her brother's words had had an impact on her. She knew that Maksim would never do her wrong. She trusted him. If he said Gar was a good man, then he was.

Perhaps manners and basic hygiene were something she could teach him.

Hopefully.

"Very well," she said, putting her sewing aside. "He's in the garden, you said?"

"Aye," Maksim said. "At least talk to him. He's going to lose quite a lot if you refuse the marriage. His life is in your hands, Mattie."

That didn't give her any sense of purpose. In fact, it put pressure on her where none had existed before. She was still angry with Gar, but she was also feeling strangely apologetic. The only thing that kept her from refusing completely was the fact that Maksim hardly spoke well of anyone, but he spoke well of Gar. And he'd also been right about something else—Gar had hurt her feelings with his honesty. Had he tried to convince her to break the betrothal? Possibly. He hadn't come right out and said it, but she had gone on assumption. She hadn't mistaken his meaning. But perhaps Gar's honesty was offending her into bitterness.

His life is in your hands, Mattie.

She wished Maksim hadn't said that.

CHAPTER SIX

"GOD'S BONES, HE'S back."

Those were Gar's softly uttered words as Winchester ran straight for him. Since he was wearing the only pair of breeches he had, even if they were something a pauper would wear, he still didn't want to surrender them to that wild dog who seemed to have a vendetta against him.

Gar was in Hensingham's lovely garden, which was a mix of flowers, a pond with fish in it, and, along the western wall, an array of vegetables. There were servants on that end of the garden and he quickly headed in that direction when the dog, accompanied by a young woman, charged through the gate at him. He made it over to the servants just in time to weave among them, walk around them, and otherwise try to keep Winchester off his tail. But Winchester was determined to get his pound of flesh and Gar was forced to yank a branch off an apple tree, using it to keep the dog away from him. He didn't want to hurt the beast, but he also didn't want to be injured, so he ended up using one of the male servants as a shield, pushing the dog away with the branch.

"Winchester!"

Someone was screaming at the dog and it wasn't the young woman who had accompanied him. That young woman seemed terrified by what was happening and offered no help. Gar looked toward the sounds of the shouting at the garden entrance to see Mattie standing there, shrieking angrily at her dog. But Winchester wasn't apt to listen. He kept growling and barking at Gar, trying to take a bite out of him, as Gar and the frightened servant kept the dog at bay.

"Winnie, you are a menace," Mattie said as she ran up and grabbed the dog around the neck. She was dragging him back when she caught sight of Agnes cowering near the garden wall. "Agnes! Come and get the dog!"

Agnes ran to her but was clearly frightened by the snarling dog. "Why is he doing this?" she said fearfully. "I have never seen him do this!"

Mattie picked the dog up, which was no mean feat considering he was probably half her weight, and thrust him at Agnes.

"Take him out," she said in a tone that sounded much like a command. "Make sure he cannot get back in here!"

Agnes couldn't quite carry the dog, so she put her arms around his body, under his front legs, and half dragged, half walked the dog out of the garden. Mattie followed, making sure to shut the gate once they were out. She stood there a moment, peering through the iron grate to make sure Agnes and the dog were well away, before brushing off her hands and turning back in Gar's direction.

By that time, Gar had released the frightened servant and tossed the branch away, making his way toward Mattie. It was a wide garden, so they had their focus on one another as they closed the gap, weaving around the flower beds.

It was Gar who spoke first.

"Thank you for saving me from that vicious beast," he said. "I do not know why he does not like me, but clearly, I must have wronged him at some point in my life."

Mattie shook her head. "He has his heart set on vengeance when it comes to you," she said. "They say that dogs know people better than people do. Mayhap he knows that there has been unkindness between us and he is trying to protect me."

Gar's manner grew subdued. "Any unkindness has been my fault," he said. "My lady, thank you for coming to speak with me. I must ask your forgiveness for any offense I caused. That has never been my intention."

"What *was* your intention?"

She was giving him the chance to explain and Gar took it gratefully, even if it was to save his career, his future. He'd never been in a position like this in his life, but here he was, making the attempt to convince this woman that a marriage between them needed to go forward. Gar was great in negotiations with the Scots, dealing with men on their level, but this was different. Now, he was dealing with a woman and completely out of his depth. She'd accused him of being manipulative before.

Now, it was the truth.

He needed her.

"I am not entirely sure what my intention was, but it wasn't hurting the feelings of a woman I do not know," he said. "The truth is that I have known about his marriage for ten years, as have you. But my focus has been on my vocation. It has been my entire life. When I assumed command of Gleann na Fola, it was a great achievement for me. The Scots… There is a deep-seated hatred there and it is my duty to protect England, and my family, from that hatred. That is all I've thought about. When I told you that my home is a cold and brutal thing, that was the truth. No one has told you just how cold and isolated and brutal it is, have they?"

Mattie regarded him, her eyes glittering as she did so. "Nay," she said. "No one has used those words."

He lifted his eyebrows. "I think that your father, and my father, want this marriage to happen so badly that they refrain from telling you what it will really be like."

Her gaze lingered on him a moment longer before she shrugged. "I would be willing to believe that," she said. "My father has not told me anything. But you… It is clear you do not want this marriage. You told me about your castle, and where we will live, so that I would tell my father to break the betrothal. Be honest with me, Sir Gar. That is why you told me, isn't it?"

He couldn't lie to her. "Aye."

"Then I did what you intended. I asked to break it."

Gar nodded faintly, averting his gaze as if thinking on what she said, on the situation as a whole. His gaze then drifted downward until it came to rest on his breeches. He immediately pointed to them.

"Thank you for these," he said. "I am wearing them, as you can see. It was a very generous gift."

Mattie looked at the breeches. "If nothing else, they will hold together until you can find a better pair," she said. "They may not fit you well, but they are well made."

"They fit me perfectly," he said, rubbing his left thigh to prove it. "You are very talented."

"They are only breeches. They were not difficult."

"Even so, you have my thanks."

"You are welcome."

The conversation lagged a little until Gar caught sight of a stone bench in the corner of his eye. "Shall we sit?" he said. "I…

I think we have a few things to discuss."

Mattie went over to the bench, sitting down as he sat down a foot or so away from her. The bench was on the edge of the fishpond and when the fish saw their shadows, they swam in their direction, looking for food. Mattie pulled off the nearest flower and tossed it into the pond, watching the fish poke at it.

"Well?" she finally said. "What did you wish to discuss?"

That was a good question. Gar thought about it for a moment before replying. "My father and your father are very angry with me right now," he said. "They did not want me to tell you the truth about Gleann na Fola, nor the living conditions. My father, in particular, is enraged at me and I do fear this incident will ruin my relationship with him."

She looked at him seriously. "Why?"

Gar shrugged. "Because he knows I was not ready for this marriage," he said. "He knows I tried to discourage you. My lady, if I hurt your feelings or damaged your pride, know that I am genuinely sorry. To be honest, I did not know how you felt about this marriage. I did not know you'd been looking forward to it. For all I knew, you were as reluctant as I, but I have since discovered that was not the case."

Mattie sighed faintly, looking off to the fish in the pond again. "Every young woman looks forward to their wedding," she said. "I am no different."

"Mayhap there is part of me that is having difficulty understanding why anyone would *want* to be married to me. I am not a prize."

She looked at him again, brow furrowed. "Of course you are," she said. "I told you that before. But if you do not want me, I cannot make you."

"It is not that," he said quickly. "I want to be clear about that. You are an astonishingly beautiful woman and you are clearly talented. You are far more of a prize than I am. I think that I would feel guilty being married to you."

"Why?"

He lifted his big shoulders. "I suppose I explained it best earlier," he said. "You deserve a prince or an earl or a courtier. Not a warlord. Christ, how could I even protect you? Even as I sit here, I think about all of the things that could happen with raiding Scots or battles or the usual danger of the borders, and there you would be, bottled up in my castle as I tried to keep you safe from harm. I would be terrified every moment that someone was going to hurt you. Or that you would be in danger somehow. And I am not used to worrying about someone close to me."

By this time, she was looking at him with big eyes because what he'd said didn't sound like a man reluctant to marry. It sounded like the words of a protective husband already.

"That… that was quite a speech," she said. "I've never had anyone I did not know worry for me so much. Are you truly afraid for me?"

He was unable to look at her. "I was thinking aloud," he said. "Other than my mother and grandmother and female relatives, I've never really had a woman I had to worry about."

"You've never courted anyone?"

He shook his head firmly. "You said something to me earlier that has stuck with me," he said. "You said you had been faithful to the betrothal. Faithful to me. I may be a mere warlord who knows nothing but battle, but the truth is that I do know contracts. I have been faithful to our contract, mainly because I did not wish to shame my family. Honor means a great deal to me. And you have been honorable to our betrothal, also. Please know that I respect you for that. I am grateful."

Mattie was watching his lowered head. The man seemed to grow more handsome with each passing second because, honestly, she couldn't seem to take her eyes from him. The way he was speaking showed that he had some vulnerability and she found that endearing. In fact, the entire conversation had been endearing, perhaps enough that she might even forgive him for offending her earlier. She dreaded baring her soul to the man, but it seemed to her that this moment called for it. He was being honest with her.

It was time for her to do the same.

"Then I am glad, if only for honor's sake, that you have been true to the contract," she said. "My lord, if we are being perfectly honest, if you do not want me, I do not know what I shall do. I am rather old to be on the marriage market and if others know that a betrothal was broken between us, they will believe there is something wrong with me."

He frowned. "I do not think so," he said. "I—"

She cut him off, though not harshly. "Aye, they will," she said. "Trust that I know more about this than you do. I have fostered in noble households my entire life and I understand the way the world of the nobility works. There will never be any question cast on you, but for me, there will be much. A broken betrothal with the House of de Wolfe means my prospects will be quite limited. If de Wolfe didn't want me, then who will?"

He looked at her. *Really* looked at her. He could absolutely understand what she was saying because he'd seen that sort of thing before. He might not have cared about marriage or politics, but he didn't live under a rock. He knew how cruel and judgmental the nobility could be.

"I see," he said after a moment. "We cannot have that."

"Nay, we cannot."

"What do you suggest we do?"

She shrugged. "I think we should go forth with the marriage."

"Do you?"

"I do."

"And you will have me?"

"If you will have me, I will have you."

He snorted, flashing a grin. "I would agree to that," he said. "But we sound like a pair of indecisive idiots."

Mattie started laughing. "We are pathetic."

"We are."

She pointed at his patchwork pants. "You even look pathetic," she said. "May I commission a better pair for you? So men will not think I allow my husband to dress like the court jester?"

He was smiling broadly. "I like these," he insisted. "They are comfortable and you made them for me. I will not surrender them no matter how much you beg."

She shook her head. "But they really weren't meant for you to wear continuously," she said. "Only until you could retrieve a better pair from your baggage."

He stood up, admiring the patchwork stitching. "I do not have a better pair," he said. "You should know that things like clothing mean very little to me. If it is durable, I wear it. I will wear it until the seams break and the seat wears out. Ask my mother."

She stood up beside him, looking at the pants with a critical eye. "Terrible," she said. "I will have to commission other breeches for you, then."

"Unnecessary."

She looked up at him. "That is not true," she said. "I will be judged harshly if I allow you to wear clothing that you wear down until it becomes indecent. You would embarrass me so?"

He was properly contrite. "Nay," he said. "Would you truly be embarrassed?"

"Probably."

He sighed heavily, a twinkle in his eye. "You are going to make me wash regularly, too, aren't you?"

"And shave."

He rolled his eyes. "God's Bones," he said. "Are you going to be one of *those*?"

"I am. You will have to live with it."

She had a gleam in her eye as she said it, one he found enchanting. He could see her sense of humor and he liked it.

Even if she was, more than likely, serious.

Perhaps this was the right decision, after all.

"My lady," he said, sobering. "I cannot promise you princely feasts, a fine home, and fine furnishing, but I can promise you that, as my wife, you will be respected and honored. I can also promise you that I will always be loyal to you and our marriage. It is not in my nature to be otherwise. Still… I know I have a good deal to learn about women and marriage in general. I will try, but I will not always succeed. I hope you will be patient with me."

Some of the softness was back in Mattie's expression. That same glow he'd seen earlier when she'd first come to repair his breeches. There had been something open and amiable about it, two traits that faded as their conversation had progressed. When he'd first seen her in the garden, she still had a hardness in her expression.

But not anymore.

"I am not entirely certain that anyone knows how to do

something they've never done before simply because they've seen others do it," she said. "I have never been a wife, but I know that I will try, also. You should know that I am used to running a house and hold. I will take charge. If you do not want me to, you should tell me now so we may discuss what my boundaries are."

He shrugged. "I am not opposed to your taking charge of Gleann na Fola," he said. "I have a cook and a man who runs the castle for me, but nothing more. It will be your domain, but do not say I did not warn you about it. It will be a… challenge."

"Good," she said. "I like challenges."

He knew she had no idea what she was facing so he chuckled, shaking his head as he did so. "I believe that," he said. "But before we can do anything, you should probably tell your father that you do not wish to break the betrothal."

Mattie nodded, turning for the garden gate, as Gar followed behind her. When she reached the gate, however, she paused and looked at him.

"My brother told me that your father threatened you if you did not go through with this marriage," she said. "You did not know that I knew, did you?"

Gar wasn't surprised to hear it. "Nay," he said. "But Maksim is very protective of you. What he told you was the truth."

She cocked her head. "I do not want you to think you manipulated me into doing what you wanted me to do in order to save you from your father's wrath," she said. "I was aware of it when I agreed. This was my choice."

"Aye, my lady."

"Just so we are clear."

"Very clear."

She rested her gaze on him a moment longer just to make

sure he knew he hadn't pulled the wool over her eyes before continuing through the gate with Gar behind her.

Out into the bailey beyond.

They had some parents to see.

Reece was beside himself with joy when Mattie, along with Gar, told him that the betrothal was once again on. He was so excited that he sent for Julia and, after that, Troy. Since the betrothal was a fragile thing, and the three parents feared that anything might tip the balance back toward a canceled contract, they decided that the marriage should be conducted quickly before either party changed their minds. Before Gar said one more stupid thing and Mattie decided once and for all not to marry him.

Julia sent for the priest in the village of Hensingham, a rector who presided over St. Mary's Church near the sea. Andreas went to personally retrieve the man, bringing him back so he could conduct a mass at the door of the great hall of Hensingham, which was traditional when it came to a wedding. In fact, the mass itself was shortened at the request of Lady Hensingham simply because she wanted to wed the two of them as quickly as possible. Once the blessing and benediction was complete, there was joy all around as the House of de Wolfe and the House of de Reyne finally became allied through a marriage.

One that didn't almost happen.

But now, it had.

And what an adventure it was to be.

CHAPTER SEVEN

"There once was a lady fair,
With silver bells in her hair.
I knew her to have,
A luscious kiss… it drove me mad!
But she denied me… and I was so terribly sad.
Lily, my girl,
Your flower, I will unfurl
With my cock and a bit of good luck!
Your kiss divine,
I'll make you mine,
And keep you abed for a fuck!"

THE GREAT HALL exploded with bawdy laughter as Gar, Andreas, and Maksim sang what was traditionally known in the de Wolfe family circle as the "Naughty Wedding Song." There were actually two or three of those questionable songs falling under that heading, but in any case, it was tradition at every de Wolfe marriage that the song, or songs, be sung. Gar and Andreas, drunk on Reese's good wine, and Maksim, even more drunk on his father's good wine, were singing it with the soldiers and sergeants that were in the great hall.

They certainly weren't singing it with the bride.

While the majority of the hall was happy and celebrating, at the dais, it was a different story. It was a somber group that sat before a mass of food, listening to the songs and watching the revelry. That included Julia, who wasn't exactly pleased with the song selection.

"Stop them," she told her husband. "I'll not have them debase this feast any more than they already have. Stop them, I say!"

Reece was trying to keep the grin off his face. He, too, would have been singing that song if he wasn't afraid of the stick his wife would use on him if he did. Troy, who had historically been at the head of those naughty wedding choruses, kept putting his cup to his lips, sipping, as if keeping his mouth busy so he wouldn't join in and offend his son's new mother-in-law.

"Let them celebrate, my dear," Reece said, trying to soothe her. "They are harmless songs. It keeps the men happy."

"And what about your daughter?" Julia said, throwing an imperious finger in Mattie's direction. "What about keeping her happy? Do you think she is happy right now?"

Reece looked over at his daughter, resplendent in a pale blue silk frock with silver and white embroidery around the neckline. It was a stunning piece, and she looked quite beautiful in it. When she saw her parents looking at her, she simply shook her head.

"I am untroubled, Mama," she said. "If he wants to sing, let him sing."

Julia frowned. "That is not a suitable song for your ears,"

she said. "This is your wedding feast. There must be some decorum!"

With that, she stood up and went to her daughter, pulling her out of the chair. As she began to lead her away, Mattie grasped Agnes' hand and pulled her along, too. There was a train of women heading for the area of the great hearth, where a man with a lute and another man with a fife had been providing music during the evening. They were part of the de Reyne army, soldiers who happened to play instruments, and Julia had made sure they played tonight.

Gar and Andreas and Maksim were striking up another chorus of a song involving an old whore named Rose when Julia began waving her hands, shouting for silence. When the men realized that Lady Hensingham was calling for their attention, they immediately shut their mouths. Very quickly, the hall fell into silence.

"Thank you," Julia said with a sarcastic tinge. "Now, the musicians will play something suitable for a *bransle.* My daughter and Lady Agnes will show you how it is done. Gar, come and dance with your wife."

It was a command. Gar immediately set his cup of wine down and went over to Mattie, who smiled hesitantly at him. He'd been having such a good time that she was concerned he might be angry with her that Julia had pulled him away from his friends, but there was no such annoyance on his face. In fact, he winked at her and took her hand, tucking it into his elbow as Julia directed the musicians, who began to play a common enough ballad suitable to that type of dance. But Mattie didn't hear the music.

All she felt was Gar.

It was the first time he'd touched her.

During the marriage mass, they'd simply stood there and listened, hands at their sides. They hadn't even looked at one another, their attention on the priest as he intoned the blessing. Even afterward, they had been congratulated by other people. They hadn't even congratulated each other. Gar had been surrounded by his father and brother, while Mattie had been embraced by her mother. Julia didn't even let her go, not until they'd reached the dais in the great hall where the hastily arranged wedding feast was spread out. Mattie sat down, there was a toast to their good marriage, and then Gar was pulled away by his father and brother and even Maksim, who seemed particularly overjoyed by the union. That had left Mattie sitting with Agnes and her mother whilst men drank and sang, and gaiety went on around her.

But something good had come out of it.

It gave her a chance to observe her new husband.

Gar loved to laugh. He laughed with his brother, his father, with Maksim. He drank, he laughed. He had big, straight teeth and a beautiful smile, one that made her heart leap strangely. He was big and handsome and seemingly bright, everything a maiden should want in a husband, but there was another side to him that she saw, too.

He was, in a word, sloppy.

He drank wine, it spilled down his chin, and he wiped it away with a hand. Then he wiped that hand on the breeches she'd made for him. He was still wearing them and the pale linen was quickly becoming dirty. At one point, he was challenged by one of the soldiers to an arm-wrestling competition, which he won with hardly any effort. But in the process of winning, he'd spilled the soldier's trencher onto his lap and onto the floor, and other than brush it away, he did nothing to actually clean it. He seemed to have no sense of cleanliness or manners, so by the time Mattie's mother was demanding he dance, Gar was filthy with stain. It was somewhat mortifying. When he winked at her, she almost forgot about it, but not quite. She was expected to stand with him. *Dance* with him. Oh, how she wanted to dance with her husband, but not the little piglet standing beside her.

Mattie was quite torn.

"Would this be a good time to confess that I do not know how to dance?"

Gar was whispering in her ear, distracting her from her thoughts. He smelled like wine. She looked at him, into those bright green eyes, and she could feel herself surrendering.

"Of course you can dance," she said. "Everyone learns to dance when they foster."

He shook his head. "Not me," he said. "I never had the ability. Everyone would laugh at me when I tried, so I simply refused to learn."

She grinned. "I will teach you, have no fear," she said. "Please do try. It is our wedding feast, after all."

He nodded, conceding the point. "For you, I will," he said. "But if anyone else asks me, they will not like my reaction."

"Gar!"

It was Julia. She was barking at him like a battle commander. Before Gar could stop himself, he shouted his response.

"Aye, empress?"

His booming voice had the entire hall laughing. Even Julia fought off a grin at his cheeky answer.

"Empress, is it?" she said. "Well and good that you have acknowledged that."

"I have, empress."

He seemed so serious about it and his reaction had Julia laughing. He was naughty, and sassy, but so adorable she could hardly become angry with him.

"I see," she said, looking at him appraisingly. "But if I am the empress, what, pray tell, is my daughter?"

Gar looked at Mattie, who was smiling up at him and he smiled in return.

"The queen," he said softly. "She is the Queen of All."

The entire hall applauded his answer, cheering the new husband's smart and submissive response when it came to two women who would be important in his life. One more than the other, of course, and the moment wasn't lost on Mattie. She flushed madly because it was a sweet thing to say and everyone knew it.

Especially her.

As the cheering died down, Julia clapped her hands quickly, businesslike, and the music began again. Since there were only three noblewomen in the hall—Mattie, Agnes, and Julia—there weren't any women for the soldiers to dance with. That was also because Julia wouldn't let the camp followers, the women who tended to warm the beds of the soldiers and cook for them, into the great hall. As she'd once told Reece, she'd rather have the dogs in her hall than the cats. Therefore, when the lines began to form for the traditional *bransle*, it was all men and two women because Julia recused herself.

The lines began to move.

Very quickly, Mattie began to see that Gar hadn't been exaggerating. He had no idea where to put his feet. Softly, she began to coach him.

"This way," she murmured. "Watch my feet. That's right. The left over the right. When we reverse, it will be the right over the left."

Gar was genuinely uncomfortable. "I am going to step on you, I know it," he said, sounding nervous. "I would much rather watch you dance than do this with you."

"Nonsense," Mattie said, smiling at him. The movement in the dance came when they were to hold hands and dance in a circle, so she took both of his hands and began to move to her left. "Follow me this way. You can do it. I have faith in you."

She was being sweet and encouraging, but Gar wanted to run. He'd done everything he could for this marriage already—he'd come under his own power. He'd relented to his father and gone through with it. But there was nothing in the laws, by God or by king, that said he had to dance with his new wife. He was about to feign a twisted ankle when Maksim and Andreas suddenly appeared on either side of him.

"Bess the Bold, the whore foretold, had hips that told a tale,
Of princes charmed and pirates fooled and pleasure bought with ale!
She found a knight, a handsome lad, and whispered in his ear—
'I've the sheath, my love, to bury your sword, and you'll none find better than here!'"

Gar burst out laughing as Maksim handed him another cup of wine. He was still holding on to Mattie with one hand, but he took the cup and downed it in one swallow. Unfortunately, he wasn't a neat man and the last few drops of it ended up splashing on Mattie.

Right on that beautiful blue silk.

Gar lost his humor in an instant.

"God's Bones," he said. "I am so terribly sorry. Please forgive me. It was an accident."

He was genuinely contrite and Mattie looked down at the bodice. It was barely speckled with two tiny drops of wine. Before she could reply, however, Julia was there, inspecting the damage. She was certain her mother was going to explode at both Gar and Maksim, but surprisingly, she didn't. She took her daughter by the hand and began to lead her away.

"Come with me," she said. "We will change you out of the garment so I can have the laundress look at it. We will find you something else to wear so you that you may return to the feast."

Mattie looked at Gar, who still seemed horrified by what he'd done. But her mother was tugging her away, so there was nothing she could do about it. She wanted to stay, to continue dancing with her husband, and perhaps he sensed that because he began to follow.

"Empress?" he said. "May I come?"

Julia glanced over her shoulder, seeing the big knight following. He had clearly decided to call her what he deemed an appropriate name for his wife's mother and, thinking it rather charming, she didn't correct him.

"It is not necessary, Gar," she said. "I will return her shortly."

But Gar didn't back off. He continued to follow them out into the night, into the bailey, with the big keep to their right. Julia and Mattie were about halfway to the keep entry when Gar caught up to them.

"Wait, please," he said, watching the women pause to look at him. "The hour grows late and I am not entirely sure I want to return to the feast because Maks will force more wine down my throat and my father will threaten to monopolize all of my attention because he will want to discuss family business, so if you are agreeable, I would like to take Lady de Wolfe to our chamber for the night."

Lady de Wolfe.

That was the first time Mattie had heard herself referred to as such and it made her feel rather warm and giddy inside. She looked at her mother, seeing that Julia didn't seem troubled by the suggestion. In fact, she nodded.

"That seems wise," she said. "It is growing late, as you said, and the men will only become more drunk. It will cease to become a wedding celebration at some point. Very well, then—you and my daughter may retreat to her chamber. I have had it prepared. I will go back into the hall and find Agnes and send her to bed. She does not need to be in the hall as the lone female among wolves."

With that, she kissed her daughter on the cheek, looking at her as if she wanted to say something more, but refraining. Her warm expression said everything words could not. Mattie watched her mother retreat toward the great hall, hearing a soft voice beside her.

"Come along, my queen," Gar said. "It has been a long day."

Mattie turned to him, smiling. "I'm your queen, am I?" she said. "Mother is the empress and I am the queen."

He nodded, taking her by the hand. "I may not know anything about marriage, or women in general, but I do know one thing," he said. "Women are the queen wherever they live and breathe. I've watched my mother and grandmother enough to know that. And every wife should be treated like a queen. My father has set that example."

Mattie giggled softly. "Good," she said. "Then he *has* taught you something about marriage."

They began to walk, heading up the steps toward the keep

entry. "He hasn't so much taught me as I have simply observed," Gar said, politely taking her elbow. "The women in my family are revered. That is simply the way of things."

"Tell me about your mother," Mattie said, interest in her tone. "Why didn't she come with you to Hensingham?"

"Because my brother's wife just had a child," he said. "The child is not thriving and my mother thought it would be best if she remained with my brother and his wife, simply to help out. If the child did not survive, she did not want to be away."

"Understandable," Mattie said. "She sounds like a caring woman."

They were inside the keep now and Gar collected one of the torches on the wall to light their way up the spiral stairs.

"She is," Gar said. "She is also Scots to the bone, as is my grandmother. There are many Scots in my family, so you are aware. I think my brothers and some of my cousins are truly men of two countries because of it. My mother's father is a clan chief called Red Keith Kerr. He's a terror."

They were nearing the top of the steps at this point, moving in the light of the torch through the darkness. "My mother's mother is also Scots," she said. "She is related to Robert de Brus, Lord Annandale."

"How is she related to him?"

"Through an aunt."

"Annandale is the Scottish royal family."

Mattie nodded as they headed down a small corridor. "Through her, I am descended from King David of Scotland," she said. "But it is a female line, so it means little."

"It is still royal blood," Gar said. "I do not know if my father knew that. He never mentioned it."

"Does it matter?"

They had reached a closed door and Mattie lifted the latch, pushing the door open to reveal a warm, fragrant, and comfortable chamber beyond. There was an enormous canopied bed in the center of it, with heavy woolen curtains all around. A fire burned brightly in the hearth, creating a warm atmosphere. Gar was rather pleased by it all and would have said so had something not launched itself at his hip.

Winchester was on the attack.

Mattie shrieked when the dog grabbed hold of the edge of Gar's blue tunic, growling and yanking at it. He wasn't actually biting Gar, but he was determined to tear the tunic to pieces. With a heavy sigh, Gar rolled his eyes and looked down at the dog as it tugged and tugged, snarling all the way.

Mattie raced over and grabbed the dog by the neck.

"Winnie, *stop*!" she commanded. "Let go this instant!"

Winchester failed to respond. He was going to rip the tunic right off Gar's body because, clearly, the garment must have also offended him at some point in its life. Gar kept his hands up so the dog couldn't bite them, but he didn't move. He just stood there, looking at the dog as Mattie tried to pull him away.

"Mayhap if we ignore him, he will exhaust himself and move on," Gar said.

Mattie was seriously tugging on the dog. "He has never done this before," she said, grunting. "My apologies that he seems to have a dislike for you."

Gar just stood there, being buffeted around slightly as Mattie tried to pull the dog away. She finally managed to do it, embracing the dog around his chest as she carried him to the door. Gar moved around her, and the dog, opening the panel so she could toss the dog out. She barely managed to make it back inside before Gar slammed the door, keeping the barking, snapping dog out on the landing. Slightly winded from the fight, Mattie pushed a stray lock of hair out of her eyes.

"Naughty beast," she said. "He really is very sweet, though I'm sure you cannot see that. He is very protective of me."

"Good," Gar said. "I'm glad. That means when I am away, you have a protector."

Mattie smiled reluctantly. "I suppose," she said. Then, it occurred to her that they were finally alone in her chamber and she began to feel a little nervous. "Now that the violence has been tossed outside the door, I suppose we should prepare for our… evening."

Gar could hear the timidity in her voice. Truth be told, he was feeling a little himself. "It seems strange, doesn't it?" he said. "We've only just met, yet we are expected to know each other as husband and wife. We've not even called one another by our Christian names."

Mattie was still smiling as she moved to the dressing table to remove the jewels she wore. "True," she said. "Everything has happened very quickly."

"It has."

"I give you permission to call me Mattie if you wish."

"Your name is Matilda."

She nodded as she moved to unfasten the necklace. "Matilda Eleanor Joan Julia Catherine Fernanda," she said. "I was named for nearly every woman in my family."

He chuckled. "I would say so," he said. "I feel rather simple with only one name."

"Gar?"

"Gareth."

"Why do you go by Gar?"

"Probably for the same reason you are called Mattie," he

said. "Something in childhood that stuck. That is my identity now. Gareth is a stranger."

The necklace came off and Mattie carefully set it on the table. "Are you named for someone?"

"Nay," he said. "But my siblings and I all have singular names. Nothing nearly as elaborate as yours."

She went to pull the pins out of her hair. "How many siblings to you have?"

"Six," he said. "Four brothers and two sisters. My sisters are young and silly and they will be thrilled to have an older sister in you. I hope you are prepared for a good deal of hero worship."

Mattie looked over her shoulder at him, grinning, as she pulled an iron pin out of her carefully coiffed hair. "How old are they?"

"Elsbeth has seen eleven years and Madeleine has seen nine," he said. "Sometimes, we call Madeleine 'Maddy,' so in order not to confuse you with my ridiculous little sister, I hope you do not mind if I only call you Matilda."

"I do not mind."

"Good," he said, watching her unwind the hair from her head in a fascinating moment for him. He'd never watched a woman groom herself before. "Because Mattie is a name for a girl. Matilda is a name for the wife of *Cù fola*. A great and noble queen."

She paused in her movements. "*Cù fola,*" she repeated softly as she translated it. "Blood dog? Blood wolf?"

"Exactly," he said quietly. "A name the Scots gave me. For fierceness in battle, I suppose."

She resumed unwinding her hair, but her movements were pensive. "And the name of your castle again?"

"Gleann na Fola."

"Valley of Blood."

"Correct."

She fell silent as she finished unwinding her hair. When it was all unpinned, she began to run a comb through it. "You said that your fortress was brutal and remote," she said. "I am coming to understand that it must be the truth. Valley of Blood Castle? It sounds like a terrible place."

Gar had been swept up in watching her comb her hair, the way it glistened in the firelight. *The woman belongs to me,* he found himself thinking. Of all the things he'd thought he would be feeling at this moment, awe wasn't one of them. He was positive he'd only feel resentment and bitterness, but that exquisite creature before him had changed his mind. At least, she had for the moment. He had no idea what he would be feeling in a day or two, but right now, it was awe.

Awe and interest.

"It has its moments of beauty," he replied belatedly to her comment. "It sits on the banks of a beautiful stream. There is peace in the valley when no one is trying to kill us. And there is an entire city of rabbits nearby. I will trap some and have a cloak made for you."

She looked at him in horror. "When I was a child, I had rabbits as pets," she said. "I cannot eat them to this day. Your offer is generous, but I am not sure I could wear a cloak of dead rabbits."

He snorted. "Not to worry," he said. "I can have something ugly killed for you so you can wear its hide. How do you feel about ferrets?"

"I had one of those as a pet, too."

"What *haven't* you had as a pet?"

She glanced at him, giggling, because his tone was one of exaggeration. "Pigs," she said. "Cows. No goats. But plenty of rabbits, ferrets, dogs, and cats."

He shrugged, sitting down on the bed. "That does not leave me much to work with," he said. "I can always shave my head and weave you something warm out of my hair."

Mattie burst into laughter. "A nice scarf, mayhap?"

"Anything you like."

She continued laughing. "Keep your hair," she said. "But I appreciate the thought."

"You are welcome," he said, grinning because he liked to hear her laugh. But that also reminded him that this should probably be a serious moment, given what they were about to face together. Perhaps this moment of levity would be a good segue for what needed to be discussed. "Now, it seems that we have a duty to attend to this evening."

She eyed him, momentarily puzzled, but quickly realized what he was saying. "Aye," she said, turning back to her reflection in the small mirror on the dressing table. "We do."

"We do."

She paused. "Does it not seem strange to you that we have only just met, yet we are expected to know each other as a husband and wife?" she said. "I have always found that a very strange thing about consummation on the night of a wedding. Perfect strangers are expected to know each other intimately."

He agreed with her. "It does seem strange," he said. "But men and women have been doing it for centuries. We are not the first and we will not be the last."

Still combing her hair, she looked at him. "May I be honest with you?"

"I hope you are always honest with me."

Mattie shook her head. "I did not mean it the way it sounded," she said. "I simply meant that we have only just truly met one another today and I hope I may always be frank with you. You will not be angry if I speak what is on my mind, will you?"

"Never, as long as it is the truth."

She sighed and turned back to her comb. "Then I will tell you that I know something of what we are about to do."

His brow furrowed. "How?" he said, the least bit miffed. "You told me that you have been loyal to the contract."

She shrugged, almost flippantly. "I had a life *before* the contract," she said. "I was six years of age and a lad my same age kissed me right on the lips. He told me he loved me. Now, I shall not tell you his name, for you may not find him and challenge him, but I will be truthful and tell you that for an entire week, he had my heart."

Gar fought off a grin. "Is that so?" he said, feigning anger. "Then I must rethink this entire marriage. You did not tell me that you were free with your kisses."

"You did not ask."

"And you think this pleases me?"

"I hope it tells you that I'm experienced when it comes to the relations between men and women. I *was* kissed."

He burst into soft laughter. "Good," he said. "Then you can teach me."

"How to kiss?"

"How to everything."

She snorted. "Do not be cruel," she said. "Kissing is, mayhap, the only thing I know about it. I will have to defer to your experience in such matters, though I must say it gives me no joy to think you *have* had experience."

"I've had no experience at all, at least not with that."

She stopped combing and looked at him, suspecting what he was telling her but not entirely sure she was right. "I do not understand."

He was sitting on the edge of the bed, looking at his hands. "I think you do."

Her suspicions were right. The way he said it, there could be no mistake, and she couldn't keep the astonishment out of her voice.

"You mean… everything?" she said.

He nodded. "Does that surprise you?"

Mattie set her comb down, the mood suddenly growing quite serious. "Do you mean to tell me that you have never done this before?"

Gar sighed faintly, looking as if he were about to confess something he wasn't entirely sure he wanted to confess. "I just… never took the opportunity," he said. "Believe me—this isn't a simple thing to admit. I debated not telling you, but now that we are being honest… it does not seem right not to tell you. You are my wife, after all. You should know everything about me. Even… this."

He seemed uncomfortable and she didn't want to make it worse by pressing him, but she couldn't help it. "But why?" she finally said. "You are young and strong and wildly handsome. Surely you… Why *not*?"

He lifted his big shoulders, as if he didn't even really know. "I've been fostering since I was six years of age," he said. "All I did was work and train, and when I grew older, all I did was perfect my skills as a knight. I was knighted three years before most men because I'd worked so hard at it. I was, and am, the perfect knight. I'm not saying that there were not women who tried to seduce me, for there have been many, and I'm not saying that I've never been kissed by a woman, for I have, but that is as far as anything ever went."

Mattie still couldn't believe what she was hearing. "Ever?"

"Ever."

"And how old are you?"

"About seven or eight years older than you are."

She shook her head in awe. "I do not mean to make you feel bad, of course, but I find that astonishing," she said. "You are so… Surely there are women who have thrown themselves at your feet. I know I would have. I think I did."

He smiled weakly. "There have been a few."

"They had good taste," she said. "But you must understand that other than my fostering, and we were very much kept from the men, my experience in seeing the ways between men and women have mostly been with my brother. He has a different woman every week and the soldiers… Well, you know what soldiers do."

"I do."

"And you have never wanted to?"

His smile grew, somewhat nervously. "I am not saying that," he said. "I *have* wanted to. But the main reason I have not is this—I told you that I had been faithful to our contract and that has been in place for ten years. That is the truth of it. Prior to that, I was a boy. There were not many opportunities for a lad of thirteen or fourteen years to bed a woman, and at that age, it simply wasn't on my mind, mostly because my father told me that if I bedded a woman and she became pregnant whilst I was betrothed to you, then he would make sure I could never father a child again. I took it to heart."

She cocked her head. "So it wasn't so much restraint or loyalty to the contract as it was fear of your father."

"That is fair."

She gazed at him for a moment longer before finally breaking into a grin. "Whatever the reason, I have to say that I am quite surprised," she said. "But I am also pleased. You saved yourself for me."

"I did."

"And I saved myself for you."

"I am grateful."

"That means we will be learning this together."

He nodded. "That is true," he said. "I hope I do not fail you."

She stood up. "How could you?" she said. "I know basically what to do, for my mother has told me. So has Agnes, who has, unfortunately, not had the same restraint I have had. She has let men… do things to her. She has done things to them and she has told me about it."

Gar's eyebrows lifted at the concerning idea of the promiscuous young woman. "I suppose hearing your friend's stories are better than knowing nothing and coming into this with terror," he said. "I think the first thing we need to do, however, is disrobe and get into bed. We can proceed from there."

He stood up from the bed, looking down at her. She was a petite thing, barely coming up to his breastbone. For a moment, they simply gazed at one another, but it wasn't awkward. There was warmth there, and interest. After a moment, Mattie smiled faintly.

"Since we've met, all has been quite formal between us, as it should be," she said. "But I think, at this point, it should not be quite so formal."

"Agreed."

"Would you like to kiss me?"

That was one of the better suggestions he'd heard all day and, without a word, he put his big hands on her upper arms and leaned down, gently slanting his lips over hers. It was just a kiss, something gentle and warm, but it was swift. He stood up to look at her, but her face was upturned to him with her eyes closed.

"Well?" he said. "Like that?"

Her eyes were still closed as she spoke. "I do not think so," she said, her eyes opening. "My father kisses like that. I do not think I like that."

He frowned, taking the criticism to heart. "I see," he said. He cocked his head thoughtfully before lifting his arms again and pulling them around her lush little body. "Mayhap we should do this the right way."

Mattie gasped as his enormous arms wrapped around her, pulling her up against him. It was as if he'd just struck flint against stone because, suddenly, there was a spark where there hadn't been before. Her body against his, heat against heat, and she was having trouble breathing as she gazed up at him.

"Aye," she said, realizing that she was quivering. "This is the right way."

"I think so, too."

That spark ignited something more. Dipping his head down, Gar kissed her forehead, and her cheek. The fragrances of roses from her hair met his nostrils and he inhaled deeply. But that sweet scent was to be his undoing—it was warm and alluring. His embrace tightened and he buried his face against Mattie's fragrant neck.

Mattie gasped again as Gar's mouth moved down her neck, roving over the soft flesh. He was smelling, but he was also tasting, very gently. She could feel his lips. Certainly, she'd asked for a kiss, but this wasn't what she had expected. In fact, his hot breath against her neck had her heart pounding so forcefully that she was positive it was about to burst from her chest.

He grew bolder.

Gar's tongue, hot and lusty, lapped at the flesh of her shoulder as his hands began to roam. They were timid, but curious. He touched the skin on her arms, his big hands gripping her then releasing her, stroking and touching. Mattie could feel his hot breath on her skin and she could hardly breathe because of it. She hadn't even known such a sensation existed. She never knew a fire like this was possible.

A fire that was beginning to gain strength.

The flames crackled softly in the hearth, sending sparks up the chimney as Gar abruptly swept Mattie into his arms and deposited her upon her bed. He gently kissed her face, moving to her chin and neck as his fingers went to work on the ties of her gown. He was clumsy about it, but persistent. Mattie finally had to untie them herself and they both giggled a little, awkwardly, but it was a sweet moment.

"Should I tell you what I'm going to do next?" he asked. "If you do not want me to do it, I hope you will tell me."

She was on her back, looking up at him. "Do *you* know what you are going to do next?"

He smirked. "Not really," he said. "I was just… exploring."

"I do not mind exploring."

"You don't?"

"Nay," she said. "And you do not have to tell me what you are going to do next. Just… do it. If I do not like it, I will tell you."

He nodded, cupped her face gently, and kissed her right cheek.

Onward, the intrepid explorer went.

The shift Mattie was wearing was the same one that had been under her blue silk gown. That was all there was between her and Gar. He was inspecting the shift, looking at the stitching, the way it lay upon her skin, and then he pulled it away a little, looking at the flesh underneath. He kissed the exposed flesh and repeated the process, like a man inspecting a new and valuable acquisition, only there was more to it.

The truth was that Gar had kissed women before and had perhaps done a little fondling, so he wasn't as much of an amateur as he'd led Mattie to believe. He knew how to kiss and how to touch, but nothing more than that. This was the moment when he would experience everything and he was soaking it in more than he'd thought he would. Mattie stared up at the ceiling as he went about his exploration, as the shift came off her shoulders, her arms, finally baring her breasts in the weak light of the chamber. She showed no signs of being embarrassed by her nudity. She wasn't even embarrassed when he pulled the shift over her hips and slid it the length of her legs.

She simply let him.

It wasn't that she was paralyzed by fear or indecision. It was simply that much like Gar, Mattie was soaking it all in. *Is this what it means to have a husband?* she thought. Because if this was what being married meant, then she was willing to embrace it. If Gar could make her feel like this, with her heart racing and her breathing coming in gasps, then she would let the man do whatever he wanted to do.

She was more than willing to let him.

As Mattie found herself overcome by her first sexual encounter, Gar was having a difficult time pacing himself. Every touch, every kiss, had him wanting to thrust his body into hers until he was satisfied. But he also wanted to go slowly because every move, every touch, every taste was something to experience. He didn't want to rush through it. Perhaps his touch wasn't entirely skilled, but it was genuine. Perhaps every kiss wasn't delicate, but it meant something. He wanted to build something with Mattie and the only way he could think to do that was to be slow and gentle with her. At least, that was his intention until the sight of her nude breasts in the firelight nearly undid him.

He'd never seen anything so arousing in his entire life.

But he didn't touch her there yet. It wasn't as if he didn't know how, or didn't have permission. He did and he did. It was a matter of putting his hand to her flesh. But it was such a personal move, something so intimate, that he was having trouble taking that step. He didn't want to frighten her or chase her away. She was new to this, too, and he wasn't sure he could live with scaring her off. As he wrestled with some indecision, Mattie abruptly reached up, took his hand, and put it against her right breast.

"Here, Gar," she whispered breathlessly. "Touch me here."

Gar's control vanished in an instant. He growled low in his throat as he descended upon her luscious body. Their lips came together in a cataclysmic clash, his mouth slanting over hers, suckling her lips furiously. Mattie's gasps of passion were muted against his mouth until he moved away from her lips and feasted hungrily at her breasts. As Mattie writhed beneath him, Gar moved to touch the unfurling flower between her legs.

For a man who had never really done this sort of thing before, he was moving with confidence. He knew what he needed to touch and what needed to happen because he had enough friends and brothers who had been quite detailed in their experiences with women. Gar knew, so he just had to put it into practice. Mattie cried out with surprise when his fingers touched the thick outer lips, matted with a fine fluff of black hair, but he maintained his hold on her nipple as he gently fondled her to allow her to become accustomed to his touch. Mattie gradually relaxed as she became accustomed to his fingers, and only when her body relaxed did he attempt to part her lush petals.

She was as slick with moisture, unbelievably hot. Gar stroked the tender folds, his entire body shaking with the power of his need. He'd never known desire like this and he could no longer hold back. It was time to make Mattie his wife in every sense of the word.

The wife he'd never wanted.

He wanted her now.

Gar finally slipped a finger into her sheath, so incredibly tight that he very nearly soiled himself at that very moment. Mattie's pants of shock quickly turned into cries of pleasure, and Gar could feel her tight passage contracting about his slick finger, pulling at him and demanding him.

He could wait no longer.

Rising to his knees, he ripped off his tunic so aggressively that he tore a seam. One boot hit the floor and the other nearly flew into the hearth. Those patchwork breeches went to his knees because that was as far as he could get them. He didn't have the patience for anything more. Climbing into the bed beside her, his big body covered hers, their flesh touching. He could hear himself groaning at the pure delight of it, warm skin against warm skin.

Now, came the core of the situation.

Joining his body with hers.

He really didn't want to be clumsy about this, so he forced himself to focus on what needed to be done rather than the actual act itself. Mattie's body was preparing itself for what was to come, so he wedged himself between her legs and rubbed his manhood against her private core to moisten himself. He'd heard that made his entry easier and he did so want to make this easier for them both. Not surprisingly, however, he had to wrestle against his natural instinct to ram into her like a stallion. It would have been so easy, but also so damaging. Finally, he pushed into her, feeling her wet heat close in around him, and it was the most amazing thing he'd ever experienced.

Little by little, he slid into her.

Somehow, he made it all the way in without any flash of pain on her part or great claps of thunder announcing they were joined. Suddenly, they were, and he could no longer restrain himself. Falling atop her, Gar began to roll his hips, thrusting into her body. Some strokes were long and hard, some weren't. It took him a few tries to find a rhythm that felt good and when he did, he thrust evenly and fully. He had her in his powerful embrace, his arms wrapped tightly around her, but eventually he loosened his grip and braced his arms on either side of her to get some leverage. But in doing so, that also meant he could look down at her body, at their bodies joined.

That was his undoing.

Mattie had soft, full breasts and he shifted his weight so he could touch her there, eliciting groans of pleasure. His free hand moved to her nipples, her shoulder, down her belly, and around to her buttocks. Soft, warm buttocks. He grasped them, holding her pelvis still as he continued to thrust into her, all the while wondering why he'd never done this before now. But in the same breath, also glad that he'd *not* done it before now. For his first time to be with Mattie, with his wife, was something no man he knew could say. But he could.

It made the moment far more magnificent.

As Mattie lay there, legs open to receive him, her breasts bouncing gently with each successive thrust of his hips, something hot was building in his loins. He knew what it was, though he'd never experienced it in this particular way, and he also knew he wouldn't be able to control himself once it erupted. And it did erupt, as fast as lightning, and suddenly he was thrusting hard, holding himself inside of her as his hot seed filled her. When he reached down to touch the place where their bodies joined to feel the magic of what was happening, his touch threw Mattie over the edge into her first climax as well.

On and on it went.

While Gar's release eventually died down, Mattie's seemed to go on, like ripples upon a pond. His hand was still on her Venus mound, his fingers still probing her, and every time he moved, she seemed to climax again. She was quivering and gasping as if she had no control over her body at all. In truth, she didn't.

He did.

And he loved it.

Still embedded inside her, he stroked her again and another weak climax rolled over her. Her legs were trembling so much that they were jerking uncontrollably. Gar finally moved his hand away just so the woman could catch her breath and he grinned as he buried his face in her neck, kissing her gently as she struggled to catch her breath.

It was finished.

Enfolded in the warmth of Gar's massive embrace, Mattie was in a stupor. Her body was limp, her mind void of any thought whatsoever as she felt the remains of Gar's arousal twitching within her tender folds. Her legs were still wide open, his significant weight covering her, and she couldn't have been more content with it all. She would have been perfectly happy to remain as they were for the rest of eternity.

No words were spoken. After that, no words were necessary. Sleep came quickly and when they slept, wrapped up in each other's arms, it was as if they had been doing it all their lives. Nothing had ever felt so natural or so right.

The virgins were virginal no longer.

CHAPTER EIGHT

Bailie Castle
Stronghold of Clan Maxwell of Westerkirk
Scotland

IT WAS COLD and dank and deadly.

Deadly because of any of the men surviving the battle in the Valley of Blood that had been brought back to the stronghold of Bailie Castle, only a few survived. Deadly because anything that touched this castle instantly turned to rot or grief or despair. Deadly in the sense that there was a cloud of gloom that hung over the place, something that had been there from the time of their forefathers. This place had never been a warm and comforting family compound.

It had always been about death.

That was partially why people stayed clear of this particular part of Scotland. The Westerkirk area belonged to Clan Maxwell and had for hundreds of years. When they had settled it back in the time of the Romans, it had been a green and fertile valley. The sun shone and the flowers grew and it was just like any other valley that attracted people to settle in it, but once they settled, the change began to occur. Generations of poor fortune and bad decisions had turned the valley into something dark and forbidding.

The English knights who came through the area months ago had quickly found that out.

It had been a shortcut to where they were going and even though they knew it was a Maxwell valley, they'd still taken the chance to travel through it, thinking it would be quicker and safer if they could simply get through it at a rapid pace. No one would be the wiser. Road conditions and the weather had forced them into that decision, which they came to regret when one of them was struck in the back of the head by a big rock that had been launched from a tree. The two knights had been taken down and brought to the Maxwell stronghold to face their sentence. The misdeed had simply been trespassing on Maxwell property, but the sentence did not fit the crime.

The sentence had been death.

After the knights had been dispatched, regardless of the pleading that one knight had done to spare them, men from Clan Maxwell had gone through their things and been able to read the dispatches they were carrying from a place called The Keld. It was the fortress of the House of de Bourne, just over the border near Keilder Water, so the bodies of the knights and their possessions—sans anything of value—had been sent back to The Keld with a decisive message.

Spies will be executed.

Unfortunately for Clan Maxwell, Ares de Bourne did not heed their message. In fact, he gathered his allies, of which he had many, and raided Maxwell lands, including Bailie Castle. The women and children were captured and the men scattered, but only temporarily. Although no one in the Lowlands of

Scotland particularly cared for the Maxwell of Westerkirk, the fact that the English had crossed the border did not sit well with other Lowland clans. That meant that the Westerkirk Maxwell found themselves with unexpected allies in this fight—and that started a series of vicious battles that went back and forth between the English and the Scots. The latest battle had been literally in the Valley of Blood and the Scots had found themselves facing an English army that outmanned them three to one.

It had been a massacre.

That particularly vicious battle had made it back to Bailie and the devastation dealt out by the English had caused the Scots to back off a little. It had been more than a month since that particular battle had taken place and the situation in general had calmed. This was not only due to the brutal nature of the last battle, but also due to the fact that the allied clans began to learn that two English knights had been killed without provocation. Westerkirk had managed to keep that detail from them, only telling them of the brutality of the English and lying about their intent. Now, Westerkirk found themselves alone in this battle against the English and that was enough to cause them to rethink this entire situation. Out of three hundred men, they were already down by half. The clan itself was facing extinction.

No one wanted that.

But the clan chief of Westerkirk had an idea and ideas in his world were dangerous things.

Ean Maxwell was that clan chief. He was young for a chief and extremely hot-headed, which was how his clan found themselves in this situation in the first place. Ean's father, Arduil, had died the previous winter of a poison in his chest, which elevated the young man to chief status, something he was wholly unprepared for. His father was a recluse, making the clan an isolated clan, but at least Arduil had been somewhat cool in temperament. That kept Westerkirk out of trouble.

But Ean had been the opposite.

His clan was dying now.

The hall of Bailie was a mix of the healthy and unhealthy. Sick men slept in the corners while those who could function took meals near the hearth. Dogs slept around their feet and filthy rushes covered the floor as the men sat and drank and spoke of the future.

What there was of it, anyway.

With Ean's plan, they weren't even certain there would be a future.

"Lad," an older man in tattered clothing said in a low and raspy tone. "I've sat here and listened tae ye speak for the past day. I've heard yer plan and I'm here tae tell ye that ye canna do what ye intend tae do. If the other clans discovered the truth, they would end us. They already want tae end us after ye refused tae tell them why ye had a fight with the English in the first place."

Ean frowned at his uncle. In truth, the man was his grandfather's brother, an old man who was wise and respected. But, in Ean's opinion, Gordie Maxwell was a fool.

"I told them the truth," he fired back to a table of men who knew he was lying even as he said it. "I told them the Sassenach wronged us."

"They dinna wrong us."

"They were on my lands!" Ean shouted. Then he jabbed a finger at his uncle. "Ye're weak, old man. Ye're too weak tae stand up against the English who want what we have."

"And what do we have, young Ean?" Gordie said, lifting a bushy white eyebrow. "Before those knights came across our lands, we at least had some peace. We had food. Men had their herds, their homes. Children had fathers. Wives had husbands. Now, the wives and children are gone and half of the men are dead. Why? Because ye punished two knights who crossed our lands and built lies around them. I still dunna know why ye did that."

"They were spies!" Ean said with the same tone he'd used in the previous statement. He was shouting at men older than him, men who had never believed he could rule well as chief. Well, he had to show them, didn't he? "They came tae see our lands and report back tae their Sassenach lord. Ye know The Keld is just over the border. Ye know they want what we have!"

Gordie looked at the others around the table. Where there used to be about thirty, there were now twelve. Most had been killed in the recent battles, but some had drifted over to other Maxwell clans where a spoiled lad didn't control their fate. No one left at the table had any love for Ean, and there had been a discussion about removing him from power, but that was always a slippery slope. Once one man was removed, another could be removed, and still another. There was no stability when the rightful chief was removed. Therefore, they were trying to mitigate Ean's damage.

But that had proven to be quite difficult.

"So ye want tae court our allies again by telling them that yer young daughter has been taken by the Sassenach?" Gordie said. "I want tae be clear on this, lad. Ye want tae lie again?"

Ean was only growing angrier. "We need victory," he said, slamming his fist on the table in front of him. "If we dunna achieve victory over the Sassenach, then all of our brethren will have died in vain. Can ye not see that? The reason I use tae draw the clans together again will not matter in the end when we have victory over the English. The lads will be proud of themselves and they'll forget why we were there. All they'll remember is the victory."

Gordie didn't think that was a good idea at all and that was evident in his manner. "Ye canna build a victory on a lie," he said. "And yer quarrel is with The Keld, not de Wolfe. 'Tis a de Wolfe fortress ye've made yer target."

That drew a smile from Ean. "The most obvious target of all," he said. "Gleann na Fola. She sits at the end of our valley. She belongs tae us."

"She belongs tae William de Wolfe."

Ean brushed him off. "The man is as old as Methuselah."

"He has forty sons and grandsons that will fight for him," Gordie said, losing some of his cool. "Old William de Wolfe doesn't need tae fight because he's got dozens of wolf cubs tae do it for him. Ye've been tae battle against the older ones. Ye know how they fight. We aren't strong enough tae overcome their armies."

Ean flew over the table and grabbed Gordie by the throat. "I'll not listen tae ye, ye old fool," he hissed. "I've already sent messengers tae the clans tae tell them that my daughter is being held at Gleann na Fola. The English are taunting us by punishing a little lass. That will rally the clans and we will descend on Glenn na Fola, once and for all. We'll overrun the place and slay every last Sassenach, men and women. All of them will die and victory will be ours. The castle will be ours. De Bourne of The Keld willna dare retaliate, nor will the rest of the de Wolfe properties because they'll know our strength."

He was squeezing, but not hard enough. Gordie hadn't

known that he'd already sent word to their other allies—and once the word was out, it wasn't as if they could refute it. That would only create more animosity against Westerkirk and their chief, who would lie to create conflict. Already, Westerkirk's reputation was hanging in tatters. The quiet, reclusive clan that everyone knew had become something volatile and untrustworthy.

It was an insult to Arduil.

"Where is yer daughter?" Gordie asked with Ean's hand on his throat.

Ean didn't like that his uncle was still able to talk and squeezed a little harder. "With her mother," he said. "The Sassenach took her."

"But they sent a message tae tell ye that the bairns were going tae the abbeys," Gordon reminded him. "Carlisle and Whitby and others. The English commander promised ye that they'd be safe."

That wasn't helping Ean's cause. "And he could have lied," he said. "The Sassenach have our women and children. They could have my daughter at Gleann na Fola. Who's tae say they dunna?"

He had a point. The English did take the women and children after the last battle, which Ean was using to his advantage. It was a lie, or it wasn't. No one really knew for sure. But one thing was for certain:

More death was coming.

And Gordie had had enough of it. He suddenly brought up a big fist and smashed it into the side of Ean's head, sending the young man flying off him. As Ean went over, Gordie stood up and kicked him in the kidneys for good measure. As Ean lay on the floor, gasping in pain, Gordie loomed over him.

"Yer father would not be pleased with ye," he said. "Ye've made liars out of all of us with yer recklessness. I'll stand with ye this time, Ean, but after this, ye'll not see me again. I cannot listen tae a fool with a taste for blood and madness. Ye make me ashamed of ye."

With that, he walked away, but not before stepping on Ean's fingers. Others followed until the entire table was empty. Ean lay there, nursing an aching head, back, and stinging fingers as one of the dogs wandered up and licked him on the face. The men around him faded into the darkness until all that was left were those licking dogs and the snap from the hearth.

Ye make me ashamed of ye.

When this was over, his uncle would be eating his words.

Ean was going to make sure of it.

CHAPTER NINE

Gleann na Fola Castle

HOW COULD SHE describe it?

Mattie didn't even know.

She could hardly comprehend what she was looking at. The valley surrounding it was beautiful enough. It didn't look like a bloody valley, but rather a verdant valley with gently rolling hills. It was quite picturesque. But right in the middle of this valley, in the point where it opened up into some smaller hills and meadowlands, sat a castle that could only be described as a big, dark box of a structure.

It looked like a cube.

The closer they drew, however, the more she could see how positively enormous it was. The truth was that she couldn't see much because she was riding in her parents' fortified carriage, which was a heavy conveyance with iron-barred windows and two benches that faced one another. It wasn't very big. The benches, fortunately, had cushions on them, more cushions still because Gar had wanted to ensure her comfort as they traveled north.

He'd insisted on it.

Even thinking about Gar had Mattie smiling. It had only been a few short days since their marriage, but those days had been full ones. There had been conversations, so many conversations, as they'd come to know one another in an environment that was worry-free and peaceful. There was no pressure of command for Gar, and Mattie was simply enamored with the man she'd married, so much so that she'd quickly become obsessed with him. She could still see that young lad who had saved her from the de Vries brat, but there was so much more to him. He was wise and humorous, a little shy at times, and he was positively mortified when she sang his praises in front of him. The man looked as if he wanted to crawl into a hole and pull the hole in after him.

Speaking of holes, he looked as if he lived in one because of those patchwork linen breeches.

That pale linen had become very dirty, very quickly, but Gar refused to take them off. Mattie had made them and he was, therefore, going to wear them. He wore them everywhere and he even tried to sleep in them. They never came off and they were becoming quite filthy, but she didn't have the heart to insist he wear something clean because the truth was that she found it very sweet that he should show tribute to her by wearing the breeches she'd made for him. Perhaps he didn't always know the right words to say, and perhaps he was clumsy with her sometimes, but he knew how to make her feel appreciated with those damnable trousers.

As they traveled toward their destination, with Mattie in the fortified carriage was none other than Winchester himself. He still growled at Gar, and still charged him, but he was becoming a little better about it and Mattie wouldn't leave him behind, so

Gar had had no choice but to bring along his mortal enemy. Maksim was riding escort as well and the dog didn't make a move against her brother, or Gar's brother, or even Gar's father, but he clearly had a loathing for his mistress's new husband. One little dark spot in what had otherwise been a smooth and agreeable experience.

"We're almost home," Gar said, coming alongside the carriage and breaking into her thoughts. "Can you see it?"

He was pointing to the north and she peered between the bars, seeing the dark-stoned structure in the distance. "Aye," she said. "I've never seen anything like it."

"Nor will you again," he said. "Gleann na Fola was not built like other strongholds, although there is one to the east that has a similar look."

"Were they built by the same man?"

Gar nodded. "Aye," he said. "He built these boxes to protect his lands and they are quite sturdy."

Gar's closeness to the carriage window brought Winchester, who barked and stuck his nose between the bars, trying to nip at Gar. Mattie was forced to pull her dog away, scolding him as she did so.

"You are a very naughty dog, Winnie," she said, frowning. "You must learn to like Gar or we are going to have a serious problem."

Gar shook his head. "I do not think he understands you."

Mattie rubbed the dog's head firmly. "Aye, he does," she says. "I swear to you, he understands my words."

"He understands food and sleep. That is what he understands."

"Have you never had a dog?"

Gar snorted. "My hall is full of them and they will eat Winchester alive, so keep him out of the hall," he said. "There is also a big orange cat that roams the upper floors and he will take delight in stalking your dog and attacking it, so it is best to keep Winchester with you at all times."

She didn't look too happy about that. "Is my dog in danger, then?"

Gar could see the concern on her face and he flipped up his visor, smiling at her. "Nay, lass," he said softly. "Your dog is not in danger. But there are those who might challenge him, so it is best to keep an eye on him. At least until he gets used to the place."

Any smile from Gar had Mattie's heart fluttering and she smiled in return. "When we arrive, will you ask your majordomo to show me the place? I should like to look around."

He looked at her strangely. "Have the majordomo do it?" he repeated as if it were an odd request. "Of course not. I shall show you the place myself. It… it's our home now, Queenie. I hope you look at it as such, someday."

Queenie. That was something he'd been calling her since the day after they were married. Julia was the empress and Mattie was the queen. *Queenie.* Mattie had been surprised by the nickname at first and, truthfully, hadn't been fond of it, but she quickly grew accustomed to it. Gar called her that out of respect, out of affection, and she wholeheartedly accepted any such attempts. From that turbulent first day to a day like today, Mattie was coming to think that she might really have a chance at a good marriage with a man she'd dreamed about for the past ten years.

She was hoping so, anyway.

"I look at Gleann na Fola as our home now," she said after a moment, her eyes glimmering warmly at him. "I do not need days or weeks or years to feel that way. I feel that way now."

He reached out a gloved hand, brushing her fingers affectionately as he gripped one of the iron bars of the window. It was really all he could do because he was a man of few words, Mattie had discovered. When it came to her, he was unsure of what to say sometimes, unused to having a woman close to him, a wife, so he often just shut his mouth and smiled rather than risk saying the wrong thing. Truthfully, she didn't mind that he couldn't say the words because he always gave her a look that told her everything she needed to know. She was satisfied with that.

For now.

Maybe someday, he could find the words.

The carriage lurched along the road, which wasn't in very good condition. It seemed that there had been a good deal of rain, so there were holes in the road and the carriage kept having to slow down to avoid them. But little by little, the great fortress of Gleann na Fola loomed closer until, finally, they where there.

They had arrived.

Because of her position in the carriage, Mattie hadn't seen the fortress prepare for their commander's return. Not only that, but there were others who had come to welcome Gar and his new wife home and that included William de Wolfe himself. The great Earl of Warenton had ridden from his seat of Castle Questing, which was about a day's ride for a young man, but William was no longer young and it had taken more than two days. Everyone had traveled slowly for him. He hated that, of course, but it had been necessary to keep him in good health, so he was the first one to greet Gar as the escort from Hensingham came in through the front gates.

"Gar!" William shouted, waving a hand to him as he stood near the gatehouse. "Welcome home, lad!"

Gar was riding beside the carriage still, with Mattie practically sitting on Winchester so the dog wouldn't bark continuously. Gar grinned at his grandfather, knowing how enthusiastic the man was about this marriage. Truthfully, he wasn't surprised to see him.

Dismounting Taches as the horse slapped him with his big, heavy tail, Gar made his way over to his grandfather.

"Greetings, Poppy," he said, a twinkle in his eye. "Whatever is the reason for your visit, I wonder?"

He was being sarcastic, his tone clear evidence that he knew exactly why the man was there, and William cast him a long look.

"Where is your wife?" he said. "I did not come to see you."

Gar snorted, gesturing back toward the carriage. "She has come, do not fear," he said. "I will fetch her to you."

With that, he turned and quickly headed toward the carriage, which had just come to a halt. The bailey was muddy, layered with dark mud and rocks, as Gar went to the carriage door, opened it—and promptly slammed it shut again as Winchester threw himself at the open door.

"Queenie?" he said politely. "Will you please secure your dog so he does not chew my face off?"

"Aye," she said, clearly frustrated at the dog's behavior. "Will you please send Maksim to me?"

Maksim was toward the front of the escort, in conversation with Andreas, as Gar let loose a piercing whistle that caught Maksim's attention. Gar simply waved him over and pointed to the carriage where Mattie's face was against the iron bars of the cab door.

"Will you please take Winchester and secure him?" she said to her brother. "I cannot have him attacking Gar at every turn."

Maksim grunted unhappily. "He's not my dog, Matilda."

Mattie kicked the door open, holding the dog around the chest as she thrust it at her brother. "*Please,*" she begged. "Take him and feed him so that I may meet my new husband's family in peace."

Maksim could see an entire host of de Wolfe knights waiting for Gar, so he growled with annoyance, took the dog from his sister, and marched off. That left Gar free to help Mattie from the carriage and not lose fingers. Instead of helping her step out, however, he scooped her into his big arms and carried her across the mud, very chivalrously.

"It would not do for your dress to become soiled," he said when she looked at him questioningly. "I know you put stock in a tidy appearance."

Mattie cocked an eyebrow. "One of us has to."

He wouldn't look at her, grinning. He knew exactly what she meant. "I am *not* taking them off."

"But they are filthy."

"They are well used."

Knowing it would do no good to argue with him, Mattie simply shut her mouth as they approached William and several other knights who were gathered around. Gar set Mattie gently on the ground in front of William.

"Poppy, this is my wife, Matilda," Gar said, sounding rather proud as he announced her. "She has made a fine addition to the House of de Wolfe and I am honored to introduce her. My lady, this is my grandfather, the Earl of Warenton. *The* William de Wolfe."

William smiled at the lovely young woman. She had such a

delicate and fine look about her, with big eyes and a pert nose, that she almost looked like something fragile and unreal. She was petite, and when she looked at him, smiling politely, he was quite certain that there was strength behind that angelic face. Something in those eyes told him so. Reaching out, he took her hand gently.

"Lady de Wolfe," he said. "I am very glad to make your acquaintance."

Mattie curtsied, a practiced gesture. "As I am glad to make yours, my lord," she said. "It is an honor."

William dipped his head in gratitude before extending a hand to the men standing around. One of them was Troy, but there were several others. William indicated the men one by one.

"Permit me to introduce you to my eldest son, Scott de Wolfe," he said. "He is Troy's twin, if you were not aware."

Mattie shook her head. "I was not, my lord," she said, bobbing a smooth curtsy to Scott. "A pleasure, my lord."

As Scott de Wolfe, a big and blond man, fair as Troy was dark, nodded his greeting, William continued to the rest of the group.

"This is Gar's cousin, Thomas de Wolfe, but he goes by Tor," he said. "And next to him is my son, Blayth, commander of Roxburgh Castle."

Mattie smiled at the big blond knight that faintly resembled her husband and another big, blond, and very scarred older knight who stood next to him.

"My lords," she greeted them. "It is an honor."

The two of them politely acknowledged her as William pointed over to another group, standing with Troy off to the east. "Those are more cousins and grandsons," he said. "There are about forty de Wolfe men of armor, but these are some of the men who serve on the western end of the border. You've already met Andreas, of course."

Mattie nodded. "I have, my lord," she said. "He is very kind."

"He's a good lad," William said. "His wife remains at their home with their children, but a few women are inside and would very much like to greet you, so let us move in that direction."

With that, he extended an elbow to her, which she took gratefully. Gathering her skirt, Mattie permitted William to escort her across the muddy bailey, which seemed to grow muddier as they approached the keep.

And what a keep it was.

Mattie's glance from a distance had only been the beginning. Now that she was up close, she could see what a truly imposing structure it was. The castle was surrounded by earthworks and berms, as she had noticed, and every berm seemed to have some level ground where outbuildings or trades were located. The level ground around the keep had some outbuildings as well, a couple of them built up against the keep itself, but from what she could see, there were literally no windows on the ground level or even the first level of the castle. It was all stone. Further up, she could see a few windows dotted around the castle, but they had to be thirty feet or more over her head. The structure itself seemed to reach into the sky itself.

No windows.

And only one door that she could see.

Like a prison.

"How fared your journey?" William asked as they headed for the only door she could see. "Well, I hope."

Mattie nodded. "Very well, thank you," she said. "Truthfully, I've never been further north than Carlisle, so this has been a bit of an adventure."

William smiled. "Do you seek adventure, then?"

"I married Gar, my lord," she said. "I do believe he is an adventure himself."

William chuckled, turning around to see his grandson walking a few feet behind them. "I like her, Gar," he said. "She understands you already."

Gar gave him a half-grin but didn't reply. William turned his attention forward to the entry to the structure, which was surprisingly small. It was a thick oak door reinforced with iron, extremely sturdy. Once they stepped inside, however, an unusual layout unfolded.

As Mattie could see, it was as if the center of the interior were hollow. An open space went all the way up to the roof, which was open. She could see the sky above. That gave it ventilation without compromising safety. The structure of Gleann na Fola was built around this small, open courtyard and there were a few staircases leading to different parts of the castle. There were also doorways that led under it, down into the vaults. There were many doors and staircases, and it reminded her of a labyrinth. She could smell the cold, dank air coming forth from the belly of the castle.

As dank as one could imagine.

Before them was a mural staircase, one that was wide and sturdy and built of stone. It led up to a landing and then doubled back on itself, and she followed William up the stairs, which ended on another landing that opened up into a large hall. It was long and wide, but the ceiling was low given the fact that it was on the first level of the castle above ground level. It was ventilated by small windows in the walls, which made it rather dark. A large hearth burned with a bright fire at the end of the room and, much as Gar had told her, dogs roamed about.

And it smelled like it.

In truth, the hall was filthy and Mattie was trying not to be horrified by it. There were dog feces against the wall, under the tables, and probably more places that she couldn't see. The fact that there were plenty of tables scattered throughout the room covered up anything else that might be on the floor. William took Mattie to what was presumably the dais because there were women there, women who came forward when they saw William and Mattie approach.

"I have her," William declared. "She does exist. Ladies, this is Matilda, Lady de Wolfe. Gar's wife."

There was a good deal of smiling going on. Mattie found herself looking at a collection of lovely women of all ages. There was much older woman with pale hair, pulled back in a bun, and pale green eyes that looked exactly like Gar's. There was another, taller woman, younger, with dark hair and a lovely face, and still another one with dark blonde hair pulled into a bun at the nape of her neck. There were others, but those were the three at the forefront.

"Welcome, m'lady," the elderly woman with the green eyes said in a heavy Scots accent. "We're so pleased tae meet ye. I'm Lady Warenton. Did ye have a pleasant journey?"

It was the great lady herself, the earl's wife. She seemed very sweet and Mattie immediately warmed to her, smiling.

"I did, thank you," she said. "I have never been this far north, so it has been an exciting expedition."

Lady Warenton's smile broadened. "That's lovely," she said. "Did ye bring yer family with ye? Yer mother?"

Mattie shook her head. "Nay, my lady," she said. "Only my brother."

"'Tis nice that he came with ye tae help ye settle intae yer new life."

Mattie nodded. "He wants to make sure I do not change my mind and run home," she teased. "He is here to see to the situation and report back to my father."

Lady Warenton took her hand, patting it. "We'll make sure that ye're well settled," she said. "We'll provide ye with any support ye need. Let me introduce ye tae some of the others."

Mattie met Scott's wife, Avrielle, and a younger daughter of Lord and Lady Warenton named Caria. But when she was introduced to Gar's mother, the mood seemed to change a little.

Rhoswyn de Wolfe wasn't, perhaps, so accepting.

"Lady de Wolfe," Mattie greeted her politely. "I am very happy to make your acquaintance."

Gar had his mother's features. Mattie could see that. He had his father's dark coloring, but his mother's fine features. Rhoswyn's gaze drifted over her for a moment, studying the woman who'd married her firstborn son, before she finally acknowledged the introduction.

"Lady de Wolfe," she said in a heavy Scots accent. "Welcome tae Gleann na Fola."

Mattie smiled timidly, simply because there didn't seem to be much warmth in Rhoswyn's voice. "Thank you, my lady," she said. "I am looking forward to coming to know the land and the people."

Rhoswyn nodded, but she was still looking at Mattie rather appraisingly. "We're in Scotland, ye know," she said. "Ye'll meet Scots here and they're not particularly fond of fine English ladies."

"*Tha mi an dòchas gun urrainn dhomh toirt orra a chreidsinn air dhòigh eile,*" Mattie said in perfect Gaelic.

I hope I can convince them otherwise.

That brought a distinct expression of surprise from Rhoswyn, and one of pleasure from Lady Warenton. It was their native language and Mattie had spoken it fluently.

"Ye speak our language?" Rhoswyn said in Gaelic.

Mattie nodded. "I do," she replied in kind. "I have learned several languages, but Gaelic will be the most helpful in my new role. I hope that I may be of some service to my husband in his duties."

"Ye will," Lady Warenton replied before Rhoswyn could, still speaking her native tongue. "I'm very happy that ye know our tongue. Ye'll do well, lass."

Mattie already liked Lady Warenton. She was kind, whereas Rhoswyn just didn't seem to warm up enough. It wasn't exactly disapproval, but it wasn't exactly acceptance, either. It was puzzling. Mattie was about to reply to Lady Warenton when Rhoswyn suddenly spoke up.

"God's Bones," she said, switching back to the common tongue. "What is my son wearing?"

The women looked over to see Gar in conversation with his grandfather and father. He was wearing his mail and protection for the most part, and it covered most of his clothing, so no one was sure what Rhoswyn meant when the woman clarified.

"His breeches," she said. "What are *those*?"

"I made them," Mattie said. "My dog has taken a disliking to Gar and tore the breeches he was wearing, so I quickly made those simply so he'd have something to wear. Now he refuses to take them off. Nothing I can say will convince him."

While Lady Warenton grinned, Rhoswyn broke away from

the women and marched up to her son.

"Those breeches," she said. "Ye need tae remove them. Ye have better breeches tae wear."

His conversation with his grandfather interrupted, Gar looked at his mother. "Why?" he said suspiciously. "Did Matilda tell you to order me to remove them?"

Rhoswyn shook her head. "Nay," she said. "But they're shameful. Terrible. Unbefitting a de Wolfe son. Remove them or I'll remove them myself."

Gar wasn't sure why his mother was being so aggressive about a pair of breeches. "I will not, nor will you," he said steadily. "My wife made them for me. She did it out of the kindness of her heart and I'll not remove them, not even for you. I am sorry you feel that they are shameful, but they are the most important thing I own."

Rhoswyn wasn't used to be refused by her children. She stared at him a moment as if she could hardly believe he'd denied her, but he had and he was clear why. Unable to do more than she'd already done, she marched off, leaving Gar bewildered. After a moment, he turned to his father.

"Why did she do that?" he asked.

Troy was watching his wife disappear down the stairs. "I am not certain," he said. "They *are* filthy, Gar."

"I'm not removing them."

Troy waved him off, as if he already knew that and it hadn't been a command. It was simply an observation. As Troy headed off after his wife to determine the source of her brusque manner, William simply smiled at his grandson.

"This is a difficult day for a mother, I suspect," he said. "Your grandmother felt the same way when your father and uncles were married. It is difficult to become the second-most-important woman in your son's life rather than the first."

Gar frowned. "But she was as much in support of this marriage as anyone."

William chuckled softly. "Until she actually met your wife," he said quietly. "That is when it became real."

Gar looked over at Mattie, who was in conversation with his grandmother and Aunt Avrielle. Caria, his youngest aunt, the adopted daughter of William and Jordan, had sauntered over and was being quite friendly to Mattie. Caria was barely a young woman herself and quite enamored with other young women, especially pretty ones like Mattie. She loved to study their clothing and hair, things she could emulate.

"I hope Mama was not rude to her," he said, sounding worried. "Mayhap I should go to her."

William shook his head. "Leave her with the women," he said. "That is where she needs to be right now. But you—your uncles and I must speak with you."

Gar looked at him. "Why?"

"We've heard some… things."

"What things?"

William put his hand on Gar's shoulder. "Come," he said. "Let us speak. You must be weary from your travels, so let us become comfortable."

With a lingering glance at Mattie, Gar did as he was told. Following his grandfather over to the nearest table, he sat down amongst his family members and others who had joined the group, men who were more than happy to pour him cups of wine and cheer his marriage. Of all the things he thought he would feel when he returned home from Hensingham, a sense of pleasure wasn't among them. Even happiness. Was he happy? Not strangely, he was. He'd been happy since the day he married Mattie. Joy the likes of which he'd never felt in his life. It was unrecognizable in his world.

But welcome.

Very welcome.

Gar was glad to be home…

With her.

ଓ

"WELL? WHAT'S WRONG?"

The question came from Troy. He'd found his wife out in the bailey, standing next to the fortified carriage that bore the de Reyne colors of blue and black. She was just standing there as the business of the bailey went on around her, as if nothing else in the world existed at the moment.

She was lost in thought.

But Rhoswyn's head came up when she heard Troy's question. She'd suspected he might come after her, and she really hadn't wanted him to, but her thoughts of finding a quiet place to cool her jumbled emotions faded away when she saw the carriage that had brought Gar's wife.

Now, she could think of nothing else.

"Why should anything be wrong?" she replied after a moment. "Everything is just as ye want it."

Troy pursed his lips wryly as he came up behind her. "You seem to have wanted it yourself until now," he said. "What's the matter with you?"

Rhoswyn knew it wouldn't do any good to avoid him. Troy was sharp. They'd been together for so long that she didn't even know where she ended and he began. It was a symbiotic relationship that few couples had.

After a moment, she shook her head.

"She's perfect," she said quietly. "Perfect and pretty."

"She is," Troy said. "And Gar is quite obsessed with her, so if you do not like the girl, keep it to yourself."

Rhoswyn sighed heavily, leaning against the carriage. "I dunna know her enough tae like her or dislike her," she said. "All I can see is a pretty, perfect English lass for my son."

Troy leaned against the carriage also, standing just a few inches from her and watching her lowered head. His Rhoswyn, a warrior in her own right, Scottish to the bone. He suspected what the problem was.

"I know you wanted a clan chief's daughter for him," he said softly. "But Gar is English. He serves the English. Papa and I discussed this at length and it is better that he marry an Englishwoman who can bring an alliance with her. It will be better for him in the end."

"Why?" Rhoswyn said, her head coming up to look at him. "I have never understood why ye thought an English wife would be better. He could have done so much good for the Lowlanders, Troy. For my people, for my father's allies. He could have made a difference."

"Did Red Keith put you onto this line of thinking?"

Rhoswyn shook her head. "Of course not," she said. "My father was glad Gar was marrying, no matter who it was. He said that a lad that beauteous needed tae find a wife in a hurry before he realized how women reacted to him and became a rake."

Troy snorted. "That sounds like something your father would say."

"I just wanted Gar tae have a wife who would value him."

Troy frowned. "And what makes you think Mattie will not?"

Rhoswyn shrugged. "Because she's pretty and perfect," she said, repeating what she'd said before. "Lasses like that only care about themselves. They will expect their husbands tae fall at their feet. Gar doesna need a wife like that."

Troy cupped her face with a big hand. "I think you are worrying needlessly," he said. "I think you must come to know Mattie yourself before you can make any judgment about her. Don't you?"

Rhoswyn did, but she was prejudiced. She really did want Gar to have a solid Scots wife, not a polished English bride. Women like that had never accepted Rhoswyn easily and she was just a little biased. But the marriage had commenced and there was no going back.

No matter how torn she was.

"I suppose," she said.

Troy kissed her before dropping his hand from her face. "Come inside with me," he said. "I think that my mother is taking Mattie around to show her the castle, but it would be nice if you went along, also. I'm sure the girl thinks that you do not like her, considering the way you left things."

"Does Gar think that?"

"Probably."

Rhoswyn winced. "Well, I canna have that," she said. "I'll go find the women."

Troy nodded, giving her an encouraging smile. "Everything will be well, I promise," he said. "Gar truly likes his new wife. She makes him happy. Give her a chance to show you that, Rhos. That's the best thing you can hope for with your son—that the marriage makes him happy."

Rhoswyn simply nodded as Troy winked at her and headed back toward the keep. She watched him go, thinking on his words and on the pretty lass her son had married.

Give her a chance to show you.

Rhoswyn supposed that was only fair. She would give the English lass the chance that other Englishwomen had never given her. Even if she'd had a rocky experience with some English-born women, that didn't mean she would have one with Mattie. And, as Troy had said, Gar's happiness meant everything.

That was all that mattered.

With a sigh, Rhoswyn headed off to find the women and her new daughter-in-law.

She had some amends to make.

CHAPTER TEN

"WHAT'S AMISS, POPPY?" Gar asked as he settled down with a cup of wine at a feasting table that had seen better days. "What things did you hear? And shouldn't Papa be here, too?"

William was seated beside his grandson, a full cup of wine in hand. "He will return in a moment," he said. "Meanwhile, your wife is with Matha and is well tended for now. We have business to attend to."

"Where is Reed? I thought he would be here."

"I sent him and Linus back to Hell's Guardhouse," William said. "With Andreas away, his castle was in need of a couple of strong knights. They were more than happy to go."

Gar grunted. "Dray will be lucky if Reed relinquishes command."

"I think Dray can convince him otherwise should it come to it," William said. "Dray is meaner and bigger and more experienced than Reed. That is why he is needed here, Gar. His sword is worth as much as two junior knights."

That was true. Andreas was nothing to be trifled with and not even power-hungry Reed could truly stand against him if it came down to it. But the way William declared that Andreas would be needed more at Gleann na Fola had Gar a little worried.

That meant something was in the air.

Gar took a big drink from his cup as he looked around the table at the other knights now gathered. His Uncle Scott was directly across from him, seated next to his son, Tor. Next to Tor were Uncle Blayth and Andreas. As they sat there, waiting for Troy to return, someone else entered the great hall.

The mere sight made Gar grin.

Atreus de Norville came to the top of the stairs, his gaze seeking out the table with the men around it. Atreus was the son of William's daughter, Evelyn, and her husband, Hector, who was the son of William's best friend, Paris de Norville. Atreus had a younger brother, Hermes, and the two of them were well known in the north. The stories of their antics, their fighting—against enemies or each other—were positively legendary. Wilder, braver, and more reckless knights had never existed and Gar was glad to see that one half of the duo was now at his disposal.

He stood up to greet him.

"Atreus," he said, embracing a man who was quite literally family. "'Tis good to see you, lad. When did you arrive?"

Atreus hugged Gar so hard that he caused the man to grunt as the air was forced from his lungs. "Yesterday," he said. "What's this I hear? You have married?"

Gar nodded, a smirk playing on his lips. "I have," he said. "A de Reyne daughter. She has come home with me, in fact."

Atreus frowned. "To this place?" he said, looking around at the dirt and dogs. "She must be positively thrilled to have such a steaming pile of dung as her domain. Do not be surprised if she runs away."

Gar grinned. "She will not," he said. "We have made a pact. She cannot run away and I cannot throw her out, so she will be forced to become accustomed to my magnificent garrison. Speaking of wives, did you bring yours?"

Atreus nodded. "Mariane and our son have come with me," he said. "You've not seen Perseus yet, Gar. A finer son has never lived."

Gar sat back down at the table, taking Atreus with him. "I believe you," he said. "Your grandfather must be thrilled."

Atreus snorted. "Paris de Norville never quite got over the fact that he does not have as many sons and grandsons as Uncle William," he said. "He tells me I must have ten sons now to try to even the numbers."

Gar laughed softly. "You'll never catch up," he said. "I intend to have ten sons of my own."

"Does your new wife know this?"

"Absolutely not," Gar said flatly. "And you'll not tell her."

Atreus started to laugh, hearing a comment against his ability to produce sons from Andreas across the table, and a good-natured verbal battle ensued. Gar was glad to be with his friends and family, but as he listened to Atreus and Andreas spar, his thoughts drifted in the direction of that lovely young woman he'd married.

He still couldn't believe it.

It was odd. Odd in the sense that when he was at Hensingham, it was as if he were on another planet. It was a different world at that castle along the sea and he and Mattie had enjoyed having time together as if nothing else in the world existed. As if there were no raging Scots, no heavy command burdens, or anything else that might weigh upon him. All was Mattie and

Mattie was all, and Gar was satisfied with that. He'd come to know a woman who almost seemed too good to be true. She was kind and attentive, and seemed genuinely interested in the things he wanted to talk about. Frankly, he never knew he had it in him to be so enamored with someone else. He'd never believed himself capable.

But he was.

Still, it was coming to feel like a dream even though he was back at his garrison and surrounded by his friends and family. It was another normal day in a year that had been full of such normal days, with one slight difference:

Mattie.

This was his world now and she was in it.

"Atreus," William said, cutting into the conversation at the table. "Dray, both of you quiet down. We have much to discuss now that Gar has returned."

Distracted from thoughts of Mattie, Gar took another sip of his wine. "Should we continue to wait for Papa?"

William shook his head. "Nay," he said. "Let us go forth with the subject at hand. Blayth has some information he came across while you were away."

Attention turned to Blayth, one of only two fair de Wolfe sons, having taken after their mother's coloring. But over the years, the dark blond hair had turned to gray. It was almost completely white these days, cropped short so that the scars on the left side of his head, horrible battle scars, were quite visible. He was the commander of Roxburgh Castle, an extremely volatile castle that tended to go back and forth between the Scots and the English, although under Blayth's command, it had remained a de Wolfe property for several years. Still, it was quite busy, as was the village around it, and sometimes Blayth heard rumors and intelligence that those at the lesser border garrisons didn't have a chance to hear. As Gar focused on his uncle, Blayth's green eyes turned to him.

"We had a visitor into Roxburgh earlier in the week," he said. Due to his head injury those years ago, he had a slow and deliberate way of speaking. "One of my mother's kin, from Clan Scott, came to tell me that he'd heard rumor that Maxwell of Westerkirk is trying to rally support behind them for another attack on Gleann na Fola."

Gar grunted. "That is not surprising," he said. "I am expecting something from them. It is only a matter of time."

"You know that Ean Maxwell is now clan chief," Blayth said. "His father was more moderate, but Ean does not have any such restraint."

"I know," Gar said. "Arduil was far easier to deal with. Never any trouble. But Ean has always been a bully of a lad. He has always tried to stir up trouble."

"More than you know," Blayth said. "He is spreading the rumor that you are holding his young daughter hostage here. He is hoping the outrage of a de Wolfe holding a child captive will motivate the clans into supporting him."

Gar's eyebrows lifted. "That's what you were told?"

Blayth nodded. "That's what Clan Scott was told to try to convince them to support a Maxwell attack against Gleann na Fola," he said. "They're using the fact that we sent their women and children south to give validity to the lie, but I'm told that some of the clans who do not really know the House of de Wolfe, or who have trouble with us, are considering it."

That was ominous news. Gar and his men could stave off the Maxwell of Westerkirk easily, but if more clans got involved, that might prove to be difficult. As Gar pondered that, he shook his head in frustration.

"So Ean lies to convince other clans to join him," he said. "The man was punished for the outright murder of two English knights and now he is claiming to be a victim?"

"This stopped being about those two knights from The Keld long ago," Scott spoke up, low and quiet. He had inherited his father's wisdom and was a man to be heeded. "Now, this about Ean's pride. It has turned into far more than paying for his actions. He's out to prove a point, to stir hatred against the English. If he can rally more clans, we may very well have a border war and that is the last thing we need."

"That is true," William said. The great Wolfe of the Border was the final word in all things when it came to the borders of Scotland. "Gar, I've taken the liberty of sending word to The Keld about this. They started this battle by requesting our assistance in punishing Westerkirk for the deaths of their knights, so I have requested they send at least a thousand men to support Gleann na Fola. If Westerkirk manages to rally support, you will need all of the help you can get."

Gar looked at his grandfather, so wise and so adored. They were quite fortunate to still have his counsel at his age and Gar knew it. He had a living legend at his disposal.

"Their last defeat was complete," Gar said. "Or so I thought. But no matter—we will be ready for whatever they intend."

Scott and Blayth looked to William because they'd discussed this very subject earlier, just the three of them. They were the senior battle commanders and while men like Gar and Andreas and Tor were very skilled, they didn't have the years that the older men had. Older men who had seen, time and time again, how badly these battles could go. Sensing the probing gazes of his sons, William looked at Gar.

"Move the women out," he said quietly. "Your new wife—let me take her back to Castle Questing. Or, better still, send her back to Hensingham. You do not want her here if a battle comes, Gar. It would be no place for a lady."

Gar wasn't stupid. He knew that. But he was struck by the revelation that he didn't want to be separated from Mattie, not now when they were just coming to know one another. That was a stupid reason, of course, but he couldn't help it. He also didn't want to appear as if he were panicking over this, which fed his reluctance.

His uncle could be wrong.

His grandfather could be wrong.

He doubted it, of course, but stranger things had happened.

"I appreciate your counsel, Poppy," he said. "I will consider it, truly I will. Atreus has just only brought his wife and son here, so he and I will speak and decide what is to be done with our families. But I am very grateful for your suggestion."

Frankly, William was surprised that Gar, the man who didn't want to be married, hadn't immediately taken the excuse of sending his new wife home. If there was still any doubt that Gar wasn't so resistant to his marriage anymore, this seemed to quash it. Young, infatuated men could be unstable creatures, indeed, so William didn't push his advice.

He simply called for more wine.

"You make the decision that is best for you and your wife," he said. "But we will be here for a few days to help you form a plan of defense for the place. Scott and Blayth have already sent out more scouts to see if they can glean any additional information."

"Thank you, Poppy," Gar said. "You have been very thorough in my absence and I appreciate it."

William smiled faintly before accepting more wine from a servant. "Now," he said. "Let us speak on more pleasant things. Am I to understand that this marriage is agreeable?"

Gar fought off a smile as the subject shifted to a much more pleasant one. "Aye," he said simply. "It is."

That answer might have been good enough for William, but it wasn't for Atreus. As Troy returned to the hall and joined the men, Atreus all but wrestled the truth about Gar's feelings on the not-so-small matter of his marriage, something that began to concern William the more he listened. Gar wasn't just agreeable to the marriage. He was enamored with it. That meant Lady de Wolfe, in spite of the danger, probably wasn't going anywhere.

Something told William that this might be an issue in the end. A new husband who did not want to be separated from his new wife.

And death on the approach.

It was a situation that bore watching.

☙

WHILE GAR WAS gathering with the male folk, Mattie was off on a tour of the castle with Lady Warenton and the other women. Gar had promised her that he would show her around, but given that he was sequestered with a group of men, that duty fell to Lady Warenton and a few others. Not that Mattie minded, to be truthful. The majordomo who tended to things in the hall had been sent back to the army by Lady Warenton because, as she said, the man did a terrible job tending to the keep. Therefore, it was Mattie and her new relatives on a grand tour of the imposing, filthy castle.

Even so, Mattie was enjoying their company immensely.

A young lady who hadn't left her side was Caria de Wolfe, Lady Warenton's youngest daughter. She had seen about fourteen years, a gorgeous young woman with dark hair and dark eyes, and she was giggly and sweet and followed Mattie closely as the women walked around the interior of Gleann na Fola, showing Mattie her new domain. At one point, Caria slipped her hand into Mattie's, smiling brightly when Mattie looked at her in surprise. That brought a grin from Mattie, who squeezed the girl's hand and kept holding it.

To Caria, Mattie was her new best friend even though Lady Warenton had tried to pry her youngest away more than once. But Caria wouldn't budge and Mattie truly didn't mind, so Lady Warenton finally backed off. She kept on with a tour of Mattie's new home, showing her all of the stairwells, the chambers, the storage chambers, the hall, alcoves, vaults, and finally the kitchens, which were in the sublevel of the keep.

As Mattie had quickly discovered, Gleann na Fola was a vast maze of stairs and chambers. Some chambers even had their own stairwell, like the master's chambers, which were on the southwest corner of the structure and included three big rooms and one smaller one. Only two ways in and out, which was designed for safety. Lady Warenton even showed Mattie a security feature that was ingenious—there was a lever at the top of the stairwell leading into the chamber that, when thrown, dropped an iron grate onto the stairwell that prevented anyone from getting to the door at the top. Evidently, other stairwells had the same feature, making Gleann na Fola one of the safer castles on the border.

Through it all, Mattie realized one thing—there wasn't one corner of the castle that wasn't absolutely filthy with dirt, mold, moss, water leakage, animal droppings, or sometimes all five.

Every stairwell was slimy with growth or slippery with water, or some other kind of organic matter, which made going up and down the stairs rather treacherous at times. That was evidently acknowledged by the occupants of the castle because most of the stairwells had a rope banister that went from the top to the bottom, something to hang on to in case one slipped. No one wanted to roll to the bottom of those stairs and break their necks.

Truthfully, the place was horrific.

Lady Warenton surely knew that, but to her credit, she didn't comment on it. To do so would be to disparage her grandson, and she wasn't going to do that. Caria, however, didn't have such restraint. She thought every surface of castle was disgusting and made sure they all knew it. Lady Warenton shushed her more than once, and Caria would obey until the next dirty situation came up and then she would comment on it all over again.

By the time they reached the kitchens, Mattie was praying that they wouldn't find the place where the food was stored and prepared in as bad a shape as the rest of the castle. The kitchens were in the sublevel below ground level, with a dedicated staircase that went straight up to another stairwell that went to the hall—long, narrow stairs where the food was brought up and down—but alongside that was a type of elevator, an enormous box tied to a rope, that could be hauled up through a space in the wall, bringing food and drink to the hall more easily than via the stairs.

Lady Warenton explained the stairs to the hall, the lever and lift system, and pointed out that that there were not one, but two wells in the kitchen. It was all very interesting to Mattie, but she still noticed that there were signs of rats all throughout the kitchen. That didn't give her great confidence in the cleanliness of their food, more so when she actually entered the kitchen proper and saw the cook.

Literally, a dirty old man.

And he didn't like the appearance of women in his domain.

"Oy!" he yelled, lifting the nearest implement, which happened to be a long wooden spoon. "What do you want here?"

Lady Warenton faced down the spoon raised at her. "Yer name is Brickie, isn't it?"

The old man's eyes narrowed. "Who are you?"

"Lady Warenton."

He frowned. "I don't care," he snapped. "Out of my kitchen! No one is allowed here!"

"I am."

Mattie stepped forward, unafraid of the threatening wooden tool. As everyone looked at her in surprise, she faced off against her husband's cook, who scowled at the properly dressed lady.

"And just who are you?" he said. "I don't know you."

Mattie cocked a dark eyebrow. "I am Lady de Wolfe," she said. "Lady *Gar* de Wolfe. Your liege is my husband and the moment we were married, this kitchen, and this castle, became my domain. I am allowed here, any time I wish, and you will like it or you will get out. Is that clear?"

Caria, cowering back by the door, stood there with her mouth hanging open in shock while Lady Warenton fought off a grin.

"Ye heard her," Lady Warenton said. "Like it or get out. We can always find another cook."

Brickie's reply was to swipe the spoon in Mattie's direction, though he missed her by a mile. Still, she couldn't back away. If she did, he would never respect her. She'd made a statement and she had to enforce it. Grabbing another wooden spoon, this one dirty with whatever he'd been using it for, she swung it at him in return.

Brickie wasn't used to someone challenging his authority. He jumped back as she lashed out at him, but only momentarily. He swung the spoon at Mattie again, and she swung hers in return, and suddenly, they were dueling with wooden spoons across the kitchen floor. It was like a sword fight, only the weapons were wooden kitchen tools.

And Mattie was going to win it.

Brickie wasn't a big man. He was small and wiry and grumpy, which was how he was able to rule over his kitchens, but the new Lady de Wolfe wasn't about to put up with his bullying. They dueled around the table in the center of the kitchen, slapping spoons, until Mattie gained the upper hand and chased him back into the buttery. Lady Warenton, Caria, and Avrielle, who had been tagging along, followed. They watched Mattie back Brickie into the rear of the buttery, unaware that Rhoswyn, who had been hunting for the women, had finally found them. Rhoswyn only caught the end of their battle as Mattie finally knocked Brickie's spoon to the ground. As the old man raised his hands in surrender, Mattie tossed her spoon aside as well.

"Now," she said, the slightest bit winded from dancing around the kitchen. "You will *not* tell me where I can and cannot go in my own home. You will not tell me, or any de Wolfe woman, that she cannot come into your kitchen. While I respect that you have been my husband's cook and will continue to be so, this is now *my* kitchen. You will do as I say. Do you understand me so far?"

Brickie was frowning. The sides of his mouth were so

downturned that they couldn't possibly go any further. "I understand," he grumbled. "But you know nothing about this kitchen!"

"I realize that," Mattie said evenly. "But you will teach me. I will listen and learn from your experience. But, with God as my witness, you had better behave yourself or I will take a spoon to you again—and the next time, you might come away with a knot on your head. Do you comprehend me?"

Brickie nodded, once, but it was enough. Mattie stood back, indicating for him to return to his kitchen, and he did so, knowing those other women were smirking at him and feeling just as humiliated as he could possibly be. It was then that Mattie looked up and saw Rhoswyn standing back by the buttery door, an expression of surprise on her face. Lady Warenton saw Rhoswyn at nearly the same time and she grasped Caria by the hand as she headed in Rhoswyn's direction.

"How much of that did ye see?" Lady Warenton asked.

Rhoswyn wasn't entirely sure. "I saw… I saw the lady chasing Brickie intae the buttery," she said. "What happened?"

Lady Warenton let her smile break through as she glanced at Mattie, just emerging from the buttery. "She did what needed tae be done," she said with pride. "Brickie is too much of a tyrant for his own good and the lady righted it. I like her, Rhos. She'll do well here."

With that, Lady Warenton headed out of the kitchens, pulling Caria along with her, as Rhoswyn and Mattie faced one another.

For a moment, Mattie didn't know what to say. Her introduction to Rhoswyn had been uncertain at best before the woman simply disappeared. Now, she was back, and Mattie wasn't sure what to say. Rhoswyn had clearly seen her take issue with the cook. Perhaps the woman thought *she* was the bully.

She was coming to sorely regret the spoon fight.

"He… he was rude to Lady Warenton," Mattie said, trying to explain. "I do not tolerate rudeness from those who serve in my household. It was inexcusable."

Rhoswyn was still looking at her rather appraisingly, but the coldness from earlier seemed to be gone. "I've got news for ye, lass," she said. "Lady Warenton can take care of herself. She's the strongest woman ye'll ever know."

"Aye, my lady. I hope I did not offend."

Rhoswyn shook her head. "That is not what I meant," she said. "Ye did what Lady Warenton would have done had this been her own home. De Wolfe women are strong. We have tae be."

"Aye, my lady," Mattie said, though she still felt as if she were verging on being scolded and sought to somehow break the ice with Gar's mother. "I… I am sorry you were unable to come to Hensingham, but I understand your most distressing reason. I do hope your son's wife and child are doing well."

Rhoswyn nodded. "Surprisingly, they are," she said. "The infant seems to be growing stronger. 'Tis a blessing."

"Indeed," Mattie said. "That is good news."

"Thank ye for asking after them."

"My pleasure, my lady."

An awkward silence briefly descended. Rhoswyn took a few steps toward Mattie, towering over her. Rhoswyn was quite tall, a strong and sturdy woman in general, whereas Mattie didn't have a height or weight advantage. For a moment, Rhoswyn simply looked her over, an appraising expression but not unkind.

The moments ticked away.

"I'm told my son is fond of ye," she finally said in Gaelic. "I'm glad he is. He dinna want tae marry, but I am glad ye changed his mind. He needs a strong wife, my lady. Can ye be that for him? Strong?"

Mattie nodded. "I can," she answered in Gaelic. "I will, I promise. I will not fail him."

Rhoswyn nodded her head. "Good," she said. Then, she reached out a hand to Mattie, who timidly took it. "Come along, lass. This keep is now yers and ye have a good deal of work tae do. But after what I've seen, I think ye can do it."

Mattie let her mother-in-law lead her out of the kitchens where Brickie was piling wood on the fire to strengthen the blaze. He didn't look at her as she quit the kitchen, but Mattie didn't care. Somehow, in this strange incident, she had earned Rhoswyn's approval. If not her approval, then at least her respect.

Perhaps there was hope after all.

CHAPTER ELEVEN

THERE WAS NOWHERE to go but up.

That was what Mattie decided the day following her arrival at Gleann na Fola. All she knew was that she couldn't live in the castle in its current state—and since Gar had told her the castle was her domain, she took him literally.

She was going to take on the daunting task of cleaning it.

God help her.

The rest of yesterday after her arrival had been dedicated to meeting more family and touring more places around the castle. Everyone had seemed more than happy to show her around and teach her about the place she would now call home. Lady Warenton, or Jordan as she asked to be called, was at the head of it all, making sure Mattie had all of her questions answered. Caria, too, stayed by Mattie's side and Mattie had to admit that it was a far warmer welcome than she had expected. She didn't mind Caria, even if the girl was a little clingy. She was sweet and helpful.

Mattie appreciated that.

But the next day, the real work began.

Since Jordan knew the villages along the borders, on both

sides, the first thing she helped with was bringing on more women to help clean. There was a small parish to the south of Gleann na Fola, with parishioners almost all farmers and tradesmen, and she was able to bring ten women to the castle by midmorning. They were promised a decent wage, as Mattie had made that clear, and they all gathered in the hall as Mattie and Jordan decided how to handle the situation. Plans were laid. Duties were given.

Meanwhile, the men were confused.

Gar watched all of it with some concern even though he'd told Mattie that she could do as she wished with the keep. He wasn't going to go back on his word, but he honestly hadn't thought she was going to start her management the very next day after her arrival. But she was. In a castle where there were usually no women, suddenly, there were more than a dozen and they were all armed with buckets of water mixed with vinegar. He could smell it. But then, he began to discover something.

The way she went about cleaning this atrocity of a castle was quite methodical.

Brilliant, even.

When Gar should have been focused on the plans of Westerkirk, he found himself watching that slip of a woman he'd been forced to marry. Last night, they'd slept in the same bed, in his great chamber, but they hardly said two words to one another before Mattie was fast asleep, exhausted from the travel and from the day's events, and this morning, he'd risen while she was still snoring softly upon the pillow. The first chance he'd had to see her was when she'd gathered her army of women in the great hall, an army that included his mother and grandmother, and as he watched with fascination, the army went to work.

It started with sweeping. So much sweeping. The dogs were chased out by the brooms, running outside, which was where Mattie wanted them. As three or four women swept, the rest of them followed with mops and brushes, scrubbing the floor behind them. More vinegar water was splashed across the floor and before Gar could get away, Mattie commandeered him for furniture moving. He sent servants to fetch Tor and Atreus and Andreas, and between the four of them, they moved the tables around so Mattie and her ladies could clean years of grime and filth off the floors.

But along with the cleaning women, there was also another addition.

Perseus.

Perseus de Norville was three years old, blond-haired and wild. He was a great-grandson of William, who took delight in the child's antics. Perseus' mother, Mariane, was a lovely woman, unafraid of hard work, and she was more than happy to pitch in and help the cause, but Perseus kept her distracted from any form of cleaning or sweeping. In fact, Perseus himself wanted to sweep, so Jordan gave him a broom and he went to work mimicking the other women. He made more of a mess rather than actually helping, but it was sweet to watch.

Until Atreus took offense that his son was doing women's work.

After that, Atreus ran off with Perseus, taking the child to attend to more manly pursuits, leaving his wife and the other women to finish with the great hall. However, it was clear that it wasn't something that was going to be finished in a day. There was so much filth on the floor that it required more scrubbing and scraping to break it free. At some point, Gar finally departed, as he had duties to attend to now that he had returned, but his thoughts were with that lovely young woman in his hall, trying to clean it of all of the man and animal filth. It was ironic, truly—well did he remember the conversation with his grandfather that had forced him into making the journey to Hensingham to collect his wife.

I do not want to focus on my wife, he'd told his grandfather.

Funny how things had changed.

Mattie had been fully aware of Gar standing near the hall entry, watching everything that was going on. She even waved to him once or twice, being rewarded with a smile. In truth, she was a little disappointed when he finally left, but she knew he had duties to attend to. Still, the mere thought of him left her with a smile on her face.

She had duties to attend to, also.

One of those duties was to leave Jordan and Rhoswyn in charge of the hall cleanup while she went down to the kitchens. She had some questions for Brickie, hoping they wouldn't have to duel with wooden spoons again for her to get any answers. Hesitantly, she made her way down into the steamy kitchens and it smelled heavily of bread. She could see Brickie and a couple of kitchen servants over by the bread oven, built of heavy stone next to the big hearth.

Brickie was taking bread out and putting it in, scolding the servants when they didn't move fast enough or efficiently enough or something. She couldn't quite understand him. But he caught sight of her near the entry into the kitchen and he scowled.

"What do you want?" he demanded.

That had Mattie doing some scowling of her own. "You will address me with respect or I will tell my husband," she said. "I've not come to fight with you, but I'll give you a fight if you do not settle down."

Brickie was still scowling, but at least he wasn't trying to fight her with the bread shovel. In fact, he stepped away from the oven and leaned the shovel against the wall before brushing off his hands.

"What do you want, my lady?" he asked.

It was only marginally more polite than the way he'd said it the first time, and it was still more of a demand than a question, but Mattie wanted to make peace, so she didn't confront the tone. She simply gave him an answer.

"Last night, I noticed that food was served upon trenchers," she said. "I also noticed that some men did not have anything at all to eat off. They just took food from the bowls and ate it with their hands."

Brickie nodded. "How else are they supposed to eat it?"

"Do you not make enough trenchers for everyone?"

Brickie looked back at the bread oven and it was then that Mattie noticed the stack of flat bread slices on a table nearby. "I have enough for those who matter," he said. "Sometimes the soldiers bring their own plates and cups to be served from."

"No utensils?"

"What's that?"

"Spoons and knives."

Brickie shook his head. "If they want a spoon, they bring it," he said. "If they want a knife, they'll bring it."

Mattie pondered that. She could see a stack of unwashed bowls near the trenchers, big bowls that food was served in, and even more on the floor. There were also platters on the floor, wooden ones, and she found herself looking under the tables as Brickie followed her around. He wasn't belligerent any longer, but he was curious. Aggressively curious. She'd pull something out to look at it and he wouldn't wait until she was finished until he was shoving it back where it belonged. When they reached the last platter that Mattie looked at, one with a chip on the side, he tried to put it back before she was done and she slapped him on the wrist.

"Cease," she hissed. "This is my kitchen and I can inspect it as I please. If you do not like it, then—"

He cut her off. "I can get out," he said. "I know. But I have a system and you're disrupting it."

Mattie frowned. "I am doing nothing of the kind," she said. "Unless your system is chaos, in which case, I am openly contributing to it by putting these back where I found them."

He frowned at her and she frowned back. "This is a castle of men," he said. "They don't care if they have spoons or knives or even bowls. As long as there is food, 'tis all they care about."

That was probably true. Gar had told her that Gleann na Fola was strictly a battle castle, not the refined palace that she was accustomed to. But her purpose in coming to the kitchen was to discover just how barbaric the feasts were. Men bringing their own bowls and knives wasn't unusual, but it all seemed so… uncivilized.

She wanted to know more.

"What about food?" she asked. "Do you serve more than one meal a day?"

Brickie shook his head. "One meal only," he said. "In the night. All they can eat."

"What do you usually serve?"

He was calming by this point, not so entirely enraged that she was in his kitchen, and actually answered the question. "The lord likes to feed the men well," he said. "Always bread, and lots of it. Always something like beans or peas or carrots, something of substance. And always meat—pork, mutton, or beef. The lord has his own pigs and cows. Sometimes he trades them for sheep."

"And you roast the meat here? In this kitchen?"

Brickie shook his head and began to walk, motioning her along. She followed him to a small, extremely fortified door in the wall. She had to duck to move through it, and the door was about a foot thick, but it emptied out into a yard on the north side of the castle. It was surrounded by a great stone wall, and it hugged the keep so that the yard itself was long and skinny, but she could see an entire herd of pigs off to the right, tucked into a shelter with a sod roof on it. There were also chickens running around, and a coop, as well as two goats that looked at her curiously.

One of them was a very pregnant female.

"Goat's milk," she muttered thoughtfully.

Brickie heard her. "Aye," he said. "The lord likes it."

She looked at him, surprised. "Does he?" she said. "That is a strange thing for a man to drink."

"Not when he has a nervous stomach," Brickie said. "Ask the lord. He'll tell you."

As Brickie wandered over to an area that had two enormous spits, both of them already speared with a side of pork, Mattie was still thinking on the goat's milk.

"Brickie, do you sell anything from the castle?" she said. "What I mean to ask is if you sell meat or milk or anything."

Brickie was checking the fires underneath the sides of pork, which were low at this time of day because the meat needed to be cooked slowly and thoroughly all the way through to reduce the risk of anyone becoming ill from eating it. He may have been a grumpy old man, but he was competent in his duties.

He shook his head to Mattie's question.

"Nay," he said. "We buy meat and vegetables sometimes because we have a lot of men to feed. Sometimes they eat more than we have."

Mattie was still looking at the goats. "What about cheese?" she said. "Do you make goat cheese?"

Brickie stirred up the embers. "There's a woman in the village that makes cheese," he said. "We purchase it from her. Why?"

Mattie pointed to the goat. "Because I can milk that goat and make cheese," she said. "I also know how to make soap from their milk. Both are products we can either use or sell. We would not have to buy them elsewhere."

Brickie looked at the goat and shrugged, turning back to his fire. He didn't seem particularly interested in her proposal, but Mattie was. She had a lot of ideas now. She went over to the pregnant goat and petted her head, though the animal was more interested in whether or not Mattie had something to eat for her. Thoughts lingering on goats, and what they meant for the economy of the castle, Mattie headed back into the kitchen with determination.

She had a man to see.

☙

"AND IF WE don't eat it, we can sell it," Mattie was saying. "You have a dozen pigs out in the yard. Why not a dozen goats? They are much more useful."

Gar was sitting on a stump in the bailey, listening to Mattie chatter on about goats and cheese and soap. She was very excited about it, but he found that all he could do was watch her. She was such a fascinating creature when she spoke, her sweet voice with a very slight lisp that was incredibly charming. She was convinced they could have a goat empire right on the Scottish borders and corner the market on cheese.

"You have an enterprising mind," he said. "In fact, my Uncle Tommy's wife has much the same mind. She has a foundling home near Kelso and that is how the foundlings make money—by making goat cheese. It is delicious."

"Truly?" Mattie said, her face alight with the possibilities. "Then mayhap she would help us build our own goat herd."

He nodded. "Possibly," he said. "But the truth is that we are not a castle that sells products, like cheese. This is a military castle, Queenie. What we have here, we eat. What we need, we buy. Our sole purpose is war."

She nodded patiently. "I know," she said. "But how do you make the coin necessary to buy what you need?"

He shrugged. "It is a de Wolfe garrison," he said. "I am provided with a monthly stipend to manage the castle. That stipend pays for whatever we need."

"Then you do not have any wealth of your own?"

He nodded. "I do," he said. "I am also paid a yearly wage as a garrison commander."

"How much?"

"Two hundred pounds a year."

"I see," she said, considering what some would consider a sizable sum. "Then you are a very rich man because I know my father has given you my dowry. My mother told me so."

Gar nodded. "He did give it to me," he said. "Why?"

"It was somewhere around three thousand pounds."

"Three thousand, two hundred."

Mattie didn't say anything. She simply wandered over and sat down on a stump next to him. Gar's gaze moved over her.

He sensed that there was something more on her mind.

"If I ask you if something is amiss with you, will you tell me?" he said.

Mattie scratched her forehead before answering. "I do not know," she said honestly. "I suppose… I suppose that I want to feel useful, Gar. I want to feel as if I contribute to our marriage beyond bringing you three thousand, two hundred pounds. I have ideas and I would like to help you, as your wife. I must *do* something. I cannot sit idle."

A smile tugged at his lips. "I am coming to learn that about you," he said. "You cannot sit still."

"Nay, I cannot."

"Then do whatever you like," he said. "If you want to have a herd of a thousand goats, then go ahead. Buy your goats if it makes you happy."

She looked at him, joy on her face. "Truly?"

"Truly."

"But there is something else."

"What else?"

"I was speaking to Brickie," she ventured. "I asked him about feasting items. You know—plates, spoons, knives. Things that are used when you provide a feast. He said you had very little in the way of those things."

Gar nodded. "That is true," he said. "I told you that we do not have fine feasts here. There is no call for plates or spoons beyond a reasonable measure."

"Could I commission some so that when we have a special guest, I will not be ashamed?"

He chuckled softly. "Commission what you like," he said. "You are my queen. This is your castle. Do what you want to do."

She brightened. "But it will cost money."

"Spend what you wish."

She stood up quickly and rushed him, throwing her arms around his neck. "Thank you," she said, kissing his cheek. "You are kind and generous, husband."

She went to pull away but he wouldn't let her go. His powerful arms were around her and he wasn't quite ready to release her yet.

"Do it again," he murmured.

She cocked her head. "Do what?"

"Kiss me."

Fighting off a grin, Mattie looked him in the eye first. Really looked him in the eye. Then, she leaned over and gently kissed his cheek. She did it again and again, moving in the direction of his mouth. When she came to his lips, she kissed him once more as a final prize. She'd only meant it to be a soft, gentle kiss, but very quickly, it turned into something more. Gar pulled her against him, his lips suckling hers, his tongue licking at her. It was clear that he wanted to kiss her deeply, but Mattie was quite aware they were in public, so she put her hands on his face to stop him.

"Not now," she whispered, her face flushed from his kiss. "There are people about."

He wouldn't be put off. "They know we are married," he said. "I am allowed to kiss my wife. *I am allowed to kiss my wife!*"

He shouted the last seven words to the bailey they were in, his booming voice reverberating off the stone walls, and Mattie shrieked with embarrassment. Gar laughed low in his throat and pulled her to him again, kissing her sweetly before releasing her.

"Very well," he said, standing up. "I do not want to create a spectacle. I will preserve your modesty, madam."

"Not for all to see, anyway," she said, looking around and seeing men in the distance, or up on the wall. "If you wanted to take me someplace private and ravage me, that is one thing. But not out here in the open."

Gar took that as an invitation.

There were several outbuildings in this particular part of the bailey, closest to the castle, and he grabbed her by the hand, towing her behind him as he marched around the corner. Mattie was giggling the entire time as he opened the door of one outbuilding, dismissed it, and then moved to the next. Finally, he found an old armory that suited his needs and pulled her inside, shutting the door securely.

Immediately, he pulled her into his arms.

Gar's mouth fixed to Mattie's and he was instantly lost. He was coming to very quickly realize that he was always lost where she was concerned. He pulled her down onto the dirt floor and, immediately, the broadcloth dress she was wearing began to loosen. His hands were warm and big and rough, and still a little clumsy, but he was learning quickly. The man who'd had no real experience with women was a fast learner. He loosened the ties on the dress and pulled it over her head as she went to work on his tunic.

All of it was coming off.

Gar's big hands lost themselves in the silken web of her hair, gripping it so tightly that she couldn't move. He had her trapped and wanted her to remain that way. Mattie gasped in response to his onslaught, fierce and powerful as he laid her on her back. They were on the dirt, but for once, she didn't really care. Both she and Gar had very quickly learned that there was a tremendous amount of attraction between them, something they were both willing to explore.

Anywhere.

Trapped beneath his big body, Mattie groaned with pleasure as his tongue invaded the honeyed recesses of her mouth.

Gar's mouth eventually left her lips, moving to the rosy-tipped breasts he had discovered on their wedding night. They were sublime, firm and full and beautifully soft. Gar lost himself in her breasts as Mattie cradled his head, encouraging him to suckle harder. This was all so new to her that she was fascinated by all of it, slipping her fingers into his mouth as he suckled her nipples. He sucked hard on her fingers, as well as her breasts, and all of that sucking sparked a raging fire between her legs. She parted them for him, pulling up the front of her dress so there would be nothing between their bodies. She could feel his hard erection against her thigh, but that wasn't where she wanted it. Grasping his manhood, she gently pulled him toward her wet heat.

Gar knew what she wanted. He wanted it, too, but he also didn't want to chance getting any dirt on her. Dirt and private parts would never do. Therefore, he stopped kissing her long enough to roll her onto her stomach before pulling her up so she was on all fours—knees and hands. When he flipped up her dusty skirt, her pert backside came into view and he growled as he descended on it, biting her buttocks gently. As he did this, he pulled her legs apart a little more so that his target was clearly visible to him. That beautiful pink flower, just waiting for him.

He didn't make her wait.

Placing his manhood against her, he thrust firmly from behind.

Feeling his full, hard length inside of her, Mattie cried out softly, biting off her screams as he began to thrust into her. This was a new position for her, but one she very quickly decided she liked. It was wildly arousing. Already, Gar could feel the tiny muscles of her sheath fluttering in preparation for her pleasure and he released her hips, running his hands up the front of her torso until he came to her beautiful breasts. Grabbing hold, he pulled her into an upright position against him, as if she were sitting on his lap, and continued to thrust.

"Do this," he whispered into her ear. "Put your hand here and rub."

He took Mattie's right hand and put it between her legs. Using his big hand as a guide, he had her probe between her dark curls, seeking the little nub of pleasure that was there, and once he found it, he began to manipulate it using Mattie's fingers. She cried out in pleasure when she realized what touching herself could do, and very soon, he didn't need to guide her at all. Instinct took over and Mattie stroked herself, bringing about a release that had her screaming. As she burst forth with a climax that shook her to the bone, Gar could feel her muscles contract around his engorged member and it was all he needed to coax forth his own release.

He put a big hand over her mouth, stifling her screams lest someone hear her and come to investigate, as he buried his face in the back of her head and spilled himself deep. He thrust hard as he did so, four or five times, each one delivering his seed to their intended mark. The first time he'd coupled with her, his release had been wondrous. But he'd bedded her nearly every night since and each time, it only grew better. In fact, he was seeing stars as he sat back on his heels, holding Mattie on his lap, impaled on him, with one hand still between her legs while the other was on her mouth.

For a moment, he just sat there and panted.

But she wriggled, slightly, and he realized he didn't want to sit there. He wasn't done with her. Still holding her fast, he used the last of his erection to move in and out of her, stroking slow and hard, and in little time, she released again. He could feel her. It made him smile as he continued to thrust, feeling the last of his erection die down, feeling her body tremble against him as he moved. As if she were made for him and him alone, she reacted to every move, every stroke, every breath he took.

He'd never known anything so powerful in his life.

Somewhere, they could hear voices. Men were walking near the outbuilding, somewhere outside, and when Gar rolled his hips back to remove himself from her body, she stopped him.

"Nay," she whispered. "Do not leave me. Stay where you are."

He laughed low on his throat, the hand between her legs beginning to stroke her again. "You like this?" he purred. "How delicious for me."

The voices were coming closer and Mattie closed her eyes, leaning her head back against him. "Do what you did before," she murmured. "Touch me… there."

His fingers probed her gently. "Here?"

She could only nod because she was so highly aroused that words wouldn't come. The soldiers came closer, looking for someone, evidently, by the way they were talking, and they were passing awfully close to the outbuilding at that point, but Mattie found that incredibly exciting. The thought of being caught in a compromising position with her husband didn't upset her in the least. As Gar quickly discovered, she liked it.

He'd managed to work her into another climax by the time the men passed within a few feet of the door of the outbuilding and when she started to make noise again, he put his hand over her mouth to quiet her. In the process of doing so, she ended up biting his hand and he found that so wildly arousing that he began to grow hard all over again. He was already still embedded in her, so it was merely a matter of rolling his hips forward and beginning that ancient, primal mating rhythm again. That very thing went on twice more as the hours of the day advanced.

Talk of goats and cheese was understandably finished for the day.

Gar and Mattie had found better ways to spend their time.

CHAPTER TWELVE

F*ERGUSON.*

Johnstone.

Those were the only clans who would consider supporting Westerkirk since Ean had sent his spies out, spreading lies, and even then, the clans had only sent about forty men total. That hardly bolstered his numbers. It was fewer than what he'd had before. But he consoled himself with the fact that sometimes, a smaller, more focused group of men could do more damage. One man, rightly placed, could bring down a kingdom.

That was what he needed to do.

Bring down a kingdom.

On a cold, bright morning, Ean and his men began heading for the Valley of Blood. Uncle Gordie had come up with the plan to destroy Gleann na Fola with the least amount of bloodshed and his plan was simple—all they had to do was get a man inside the castle. Everyone knew that Gleann na Fola was virtually impenetrable, which meant the man couldn't scale the walls or dig underneath it or breach it in a normal fashion. The man that got inside the castle was going to have to use luck and intelligence, and, unable to come up with a suitable candidate,

Gordie decided that it should be him. He might have been an old man, but he knew how to operate.

Therefore, he was traveling with his warriors this morning.

The ground was wet and dew lay heavily upon the land. As the sun began to rise, all of that moisture glistened like diamonds on the hillsides as they made their way toward the northern end of the Valley of Blood. They had scouts out in front of them ensuring that their path to their destination was unimpeded or, at the very least, kept them safe from English patrols. And there were plenty of those all around, as was normal with the House of de Wolfe. They always had a dozen patrols at any given time along the border, ensuring that the Scots stayed on their side.

Ironically, Gleann na Fola was on the Scottish side of the border. It just happened to belong to the House of de Wolfe, all in the name of keeping the Scottish border secure. The House of de Wolfe had several castles in Scotland and there wasn't one clan that had tried to run them out over the years, mostly because William de Wolfe was married to a woman from Clan Scott and there were several clans that viewed that as both a kinship and an alliance. But there were also several that didn't.

One of those was Maxwell.

Bailie Castle was about a day's travel from the heart of the Valley of Blood. If a man traveled swiftly on foot, he could make it in good time, and it was Ean's intention that they should make it to the southern end of the valley by nightfall. That would give them an entire night to lay forth their plans and somehow manage to get Uncle Gordie inside. Gordie happened to know the castle from when he was a young lad, so he knew the fortifications and he knew the layout. When the House of de Wolfe took charge of the castle, however, they'd reinforced the fortifications and dug berms into the side of the hill that the castle was on, so now it was an incredibly fortified location. However, Gordie was confident that he could somehow get inside.

Or die trying.

The truth was that almost three hundred Scots could do some damage, but not enough.

Not enough to truly hurt.

And they needed to hurt.

"Lad?" Gordie was walking next to Ean now, something he'd not done since they left Bailie. There was tension between them, something not easily dissolved, but Gordie was the more reasonable of the two. Things had to be said. "I've been thinking about our approach tae Gleann na Fola."

Ean was looking straight ahead, at the rolling hills to the south. Beyond them was the valley they sought. "What is it?" he said.

Gordie glanced at his stubborn nephew. "We spoke of breaching the castle," he said. "We've spoken of me getting inside. I was there as a child, several times. I know that castle."

"Go on with it. I've not got all day."

Gordie shook his head faintly at the sheer belligerence of the man, even when dealing with someone who was, by all accounts, putting himself in danger for the very clan that Ean ruled over.

"Did ye ever stop tae thing *how* I'd get inside?" Gordie said.

Ean looked at him, frowning. "Of course I have," he said. "I'm not daft."

"Then tell me how."

That only seemed to make Ean angrier. "Dunna be stupid," he said. "That's why we're going tae build ladders. Tae get over the walls. That's how we'll get ye inside."

Gordie sighed faintly. "Nay, lad," he said. "That's *not* how I'll get inside. That's how ye'll get every man killed."

Ean suddenly came to a halt and grabbed Gordie by the arm. "Then what are ye saying?"

Gordie pulled his arm out of Ean's grip. "I'm saying that building ladders tae mount the walls will only get men killed," he said. "Our brethren will be climbing the ladders as the Sassenach fire bolts at them. Do ye want that?"

Ean was close to exploding. "Then what do ye want tae do, old man?" he barked. "We spoke of mounting the walls back at Bailie and ye never said a word about it. What now?"

Gordie was truly ashamed for his brother that the man's son was such an imbecile. "Because I dinna want tae correct ye in front of the men," he said. "Ean, the only way this will work is if ye draw out the Sassenach. Ye have tae make them want tae open the gatehouse. Once they do that, we can fight them. Otherwise, they're going tae murder us."

Ean wasn't quite following him, but at least he wasn't refuting his idea. "Draw them out?" he said. "How? They willna want tae leave the castle once we arrive."

"They will if we raid the village tae the south."

Ean stared at him, all of the fury suddenly drained from his face. "A raid?"

Gordie nodded. "Aye," he said. "A few of us raid the village and when the English come tae chase us off, the rest of us rush the gatehouse. We can get in that way. They'll never know what happened until it's too late."

Up ahead, one of Ean's men was shouting at him, waving his arms, trying to catch his attention. Both Ean and Gordie turned in the man's direction, seeing that he was excited about something.

Gordie gave Ean a push.

"Go," he said quietly. "Tell the men what we intend tae do. Send about ten or so intae the village and tell them tae burn it. Do what they can. It has tae be enough tae draw the Sassenach out of Gleann na Fola."

He was going to let Ean claim the idea, which was as it should be as far as Ean was concerned. With a lingering glance at his uncle, he ran on ahead, to where his youngest and bravest warriors were gathering, and told them of the raid on the village south of Gleann na Fola.

Something to lure the Sassenach out of their castle.

Something that would start the chaos they intended.

The plan was set.

CHAPTER THIRTEEN

"AND THEN WE can make goat cheese, for eating or for selling," Mattie said. "According to Gar, this castle relies solely on the stipend provided by the Earl of Warenton. It would be nice if we could earn our own money or at least be more self-sufficient."

She was speaking to Jordan, Rhoswyn, Avrielle, and Mariane. Caria and Perseus were playing games with each other and not particularly paying attention to Mattie, but she didn't care. She wanted to know what these women thought, older and wiser than she was and women who had their own castles to manage. She held her breath with anticipation as the women seemed to seriously consider her suggestion.

"I like yer spirit, lass," Jordan said. "There is always something more a castle can be doing tae help itself. Castle Questing is the heart of the de Wolfe empire and we generate income with sheep and cattle, but also by training royal troops. The Crown pays handsomely for that."

"Mae has her foundlings make goat cheese," Rhoswyn said. When Mattie looked confused about whom she was referring to, she quickly clarified. "Mae is the Countess of Northumbria.

She is married tae Tommy, Lady Warenton's youngest son. My husband's youngest brother."

Mattie nodded. "Gar told me about her," she said. "I think it is a very good idea."

"As do I," Rhoswyn said. "Ye have a head on yer shoulders, lass. I like tae see that. Ye're thinking of ways tae help Gar."

"I am," Mattie said. "Though I am not entirely sure he appreciates it. I do not want to push him to do something he does not want to, but he did give me charge of the castle. And I say a castle should try to earn money for itself."

"Agreed," Avrielle said. Scott's wife was a lovely, elegant woman with a refined look about her. She smiled at Mattie. "Every property of ours is a working castle. Castle Canaan, to the south, has miles of orchards. I believe we supply apples and pears to most of Cumbria."

Mattie was feeling bolstered by their support. She honestly wasn't sure how they would perceive her trying to change things at Gleann na Fola so soon after her arrival. And speaking of change, there was something else she wanted to do.

Perhaps now was a good time to discuss it.

"Then I appreciate your words of wisdom," she said. "But there is something else I would like to do and I am not entirely sure how to go about it."

"What is that, lass?" Jordan said.

"I'd like the hall… during meals… to be a little more civilized."

Jordan cocked her head curiously. "What do ye mean?"

Mattie looked out at the great hall. The women were seated on the dais, but at one end of the table. All of them, together. Gar, his brother, father, uncles, and cousins were at the other end, laughing and drinking. Even Maksim was there, integrating into the group, which Mattie thought was rather nice. At Hensingham, Maksim was the only knight. He didn't really have any other friends to eat and drink with. Such was one of the curses of being a peaceful castle—it could be lonely and she knew that Maksim was lonely from time to time, which was why he tended to chase women. But here—here, he had an entire group of elite knights to feast with and he seemed quite happy about it.

Mattie was happy for him.

But it didn't solve the problem of the great hall, as a whole.

"We took the first step today by scrubbing the hall," Mattie said. "I cannot thank you enough for your support and guidance in the matter."

It was Rhoswyn who answered. "Lass, the fact that ye were brave enough tae tackle this cesspool of male stink immediately invited our support," she said. "We were happy tae help, but we've already decided that the hall must be cleaned again tomorrow. One pass over this mess isna enough."

Mattie smiled faintly. "Thank you for that," she said. "I was thinking the same thing, but I did not want to send Gar into apoplexy by scrubbing his hall twice. I doubt it has been scrubbed once in the past twenty years."

Jordan snorted. "Twenty years?" she said with disgust. "I was thinking fifty years."

The women started laughing, watching as one of the dogs jumped up on the other end of the table and started tearing food from Andreas' trencher. Andreas grabbed the dog by the scruff and put it back on the floor as the women's laughter grew.

"God's Bones," Mariane said, shaking her head at the spectacle. "What a barn this place is."

"And that is exactly my point," Mattie said. "I do not expect to make this place a palace, but I would like to at least make it more civilized. No dogs on the table. A clean floor every week. Commissioning a smithy to make spoons and knives that can be used by guests who come to visit. As an example, look at what we have in front of us—a trencher or a bowl. No spoon. No knife. I am told that men bring their own because none are supplied."

Jordan wasn't unsympathetic. She glanced at Rhoswyn, at Avrielle, women who both oversaw multiple de Wolfe castles. They, too, weren't unsympathetic, but they were also realists. They knew how warring castles functioned and they suspected that Mattie did not.

"There are different kinds of castles, dearest," Jordan finally said. "Some are more oriented toward battle, like this one is. Others are peaceful and more focused on commerce, mayhap. What of yer home? Did ye see much battle?"

Mattie shook her head. "None," she admitted. "Our home is a fine and peaceful place. My mother is very proud of her hall. It is a glorious room with banners hung from the rafters and she has enough pewter spoons and knives for over one hundred guests. The feasts she gives are legendary in Cumbria."

That explained a lot. That was the world that Mattie knew and it was natural for her to want to shape Gleann na Fola's hall into something similar. But the de Wolfe women could see, just by looking at Mattie, that she was like a babe in the woods when it came to a military castle. She only knew her world, not her husband's.

Sometimes, those two worlds could collide.

"It sounds like a lovely place," Jordan finally said. "Have ye spoken tae Gar about making his hall a finer place?"

Mattie nodded. "A little," she said. "I told him that I wanted to commission spoons and knives for our guests and he told me that I could."

Jordan smiled. "Good," she said. "I can help ye if ye wish."

"I would like that very much, Lady Warenton."

Another servant came around bearing more wine, pouring it into the women's cups. Next to Mariane, Perseus was growing tired and began to cry as Caria struggled to entertain him, so Mariane excused herself and her fussy son, heading off to bed. Atreus, seated with the men, saw his wife carrying their son away and went after them, escorting his little family to bed for the night. That had Gar up, moving over to where his wife and mother and grandmother were sitting.

"Queenie, come," he said, pulling his wife out of her seat. "The women have had you long enough. I want you to sit with me."

Mattie was swept along by her tipsy husband, but his mother stopped him. "She's had a busy day, Gar," Rhoswyn said. "Why not let the lass go tae bed now? She doesna need tae sit around with a bunch of smelly men."

Gar frowned at his mother. "I am *not* smelly," he said, but then sniffed the armpit of his tunic and shrugged. "Mayhap only a little. Do you not wish to sit with me, Queenie?"

Before Mattie could answer, Jordan spoke. "What's this ye call her?" she said. "Queenie? Why do ye do that?"

Gar smiled at Mattie as he answered. "Because she is my queen," he said. "Her mother is the empress. You should see the way that woman rules Hensingham. It is only right that Gleann na Fola have a queen."

With that, he pulled her away before his grandmother could say anything further, planting her in his chair in the midst of the men. Maksim was there, watching his sister with her new husband and genuinely astonished at the behavior. He had been for the past several days. The two of them traveling together had been a spectacle of flirting and coy glances. If Gar wasn't looking at her, he was talking about her. That man who'd never wanted to marry couldn't think of anything else. Even now, as Mattie was seated in Gar's chair, all Gar could seem to do was hover over her. He held her hand tightly, as if she were going to slip away.

"My lady," Andreas said. "Gar tells us that you have ideas for generating revenue here at Gleann na Fola. He says that you are going to make him rich."

Mattie smiled, embarrassed, as all eyes turned to her. "I do not think we shall be rich," she said. "But I think that I could make the castle more self-sufficient."

"With what?"

"He did not tell you?"

Andreas shook his head. "All he told us was that you were brilliant."

Mattie looked at Gar, who was gazing at her with a rather besotted smile on his face. "I see," she said. "Since he did not tell you, then I shall. My idea was to have a herd of goats and make cheese and soap. That which we do not use, we can sell. It is always wise for a castle to have a source of income, is it not?"

She sounded bright and the men around the end of the table nodded in agreement as Gar puffed up proudly.

"You see?" he said. "She is brilliant."

"Indeed," Andreas agreed. "She is also a woman of action because she cleaned this hall today in a way the hall has probably never been cleaned before. That took bravery."

"Fearlessness," Tor chimed in. "Any woman who would

take on such a challenge is positively legendary."

While Mattie was left flushing with the flattery, Gar frowned at his family members. "Get out," he told them. "If you insist on insulting me, get out. I'll not feed you any longer."

"It is Poppy who feeds us," Andreas pointed out, grinning. "He pays for your food and drink here. At least the lady is trying to come up with ideas to make you self-sufficient and not dependent on your grandfather's wealth."

Gar wasn't at all pleased with that crack. "You have no cause to point fingers," he said. "Hell's Guardhouse takes plenty of Poppy's money, so do not act as if you refuse all coin from Poppy and use your own. You do *not*."

"I do," Andreas insisted. "I must use my own money because I take Poppy's money and gamble it away while I am in London."

The table roared with laughter. Even Mattie was grinning, looking up at her husband, watching his face, watching every move he made. She was clearly studying him, making sure the insults flying around weren't seriously upsetting him. She was learning about him, about the way he interacted with his family, and she could see how much love and camaraderie there was between them. Given that all she had was her parents and brother, she realized that she was envious of that. She was envious of the giant de Wolfe family. But if she was feeling that way, she could only imagine what Maksim was feeling.

In fact, as she watched Gar shake a fist at Andreas, who laughed in the face of it, she caught sight of her brother sitting at the edge of the frivolity. He had a cup of wine in hand as he viewed the goings-on as simply an observer, not a participant. If their mother was the Empress of Hensingham, it was Maksim who was the emperor—not Reece. Maksim reigned over the castle and its occupants, which was why Mattie had been mildly surprised that her father had allowed his only son to accompany her to Gleann na Fola. Reece's reason, at least in public, was that he needed to make sure Mattie was settled well, but that wasn't the real reason, she suspected.

There was something else.

A castle couldn't have two kings.

Perhaps he was hoping Maksim would want to stay at Gleann na Fola.

Unfortunately, Maksim's time here seemed to be having the opposite effect. He wasn't the emperor here. He was the low man in the hierarchy and he wasn't used to that. As Mattie watched, Maksim suddenly downed what was left in his cup and left the table, heading out of the hall.

Mattie followed.

She gave Gar the rather indelicate excuse of having to find the privy and he quickly let her go. No man stood in the way of a woman's business. Mattie followed Maksim out of the hall, finally catching up to her brother when he was down near the gatehouse where the men from Hensingham had set up a small encampment away from the gate. The first thing she saw as she approached the cluster of canvas tents was Winchester, tied up next to Maksim's pristine blue tent.

Pristine because it was never used in battle.

Or anywhere else.

Winchester was very excited to see his mistress. The dog cried and barked and leaped vertically, straight up in the air, until she finally went to him and hugged him. Untying the rope around his neck, she headed into Maksim's tent with Winchester on her heels. The first thing the dog did was run to Maksim's bed and jump on it, getting the coverlet and pillows dirty. Maksim, who had been bent over a large trunk, scowled at both his sister and the excited dog.

"If I'd wanted that filthy animal on my bed, I would have untied him myself," he said. "What are you doing here? Why aren't you with your husband where I left you?"

Mattie ignored the bad attitude and went to sit on the bed next to her dog. "Because I wanted to speak with you," she said. "I've not spoken to you since we arrived here."

Maksim turned back to his trunk, digging around. "That is because you were with your husband," he said. "That is where you should be."

"Are you angry with me?"

He paused and looked at her. "Nay," he said. "Why? Should I be?"

"You are acting like you are."

He frowned and returned to his trunk. "No one is angry," he said. "Go back to the hall. Gar will wonder where you have gone."

"Maks, what is wrong with you?"

He was still rummaging through the chest. "I told you that nothing was wrong," he said. "I am not angry with you. Go back to your husband, his family, and this life that has chosen you. You are a warlord's wife now, Matilda. Your life is going to change forever."

"Is that a bad thing?"

He paused again, thinking on her question. "Nay," he finally said. "But it will be different."

Mattie watched him resume his quest for something in the trunk. Even though he'd said he wasn't angry with her, something about him still seemed off.

"Will you at least stay here awhile?" she asked. "It would do me good to see at least one person from home. This is a very big place and although everyone has been kind, it is still daunting to me. I would like it if you could stay awhile. Mayhap you would even meet a young woman to marry. I am not sure how I ever became betrothed before you, but imagine if you were to meet a de Wolfe bride. Then you would be part of the family, too!"

She said it with some excitement, but Maksim didn't rise to that level. He finally found what he was looking for and pulled forth a heavier tunic, something warmer against the cooler temperatures of the night.

"Family," he muttered, shaking out the tunic. "You do realize that we have no family at all. No cousins, no uncles. We live in a castle that has not seen a battle in decades. Father has grown soft, our soldiers are bored, and I… I am a well-trained knight, Matilda. I have had the finest education, yet I sit and rot at Hensingham."

Mattie's brow furrowed with concern. "I've never heard you talk this way," she said. "Are you unhappy, then?"

He had to think seriously on his answer. "Unhappy?" he said. "Not exactly unhappy. But seeing Gar with his cousins and brothers and family, how much they adore each other, how seasoned and experienced they all are, has made me realize just what I have missed. Do you know I've only seen one skirmish in my entire life? Papa sent me to Berkhamstead Castle and all it ever was during my tenure there was a royal prison. The only skirmish I've ever seen was there, when some unruly warlord tried to break his son out of prison. The skirmish was easily put down. But I trained, I learned, I went through the motions of being an excellent knight, but the truth is I'm not."

"You are!"

He shook his head firmly. "I am not," he said, throwing a finger in the direction of the great hall. "*Those* men are excellent knights. They have seen death in battle. They've suffered. They have a camaraderie that I can only dream of because I've not fought with them. I've not fought with anyone. I do not know why I am even telling you this. You cannot possibly understand."

Mattie was listening to him seriously. "I know what it means to belong to something," she said. "You and I, Mama and Papa… We belong to each other. We belong to the legacy of Hensingham. Is that not something, small as it is?"

Maksim shrugged. "I suppose so," he said. He finally sat down on the bed next to her, his shoulders slumped. "But I want more, Mattie. I did not even realize that until we arrived and I saw all of the knights and the way they were with each other. You asked me if I was going to remain here for a while—the truth is that I will stay permanently if Gar will allow it and I am not sure how Papa will take the news. I want to live the life I was trained for. I do not want to return to a castle of boredom."

Mattie could understand that, somewhat. Everyone wanted to feel as if they had a purpose. She put her hand on her brother's shoulder.

"I think Gar would love for you to stay," she said quietly. "Remember that he said he's been having trouble with the Scots. I'm sure he can use every good knight he can find."

Maksim nodded, pondering what the future at Gleann na Fola might hold for him. "I think Mama will be worried for me," he said. "I do believe she is content for me to remain at Hensingham, safe and under her care. I think this is what she envisioned for me."

"But you do not," Mattie said softly.

Maksim shook his head. "Nay," he said. "I do *not*. If I am to have a legacy, then I must build it. Your marriage to Gar has given me that chance."

Mattie smiled at him. "I hope so," she said. "I think my marriage to him has given us both a chance at a different life. A different legacy."

On the bed beside Mattie, Winchester let out a sigh of contentment and they both looked over to see the dog lying on its back, limbs curled, snoring away.

Maksim shook his head reproachfully.

"That stupid beast has done nothing but bark since yesterday," he said. "Since we do not want him attacking Gar and tearing his breeches again, I've been forced to keep him here and listen to him bark all night."

Mattie cocked her head thoughtfully. "I've been trying to get those breeches off him since he first put them on."

Maksim let out a snort of disgust. "God's Bones, Matilda," he said. "Do not say such things in front of me. I do not need to know *that*."

Mattie realized what he meant and she laughed. "I simply meant that they are filthy and he will not remove them, not even for cleaning," she said. "But if I let Winnie run free…"

Maksim could see where she was going with that line of thought. "Then he'll find Gar and rip the breeches off for you," he said. "You are a devious girl."

Mattie laughed again. "Mayhap when the situation requires it," she said, rubbing her dog's belly affectionately. "In fact, I think I will take him up to the hall. Mayhap he can even tear those breeches to shreds tonight."

That had Maksim grinning at the thought of Winchester tearing Gar's breeches off in front of a hall full of men. Mattie stood up from the bed, pulling with her Winchester, who was more than happy to go with his mistress. Maksim stood up to follow because if there was going to be a spectacle in the hall, he wanted to be present for it. Just as the two of them, plus the dog, reached the tent opening, they could see a good deal of commotion going on at the gatehouse. There was yelling, and people calling for Gar, as an exhausted man in tatters came through the gatehouse. Several soldiers were pulling him toward the keep.

Mattie watched curiously as Maksim pushed past her, coming out of the tent. He stood there for a few moments, watching the scene, before tilting his head upward as if looking to the sky.

"I smell smoke," he said.

Mattie looked at him. "There are a dozen fires in this bailey," she said. "That is what you smell."

But Maksim shook his head. "Nay," he said. "It is blowing in from the south."

"What does that mean?"

He snorted. "That there is a fire to the south of us," he said, stating the obvious. "Get back up to the keep, Matilda. Take the dog with you. There's something in the air and you should be safe inside."

Mattie nodded and started walking for the keep, quickly, making sure Winchester was right at her side. The dog stuck closely to her, all the way into the great hall, where the man in tatters was now speaking with Gar and William and the rest of the de Wolfe men. Mattie remained on the edge of the hall, watching carefully, but still making her way over to where the women were still sitting. By the time she reached them, Jordan was on her feet.

The woman's gaze was locked on her husband and the

disheveled man he was speaking with.

"My lady?" Mattie said timidly. "What is amiss? Do you know?"

Jordan shook her head slowly. "Nay, lass," she said. "But it is clearly something."

Rhoswyn and Avrielle came to stand next to Jordan also, all of them watching the men. When a few of them broke off from the conversation huddle and dashed from the great hall, Jordan seemed to know, instinctively, what to do.

"We go tae work," she said quietly, turning to the women around her. But her focus was on Mattie. "I dunna mean tae usurp yer position as Lady of the Keep, but would ye like for me tae organize an area for any wounded we may have?"

Mattie looked stricken. "Wounded?" she repeated. "Has something happened, then?"

Jordan shook her head. "I dunna know," she said. "But I suspect something is either happening or will happen, so we must be prepared. There may be those in need of help. May I organize it for ye, lass? Unless ye'd rather do it yerself."

Realizing that there was some kind of battle at hand, Mattie felt sick to her stomach. Sick and frightened. Even so, she understood the value of what Lady Warenton was offering: a woman who had seen such things time and time again.

Mattie never had.

Quickly, she nodded.

"If you would be so kind, my lady," she said. "Please tell me what to do and I shall do it. I will gladly learn from you, if you will teach me."

Jordan smiled, putting a gentle hand on Mattie's cheek. "Good lass," she said. "Now, ye can take charge of the hot water and bandages. The cook may know where they are and how tae help, so see Brickie and ask for his assistance. Rhos and Avie and I will take charge up here."

Taking Winchester with her, Mattie fled the hall, heading down to the kitchens to get the hot water to boiling. She could do that, couldn't she? Manage something as simple as water and bandages? She could. And she was going to do it to the very best of her abilities.

She was going to make Gar proud of her.

Because, God only knew, she was facing something she'd never faced before.

And it would end up being nothing she could have ever imagined.

CHAPTER FOURTEEN

"ARE WE READY?"

The question came from Gar, spoken to Andreas, Tor, Maksim, and Atreus, who were acting as his commanders because Reed and Linus, usually the men to handle his army, were on duty at Andreas' castle. Therefore, the organization of the men had fallen to them and they took the duty happily. In truth, it was more Tor and Atreus because Maksim wasn't hugely experienced when it came to forming an army for an offensive, so he mostly watched and pitched in where he was directed. He was eager, but also somewhat timid. He had about fifty de Reyne men that he'd brought from Hensingham, but the troops, as a whole, weren't his and he was uncertain when it came to directing them. As this was going on, Andreas had mostly been at the gatehouse, monitoring the village burning in the distance.

Everything seemed to be in flames.

"The men are ready, Gar," Atreus said, answering his question. "Give the word and we shall move them out."

Gar nodded. He could see his troops near the gatehouse, about eight hundred of them, ready to move out and into the village. According to the old villager who had escaped the devastation, there were Scots in the little town, burning and stealing. He wasn't sure how many, but there were several. They were terrorizing everyone. The old villager lived on the south side of the settlement and he seemed to be one of the first hit, barely able to remove his possessions from his home before the fire closed in and burned everything.

A fire that had seemingly taken over the entire village.

Gar was focused on that glow in the distance.

"This could be a simple raiding party or it could be a ruse," William said, coming to stand beside Gar. "Have your men checked the trees off to the west and the north?"

Gar nodded. "They have," he said. "The problem is that it is night, with only a half-moon, so it is difficult to see."

"But they checked for signs of men?"

"Aye, Poppy, they did," Gar said. Then, he looked at him. "Does something have you concerned?"

William shrugged. "Every move by the Scots has me concerned," he said. "I would not have lived as long as I have if I had not been concerned about everything."

"True," Gar said. "Do you want me to send more men into the trees to check again?"

"Not if you are confident your men were thorough."

"As thorough as they can be," Gar said. "We've had patrols out all day, but not to the south. The Scots must have slipped past my patrols and made it to the village."

"Then you must be extra vigilant," William said. "They want something, badly enough that they've circumvented your patrols. It's possible that the village was the intended target, but it's equally possible it wasn't."

"What do you mean?"

William shrugged again. "They might be trying to draw you away from the castle," he said. "Mayhap the castle is their true target, or mayhap it is the army itself once it is removed from the safety of the curtain walls. In any case, you should leave your father or one of your uncles behind. You will need a competent knight in command while we are out tending to the village."

Gar glanced over his shoulder at his father, Uncle Scott, and Uncle Blayth in full battle gear. It took him a moment to realize that his grandfather was also dressed in battle protection from head to toe, which was William de Wolfe's usual uniform. The man might be exceedingly old, but given his decades of experience on the Scots border, he knew what they were capable of and he knew how to handle them. But that didn't mean Gar wanted his extremely elderly grandfather going to battle with him.

William was too valuable for that.

"Poppy," he said. "I would be honored if you would remain. If the Scots are going to be wily, there is no one in England with more experience in dealing with them. You are most valuable to me here."

William, who was still eyeing the glow of the burning village in the distance, turned to look at him. "I would serve you better in the field," he said. "Leave Blayth behind to command Gleann na Fola. I will go with you."

Gar truly didn't want that. Unfortunately, William had a habit of riding with the army, still, and Gar wasn't entirely sure he could keep him away. He looked beseechingly at his father, who understood the dilemma because Troy dealt with the same thing—his elderly father wanting to battle. All of the sons and grandsons with garrisons did. No one could tell him otherwise.

Except one.

Troy knew they needed help.

As Troy headed to the keep to seek reinforcements, Gar returned his attention to the army before him. They were ready to move out, but the portcullis had yet to be lifted. The gates were open, however, and the drawbridge was down, spanning a moat that was filled with more dead things and filth than any moat Gar had seen, ever. It was a horrific trap of muck and disease, one that protected Gleann na Fola quite ably.

It was time to get on with it.

"We've delayed long enough," Gar finally said, turning to Andreas, Tor, Maksim, and Atreus. "Prepare to lift the portcullis and move out. Get the men moving."

The four knights headed down to the gatehouse where their horses were waiting. Scott and Blayth moved past Gar, following the others, and Gar knew that they were looking forward to the fight. They were knights to the bone and any skirmish with the enemy was something that fed them. It had been part of their lives since they were small children. As Gar put his helm on, adjusting the mail around his neck to ensure it was covered, he could hear Troy behind him.

"Papa!" Troy called. "Mama has great need of you. You must come!"

William put his own helm on, turning to Troy. "What is it?"

Troy shook his head, coming alongside his son. "I do not know," he said. "But she has asked me to fetch you."

William shook his head. "I cannot," he said. "The army is moving out."

"If you do not go to her, she will follow you all the way to the village. You know that."

William did. With a heavy sigh, he turned around and

headed for the keep while Gar and Troy made haste down to the gatehouse. When their reached their horses, they saw William's dark steed standing quietly off to the side and they told the soldier holding the animal that William would not be coming, so the man turned back for the stables. It might not stop William completely, but it would slow him down if Jordan couldn't manage to keep him inside.

Mounting their horses, they decided to wait until the rest of the army was through and then bring up the rear so that the back of the army wasn't left vulnerable. No one was sure what the Scots were doing, but no one trusted them, either.

This could be a simple raiding party or it could be a ruse.

Gar was about to find out which very quickly.

Things were about to turn deadly.

☙

MATTIE WAS WATCHING.

From the roof of the keep, which was flat, she could see the gatehouse and the burning village in the distance. Caria was with her, and together the two of them watched the activity below. Jordan, Rhoswyn, and Avrielle were down in the hall because they didn't want to watch the army leave. They'd seen it too many times, watching their husbands ride to battle, and they didn't want to see it again. It was too anxiety-inducing. But Mattie had never seen such a thing, so she very much wanted to watch it. Her husband was down there as well as her brother. Maksim had expressed his wish to stay at Gleann na Fola so he could do what he was trained to do, but he probably hadn't expected it so quickly.

It was a clear night above, icy, with a scattering of stars across the night sky. Caria was cold, so she pressed against

Mattie to keep warm as they watched the army trickle out. What they didn't know was that William had been recalled to the keep by his wife and, even now, was arguing with her about riding out with the men. Jordan wanted him to remain and help her should the need arise and he wanted to do his duty. That was where the rub was because Jordan was convinced that he'd already *done* his duty—many times over and for many years—and didn't need to ride out in a skirmish. He thought she was wrong and she thought she was right.

It was an argument they'd had before.

But Mattie and Caria weren't aware of it. They were simply watching the spectacle below. The night was dark and spooky and the distant fires in the village had phantoms rising out of the smoke. Even if Mattie had never seen her husband or brother ride to battle, the impact of the moment wasn't lost on her. It was a night of ghosts.

She was frightened.

"What do you suppose will happen?" Caria asked, shivering against Mattie. "Will they return soon?"

Mattie had her arms around the girl, mostly for warmth. "I hope so," she said. "It is a cold night and they must all get back to their beds."

Caria lifted her head to look at Mattie. "Will everything be well, do you think?"

Mattie nodded, her focus still on the gatehouse. "I think so," she said. "They are all very brave and strong. They will chase the Scots away in no time. I think—"

She was cut off by an abrupt action at the gatehouse. The last of the army had just trickled out and the portcullis was still up, but suddenly, men were running through it. There were soldiers in the bailey, on the inside of the wall, and the men running through were attacking the soldiers. Abruptly, there was a fight going on, but some of the men running in through the gatehouse were heading for the keep.

And they were armed.

Seized with panic, because she truly didn't know what was happening, Mattie released Caria and ran for the stairwell that led to the lower floors. It was a spiral staircase and she took it far too fast, slipping somewhere between the second and third floors and sliding all the way to the bottom. It did, however, get her to the floor where the hall was located quite fast, and she managed to get her feet underneath her and run like mad for the great hall.

She burst into the hall about the time soldiers were running in to inform William that the gatehouse had been breached. That had William drawing his sword and ordering the women to the upper floors where they would barricade themselves in their chambers. Rhoswyn took hold of Jordan while Avrielle, spying Mattie running into the hall, shouted at her to return to her chamber immediately and bolt the door. Caria, who had come down after Mattie, ran to Jordan and helped Rhoswyn move the old woman more quickly. As William and the soldiers headed down the main stairs to the keep entry, the women rushed upstairs.

Everything was chaos.

Avrielle ran with Mattie into the master's chambers on the floor above. She didn't have time to safely retreat to the chamber she and Scott shared, so she sought refuge in Mattie and Gar's, throwing the gate at the top of the stairwell and then bolting the heavy oak door once she and Mattie entered. There was another door, however, in the smaller servants' alcove that led to a very narrow, and very steep, set of stairs that went between the kitchen and all the floors. Mattie rushed to that door and threw both of the big bolts on it, making sure the chamber was secure from any incursion. Once that was done, she ran into the main chamber again, eyes wide with fear.

"What else shall we do?" she asked, breathless.

Avrielle was over at the narrow window that faced the western part of the bailey and the gatehouse. She could see a great deal of fighting down below because the army, realizing the gatehouse was rushed by Scots once they'd gone through, had returned and now there was fighting all over the place. It was even up on the wall walk—some Scots had managed to make it up there.

"We'll be safe here," Avrielle said calmly, watching the turmoil unfold. "Even if they try to burn the doors down, they are reinforced with an iron cage. They will not be able to make it into the chamber."

On the bed, Winchester awoke at the sound of voices and rolled over, spying his mistress and another woman in the chamber. He yawned and climbed off, coming over to Mattie for a pat, but she couldn't seem to manage it. She was terrified. Timidly, she went to stand next to Avrielle and together, they watched the madness below.

"I've never seen a battle before," she said, voice trembling. "I've lived my entire life in castles that never saw any fighting. This is new to me."

Avrielle looked at her, smiling faintly. "You are married to Gar now," she said. "I do not mean to be a doomsayer, but this will not be your last battle."

"You've seen many?"

Avrielle nodded. "Many," she said softly. "That is what it means to be married to a de Wolfe. They are the last line of defense between England and anarchy. Between peace and war. Without them, the north would be overrun, or worse. You have assumed a noble calling, my dear. The wife of a de Wolfe knight is not something to be taken lightly. It is something to be honored."

Mattie let those words sink in a little. "Have you been married to your husband for a long time?"

Avrielle put her arm around Mattie's shoulders. "Long enough," she said. "Before that, I was married to another knight, a warlord, whom I lost in battle."

Mattie looked at her sharply. "I'm so very sorry," she said. "How awful for you."

Avrielle shrugged. "It was at the time, of course," she said. "And it is not easy to watch Scott go to battle time and time again. There is always a chance he will not return. But we must be brave. *You* must be brave. That is the best gift you can give Gar—your bravery in moments like this. When he returns, do not greet him in a flood of tears. Greet him with a smile and welcome him home. Let him see your strength."

Mattie sighed heavily. "I do not know if I have any," she said. "I've never had to show it."

Avrielle gave her a quick squeeze. "You will," she said. "It is there. You simply have to find it within you. Look—the battle is dwindling already. See?"

She was pointing from the narrow window and Mattie could, indeed, see that men were running from the gatehouse and the English were giving chase. What had started quickly was now just as quickly over. They could see men lying around on the ground and still other able-bodied men helping the wounded.

"Should we go down into the hall?" Mattie asked. "It looks

as if there are wounded to be helped."

Avrielle could see that. "I will go and see," she said. "That smaller door in the alcove—where does it go?"

Mattie looked over at the small, sturdy door. "A stairwell," she said. "The servants use it, so it has a landing at every level."

Avrielle moved over to it, throwing the bolts and carefully peering down the stairwell. "I do not hear anything," she said. Then, she looked back into the room until she spied something. "Bring me that taper, my dear. I must have a little light so I do not kill myself on these stairs."

Mattie ran over and struck a flint and stone, lighting a fat yellow taper, which she then carried over to Avrielle.

"Here," she said, carefully giving it over. "May I go with you?"

"Nay," Avrielle said. "Stay here until I send for you."

"Are you certain?" Mattie said anxiously. "I can carry a dagger and protect us both."

Avrielle grinned. "Sweet lass," she said. "Nay, you will stay here. I will send for you if it is safe."

With that, she slipped through the door and disappeared down the treacherous stairs. Mattie watched her go, then listened until she could no longer hear the footsteps. Shutting the door, she bolted it again and went back to the window, seeing that there was no longer any fighting, only men milling around and wounded being moved. It was clear that peace had been restored, so she moved away from the window and went to sit on the bed. Winchester, who had been following her around more or less, jumped up beside her. Absently, Mattie stroked the dog, wondering if she should do as she was told or if she should go into the hall and help. She was the chatelaine, after all. This was her home. She knew that Avrielle had meant to protect her, but by protecting her, she was keeping her from doing her duty.

She couldn't sit around, idle.

Leaving Winchester lying on the bed, Mattie went to the main chamber door, unbolted it, and stepped through.

She had tasks awaiting her.

Be brave, Avrielle had said.

That was exactly what she was going to show Gar.

Her bravery.

ↄꞵ

GAR WAS TRYING not to feel stupid.

His grandfather had asked him if his men had checked the woods to the west and north of Gleann na Fola and he'd confirmed that his men had.

But evidently, not very well.

Thank God the army had only just cleared the gatehouse when a host of Scots poured from the trees and rushed in through the open portcullis. Gar and his men hadn't been so far away that they hadn't seen what had happened and had been able to turn about immediately. The offending Scots got more than they bargained for and the battle was short-lived.

Mercifully.

Still, there were many wounded because they'd been caught off guard. The wounded were mostly the soldiers left behind, men who had been unexpectedly forced to defend their castle. The best news of all was that even though the Scots had tried to make it into the keep, William had made sure both access doors were bolted, so no one was able to make it inside. The keep itself contained a small armory, purely for situations like this one, and he'd made it to the roof along with a couple of soldiers with crossbows. When the bolts started flying, the Scots beat a hasty retreat.

No one wanted to be hit by flying bolts.

Now, they had a hell of a mess to clean up.

There were eleven wounded, all of them moved into the great hall, into a warm spot by the enormous hearth, which was churning out both heat and smoke into the hall. The surgeon for the army, a man named Holt who also doubled as the castle's ale master, was moving among the injured, the worst of which was a soldier who had fallen from the wall walk and broken his left shoulder, left arm, and left hip. Because of the height of the fall, the bones had been smashed and protruded through the skin, so it was a serious situation for him. But overall, the damage wasn't bad.

In truth, it could have been much worse.

Gar saw his Aunt Avrielle in the great hall as the wounded were brought in and she informed him that his wife was perfectly safe and unharmed, and that brought him a huge sense of relief. When he and his men realized the Scots had been waiting for them to leave the castle, waiting for the moment when they could charge through the open gate, he'd been terrified that Mattie would somehow be injured or even killed in the rush. He'd fought his way to the keep only to realize it was locked up, which gave him the strength to fight on and not rush straight to Mattie to make sure she was well.

But now, the rush of battle was over.

Exhausted, but still feeding off a battle high, Gar stood at the top of the stairs of the great hall, watching people move about as they tended to the wounded. He could see his grandmother, mother, and aunt as they helped the men. Things they'd done a thousand times before, to a thousand different men, carefully ensuring they would live to see another day. Avrielle was particularly good at it, as Scott was an excellent healer and she'd learned a good deal from him over the years. Gar derived a strange sense of comfort watching the women of his family tend to his men as the world righted itself after the fight.

But then, he caught sight of someone new.

It was Mattie.

She was kneeling alongside the surgeon as he discussed a gash on a man's forearm. Mattie was very attentive, listening closely, but as Gar watched, it became clear that the surgeon asked her to stitch the wound. He was pointing at the gash, pointing at the box she was carrying around, which happened to be the surgeon's box with a sewing kit in it. The surgeon took something out of his bag, told Mattie to stitch the wound, and then moved to the next patient.

"She's trying very hard, ye know."

The soft voice came from his right and he looked over to see his mother standing there, watching Mattie just as he was.

Gar smiled faintly.

"She is a woman of determination," he said. "But I do not think she has ever tended wounded after a battle."

"She hasna," Rhoswyn said. "She came down here, asking tae help, but she has no experience, so she is shadowing the surgeon."

Gar scratched his head dubiously. "I think the surgeon just asked her to stitch a wound," he said. "She looks a little… green. I can see it from here."

Rhoswyn chuckled softly. "Ye should have seen her with the man who fell from the wall," she said. "She wanted so badly tae help, but she caught sight of the bone sticking out of the man's shoulder and gagged twice before yer mother sent her tae help someone who wasn't quite so mangled. But, God love the lass, she dinna fold. She's still trying."

Smiling faintly, Gar watched Mattie pull forth needle and thread in preparation for stitching up the gash. As he watched, she took another look at the wound and gagged, trying to cover her mouth with her hand.

"Brave," he muttered, snorting quietly. "She's very brave."

"She is," Rhoswyn said. "And I suspect she's doing it because she knows that's what's expected. I dunna think she wants tae disappoint ye."

"She could never do that."

Leaving his mother, Gar headed over to where Mattie was staring down the laceration on the man's arm as if she were looking straight into the jaws of hell. She still had her hand over her mouth, swallowing hard, trying desperately not to get sick.

"Queenie?" he said softly.

Mattie's head snapped up, her gaze fixing on him. "You are well," she said, sounding relieved. "I mean to say that you look well. Are you? Do you need assistance?"

Fighting off a grin, he shook his head and knelt down next to her, leaning over to kiss her on the head. "I only need to see you," he said. "It looks as if you are doing good work. I am proud of you."

She smiled wanly. "Are you?" she said. "I've never done this before, but I think I am getting better at it."

He didn't want to dispute her, but once she threaded the bone needle, she just stared at the open gash, trying to figure out how to sew the thing up. She lifted the needle as if to start it, but hesitated.

Gar took pity on her.

"Do you have any ale or wine?" he asked.

She nodded, letting out a most unladylike burp as she pointed to an earthenware bottle next to her. "Aye," she said, covering her mouth discreetly and hoping Gar hadn't noticed. "The surgeon gave this to me. He told me to give it to the men to ease their pain."

Gar reached over her and took it. "Nay," he said quietly. "This is what you do. Watch me."

He took it and poured it right onto the open wound. The soldier groaned, Mattie gasped, and Gar took the needle from her and very swiftly stitched up the flesh that was still stinging with the wine. His stitches weren't the neatest, but they were swift and in no danger of pulling. He made a row of five of them as Mattie watched with morbid fascination. Finishing the last one, he tied it off and cut the end.

"Now," he said. "Bandage it up tightly. It is a deep cut, so you will want to check it in the morning to make sure poison isn't setting in. When you do check it, rinse it with more wine. That keeps the poison away."

Mattie nodded unsteadily, picking up some boiled linen from the surgeon's bag. Without a word, she wrapped the arm very carefully, and very slowly, starting over at least three times because she wanted to get it perfect. Gar watched her, thinking she had a lot to learn about battle medicine, but very proud that she wanted to learn. She wasn't going to give up, no matter how horrified or sickened she felt. When she was finally finished, Gar inspected the bandage with approval.

"You did an excellent job," he said. "Is this truly your first time tending battle wounds?"

Mattie nodded. "My very first time."

"I would have never known it."

She gave him a long look. “Not much you wouldn’t,” she said. “But it is kind of you to say so. I will get better, I promise.”

He smiled, kissing her head again before standing up. “You are already quite excellent,” he said. Then, he pointed to an older man slumped against wall. “Can you tend to him? See what his wound is and tend it accordingly now that I’ve shown you how.”

Nodding eagerly, Mattie moved to the older man with the dirty white hair to his shoulders. He had his face turned away, his eyes closed, and she looked him over to see what his injury was and came across a swollen jaw and broken teeth.

“His mouth,” Mattie told Gar. “What do I do?”

Gar peered at the man, but he could only see the side of his face. “What is amiss?”

“Broken teeth.”

“Ah,” Gar said in understanding. “Have him rinse his mouth with wine and ask him if he wants you to bind his jaw. We cannot usually do much for men with head wounds.”

Mattie asked the man gently if he wanted any help, but he shook his head and told her he only wished to sleep. She didn’t push him and Gar didn’t seem to think it was horribly important, so they moved on to the next man.

“Look at his wrist,” Gar pointed out. “See that it is swollen?”

Mattie nodded. “I do,” she said, visually inspecting it. “What should I do?”

“Wrap it tightly with the boiled linen,” Gar said. “We may ask the surgeon if it needs a splint, but for now, simply wrap it tightly so it will not move around. In battlefield medicine, sometimes there is not time to give a man a full measure of attention. Sometimes you must do what you can and move to the next man until time allows.”

Again, Mattie endeavored to wrap a man's wrist when she really had no idea what she was doing. The first time she did it, she wrapped it so tightly that the man's fingers turned purple. Gar gently pointed that out, so she unwrapped the wrist and then did it again, this time without cutting off the blood supply.

By the time she was finished, there were no more wounded to tend. Between Jordan, Avrielle, Rhoswyn, Mattie, Gar, and the surgeon, everyone was adequately tended. The situation had calmed down significantly and by the time the sun started to rise in the east, Gleann na Fola was relatively peaceful. William had sent about a hundred men into the village to tend to the fires and help the villagers, and Atreus and Maksim went with them. There were many villagers who were significantly displaced and after much discussion with his father and uncles and grandfather, Gar finally gave permission for the villagers to come into the castle walls for protection. At dawn, a tide of humanity began to trickle in.

That meant more work for everyone.

Mattie hadn't slept all night, like everyone else, but she didn't seem tired. She was determined to ensure the villagers had a hot meal as the soldiers helped provide adequate shelter with spare tents and tarps strung up to create makeshift roofs. Mattie and Brickie, working together this time, organized two enormous iron pots of water into which went beans, peas, and leftover pork that Brickie had roasted a couple of days before. Carrots went in and plenty of salt, all of it boiled until a thick stew was created. By noon, the pottage was ready to be distributed and hungry, burned villagers were grateful for the meal. The wounded, too, were fed the nourishing stew.

And Mattie supervised it all.

She spent all morning outside in the elements, which turned

out to be a cold wind on a sunny day, making sure the kitchens of Gleann na Fola produced enough food for the hungry. At one point, Jordan and Avrielle offered to help, but she turned them down. She wanted to do it herself and they let her, finally retreating to bed after a long night and long morning while Mattie remained outside, directing the feeding of the villagers.

Gar, for his part, split his time between making sure his bailey was still functional for the soldiers, since he considered the castle still on alert, and also retreating to the kitchen yard to make sure his wife wasn't collapsing from exhaustion. By midafternoon, the villagers were fed and settled, the wounded were sleeping, as were most of the knights and half of the army, but Mattie remained at her post.

Gar knew she must have been bone-tired because he was, but she wasn't going to surrender to something as mundane as sleep. Not when there was work to be done. He watched her work until she nearly tripped whilst gathering more water for the stew and that was when he put his foot down. His lovely, naïve, and completely dedicated wife had warmed his heart in a way he couldn't have imagined. She was trying so hard to be helpful, to do the right thing in a situation she'd never experienced before, and he couldn't describe the gratitude he felt toward her.

Or the feelings.

But he knew they were strong.

"Queenie?" he said quietly, coming up behind Mattie as she stood near one of the nearly empty pots of stew. "Everything is in hand now. I think you and I should try to get some sleep."

Mattie looked at him as if surprised by the request. "I am well enough," she said. "I do not need to sleep now."

It was a lie. Her eyes had dark circles under them, but to

Gar, she'd never looked more beautiful. He felt as if he was seeing a woman, *really* seeing a woman, for the first time in his life.

Brave.

That was the highest form of praise he could give her.

"Mayhap you do not, but I do," he said after a moment. "And I do not want to go alone. Will you at least go with me and sit with me until I fall asleep? I've just been to battle, sweetheart. I could use your comfort."

The last part was manipulative, but he wanted to say something that would get her upstairs with him. Once he had her in bed, he'd make sure she didn't leave, so it was with resignation that she agreed to go with him, leaving Brickie to supervise what was left of the food line.

Quietly, they made their way up to the master's chamber. When Gar opened the door, Winchester's head popped up from the bed and, after a startled moment, the dog jumped down and ran at Gar. Truthfully, Gar had had no idea that the dog was even here, but Mattie's strong commands to the animal at least had him backing off any attack. Mattie pointed to the hearth and told the dog to go lie down, which he did, but all the while, he was watching Gar like he wanted to eat him. Gar didn't really want to be worried for his life in his own bed, but if the dog wasn't advancing, he would be gracious enough to allow the beast to remain. He knew it would make Mattie happy.

She might even want to stay and sleep.

It was a chance he was willing to take.

Luckily for Gar, once Mattie's head hit the pillow, she went out like a doused candle. She was instantly, and deeply, asleep. He pulled her into his arms and promptly fell asleep next to her. They slept the afternoon away and when Gar finally opened his eyes again, it was dark outside. It was nighttime and he could hear the soldiers' distant calls on the wall in the course of their regular sentry duties. Everything seemed normal, thankfully. In his arms, Mattie was sleeping like the dead and he gave her a squeeze, preparing to pull her closer, when he realized something very strange.

It wasn't Mattie at all.

It was Winchester.

Somehow, the dog had gotten onto the bed, in between him and Mattie, and now was wrapped up in his arms with his wife snoring softly on the other side of the bed. Gar opened his eyes in shock and found himself staring at a sleeping dog's head, with Winchester's teeth inches from his face. The dog was as content as a baby in its bed, snug with his new master.

Realizing that, Gar laughed until he cried.

CHAPTER FIFTEEN

IT WAS WARM and quiet.

Gordie had spent the day leaning against the wall and pretending to be asleep while the Sassenach world went on around him. Ever since they found him just inside the gatehouse, lying on the ground and wearing clothing that had been stolen off a dead English soldier, he lived in fear that his ruse would be discovered.

So far, it hadn't been.

Not that it wouldn't be at any given moment, but he'd managed to carry on the pretense of being a wounded English soldier since the fight at the gatehouse. That skirmish had had the sole purpose of getting him inside and it had worked. What they'd had to do, however, was kill an English soldier so they could take his clothing, and so far, Gordie had not heard anyone speaking about a missing English soldier. Ean and the men had carted the body off when they retreated to the north, so the body more than likely would not be found anytime soon, if at all. Things always tended to be a little chaotic after a battle as it was, so it was no surprise the English had not yet discovered that they were missing one of their men.

Hopefully, that would hold out until Gordie did what he needed to do.

The plan was this—Ean and the others were to retreat to the north and find a good hiding place. No one was sure if the English would send out patrols after them, but so far, they hadn't. They seemed to be more concerned with repairing the gatehouse and tending the wounded. If there were no patrols, then Ean and the men would return tomorrow at sunset, whereupon Gordie would make his way to the postern gate and unlock it. The postern gate of an otherwise strongly fortified castle was used primarily by the kitchen and, in the case of Gleann na Fola, the door was so small that it looked as if it had been made for children. Gordon remembered this from the days when the Scots used to hold the castle, back when he was a child. However, if the English had bricked it up to ensure there was only one way in and one way out of the castle, then Gordie's plans were for naught.

He would have to figure something else out.

Meanwhile, he intended to stay exactly where he was, pretending to be a wounded English soldier, presenting a head wound that Ean had given him. They had to make Gordie look as if he had actually been injured, so a blow to the jaw had been the way to do that. It created enough of a bloody mess, and a mild injury, without actually debilitating him. The man needed to have his wits about him if he was going to execute the plan and, until sunset, it was going to be a waiting game.

But when the time came, the old man would be ready.

And so would the Scots.

CHAPTER SIXTEEN

IT WAS MORNING.

Gar awoke to Winchester sleeping on his legs now and an empty bed. It had to be close to dawn at this point and he yawned, lifting his head slightly to see where Mattie was, only to discover her over by one of the narrow windows that looked out toward the east. There was a tiny bit of light in the chamber from the hearth, a small flame that had been stoked up from the embers, so he could see the hair lifting from her face in the slight breeze.

"Queenie?" he muttered sleepily. "What's wrong, sweetheart?"

Mattie looked over at him, smiling weakly. "Did I wake you?"

"Nay," he said. "I usually awaken before dawn. But why are you awake?"

She shrugged, turning her face back to the window. "I had a dream," she said. "Something about my mother and father, but when I tried to speak to them, they faded away."

He sat up in bed. "You had a dream about Hensingham?"

"I think so," she said. "It was a castle. I assume it was

Hensingham, though it might have been Prudhoe."

"Why Prudhoe?"

"Because that is where I fostered," she said. "Sometimes I dream about it. I don't know why, but I do."

He threw his legs over the side of the bed. "Because it was important to you, once," he said. "I dream of Castle Questing sometimes, of the holiday celebrations we have there. You've never known a Christmas or Martinmas as crowded as those at Castle Questing. All of those de Wolfes jammed into one place and it looks like a parade for the king."

She grinned. "I am looking forward to it," she said. "Our family celebrations were always small."

"You have no close family, do you?"

She shook her head. "Not really," she said. "The de Reyne family of Ashington is a distant cousin and there were times we visited them, but we were never close."

"There are also de Reynes at Throston Castle."

"I know," she said. "But, again, distant cousins. I think I've met them once."

He stood up wearily, completely nude. "You needn't fear lonely gatherings any longer," he said. "From now on, you will have more family than you can count."

"I look forward to it."

He stood there, glancing around the chamber. "Speaking of looking," he said, "where are my breeches?"

Those horrible patchwork breeches. Mattie moved away from the window, going over to a small table that had been moved into the chamber so she could store her things, and picked up the infamous breeches.

"Here," she said. "I noticed that they were tearing in places, so I wanted to sew them up before they fell apart and you were accused of indecency."

He grinned, reaching out for them and feeling that they were also damp. "You washed them?" he said incredulously.

Mattie nodded. "A little," she said. "I tried to remove some of the dirt and stains, but it is difficult without proper washing facilities."

He was inspecting the stitching she'd done, reinforcing the seams, when he suddenly came to something on the waistband. Brow furrowed, he peered closely at it, realizing that it was writing.

Queenie.

He smiled broadly.

"What is this?" he said, lifting it to show her. "Are you signing your work now, like an artist?"

She grinned. "Nay," she said. "It is so you will take me with you to every battle, or at least every battle where you wear those breeches. It is so I can watch over you, even when I am not by your side. It is so you will remember whom to return to."

The conversation took an abrupt turn, from light and humorous to serious, all in an instant. The smile faded from his face as he looked at the stitching once again, spelling out his nickname for her. Emotions he'd never experienced before washed over him, those of delight and joy and even sadness. Sadness that now he did have someone to return to and he was aware of a feeling of fear that there might be a day when he didn't return to her. Surely, she must have felt that fear too, or she wouldn't have put her name on those dirty breeches.

"Oh… Queenie," he said, lowering the breeches and going to her, wrapping her up in his powerful embrace. "I will always return to you, sweetheart, I swear it. You needn't worry."

Mattie was holding him tightly, feeling his big, warm body

in her arms, the skin of his chest against her right cheek. "You do not know that," she said. "I saw the battle yesterday. I saw the wounded in the hall. I knew there was a chance you might be one of them, or worse. But I realized something else, too."

"What?"

"That it was foolish of me to clean the great hall," she said. "It is foolish of me to want to turn this place into something other than what it is."

"What do you mean?"

In his arms, she sighed faintly. "I cannot turn it into what Hensingham is," she said. "My family home is not a warring castle. It is one of grace and teaching and our days are full of making it a lovely place that a woman would be proud of. But Gleann na Fola isn't like that. You tried to tell me, but I did not listen. Now, I've seen for myself. It would be like trying to turn you into a priest. Some things are better left the way they are."

He snorted softly, a smile rippling across his face. "You were not foolish to clean the hall," he assured her. "It needed it. It was not a place for decent people until you worked your magic on it. I am very proud of you."

She looked up at him. "Are you?" she said. "I am trying very hard to be the kind of wife you should have."

His smile was gentle as he cupped her face between his two enormous hands. "You *are* the kind of wife I should have," he murmured. "Everything about you is the wife I need and should have. You are the bravest woman I know. I watched you with the wounded. I saw how wonderful you were with them. If there was any doubt in my mind that our marriage was the right thing to do, watching you gag while you tried to stitch a wound erased any uncertainty I have ever had. You cannot know how much I admire you, Queenie. Or how much I feel for you."

She went from being flattered and reassured to being surprised by his last sentence. "What do you feel?" she asked.

"What do *you* feel?"

"I asked you first."

He grinned, coyly. "I think I like you."

"I think I like you, too."

He started laughing, hugging her tightly and kissing her on the top of the head. "Good," he said, releasing her. "Now that we have established our mutual like, I feel as if we at least have an understanding between us."

He started to pull the breeches on and she pointed to her name in the waistband. "We do," she said. "You are my property and do not forget it."

He paused, looking at her with a twinkle in his eye. "I would never forget such a thing, madam," he said. "I am very proud to belong to you."

A smile crept over her lips. "And I, you."

The twinkle turned to something else, something smoldering. The breeches suddenly hit the ground and Gar was on Mattie again, his mouth fusing to hers as his arms went around her. She responded to him, readily, something that was becoming natural to her. She'd quickly learned to love their physical relationship, the exploration, the satisfaction of it, and she was never reluctant when he wanted to bed her.

In fact, just the opposite.

Since Gar was already nude, he pulled off her sleeping shift, leaving her naked body exposed to his hungry eyes. She had a delicious figure, soft and round in the right places, and already he was suckling her breasts and fondling her buttocks, pulling her up against him. She had such soft skin and he lapped it up, hungry for her. Nothing on earth fueled him like she did.

He'd learned that the first time he ever touched her.

There was much kissing and fondling going on, the touching of nude bodies. Mattie had only just become comfortable touching his body, though she was still somewhat timid. When she put her hands on his erect manhood, he whispered encouragement to her. She caressed him gently, stroking his length and feeling him shudder in delight. Unable to wait any longer, Gar went to lay her on the bed, but Winchester was sleeping right in the middle of it. Rather than move the dog, he simply turned her around, braced her arms against the bedpost, and lifted her buttocks up against his pelvis. His male organ, hard and demanding, thrust into her from behind.

Since Gar was so much taller than Mattie, he had to bend his knees significantly in order to thrust into her, but that quickly became an untenable position, so he gripped her pelvis and lifted her off the ground. It was nothing for his considerable strength. Mattie gripped the bedpost, bracing her feet against him as he drove into her soft and yielding body. He had a firm grip on her hips, holding her against him as he moved, but his gaze was on her slender back and supple buttocks. The way her waist narrowed and then flared out at her hips was a glorious sight.

It was driving him mad with desire.

At some point, he released her hips so she could stand on her own and he bent over, wrapping a big arm around her torso and holding her against him as his free hand roamed her breasts, delighting in the silken texture. He was thrusting so hard that Mattie ended up bracing her arms against the mattress, which bent her nearly in half, her buttocks almost facing the ceiling. It was a much better position for Gar and he moved his fingers to the curls between her legs, stroking her, listening to her gasp with pleasure. He felt her release begin and he answered in kind, spilling his seed deep into her womb.

Still embedded in her, he held her close, kissing her back, stroking her breasts gently, absorbing everything about the woman that he was so obsessed with. Every movement, every breath, every sigh was ingrained in his brain. As he stood there and held her, his body still joined to hers, his mouth was against her shoulder.

"I think I love you," he whispered against her flesh.

Eyes closed, trying to catch her breath, Mattie smiled at his confession. "I think I love you too," she whispered, reaching between her legs to touch him as he was still joined to her. "Most assuredly, I think I do."

CHAPTER SEVENTEEN

NO ONE HAD bothered him, no one had moved him.

Gordie was in the same place he had been since first being dragged into the great hall of Gleann na Fola. He'd been feigning unconsciousness since last night and other than check his breathing from time to time, he'd been largely left alone by the women who were tending the wounded. An older woman with a Scottish accent had tried to rouse him to take some nourishment once, but he hadn't stirred, so she left him alone.

And that was what he wanted.

He could hear what was going on around him, however. He could hear when wounded men were moved away or when they were able to get up on their own. He wasn't sure how many were left, but he was one of them, and toward the evening meal, two soldiers carried him out of the hall and into a chamber that was quite warm. The hearth was blazing as they deposited the rest of the wounded from the hall into the smaller chamber so that they wouldn't be disturbed and so the surgeon could tend them more easily.

When he was certain there was no one left in the chamber except for the wounded, he dared to open an eye to see where he was. It was a tiny chamber, in fact, and he lifted his head to see that there were four other men in the room with him. Out of all of those wounded from the battle, only five were left, including him. The fire was burning brightly, staving off the ice radiating from the old stone walls, but Gordie was more concerned about where, exactly, he was and how he could escape the keep and get to the postern gate. This chamber had no windows, so he couldn't see what time it was by the setting of the sun, but he knew they had been moved out of the hall because the evening meal was approaching.

That meant it was nearing sunset.

He had to get out of that chamber.

Gordie lowered his head, lying back down and wondering what he should do next. He was afraid that if the surgeon or one of the women returned and found a wounded man missing, they might go looking for him. If they found him before he was able to open the postern gate, then all of the work to get him to this point would be for naught. However, given the fact that he knew he had to act quickly, he simply couldn't wait around any longer.

His clan was waiting for him.

Sitting up again, Gordie looked around the chamber to see if there would be any witnesses to his leaving. The four men seemed to be sleeping, or at least their eyes were closed, and given that these were the most severely injured in the battle at the gatehouse, they weren't in any condition to do anything other than rest. Gordie climbed to his feet, silently, making his way to the chamber door and peering outside to see if there was anyone around.

There wasn't.

Quietly, he made his way out of the chamber, realizing that

he was on the lower level of the keep. The entry was directly to his left and although he thought he heard a servant moving around off to his right, he didn't see anyone. He did, however, hear voices on the level above because the big staircase leading up to the hall was directly in front of him. He could make it to the keep entry undetected if he went at this very moment, so he did. For an old man, he moved swiftly. Yanking open the entry door, he bolted out into the dusk.

Now, he knew where he was. There were men around, but no one close by, at least no one who might stop him. He was still dressed as an English soldier and that was his saving grace. Trying not to appear suspicious, or if he were running, he made his way around the east side of the keep, spying the kitchen yard directly ahead.

Unfortunately, there were people here.

That brought him pause. Indecisive, he turned toward the south where the bulk of the lower bailey was. It was where the gatehouse was located, where he'd entered, and he could see that the lower bailey was full of people. There were makeshift shelters down there. Back toward the north where the kitchen yard was, several people were milling around and he could see that they were receiving food from two enormous iron pots that were bubbling over the open flame. Fortunately, everyone seemed focused on the food and not on an English soldier walking timidly toward the kitchen yard.

Then, he saw it.

The postern gate was off to his right.

The ground sloped here and there was a path down to the gate, through the berms. He didn't remember these defensive features from when he was a lad, but, indeed, a muddy path led down the slope and to the small postern gate, which didn't seem to look any different than it had when he was a child.

But one significant thing had changed.

Over the years, mud and earth had built up around the base of the gate so that when Gordie was able to throw the bolt to open it, the gate hardly opened wide enough for a man to pass through. There was too much debris built up at the bottom of it. Realizing this, Gordie looked around for something to clear the dirt away and only came up with a rock. Given this area was an ancient riverbed, there was good deal of rock around, the same rock the castle had been built out of, so he took that rock and began clearing the dirt away.

By some miracle, nobody noticed.

Working quickly, and getting mud all over himself, Gordie managed to clear away enough mud that he was able to pull the postern gate almost all the way open. It was smaller than he remembered—or perhaps he was simply larger and it therefore seemed smaller than he remembered—but he was able to get through it with no problem. That small, thick, highly fortified door led to a steep slope outside the walls, with a slippery path descending to the moat below.

The moat.

That was going to be a problem because it was a clogged mess of debris. Gordie wasn't sure how deep it was, but it was so disgusting that no man in his right mind would try to cross that swamp.

Except Ean.

Gordie began hoping his nephew would show himself soon because he wasn't sure how long the English would stay oblivious to the postern gate being opened. Therefore, he made his way back to the gate and pulled it closed, as much as he could without shutting it completely. At least this way, it would look closed to anyone glancing at it. He had to keep it this way until the clan arrived.

As the sun set completely, Gordie sat by that little gate and waited.

And waited.

If they managed to pull this off, it would be a damn bloody miracle.

CHAPTER EIGHTEEN

"CLEAN UP AND wash your hands before sup."

Andreas, Tor, Maksim, and Atreus heard the command, but they couldn't quite comprehend it. They looked at Gar as if the man had grown another head.

"What did you say?" Andreas finally said, speaking for the group of confused men. "We're supposed to *wash* our hands?"

The group was in the great hall after the sun had set, all of the settling down in preparation for a fine meal, but Gar's order had them puzzled. However, simply by the look on Gar's face, they knew the man wasn't bluffing.

He was damn serious.

"You heard me," he said. "Mattie wants the hall to be a cleaner place of refined men and that is what we are going to do. Have a servant bring you a bucket of water so you can wash the dirt off your hands. And wash your faces while you're at it."

After the command sank in, the men looked straight at Maksim. As he was the lady's brother, perhaps they were looking to him for clarification, or perhaps they were even looking at him in outrage because this was *his* sister, after all, but Maksim threw up his hands in surrender.

"I have nothing to do with this," he said. "But I will say that Matilda is behaving like my mother, who likes men at her table clean and shaved. If Matilda expects me to shave right now, she will be sorely disappointed."

Gar shook his head. "I did not say that you had to shave," he said. "But Mattie has worked very hard to clean this hall and I think we should help her. She doesn't want to eat with a bunch of smelly, dirty men, so we will indulge her. And given that everyone at this table except for Maks has a wife, you know what I mean. Do as you are told. We must make the women happy."

Andreas and Tor shook their heads in annoyance. Atreus actually groaned, but he understood. Begrudgingly, they sent a servant for water and waited until the man returned with a steaming bucket of the stuff. As they took turns splashing around in it, washing off dirt and blood from yesterday's battle, William, Troy, Scott, and Blayth joined the group. When they saw all of the bathing going on, at the table no less, they looked at Gar in confusion. Gar simply pointed to the bucket.

"Mattie wants those who eat at her table to be clean," he said. "I would suggest you follow suit and wash your hands and face also."

The older men started grinning, looking at each other and trying not to break down into laughter. Given the fact that it was well known that Gar was one of the more slovenly de Wolfe knights, hearing him demand that everyone around him wash was quite ironic. However, they obeyed, taking the bucket from Atreus and washing their hands and faces, making sure they were clean enough for Lady de Wolfe's table.

It was all quite hilarious.

But also quite touching.

"I think the newest Lady de Wolfe has worked some magic on your son," William muttered to Troy as the man wiped water from his eyes. "I must say that I am impressed."

Troy wiped more water from his eyes and looked at his father. "He has gone from resisting the marriage to doing her bidding all quite swiftly," he said. "I am not only impressed, I am astonished."

"This is good for him, Troy."

Troy nodded quickly. "I know," he said. "I wasn't implying otherwise. But this new behavior… I wasn't sure he had it in him, frankly."

William grinned, watching Gar inspect Andreas' hands to see if they were clean enough. "When I think of the frustration that lad caused us during the buildup to this marriage, I confess that I am more than relieved," he said. "He is trying to be a good husband. That is all I can ask for."

Troy was watching Gar also. "Rhos told me that Mattie had never tended wounded before," he said. "She said that it was quite difficult for her, but that she persevered. She seems to be trying very hard, also. Thank God."

William nodded sincerely. "Thank God, indeed," he said. "I realize it has only been a few short days, but marriage seems to agree with them both."

"It does," Troy agreed. "She has been a good influence on him. She's pretty enough, of course, and I knew that would have his attention, but she seems to have a good heart, too. She reminds me a little of Helene, in fact."

Helene was Troy's first wife, mother of Andreas, who was killed in a tragic accident many years ago along with Troy's two young daughters, Arista and Acacia. Helene was a daughter of Paris de Norville, grandfather to Atreus, and her death, and the death of her younger sister at the same time, devastated the de Norville and de Wolfe families. Talk of Helene was therefore minimal, though over the years, Troy had spoken of her more freely. Time had a way of healing grief to the point where the agony of it wasn't as sharp as the good memories, so when Troy spoke of Helene, William listened.

"Helene?" he said. "Truly? Why?"

Troy shrugged. "Her size," he said. "Helene was small like Mattie is. But I also see Helene in Mattie's manner. She seems so determined to do good, to do the right thing. She is trying very hard. That was Helene."

William smiled faintly at the memory of the delicate, lovely Helene. "It was," he said. "She was always trying to please people. She seemed so fragile that to raise your voice to her was to crush her. I know that Paris had a difficult time being stern with her."

"He was stern enough to me when I wanted to marry her."

The marriage of Troy and Helene was legendary in the history of the de Wolfe and de Norville families. The pair had been in love since childhood, then Helene found herself pregnant and unwed and when Troy asked her father for her hand, a series of violence and hilarity ensued. It almost broke William and Paris' friendship initially, but fortunately, their bond was stronger than an irate father and a pregnant daughter.

Still, it was a memory to look back upon with relief that it was well in the past.

"Ah," William said as he reflected on that event. "It all turned out well in the end. You married Helene and had Andreas and Arista and Acacia."

Troy nodded faintly, thinking of his daughters, twins, who had been lively and sweet. "The girls would have been married by now," he said. "I think on that sometimes. I wonder about the husbands they would have had, the grandchildren I would have been given."

"You are going to have plenty of grandchildren from Andreas and Gar," William said, not wanting to venture too far into a sad memory. "Because if Gar is behaving like this, my suspicion is that he is very pleased with his new wife."

Troy chuckled. "I will have a grandchild by this time next year."

"If not sooner."

Troy continued to snort, thinking on Gar as a father. He was young, that was true, but Gar had been born old. *An old soul*, his mother had called him. Even as a young child, Gar had possessed an innate wisdom, something that saw him grow up quickly and become knighted a full three years before most men. He was dedicated and wise, even if he did live like a pig. Or, at least, *had* lived like a pig.

But no more.

Gar was maturing right before Troy's eyes.

Funny how things like that happened when one met the right person.

As Troy and William reminisced about the past and discussed Gar's future, Gar himself was focused on the men who had graciously agreed to wash their hands and faces before Mattie arrived. Even if they didn't have much of a choice, they'd done it anyway, simply to make Mattie happy, and Gar appreciated that. As Andreas lugged the dirty water away from the table, and Tor and Atreus went on the hunt for more wine, Gar found his attention drawn to Maksim.

His new brother.

The truth was that although he knew Maksim, he didn't

know him extremely well. They were colleagues, fellow knights, allies, and had spent some good times together, but his interest in Maksim now was in getting to know Mattie through her brother's eyes. Maksim could tell him more about his wife and Gar thought that would be helpful.

"Is there anything else I should be doing for your sister to make her happy?" Gar said as he sat across the table from Maksim. "Anything I am missing?"

Maksim snorted. "Why not ask her?" he said. "She has never had an issue with being honest about what she wants or doesn't want."

Gar shrugged. "I cannot ask her everything about herself within the first few weeks of knowing her," he said. "I thought that you could tell me something about her that I should know."

Maksim could see that he was being earnest about it. "She is a woman who knows her mind," he said. "I do not know what I can tell you about her that you should not discover on your own. But I do want to thank you."

"For what?"

"Not breaking her heart."

Gar grinned, remembering those words from Maksim back at Hensingham. "It was a touchy situation there for a time," he admitted. "But I am glad that I married her. I thought you would like to know that."

"It is good to hear."

"You will tell your parents, too, when you return home."

"I will," Maksim said, but it was clear that there was something more on his mind. "In fact, I was wondering… would it be too inconvenient if I did not return right away?"

Gar shook his head. "Not at all," he said. "But why? You do not want to go home?"

Maksim sat forward, resting his elbows on the table as he faced Gar. “I spoke of this to Mattie, but I will tell you also,” he said. “The truth is that Hensingham is a quiet castle. I’ve never faced a battle there. In fact, yesterday’s battle was only the second one I’ve ever faced in my life.”

Gar’s eyebrows lifted. “Truly?” he said, surprised. “I did not know that.”

“Now, you do,” Maksim said. “I fostered like everyone else. I trained for battle like everyone else. But until yesterday, I’d only seen one actual skirmish. Knowing that Gleann na Fola is a busy castle, and a military establishment, I was hoping you’d let me stay on here and gain some experience. I cannot go to my grave as a knight saying that I’ve only experienced battle twice. I would be ashamed.”

Gar smiled. “I do not mind at all,” he said. “I would be fortunate to have you. In fact, I can arrange for you to serve at other de Wolfe properties if you wish to gain more experience. Gleann na Fola is remote, and we do not always have trouble with the Scots, so another castle, eventually, might be to your liking.”

Maksim seemed both relieved and encouraged by Gar’s response. “That is extremely generous, Gar,” he said. “I would appreciate that.”

“Then it is settled,” Gar said. “You can stay here until such time as you feel like you want to go elsewhere, but meanwhile, I am certain Mattie will be thrilled to have her brother here. So will I.”

Maksim was pleased. “Excellent,” he said. “Now, you must assign duties to me like everyone else. I will need something to do. I cannot simply lie around and eat your food and drink your wine.”

"Do you want to start tonight?"

"Anytime you say."

Gar gestured to Andreas, who was returning to the table. "All of the knights are inside right now, my brother included," he said. "Of course, I have senior soldiers all around, at the gatehouse and on the walls, but you can start by walking the grounds and familiarizing yourself with this castle and the posts that are set. You'll need to know that if you are to serve here."

Maksim was already on his feet. "I'll do it now," he said. "Shall I take the night watch, then?"

"Aye," Gar said, his eyes twinkling at Maksim's eagerness toward duty. "I'll send word to the sergeant at the gatehouse that we have the addition of a new knight. Once you've made your rounds, go to the gatehouse and find a man named Winebald. He'll answer any of your questions. For now, let him take the lead until you become more familiar with how we do things around here."

Maksim was more than happy to do that. "I will," he said. "Is there usually a knight in command on night watch?"

"It is usually my brother, Reed, but he is not here at present."

"Understood," Maksim said. His next words were sincerely delivered. "Thank you, Gar. The opportunity is appreciated."

"You are welcome," Gar said. "I hope we do not bore you to death."

"I sincerely doubt it."

As Maksim headed out, Gar summoned a servant and gave him a message to give to the sergeant at the gatehouse regarding the addition of Maksim. Andreas, Tor, and Atreus were just sitting down again, with wine in their hands, as Mattie appeared.

Clad in red silk, she looked astonishingly beautiful. In fact, Gar had never seen such a well-dressed woman in his hall and he rose to his feet as she approached.

He could hardly believe she belonged to him.

"My lady," he said, a gleam of appreciation in his eye. "May I compliment you on your beauty? You positively shine, Mattie."

The way he said the last few words caused Mattie to blush furiously. There was a seductive lilt to them. The truth was that after spending most of the day in the kitchens with Brickie, with whom she had come to a tentative truce, she had retreated to the chamber she shared with Gar because she wanted to wear something special for the evening meal. She just felt as if the occasion called for it, given the fact the man had told her that he loved her, and she wanted to look pretty for him. It seemed as if every day with him was getting better and better, and looking her best just felt natural.

She was happy and all was well in the world.

"I am glad you think so," she said as he lifted her hand to his lips for a sweet kiss. "Because all of those trunks we hauled from Hensingham contain garments such as this and I will be wearing them to please you."

"Good," he said, helping her sit. "I am glad we did not lug those heavy trunks around in vain."

Mattie giggled. "We did not, I assure you."

"You are worth it."

With that, Gar commandeered a cup of wine for her and now that the lady of the castle had made an appearance, the meal could begin in earnest. Jordan, Caria, Rhoswyn, and Avrielle eventually joined those at the table, though Mariane remained with Perseus, who seemed to have caught a bit of a cough, so he was prescribed hot, watered wine by Jordan and told to stay in bed. Difficult as it was to keep a three-year-old in bed, Mariane was doing her best with it.

Life, at Gleann na Fola, was settling into something warm and wonderful. As Mattie looked around the table, she already felt a kinship with these people. They'd been through a wedding and suffered a battle together, most of them. There was a bonding experience in both of those events and for the first time since coming to Gleann na Fola, Mattie was starting to feel as if, perhaps, she actually belonged.

She sincerely hoped so.

But that sense of peace was about to change forever.

CHAPTER NINETEEN

IT WAS ANOTHER icy night.

Maksim found himself looking up at the sky as he walked the berms of Gleann na Fola's bailey, seeing the stars as brightly as if they were within arm's reach. If he reached up, he could probably capture one.

Ironic how everything just seemed brighter now.

He was going to remain at this warring castle, fulfilling the hopes he'd relayed to his sister. He was quite excited about it. As he headed along the east side of the keep, gazing up at the stars, he reflected on his life at Hensingham versus the life he hoped to have at Gleann na Fola. He knew his father wouldn't be pleased with his decision, mostly because Reece wanted his son and heir at home, with him. He wanted Maksim presiding over the peaceful castle just as generations of de Reyne heirs had done before him.

But Maksim wanted more.

As he'd told his sister, he hadn't realized what "more" he wanted until he came to Gleann na Fola and saw a completely different life led by knights who were entrenched in struggle every day of their lives. They were doing what they'd been trained for, and Maksim had the same training, only his life was safe and boring. He didn't want safe and boring any longer.

He wanted purpose.

Now, he was going to get it and he was genuinely pleased at that. He was pleased to become part of a group of seasoned knights. Maybe that meant he wasn't the prince of his domain any longer, like he was at Hensingham, but he could live with that. Maybe he'd even find a de Wolfe bride somewhere among the dozens of granddaughters of William de Wolfe, as Mattie had suggested. His sister had just married a grandchild.

Why couldn't he?

The thought brought a smile to his face. Mattie seemed genuinely happy and he didn't realize that he wanted that, too, until he saw how well she'd taken to this marriage. Now, he wanted what his sister had. He'd never realized what he was missing until the introduction of the House of de Wolfe into their lives. As it turned out, he'd been missing a great deal.

He intended to catch up.

Shaking himself from his train of thought, he began to focus on the world around him. Gar was willing to give him the night watch, but he at least needed to know what he was watching. Every nook, every seam, every stone. Therefore, he paid strict attention to the berms inside the walls and the slope of the hill that the keep sat upon. He paid attention to the fact that the walls were downslope from the keep and in some places, that made the top of the walls almost level with the keep itself. It was a good strategic position because if anyone ever mounted those tall walls, archers could easily pick them off from this level. Maksim digested what he could of the slopes and angles on this first pass before moving on.

The kitchen yard was to the rear of the castle, as the kitchen itself was underground, in the sublevel. There was a door leading into the kitchens from the yard and there seemed to be a good deal of activity in the yard itself as two enormous cauldrons bubbled away on open fires. There were people milling about, filling up bowls or small pots with whatever was steaming in those cauldrons, and Maksim observed the activity for a minute or two before something else caught his attention.

A small gate downslope.

The little gate was in the shadows of the wall, away from the torches that had been lit to stave off the night, and could have easily been missed. As Maksim's vision adjusted to it, he could see some kind of activity at the gate. Curious, he left the kitchen yard and went down the slope, approaching the little gate just as someone pushed it open. It was so dark that he couldn't see who it was, never imagining it wasn't a soldier or someone else associated with the castle. By the time he reached the gate, another man came through behind the first one, both of them standing tall and seemingly startled to see him. He only saw the flash of a weapon as it was raised, reflecting the weak torchlight, but by that time, it was too late for him to react.

It wasn't anyone associated with the castle.

It was the enemy.

A dirty, sharp ax plowed into Maksim's chest before he even realized what had happened. Whoever landed it tried to remove it, but it was wedged deep into his sternum. They left it in the bone. But that same person pushed Maksim out of the way, so he fell down, rolling down the slope and ending up at the base of the wall as a steady stream of Scots poured in through the open postern gate.

But Maksim was still conscious, at least for the moment. That wasn't going to last and he knew it. With his dying breath, he bellowed the only thing he could. The only alarm he could give.

Maksim de Reyne spent his final moments on earth as a true warrior.

Just the way he'd wanted.

"*Breach!*"

ᏣᏰ

"SCOTS ARE IN the compound!" a panicked soldier shouted into the hall. "To battle stations!"

The knights on the dais heard the cry and suddenly, everyone was on the move. They had been sitting around, enjoying a fine meal of pork and beans and good conversation, when the alarm came. Gar bolted to his feet, pulling Mattie with him, and the men with wives at the table immediately began escorting the women to the stairwells that led to the upper floors. Jordan took charge of Mattie because Gar had to go, and together, the women raced up the stairwell to the master's chamber while Rhoswyn, Caria, and Avrielle went up a separate staircase.

The great hall cleared in seconds.

Unfortunately, the fight was right at their door. The Scots had indeed breached the compound and were trying to get into the hall, into the castle itself. Yet again, they were trying to take the fight straight into the hall. With the entry door open because people were going in and out, they managed to make it inside, but there was a massive fight at the door. Unfortunately, the knights weren't armed. No one had come to the hall with weapons simply because no one had expected they would be needed. The castle was well manned, and Gar's men were vigilant, so there was no reason to come to the hall armed for war.

Now, they were wishing they had.

The younger knights were at the forefront of the battle at the keep entry. Andreas, Tor, and Atreus managed to hold back a tide of Scots as the older knights behind them—William, Troy, Scott, and Blayth—caught anyone who slipped past their net. Gar had managed to make it outside, racing to the small armory where he and Mattie had made love, and grabbed what weapons he could. Racing back to the entry, he speared two Scots immediately, clearing the way for him to provide swords to Andreas and Tor. As those two began cutting through Scots, he was able to get weapons to the rest of them, which left him without a weapon.

But that didn't matter.

Gar was fighting with fists and feet at that point.

Suddenly, a wave of armed soldiers descended on the keep entry because that seemed to be where the majority of the Scots were concentrated. There were dozens of them. They were wet and smelly and it occurred to Gar that, somehow, they had crossed that horrific moat and made it in. If they hadn't come through the gatehouse, then they'd either gone over the wall or come through the postern gate because those were the only ways they could have entered. Gar cursed himself for being caught off guard, but he couldn't dwell on it. He had to stem it. However the Scots had managed to do it, the breach was probably still open.

It was imperative that they close it.

"Atreus!" Gar boomed. "Find the breach!"

Atreus was a madman with a sword. He sliced through men, kicking and stabbing and punching, and finally made it outside. As Atreus took off, taking soldiers with him, Gar retreated to the armory and collected a big broadsword.

Returning to the entry, he could see that the fight had spread out more now. There was fighting both inside and outside the keep and that included William doing battle with a particularly large Scot just outside the keep door.

Gar wasn't going to tolerate that.

He knew his grandfather would be furious with him for interfering, but watching his elderly grandfather fighting for his life wasn't something Gar could ignore. No one was wearing mail or protection, him included, so they were all particularly vulnerable. That was what concerned him the most.

He didn't want to see an old knight get carved up.

Gar had his focus on William as he approached the keep entry. He was several feet away, preparing to swing wide and come around, approaching his grandfather's opponent from behind, when the big Scotsman suddenly thrust a fist right into William's throat. He was a tall man, with a long reach, and with fighting in such close quarters, it wasn't surprising that he was able to get close enough to William to strike him. But that move had Gar rushing the man as William staggered back and stumbled to one knee. Gar was so focused on bringing his broadsword to bear on the Scotsman's neck, which he did ably, that he failed to see a second Scotsman coming up behind him.

But he certainly felt it when a big, dirty blade plowed into the right side of his torso.

Instinct had him whirling around, using his own blade to slice his attacker at the throat. As his enemy fell away, nearly decapitated, Gar put his hand to the gash in his side and came away with an extreme amount of blood. He turned, trying to get a look at it, and all he could see was his patchwork breeches covered in it, all down the right side.

It was a bad wound.

But he wasn't going to stop. His castle had been violated and he was going to fight until he could fight no more. He was just about to go after another Scotsman when he felt hands on his arm, stopping him from proceeding.

"You're wounded, lad," William said calmly. "Come back inside. Let me take you to your grandmother."

Gar refused. "I cannot," he said. "I must defend my castle."

He tried to pull away but William held him fast. "Lad, you must come with me," he said. "You are bleeding heavily. Let your grandmother tend your wound."

Gar looked at him, his face already pale as the blood loss was starting to weigh on him. "I am wounded because you are out here doing something you should not be doing," he said angrily. "No one wants you fighting any longer, Poppy, but still, you insist. That means we must all watch you in battle to ensure you are not killed. The great William de Wolfe must be protected at all costs, so *you* go inside. Go inside where it is safe and let the younger men do the fighting."

He tried to pull away again, but William wouldn't budge. He wasn't going to let Gar's furious words hurt him, true though they might be.

"Come along," he said, moving toward the door and trying to drag Gar with him. When William saw Scott nearby, he shouted to him. "Scott! To me!"

That was a cry that was never disobeyed, not by any knight or member of the de Wolfe family. When William gave an order, men obeyed. Therefore, the command had Scott immediately rushing to his father, seeing the horror of a very bloody and pale Gar.

Scott was instantly at Gar's side.

"Let me see the damage," he said, lifting Gar's tunic. What

he saw had his features tightening with concern. "We must get him inside, Papa. *Now.*"

Gar was weakening. "I cannot," he said, his voice with less force than it usually had. "My castle is under siege."

"There are many men to defend it," Scott said. "You need help, Gar."

Between Scott and William, they managed to pull Gar inside the keep, but he was still resisting.

"I will survive," he insisted. "My castle may not. I must command this battle."

"I will have Andreas do it," William said calmly. "He knows the Scots. Your castle will be safe."

Gar was starting to fail. He seemed unable to move his legs adequately as the blood drained from him. "T-tell him I…" he stammered, feeling extremely lightheaded. "He must… My wife is here… Tell him he must…"

That was as far as he got before he passed out completely.

The battle for Gleann na Fola raged on.

CHAPTER TWENTY

"AS NEAR AS we can deduce, someone opened the postern gate and the Maxwell was waiting," Troy said grimly. "Maksim must have tried to stop them because we found him with an ax in his chest near the gate. We managed to kill about half of the Scots, but the rest of them ran off by morning. That was three days ago and we've not heard anything from them, or any of their allies, since. But one thing is certain—the Maxwell of Westerkirk did not do this alone. They had help."

It was daybreak on a misty morning as the bulk of the de Wolfe command structure stood around the dais in the great hall of Gleann na Fola, discussing the breach that had been so very costly. William had sent word to de Wolfe allies in the north right after the event, so gathered around the dais were men that had been allies and family of the House of de Wolfe for years. Decades in some cases. But this was a crucial moment for all of them. The Maxwell of Westerkirk had managed to hit them, and hurt them, and it was time to strike back and erase the despicable Scots from the earth once and for all.

This was a war council.

Ryston and Dalton de Royans, close allies of de Wolfe and

lords over a castle along the border known as The Lyceum, were the first ones to answer William's summons. By sheer proximity, they were the closest. Joining them were John de Longley, son of Adam de Longley, Earl of Teviot and lord of Northwood Castle, which was where William had been the captain of the guard for many years before becoming a lord in his own right. The House of de Longley was family to the House of de Wolfe. Adam had been knighted by William, long ago, and his only son, John, was a tremendous commander. He had addressed William as "Uncle William" his entire life and now stood at the ready to help a man he loved very much.

And help was most definitely needed.

Last to join the war council on this short notice was William's youngest son, Thomas. As the Earl of Northumbria, a title he'd acquired through marriage, Thomas was the most excitable of William's sons and a warrior with no equal. He took every battle personally, which meant everything he did was fed by emotion.

Including now.

Thomas was absolutely furious.

"To be perfectly clear, the Maxwell of Westerkirk started this entire situation," he said. "They murdered de Bourne knights."

Troy nodded. "They did."

"And when they were punished, they told their allies that *they* were the victims of English aggression."

Troy shrugged. "That is simplifying it, but aye, that's what they did."

Thomas threw up his hands. "And now, the western section of the border threatens to explode because of what they've done."

Troy drew in a long, sorrowful breath. "Aye," he said quietly. "We nearly destroyed the entire clan in an earlier skirmish. We captured one hundred and sixty-seven of their women and children and sent them into England to be sequestered in a few abbeys. One would have thought that Westerkirk would have surrendered at that point, but they did not. They called on their allies to oppose us. They staged an attack on the gatehouse, which somehow led to a spy being planted in our midst. We are still trying to determine just how and why that happened, but we believe that spy opened the postern gate so they could breach the castle."

"It was clever of them," Thomas said, shaking his head with regret. "They may have been small in number, but they are very determined."

Troy nodded, looking to his father, who was sitting while most were standing. During the battle three days ago, he had been sorely taxed and still hadn't really recovered. William wasn't thrilled with the term "clever" that his son had used, but it was the truth.

The Scots had been damn clever.

"They were either clever or very fortunate," William said after a moment. "Or both. We had men all over the walls, outside the walls, and everywhere in between, but they still managed to breach. We lost an excellent knight in Maksim de Reyne. I'm told he was the reason we knew the castle was breached in the first place. Without his sounding the alarm, it could have been worse."

"It *is* worse," Thomas said, eyeing his father, his brothers. "They killed a knight and six soldiers. They also badly wounded Gar. How does he fare, by the way?"

William sighed heavily, indicative of the sadness he was

feeling. He looked at Scott, who had a more in-depth knowledge of Gar's injuries, which were extensive.

Extensive and potentially fatal.

"He is not well," Scott said. "The blade cut into the right side of his torso and was buried deep. It punctured innards and did damage. But the worst part is this—we've known the Scots to wipe their blades with feces on occasion and we think this blade was one of them, for the poison set in almost immediately. Gar has been quite ill since it happened and my mother and I have been working extensively to ensure that the poison does not kill him. Other than that, all we can do is pray."

It was grim news, something none of them wanted to hear. Andreas, in particular, was devastated and he kept flicking tears from his eyes. Reed, who had been recalled from Hell's Guardhouse, and another brother, Corey, were equally upset. They wouldn't even wipe their tears away as Andreas was doing, letting them run down their faces or drip off their chins like some macabre badge of honor. On the dais, Troy stood next to his brother, stoic and morose. He was a moody man to begin with, and the wounding of his eldest son with Rhoswyn, his shining star, was not sitting well with him.

He wanted blood.

"And that is why you have all been summoned," Troy said, his jaw twitching with emotion. "Westerkirk started this when they murdered two English knights, but now they have tried to murder my son. My wife's father, whom you all know to be Red Keith Kerr, has told us that Westerkirk was helped in this attack against Gleann na Fola by the Maxwell of Davington and Merrylaw. It seems that Ean Maxwell's lies did not convince other clans that he sought assistance from, according to Keith, so others will not face my wrath. In fact, they have my gratitude for not answering. However, as we speak, Red Keith's men are moving to form a net around Westerkirk so that any Maxwell who try to escape will be caught. We will move our armies up the Valley of Blood and sweep into Westerkirk from the south and destroy Bailie Castle once and for all. If we can capture Ean Maxwell alive, then we shall, because I intend to make an example out of him. The man wanted blood. He is going to get it, and it is going to be his own."

Determined words from a grieving father, but no one in the room disagreed with him. That was what they'd all come for and it was time to finish the job.

"Then we must be prepare to move out before dawn," Thomas said, his loud voice lifting to the group of seasoned men. "Ryston, you and your brother will take the lead. I fear that the rest of us may be too emotional about the situation, so you will organize the front line and send out scouts. Westerkirk managed to evade our scouts before, so make sure they do not evade yours. We need to know where they are and what they are doing, and you will make contact with Red Keith and his men. Coordinate information."

Ryston and Dalton, sons of the great Torston de Royans and part of the powerful de Royans family, nodded smartly. They were seasoned knights with plenty of battle experience, so they understood the assignment well. After that, Thomas' attention moved to John de Longley.

John was a big man, not particularly tall, but strong and noble. He was well liked by everyone and had the heart of a warrior, something his father had, but something that had evaded his grandfather and other men in the family. Most of his ancestors had been politicians, not soldiers. When he saw Thomas' attention, he put his hand on the hilt of his sword, indicating his readiness.

"Whatever you desire, my lord," he said. "Command me."

"Command *me*."

Another voice came from the hall entry and everyone turned to see something that had been a staple of the wars in the north for decades. It drew smiles from some, looks of annoyance from others. Paris de Norville, the former captain of Northwood's armies, approached the dais. Seeing his grandfather, Atreus joined him, both of them coming to stand next to John, who was technically their liege.

Except Paris was in charge.

At least, he thought he was.

"Now," Paris said, looking at the de Wolfe men before him. "You will command *me*. I've brought a thousand Northwood men here and I intend to tear up Westerkirk until there is nothing left to tear. I will cut off heads and put them on pikes for all to see. I will fillet their hides from their bodies and plaster them across every clan village from Lockerbie to Coldstream. I will send a message that if one more English knight is murdered by Scots dogs, then I will burn up the north and leave no survivors. Well? Command me to do it and I shall. What are you waiting for?"

He meant every word. Paris de Norville was a legend almost as much as William was and the pair had been friends since their youth. They were brothers in every way but blood and any affront to William was an affront to Paris. He was also as old as William was, and his health hadn't been the best as of late, but his pride was monumental so in a situation like this, there was no possibility he was going to stay out of it.

He was out for vengeance.

And the knights knew it. Scott, Troy, Blayth, Thomas, and

their siblings had all grown up with Uncle Paris. Two of them had married into the de Norville family, so Paris truly was their kin. Much like William, Paris was far too old to be riding to battle, but it was something that was part of their very fabric. Old knights couldn't shirk their duties and age didn't matter.

But it did.

No one was quite sure how to convince the elderly knights to remain behind.

"Your presence here is revered, Uncle Paris," Thomas finally said, trying to be diplomatic. "You know we cannot go into battle without you."

Paris puffed up, feeling appreciated. "As long as you know that," he said. "Now, what would you have from Northwood's army?"

Thomas glanced at John, who simply shrugged. There was no getting around Paris's thinking he was in charge. "Northwood will form the center of the army, of course," Thomas said. "But I need you to speak with my father so that a strategy will be worked out. Meanwhile, the other knights will prepare the army while we wait for your direction. Will you do this?"

Of course Paris would. He was being asked to direct a battle and he would do just that. As he headed over toward William, Thomas began waving at the knights, silently commanding them to hurry outside while the old men conferred. That way, the elderly knights were out of the way and the real work with the army could begin.

With a purpose, the men headed outside.

As William and Paris began to talk strategy, Thomas took Blayth outside with him and the other de Wolfe knights to begin forming their ranks. That left Scott and Troy alone, standing near the table where William and Paris were sitting.

The hall, so full of knights in armor not moments before, was now oddly still and silent.

It was a painful, fragile silence.

"I'm going to return to Gar for a while," Scott told his brother quietly. "Will you come with me?"

Troy had been staring at the entry door, watching his sons as they filtered out with the rest of the knights. He heard his brother's question and it shook his composure a little.

"Andreas is not taking this well," he muttered. "Neither are Reed and Corey. You know that Corey nearly lost his infant son recently."

"I know."

"He cannot take much more of this grief."

Scott's gaze fixed on his twin brother. They were separated by minutes in the birthing order and couldn't possibly have been more different, but when it came to the love of family, they were the same.

They had shared much heartache together.

"He can," Scott murmured. "He will if it comes to it. And so will you. You and I know better than anyone that life goes on."

Troy looked at him. "Not if Gar dies," he said. "I have decided that if he dies, I will go with him."

Scott frowned. "What do you mean?"

"You *know* what I mean."

Scott did. He also knew that Troy wasn't being overdramatic. He meant it. "You would do that to Rhos?" he asked softly. "You would do it to your children? And how do you think Gar would feel about that? For him to be the cause of his father's death?"

Troy's jaw was twitching furiously and as Scott watched, tears sprang to the man's eyes. "I suffered the loss of two children before," Troy said hoarsely. "Little girls who'd not yet lived their lives. But to suffer the loss of a son… a young man who had finally found happiness in life… I do not think I can take it. I cannot accept it. I do not want to be left behind to pick up the pieces that he will leave when he goes. I cannot do it again."

Scott could hear the pain in his voice. He put a gentle arm around his brother's shoulders, trying to comfort him.

"And I have lost a son," he whispered. "I lost Andrew when he was young, just as you lost Arista and Acacia. Could I stand to lose Tor or Will? Of course I would not want to weather that. No parent does. But you must think of what you would leave behind. You have other sons who would know you took your own life. What message would that send to them? That their father was not brave enough to face death? How do you think that would make them feel, losing Gar and then losing you?"

Troy's head was down as he wiped at his eyes. "I know," he muttered. "I know, but I cannot stand the thought of losing Gar. It will destroy me."

"He's not dead yet," Scott said. "Mother and Rhoswyn have been pouring rotten tea into his mouth every chance they get. If anything can heal him, that can. It will. You must have faith."

"That is something I have little of these days."

Scott knew that, but he didn't say so. Troy's faith had always been tenuous, at best, so it was difficult for him to lean into it. He gave his brother a final squeeze before dropping his arm from his shoulders.

"Come with me," he said, pulling at him. "Let us go see to your son."

Troy simply nodded, dumbly, for lack of a better reply. He let Scott escort him from the hall to the stairwell that led up to the master's chambers. As the two of them headed up the steps, William and Paris watched them go.

The older men hadn't heard the conversation, but they didn't have to. It was enough to see Troy's tears and Scott's gesture of comfort. Sometimes being a parent was particularly painful and it was something all the men lived in fear of.

Losing a son in battle.

It was the great horror they hoped they never had to face.

"How badly off is Gar?" Paris asked softly.

William rubbed his one good eye wearily. "Bad," he muttered. "Very bad."

"Should I see to him?"

It was well known that Paris was an excellent healer. He had been since his youth. William stopped rubbing his eye and looked at him.

"I thought you were marching with the army?" he said.

Paris shrugged. "They do not want me," he said. "I know they do not want me, so I go. The more they don't want me, the more I go. But seeing to Gar would give me an excuse not to go."

William stared at him a moment before breaking down into soft laughter. "You are a conceited devil," he said. "Would I rather have you see to my grandson than ride to battle? Of course I would. But I did not want to ask."

Paris smiled faintly. "You know you can always ask me anything," he said. "Whether or not I do it is another matter."

"You have been that way your entire life."

"Would you have me any other way?"

William shook his head and stood up. "I would not," he said. "At least you are predictable in that way. Now, let us see to Gar. It gives me comfort knowing you will help him if you can."

Paris stood up beside him, wearily. "I will always help if I can," he said. "But I am sincerely sorry this happened to Gar. I like him, William. He's a good lad."

William was trying not to let his sadness overwhelm him. "He is," he said. "But his wife… You've not met her yet, Paris. She has been incredibly good for him. Her brother was killed when the Scots breached the castle and now with Gar wounded, she has a very heavy burden to bear."

Paris could see the pain in William's expression. Paris may have many qualities, but a lack of empathy wasn't among them. He was surprisingly compassionate even if he didn't show it.

But he would show it now.

"Then let me see if I can help ease it," he said quietly. "Take me to her."

William nodded, heading toward the stairwell that led to the upper floors with Paris on his heels. His wife and Scott were competent healers, but Paris had knowledge that ran deep. William could only pray it was deep enough to spare Gar because he couldn't stomach the alternative.

God help them, he hoped it was a tragedy they would all live through.

☙

HE LOOKED LIKE he was sleeping.

Sitting in a chair next to the bed she and Gar shared, Mattie could only stare at the man who, she was told, was stable for the time being. But that could change. The fever he'd had since yesterday was moderate, but fevers were never a good thing, especially when it came to an injury. Mattie didn't know much about injuries, only what she'd seen after the Scots had rushed the gatehouse, but she knew that the injury Gar had suffered was worse than anything she'd seen to date.

She knew it was bad.

When they'd first brought him up to the chamber, she'd tried to help, but her shock had gotten the better of her and, had Jordan not forced her to sit down, she probably would have made a fool of herself and fainted right onto the floor. Instead, she sat in a chair like a weakling, watching people who knew what they were doing tend to her injured husband, who was coming in and out of consciousness at that point. He came out long enough to extend a hand to Mattie and assure her that all would be well, but those were the last words she'd heard from him.

He'd been silent for almost three days.

Three days that started with Jordan and Scott inspecting the biggest, most horrific gash that Mattie had ever seen. She could only look at it for a couple of seconds before her gag reflex kicked in and she had to look away or risk getting sick. She was terribly embarrassed at her reaction, but the truth was that she'd never seen so much blood on a human being in her life. Suddenly, *Cù fola* took on a whole new meaning.

Blood wolf.

Someone had bloodied the Wolfe.

Between Scott and Jordan, they managed to cleanse the wound with wine before stitching it tightly with what turned out to be fifty-five sutures. Mattie had heard them say so. Fifty-five sutures in Gar's trim torso. Once the cleaning and stitching was done, she had, indeed, vomited.

She simply couldn't help it.

After her husband had been tended, and his torso wrapped tightly, the situation had settled down until Troy appeared later that night to gently tell Mattie that Maksim had been killed in the attack. At first, she hadn't really understood his words. They made no sense. It simply wasn't possible that Maksim could have been killed, because he was a skilled knight. She had only just seen him yesterday. Moreover, he had been excited to establish his legacy, so he couldn't be dead due to something as random as a Scots raid.

But he was.

Still, she refused to believe it.

Against Troy's better judgment, he heeded her request to see her brother for herself and took her down to the sublevels, near the kitchen, where they were storing the dead in the cold, dark vault. There were about a dozen bodies down there, covered up, and Troy took her to one in particular that was on a table. Carefully, he peeled back the blanket that was covering the head to reveal that it was, in fact, Maksim. He had been dead for several hours, so his face was mottled in color and his mouth was open, his jaw tightening in the throes of decay. It hardly looked like her brother at all, but it was.

Maksim was actually dead.

Throwing herself across her brother's corpse, Mattie wept hysterically.

She wasn't even sure how long she remained with him, weeping, apologizing over and over. She didn't know why she was apologizing to him, only that she was. She was sorry for the life he would never lead, the children he would never have. She was sorry for all of those things, but most of all, she was sorry to lose her only sibling. They'd come to Gleann na Fola with such hope.

Now, hope was gone.

The pain was unbearable.

When Troy had duties to attend to, he stayed with Mattie in

that icy vault as she expended her grief. Since Gar couldn't, he felt obligated to. For Mattie, it seemed like a horrible nightmare she was praying to wake up from. She didn't even remember how she'd come back up to the master's chamber where Gar was sleeping on the bed, only that she was suddenly there and she had left her brother behind in that freezing vault. Another look at Gar on their bed, his torso bound up and his skin pale with blood loss, and she burst into tears all over again. She managed to make it over into a corner in the servants' alcove, huddle down, and weep inconsolably.

In the stillness of the chamber, it was a heartbreaking sound.

Winchester, who had been under the bed, came to her and lay down next to her as her grief found an outlet. Jordan tried to coax Mattie into coming out and sitting by Gar, but Mattie wasn't ready to do that yet. She'd had two horrible shocks, one after the other, and she was coping with it the best way she could.

Unrestrained tears.

Jordan finally left her alone and simply let her cry it out.

That lasted for about six hours. Mattie wept until she could weep no more, now having to resign herself to a world her brother wasn't in. Worse still, she had to tell her parents and she knew how it would destroy them. Especially her father. But she eventually came out of the alcove, apologized to Jordan for her weakness, and took a seat next to the bed where Gar was starting to show signs of a fever.

Since nearly the moment he was injured, Jordan and Scott had begun brewing something they called "rotten tea" that smelled awful but was said to kill the poison associated with wounds. It was made from the blue mold that grew on bread and then steeped with water to create a brew. At least, that was what Mattie had observed. The process seemed mysterious. All she really knew was that her trust was in Gar's grandmother and uncle, and they seemed to know what they were doing when it came to healing her husband.

He was in the hands of experts.

Mattie's duty was much simpler. It was her job to use cool water and rags to bathe Gar's face and arms, trying to keep his temperature down. She worked diligently at it, only stopping when Jordan forced her to rest. But she couldn't sleep, and neither could Winchester, and over the past day or so, the dog had taken to crawling into bed with Gar and lying by his side. Mattie would remove him, but somehow, he would find his way back up again. Finally, she simply left him, bathing her husband's hot brow with cool water as Winchester lay next to Gar with his head on the man's shoulder. He seemed to sense that something was terribly wrong and, truthfully, it gave Mattie comfort to have him there.

At least he wasn't trying to bite Gar anymore.

She was grateful for small mercies.

Her now-placid dog reminded her of the breeches he'd destroyed and her attention would drift, every so often, to the patchwork breeches that were now hanging over the back of a chair. The entire right side of them had been stained with Gar's blood, but at some point since Gar was injured, Jordan had given the breeches over to a laundress, who'd soaked them in icy water and then in vinegar to remove the bloodstain. They did something else to the stain to try to remove it, but even with all of that, the stain's yellowish outline remained.

But so did the breeches.

No matter what Gar put them through, they were enduring.

Just like Mattie's love for Gar.

She took such comfort in that bit of clothing. She'd once regretted making them, but no longer. Now, they signified something solid and important. As the hours passed and Gar seemed to linger in a fevered state, Mattie made sure those breeches were just where he could see them should he suddenly awaken and want to get out of bed. But… as the hours passed and Gar didn't awaken, it was difficult not to feel despair.

Those breeches became a symbol of what had been.

She prayed they wouldn't become a symbol of loss.

The third day after Gar's injury, Mattie was sitting on the bed next to him, bathing his sticky forehead with cool water as Jordan slept in a nearby chair and Winchester lay across Gar's feet. Mattie knew that men had arrived over the past couple of days, men with armies, more knights coming in and out of a castle that was under repair, but she didn't pay any attention to what was going on. It didn't matter as long as Gar remained as he was, drifting on a sea of limbo, between life and death. All Mattie cared about was bringing him into the shore where she was waiting.

She was willing to do anything to bring him back to her.

"There once was a lady fair,
With silver bells in her hair.
I knew her to have,
A luscious kiss… it drove me mad!
But she denied me… and I was so terribly sad!"

That was all she remembered of the song that Gar and some of the others had sung at their wedding, and she sang it off-key, but it was enough to bring Jordan out of a deep sleep. Her head came up, her eyes still half closed, as she recognized the tune of the naughty wedding song.

"God's Bones, lass," she said sleepily. "Dunna tell me he taught ye that song?"

Mattie looked over at her, grinning. "He did not exactly teach me," she said. "But he sang it more than once at our wedding. I just remember a few words."

"Good," Jordan said flatly. "When he wakes, remind me tae beat him for singing that song in front of ye."

Mattie laughed softly. "I did not mind," she said, looking at Gar again. "I like to think that he sang it because he was happy. I was just trying to remind him of that."

Her smile faded and Jordan watched the expression on her face, a young woman trying so hard to be courageous when her happiness hung by a thread.

"Then I'll let ye sing it again if it pleases ye," she said. "But dunna ask me the rest of the words. A lady should not know such words."

Mattie smiled weakly. "I will not ask," she said. "But… if I may, I do have a question."

"What is it, lass?"

"Have you ever seen anyone injured this badly recover from it?"

Jordan nodded without hesitation. "Of course," she said. "Mattie, there is always hope. Let me tell ye a story about Poppy. Ye've noticed that he's missing an eye."

Mattie nodded. "Aye."

Jordan pulled her old, tattered shawl more tightly around her shoulders as her mind wandered to the memories surrounding William's missing eye.

"I was pregnant with Scott and Troy," she said. "William

had been in London serving the king and part of those duties had him in Wales. The details of the battles are mostly lost tae me now, but he received a bolt tae the eye in one particular fight. That is how he lost the eye."

Mattie frowned, sympathetic to such a horror. "That is awful," she said. "How in the world did he survive it?"

Jordan sighed. "That is the question," she said softly. "The bolt should have gone through his head, but only by the grace of God, it dinna. But it destroyed the eye well enough. By the time I reached London, William was in a terrible state. He was feverish and quite ill. I lay with him, I talked to him, I pleaded with him. Truly, Mattie, he should have died. But he dinna. 'Tis amazing what love can do."

Mattie looked at Gar. *'Tis amazing what love can do.* She'd told him once that she was fairly certain she was in love with him. Perhaps that was not when he'd needed to hear it.

Perhaps he needed to hear it now.

A knock on the door roused Jordan out of her chair as Mattie remained on the bed, looking at Gar. As the older woman toddled over to the door to answer it, Mattie leaned down, her lips next to Gar's left ear.

"I love you, Gar de Wolfe," she whispered, kissing his ear. "If you need something to believe in, something to bring you back, then believe in us. Believe in what we can be, together. Believe in the children we shall have and the legacy we shall create. I promise you that our love will outlast the sun."

Tears sprang to her eyes, but she quickly blinked them away. She hadn't wept in an entire day and she was trying to stay strong about it. Behind her, the chamber door opened to reveal William and a man who was probably as old as William was. He was big, his thick hair cropped and gray. As William put his arm around Jordan's shoulders, the other man came right up to the bed, acknowledged Mattie with a nod, and then bent down to lift up both of Gar's eyelids, one after the other.

As Mattie watched curiously, he felt Gar's pulse, checked his temperature, and then asked Jordan to help him inspect the wound. Since Mattie didn't want to see it again, she came off the bed and took Winchester with her because the dog was still lying on Gar's feet. She and Winchester went over to a chair near the hearth, making sure they were turned away from Gar as Jordan unfastened the wrapping around his torso to show the man the injury. When they finally fell away, she heard the man hiss.

"Did they try to slice him in half, then?" he demanded. "A little more force and Gar would be in two pieces."

Mattie tried not to gasp, but she couldn't quite help it. She turned her head away, trying not to weep yet again, as Jordan frowned at the man.

"If ye wish tae upset his new wife with yer flapping lips, then ye've accomplished yer goal," she snapped. "Ye dunna have tae say such things, Paris. We know what it looks like."

Paris.

Mattie had heard that name before. Paris de Norville, William's oldest and dearest friend, and commander of Northwood Castle's army. Clearly, he had arrived with the gaggle of men who had come over the past day or so and now, he wanted to see to Gar. As Mattie sat there, head turned, she could hear the elders behind her.

"I was not trying to upset Lady de Wolfe," he said, contrite. "It was simply my anger at the Scots speaking."

Jordan eased up on her angry stance. "Ye're in good company because we're all feeling enough," she said. "We've cleaned the wound well and stitched it up, but there is poison. I fear we'll have tae reopen it and clean it."

"Have you given him the rotten brew?"

Jordan nodded. "Twice," she said. "He's not been awake enough tae drink much of it and the last time we tried, he nearly choked."

Paris nodded, his expression serious as he looked at Gar. "We must get the brew in him," he said. "I will stay and assist. I have a willow powder in my bags. That will help with the fever."

"Then bring it," Jordan said. "I'll send for more wine and boiled linen if we are tae clean out the wound again."

Paris nodded, then he glanced over his shoulder at Mattie, sitting near the hearth. "Lady de Wolfe should not be here when we do it," he said quietly. "William? Will you take Lady de Wolfe in hand while we work?"

William had been listening to the conversation and he knew what Paris meant. He, too, glanced at Mattie before moving closer to the bed, addressing Paris and Jordan directly.

"I will take her with me when I see to the army," he said quietly. "I have a feeling that seeing Gar's wife will help spur on the men. They are already seeking vengeance for Gar. Now, they'll seek it for Mattie."

"Ye're not riding with them, are ye?" Jordan asked, but it really wasn't a question. It was a directive. "I'll need ye here, English. We have much tae do with Gar."

William's gaze found his wife across the bed. "I am riding with them," he said softly. "But not for the reason you think. The younger men can do the fighting. But this is a highly sensitive and political action and I must be there to ensure nothing happens that could ignite the border into a larger war. With Edward having difficulty with the Scots, and a failed alliance with the German king, our actions against Westerkirk may have farther-reaching implications. I know you understand that."

Jordan's gaze was locked on William. "Ye dunna need tae bear a sword," she said, clearly unhappy. "But if ye simply intend tae manage the situation, then I have no quarrel with ye."

This was usual with them. William didn't need her permission to do his duty and they both knew it, but he didn't want her fighting him on it. An agreement from her was as good as permission. It was a dance they'd danced many times over the decades, especially as he grew older but still wanted to ride to battle.

She thought he was too old.

He didn't.

"I am simply going to watch the situation," William confirmed. "And I am going to watch the overly emotional brothers of Gar to ensure no one becomes a danger to himself. Grief can breed recklessness."

That made sense. The family was having a difficult enough time with Gar's injury. They didn't need another young de Wolfe knight falling. As Jordan nodded in resignation and returned her attention to Gar, William made his way over to Mattie.

Somehow, she looked so small and pale sitting in that chair. There was another chair next to the hearth and he sat in that one, facing Mattie. She gazed back at him with an expression somewhere between anguish and fear.

William smiled faintly.

"I have need of you, my lady," he said.

Mattie sat up straight. "You only need tell me, my lord."

William glanced at the windows that overlooked the west side of the castle. Although he couldn't see anything, he could still imagine the view from that window, a view of a big army that was forming below.

"Many men have come to punish those who hurt Gar and killed your brother," he said. "If I've not expressed my sincere sadness at Maksim's passing, please allow me to do so. He was a fine knight."

Mattie's eyes filled with tears. "He was," she said. "He so wanted to belong to the House of de Wolfe. He envied the closeness the knights had, the camaraderie, and he just wanted to be part of it."

"And he was," William assured her. "He was a fine addition, and he died doing something very heroic. If it had not been for his alarm, the castle breach could have been so much worse. His actions saved many people, Mattie. That is what I will tell your father, if you will let me."

Mattie nodded, blinking, and the tears spattered. "I would appreciate that," she said. "I have been wondering how I am going to tell my parents."

"I will do it," William said. "But first, I want you to do something for me."

"Anything, my lord."

William held out a hand to her. "Go outside with me and see to the forming of the army," he said. "The men know you are Gar's wife. They also know you are Maksim's sister. Let them see you as a tribute to both men. Let them see what they are fighting for. It will inspire them."

Taking a deep breath for courage, Mattie took William's hand and as he stood up, he gently pulled her to her feet. She was wiping the tears away as he led her to the door, his final glance toward the bed showing that Paris was already starting to remove the stitches that Jordan and Scott had so carefully put in. He was removing Mattie just in time.

She didn't need to see that.

Leading her down the stairs that ended in the great hall, William found himself trying to tamp down his own anger at what had happened. He was usually quite levelheaded about critical situations, but every time he looked at Mattie's lowered head, he started to feel rage all over again.

But this time, it was at himself.

This was his fault.

He was the one who had insisted on the marriage. He'd bullied Gar into it. He knew he had, but he'd justified his actions by telling himself that this was a necessary alliance. It was necessary for Gar to marry well. Fortunately, Gar had seemed pleased with the marriage, only to be cut down trying to protect his grandfather, who didn't have the sense not to engage men half his age in battle.

Aye, that was his fault, too.

He knew that.

William found himself praying that he hadn't created this marriage only to see it end in tragedy. He wasn't sure he could live with himself if he had.

And he wasn't sure Mattie could live with the results, either.

CHAPTER TWENTY-ONE

Bailie Castle

THEY KNEW THE English were coming.

There was no doubt.

Truthfully, they'd been very lucky in their efforts against them. They'd managed to rush the gatehouse and plant Gordie as a spy, and Gordie had been able to open the postern gate, allowing the Maxwell to, yet again, rush inside of Gleann na Fola. Hiding after the rush on the gatehouse had been tricky for Ean and his men because the English had heavy patrols scouring the countryside, but they'd managed to keep out of sight until they needed to cross that horrible moat and pass through that tiny, odd postern gate.

Aye, they'd been damn lucky.

But that luck wasn't going to hold.

After the battle at Gleann na Fola, they'd retreated just after sunrise with less than half of the men they'd come with, and that included Gordie. The uncle that Ean had had a contentious relationship with, the same uncle who had made it possible for Westerkirk to breach Gleann na Fola, had fallen shortly after the battle began. He'd taken a sword to the neck, which nearly decapitated him, and Ean had seen his body somewhere later in the fight.

He'd had to leave him behind when they fled.

Unable to take Gleann na Fola because of all of the English protecting it, the Scots had retreated north through the Valley of Blood and into Westerkirk, where what remained of Bailie Castle waited for them. But that was all that waited for them. Given the battle that had seen their women and children taken, there was literally nothing else, and considering the English would undoubtedly follow them, they fully expected the castle to be razed.

No survivors.

But Ean wasn't going to wait for an English death.

He was going to go out *his* way.

"What now, lad?"

The clan chief from Maxwell of Merrylaw asked the question. He was the only chief that had joined the raid against the English. Brend Maxwell was young, and nearly as hot-headed as Ean, and he didn't much like the English or respect any treaties that his forefathers had agreed to. The stealing of women and children, and the holding of Ean's young daughter hostage, didn't sit well with him, but he'd lost thirty men in the assault and considering his clan was quite small, it was a heavy loss for him.

Now, he wanted to know what the future held.

"Well?" he said again. "What now, Ean?"

Ean was nursing a nasty gash on his right thigh, one that ran from his knee to his hip. Poison was developing in it, but he was ignoring it. He was young and strong and based on that belief, he would survive it. He wasn't going to let the English take his life the way they'd taken so many others'.

But Brend's question had him on the defensive.

"They'll come here," he said, smacking the old, broken table they were sitting at. "They'll come straight tae Bailie, but we willna be here."

Brend cocked an eyebrow. "True," he said. "I will be home. But where will ye be?"

Ean waved his hand. "Gone," he said. "I'll go with ye tae yer home. We'll stay there and wait out the Sassenach before we go against them once more."

But Brend shook his head. "I think not," he said. "I'll not let ye bring the Sassenach tae our door. I've a family tae think of."

That wasn't what Ean wanted to hear. "As do I," he said. "Those bastards at Gleann na Fola still have my daughter!"

Brend inhaled slowly, indicative of a man with something to say. "About that," he said. "Gordie, God rest him, told us that never happened. Ye lied about it."

Ean's eyes widened. "That's not true!"

"Then where is yer daughter?"

"In their vaults!"

Brend knew Ean. He knew the man wasn't going to confess his fabrication, stubborn fool that he was. It was like dealing with a child.

"Then I'll ask ye the same question again," he said. "What now, Ean?"

Ean was red around the ears, indicative of his level of anger. "They'll come now," he said. "They'll come tae Bailie, but they'll get nothing."

"My mother could climb over yer curtain wall," Brend said. "The Sassenach will be able tae mount it and then they'll be in yer lap. Do ye not have a plan for that?"

"I have a plan."

He didn't elaborate, frustrating Brend. "What is it?" he said. "Or must we guess? Ean, do ye even know where the Sassenach are? Do ye have scouts watching the south, scouts who can warn us when the army approaches?"

"We dunna need scouts."

He was being incredibly evasive and Brend had suffered enough. Without another word, he stood up from the table and motioned to his men, well-seasoned Lowlanders wearing their traditional long woolen tunics, and headed from the hall. Ean watched them go, his mouth open in shock, but more than the abandonment he was feeling, he was also feeling outrage.

Outrage that his world was coming to an end and he had no one to stand with him.

Around his table, only two men remained. The rest had either been killed at Gleann na Fola or they'd deserted him. Those two men, his cousins, were looking at him with trepidation. They weren't Gordie or Brend. They were young men, barely having reached manhood, and they had no idea what to say. No one knew what Ean was going to do now or what he wanted.

But Ean was about to show them.

With a gleam of madness in his eye, he stood up and went over to the hearth. There were a couple of torches leaning into the flame, so light would always be available in the darker recesses of Bailie, and he picked up one of those torches. The burning end was soaked in fat, spewing black smoke into the chamber when he pulled it out. Heading over to one of the support columns that held up his ceiling, Ean held the torch against a dry patch of splinters long enough for it to ignite.

The column began to burn.

Ean still didn't say a word.

He simply fled.

ଓ

RED KEITH'S CIRCLE of men to the west of Westerkirk lands netted thirteen men from the Maxwell of Westerkirk, but the English army heading north captured more.

It was like trying to herd chickens, however.

There were almost two thousand knights and soldiers marching on Westerkirk and they had absolutely no resistance until they reached Bailie Castle. Even when they arrived, however, the resistance was minimal because the castle itself was in flames. Flames that were seen for miles before the de Wolfe army reached them, and once they arrived, the de Royans brothers, along with Blayth and Thomas, sent men into the compound to root out anyone else who was there and take them prisoner.

It was a chaotic scene as the de Wolfe men chased down Scots, fighting with many, while still others just simply gave up. While that was going on, the men from Northwood spread out to the east and north, sweeping through a few small communities and coming up with eleven Maxwell clan members who were in hiding.

A long day turned into a long night.

William, at the head of the dragon, wanted to make sure everything they did was clean and as ethical as it could be because he'd kept peace on the border for sixty years. He wasn't going to jeopardize it now over a rogue clan chief. Along with Scott and Troy, he'd made his way into the bailey of Bailie Castle, surveying the carnage and the fire as the keep burned, when Scots suddenly came out of the piles of debris that were stacked around the ward and attacked. William found himself fighting off a few rabid Scotsmen as Scott and Troy and a collection of de Wolfe soldiers backed him out of the danger zone.

But he'd taken a good nick to the forearm.

All he could think of was the fact that he'd promised his wife he wasn't going to bear a sword. He was simply going to manage the situation, he'd told her, but here he was with a sizable nick on his left wrist and, as it turned out, a broken bone in his hand from the impact of the sword that cut him. Scott had to give him three stitches in the nick and wrapped his hand up with some wood to keep it straight and protected, but William hated the fact that he looked like a bloody invalid with the big bandage on his hand.

Still… it could have been worse.

As the night turned to dawn, the Northwood army returned bearing their prisoners and the de Wolfe army had collected any captured Scots from Red Keith Kerr and his men. They were all brought to the de Wolfe encampment, which was just outside of Bailie Castle. The castle itself continued to burn even now as the fire moved from the keep to outbuildings, to anything else that was flammable.

The entire countryside smelled of smoke and despair.

William was waiting for news that Ean Maxwell was among the many Scots captives. Standing at the door of his tent at sunset, he was nursing a sore back and shoulders from the unexpected fight in the bailey. Truthfully, he still hadn't recovered from the battle at Gleann na Fola Castle. His body didn't recover like it used to, and his ailments, coupled with the injury to his left hand, when his dominant hand was the left one, had him feeling somewhat under the weather.

Everything hurt.

It especially hurt when he inhaled deeply, so he tried to avoid doing that. He was starting to think that maybe his wife was right and that he shouldn't be fighting at his age, but the truth was that he didn't know anything else. This was his life, the life he'd chosen, and it was in his blood. But he didn't want that blood spilled any more than Jordan did.

Perhaps it was finally time for him to hang up his sword.

As he mulled over that very depressing probability, he could see four of his sons moving in his direction. Behind them came a man he didn't recognize, a Scot in a long tunic, and then behind him came Andreas, Tor, Reed, and Corey. Eight de Wolfe knights and one Scotsman.

Something told him that this was the very Scotsman he'd been waiting for.

He stepped back into his tent to wait.

In a short amount of time, Scott and Troy stepped through, followed by Blayth and Thomas. They faced William as he poured himself a measure of wine before sitting heavily on a cushioned chair. But even that hurt his old body and he winced, trying to get comfortable.

"What's wrong, Papa?" Scott asked. "Are you in pain?"

William shrugged. "At my age, always," he said, making light of it. He gazed at the four enormous men facing him, fondness glimmering in his eye. "I miss seeing Atty and Edward with you."

Atty, or Patrick de Wolfe, was the Earl of Berwick, commander of Berwick Castle, and Edward was an advisor to the king who spent most of his time in London. Patrick was between Scott, Troy, and Blayth in the birth order, the biggest de Wolfe brother who was hell on the field of battle. To the family, he was the gentle giant, but to the enemy, he was the knight no one wanted to face. Edward was a capable knight, but he was, and always had been, the family diplomat.

"Sadly, there was not enough time to wait for Atty to join us all the way from Berwick," Scott said. "We did send him word on our actions, however. He knows what has happened. And Edward is in London."

"He does not usually ride to battle," William said. "He fights more difficult battles, I think. Political intrigue is always the most difficult battle."

"True," Scott said. Then, he gestured toward the tent opening. "We've brought you a gift, Papa."

"What?"

"Ean Maxwell."

William's eye lit up. "You found him!"

"Aye," Scott said. "He tried to evade us dressed as a woman, but he was betrayed by one of his own men. He is not particularly happy right now, but we knew you would want to see him."

William was out of his seat. "See him, aye," he muttered. "And tell him how unhappy *I* am about what he's done. Bring him in."

Scott nodded to Thomas, who was standing near the tent flap. Thomas stepped out and when he stepped back in, he had a squirming captive in his grip. It was a surprisingly young man with dirty, dark hair and a bloodied face.

Thomas shoved the man down to his knees before William.

"Murtairean Sassenach!" the man yelled. "Marbhaidh mi thu ma gheibh mi cothrom!"

English murderers! I will kill you if I get the chance!

Given that he was married to a woman who fluently spoke

the language, and William had been dealing with Scots for more decades than he cared to admit, he knew exactly what the man had said. So did his sons, who looked less than pleased. In fact, Thomas slapped the captive on the back of the head, hard enough for the man to face-plant into the ground. Then, Thomas reached down and yanked him up by the hair.

"Speak more respectfully to the Earl of Warenton," Thomas hissed.

Now, it was making some sense as to why the young man had a bloodied face. He couldn't control his mouth and had received the appropriate warnings. William watched him squirm.

"You are Arduil Maxwell's son?" he asked.

The young man looked at him, pure hate in his eyes. "Aye."

"Then you are Ean."

Ean's response was to spit in William's direction, which brought a kick to the kidneys from Troy. As Ean went down in agony, William watched him without an inkling of compassion.

"You have been creating havoc," he said. "You should have realized your defeat when we took your women and children, but still, you tried to fight. Now, your clan is destroyed and you are my prisoner. I will, mayhap, not be so inclined to show mercy, young Ean."

Ean was gasping as the pain in his back started to subside a little. "That is of no consequence tae me," he breathed. "Ye're a Sassenach bastard and I'll fight ye until I die."

"That will not come for a long time yet."

Strangely, that brought Ean pause. He lifted his head, looking at William. "What do ye mean by that?" he said. "Kill me! I demand it!"

William shook his head. "Nay," he said. "Why would I

make you a martyr to your people?"

Ean struggled to sit up. "Ye Sassenach dog," he said, spittle flying from his lips. "Just kill me! Hang my body from a pole! Are ye a coward tae not destroy yer enemy?"

Thomas raised a hand again and Troy lifted his big boot, but William stopped them. He was looking at this young, arrogant Scotsman, seeing him for what he was—a frightened child who had taken on a man's game only to lose. But he wasn't a fool—he knew what the value of his death would be for his men. William had already stated it—executing Ean would make him a martyr, which was what he wanted.

William wasn't going to give it to him.

No matter how much he wanted to.

"I've heard that you told your allies that your young daughter was a captive at Gleann na Fola," he said, almost casually. "That was how you were trying to solicit their help for your attack on the fortress. Although it wasn't true, I can tell you what will be true now. There will, indeed, be a member of your family held captive by the House of de Wolfe because *you* are going to be my captive. I'm going to put you in the bowels of Castle Questing and let you rot. No martyrdom, no victory, no legend to your people. Just four cold walls and a lifetime of darkness. That is the price you pay for attacking a de Wolfe. And I will be certain to tell your allies how you cried all the way to your cell, like the child you are."

With that, he flicked his hand at Thomas and Blayth, who lifted Ean to his feet. The young man began to curse and spit and kick, so much so that Thomas had to throw him into a choke hold as they carried him out. William listed to the screaming fade from a man who hadn't gotten what he wanted. It had been William de Wolfe who emerged the ultimate victor.

Though William would never know the man named Gordie who had nearly turned the tides, and he would never know what, exactly, happened with the rush on the gatehouse to ensure Gordie could complete his task, none of that mattered because, in the end, the House of de Wolfe was triumphant.

And that was why William had come to Westerkirk.

To ensure everything happened the way he wanted it to.

"Well done, Papa," Scott said, breaking into his thoughts. "Making that man a martyr to the Scots would have had lasting consequences."

William looked at his eldest. "I knew Arduil," he said. "Troy, I think he was an ally of Red Keith at one point, was he not?"

Troy nodded. "He was," he said. "But not in the last years of his life. The man lived like a hermit. When Ean took control of the clan, we thought that might change, but it did not. Ean did not want allies with English relatives."

William snorted at the irony of that. "On the border, one can hardly avoid such a thing," he said. "Speaking of Red Keith, where is he? I've not seen him to thank him."

Troy scratched his head wearily. "The man may be willing to help us, but socializing with us is another matter," he said. "He's still a Scot, not a traitor, as he so eloquently put it to me."

William grinned. "He's an old man, set in his ways," he said. "I remember when we laid siege to Monteviot Tower, where you first met Rhos. Now, *that* was a battle."

That had Troy grinning, looking at Scott, who smirked and rolled his eyes. "The same battle where we saw naked Scots arses, and piss poured on young knights who challenged the Scots," Troy said. "Aye, *that* was a battle. It was a good day."

William continued to grin, thinking back on that particular

battle, seemingly so long ago. "All of us were there," he said in quiet reflection. "I think that is one of the last battles I can remember that had everyone of us in attendance. De Wolfe, de Norville, Hage. There were many."

Troy nodded. "Old knights from Northwood were there, also."

William's smile faded. "I will admit that a battle march has never seemed the same without Paris and Kieran," he said. "I do not mean they were any better, of course, just… different."

Scott went to his father and put his hand on the man's shoulder. "If Kieran were here, he would tell you that your time for battle marches is over," he said. "I do not know how we are going to explain your injured hand to Mama, but we had better think of something. She is going to be furious."

William looked at his hand, tightly wrapped. "I know," he sighed. "I will come up with an explanation. I always do."

Scott patted his shoulder before moving for the tent flap alongside Troy. "Try to get some sleep, Papa," he said. "We have everything under control. You needn't worry."

"I never do."

With that, the men quit the tent, heading out into the encampment to go about their duties. William put his head back, against the back of the chair, but he was too achy for sleep. He stood up from the chair, wearily, and walked to the tent opening. He watched his sons fade into the encampment, which was starting to settle in for the night.

Yet another encampment on yet another battle march.

William wasn't sure why he was feeling nostalgic, but he was. He suddenly missed Kieran very much. Kieran Hage had been in innumerable battles with him and William had always drawn comfort from the fact that he knew Kieran was fighting beside him. The man could swing a sword better than anyone, stronger than any man alive, and wiser than God himself.

He felt Kieran's presence strongly tonight.

Wandering out of the tent, he found himself thinking heavily on Kieran, walking around the tent and looking at the smoldering ruins of Bailie Castle. He could, of course, claim it as a spoil of victory, and he very well might, but tonight was more about vengeance than anything else. He wondered if Gar were even still alive. As he walked toward the castle beneath the dusk as it transformed into night, he thought on his grandson, who had been the beginning of a new life for the boy's father. William loved all of his grandsons equally, but there was something special about Gar. Perhaps it *was* because he represented a new life for Troy after the horrific loss of Helene. Gar had been a symbol of hope to the entire family, a light that brought them out of a very dark time.

He just couldn't face the thought of losing him.

There was a small hill to the west of Bailie and that was where William found himself, gazing up at the stars. They were so clear tonight that he swore he could have reached up and grabbed one. He was going to miss nights like this at the end of a battle, when the surge of excitement in his veins had cooled and he would give thanks that he had survived yet another fight. He was going to miss the camaraderie of the knights, of his sons, as they shared their stories and bonded over victory.

He was going to miss it all.

"He was wrong, you know."

It was a faint voice upon the breeze. In fact, William wasn't sure he'd even heard the words. Maybe he had imagined them. He looked around, knowing he was quite alone on the hill.

"Gar was wrong, William."

Now, he *was* imagining things. He heard those words more clearly and his heart began to pound, just a little. Maybe it had finally happened—he was finally losing his mind and there was nothing he could do to stop it. He thought that he should probably make his way back to his tent before he started foaming at the mouth and baying at the moon, but as he turned for the encampment, he caught sight of a shadow over in the trees to the south.

A shadow that was moving.

William wasn't armed, but he wasn't frightened. At least, not of an armed man. He was more frightened of losing his mind. As he stood there and watched, the shadow came closer until the moonbeams finally illuminated it.

Then, he could see it clearly.

A distinct shock rolled through him.

"God's Bones," he muttered. "It has happened. It had finally happened."

"What has?"

"I'm mad. I am genuinely mad."

"You are not mad, but you *are* seeing things."

William didn't say anything for a moment. He couldn't because there was a lump in his throat.

"Kieran? Am I truly seeing you?"

Kieran Hage was fighting off a grin. He was the color of the moonbeams, cold and pale, all shades of black and gray and white, but he looked the way William knew him in his prime—the most powerful man in England. He was young and strong and handsome, not old and ill as he had been at the end.

This was the Kieran that William would always remember.

"You might be," Kieran said. "Then again, you might not be. I may be a dream beneath the moonlight."

"Not to offend you, but when I dream of someone beneath the moonlight, it is not you."

Kieran grinned. "I am not offended," he said. "But I did come to tell you something."

"What?"

"That Gar was wrong when he told you that you were too old to be fighting," Kieran said, his smile fading. "And he was not injured because of you. He was injured because of a Scotsman."

William sighed faintly, still trying to figure out if this were some kind of fever dream, but he was quickly becoming overwhelmed with emotion.

"How do you know this?"

"Because I do," Kieran said. "Will you truly question an apparition?"

"It *is* you, isn't it?"

"It is."

William blinked his eye and the tears rolled down his cheek. "My God," he said hoarsely. "I have missed you so much."

Kieran's smile turned gentle. "And I have missed you," he said. "You remember when I lay dying and you came to me? You told me that I was free to let go. You told me that you would ensure our grandsons remembered me. You gave me permission to leave."

Tears continued to roll down William's face. "I remember."

"That was the kindest thing you have ever done for me," Kieran said. "Those were words I needed to hear. And now, I'm going to give you words that you need to hear."

"What words?"

Kieran took a step closer, his dark gaze intense. "That you are the greatest knight England has ever seen," he said seriously.

"I know you are thinking of hanging up your spurs. I know that Gar's words were hurtful. And I know that every time Scott or Troy try to tell you to stay out of a battle, it hurts you. I am here to tell you that you should fight to the end, William. They are only thinking of you, that is true, but they are doing it in a selfish way. They do not want to see you injured or killed. They do not want to lose you. But you were born for battle. You were born for nights like this, when a clan chief needs to be taught a lesson that only you can teach him. Your sons love you, but after all these years, they still do not understand you. Do not let them make you anything less than what you are. If you want to fight, then fight. But if you want to rest, then rest. You have earned the right to choose. Do not let others do it for you."

William wiped at his face, but the tears kept falling. "That is wisdom I have missed desperately," he muttered. "Paris tries to give me advice, and most of the time it is good advice, but it is not the same. Tell me something, Kieran."

"Anything."

"Am I dead right now? Is that why you are here and we can have a conversation?"

Kieran laughed softly. "You are not dead," he said. "You are merely sleeping. And this will be a dream you will not remember, at least not in detail. But the next time there is a battle, my words will come to you. I'm still with you, William. I have been with you at every battle you've ever fought, right by your side, whether you could see me or not."

That reassurance brought more tears to William's eye again. "I know," he said. "I think I've always known. I felt you tonight and here you are."

"I am always here, just out of your line of sight," Kieran said. "But I cannot stay. I wish I could, but I cannot. I just wanted to speak to you, if only for a brief moment. You have had a difficult time as of late."

"Difficult, indeed," William agreed, thinking on Gar, possibly dying back at Gleann na Fola. "Kieran, what about Gar?"

"What about him?"

"Is he going to survive?"

"This, I cannot tell you, but there is every reason to hope."

"Hope," William muttered. "Sometimes that is hard to come by."

"I know," Kieran said. "But you must have faith. That is what hope is born from."

William pondered that advice, drawing a tremendous amount of comfort from it. It was as if Kieran had never left, now standing here, carrying on a conversation. It took William back to years past when he had Kieran's steadying influence around. As he had told the man, he'd missed it terribly.

Even after all these years.

"Thank you," he finally said. "That means a great deal."

"I am glad."

"I could continue this conversation with you all night."

Kieran's expression was gentle. "As could I," he said. "But there is something more I wish to say to you before it ends."

"What is it?"

"Thank you for keeping every promise you made to me on my deathbed," Kieran said softly. "You are a man of your word. A man of honor. A friendship like ours will continue in eternity because a bond like ours cannot be broken."

"Agreed," William whispered. "But what about Paris?"

Kieran's features twisted into an annoyed expression. "Him, too, sadly enough," he said. "The three of us are destined to go through eternity together, I fear."

"You know that he married your widow."

"I know."

"And you are not troubled by it?"

Kieran shrugged. "I was her great love," he said. "Paris is her great salvation. She was very lonely, William. I cannot be angry that he is taking care of her. Above all else, she must be happy."

"Good," William said. "I always wondered what you would think."

"Now, you know."

"I do."

William realized that Kieran was starting to fade a little. The moonlight that illuminated him seemed to be undulating and changing, the brightness going out of it. That told William his time with Kieran had come to a close.

"Are you leaving now?" he asked.

Kieran nodded. "I am," he said. "But we will see each other again."

"In this life or in the next?"

"Both."

William fought down the lump in his throat. "Then I look forward to it, wherever our next encounter may be," he said. "Thank you, Kieran. For everything, I thank you."

"I could say the same," Kieran said. "And I have. Until next we meet, my dear friend."

William lifted a hand to bid the man farewell. His heart was aching, but it was also fortified by the unexpected appearance of the man he loved as a brother. As he watched, Kieran faded back into the shadows of the trees and disappeared.

The night was lonely once again.

"Papa? Papa, wake up."

Suddenly, William opened his eye and was back in his tent, in the chair he'd been sitting in. He'd leaned his head back to rest on the chair and he was still here. He looked up to see Troy was standing over him.

"Papa?" Troy said, peering at him. "Are you well?"

It took William a moment to orient himself. He looked around as if he had no idea where he was before realizing that he was in his tent near Bailie Castle. *Still* in the tent and *still* in the chair he thought he'd climbed out of. Wearily, he rubbed his eye.

"God's Bones," he muttered. "I did not realize I'd fallen asleep. I must be more exhausted than I thought."

"I know," Troy said. "And I'll help you to bed, but I had to come and tell you that we just received a missive from Gleann na Fola."

William stood up wearily. "What missive?"

"From Uncle Paris," Troy said. "He wanted to tell us that Gar's fever broke."

William looked at him in surprise. "He is recovering?"

Troy nodded, a rare smile on his face. "He must be," he said. "Uncle Paris would not have sent the missive otherwise, I'm sure. But he wanted us to know. My son is going to live, Papa. He's going to *live*!"

William put his arms around Troy, who hugged him in return. They shed tears of joy at that moment, rejoicing in news that was most welcome. It seemed that all things came together at that moment, the way they were supposed to, and there was reason to celebrate. The appearance of Kieran, which William did not remember, was only a foretaste of that faith he'd encouraged William to have. After that, the rest fell into place.

A battle of vengeance.

Justice dispensed.
An unexpected visitor.
And a young knight who would live to see the next day.
It was a grand celebration, indeed.

CHAPTER TWENTY-TWO

Gleann na Fola Castle

SOMEONE WAS SNORING in his ear.

It was rhythmic, almost soothing… in, out… in, out… but it was becoming louder, enough so that he simply couldn't sleep through it any longer. Additionally, he could feel hot breath on his cheek and it wasn't pleasant. Disgusting, actually. When he opened an eye, all he could see was pale hair and part of a snout.

Even half asleep, he knew what it was.

"God," he muttered with revulsion, putting a hand up and feeling the dog that was lying on him. "Queenie?"

On a chair next to the bed, Mattie had been sleeping with her head on the bed and her left arm across Gar's thighs. She heard her name but thought she was dreaming until Gar stirred slightly and called her again.

"Queenie, move the dog, please."

Head up like a shot, Mattie stood up so fast that her chair tipped over. Instantly, she was hovering over him, yanking Winchester away from Gar as the dog wondered what he'd done wrong to be treated so poorly.

"Gar?" Mattie gasped, her hand on his forehead, which was surprisingly cool. "I'm here, my love. I'm here."

His eyes were still closed, but he put a hand up to grasp hers and she held it tightly, trying desperately not to weep because he was awake. And moving. And talking.

It was a miracle.

"Where am I?" he asked, tongue thick.

She kissed his hand. "Home," she said. "You are home. How do you feel?"

He twitched, trying to move a little, and grunted in pain. "I think I've been better," he said. "What has happened?"

Mattie stroked his brow in a comforting gesture. "What do you remember?" she asked. "Do you remember the battle, here, at Gleann na Fola? When the postern gate was breached?"

Gar's eyes rolled open, crusty and bloodshot. "The breach," he muttered as the cobwebs of his mind began to clear a little. "Aye… I remember it. I remember seeing my grandfather struck by a Scotsman. I went to save him and… I do not remember what happened. Is Poppy well? Did he survive?"

Mattie nodded. "He not only survived, but he took the army into Scotland and razed the castle at Westerkirk," she said. "The army was victorious."

He looked at her, then. "Westerkirk?" he said, confused. "How long have I been unconscious?"

"About six days."

Before he could reply, Winchester managed to jump on the bed again and the chamber door opened, revealing Jordan and Rhoswyn. Mattie bolted to her feet.

"Look!" she said excitedly. "He is awake!"

Jordan and Rhoswyn rushed to the bed, seeing for themselves that Gar was lucid. Rhoswyn was so happy that she nearly wept with joy, taking her son's hand and kissing it as Jordan bent over him and put a gentle hand on his forehead, making sure the fever was completely gone.

It was a moment they'd worked so hard for.

Mattie stood back, watching everything with more relief than she could express. The days had been so dark and hope had been such a difficult thing to come by, so to see Gar awake and speaking to his grandmother was almost more than Mattie could bear. Tears of happiness sprang to her eyes and she kept wiping at them, watching Gar with his mother and grandmother, until Rhoswyn held out a hand to her.

"Mattie, love," she said. "Come here. Dunna stand back there."

Mattie came alongside the bed and Gar reached out to grasp her hand. "My beautiful Queenie," he said. "Mama, I would like a moment with my wife. Can you fetch me something to drink? I kept having dreams that someone was trying to force spoiled milk down my throat, but I find that I am quite thirsty."

Rhoswyn chuckled. "Ye dinna dream that, lad," she said. "Someone *was* trying tae force ye tae drink medicine, but it did ye good. It worked."

He curled his lip. "Whatever it was, it was awful," he said. "I take it that I was wounded?"

Rhoswyn's smile faded. "Ye dunna remember?"

Mattie looked up at her. "He only remembers helping William," she said softly. "He does not remember anything after that."

As Rhoswyn nodded in realization, Mattie returned her attention to Gar. "You have a wound to your torso," she said. "Your grandmother and Uncle Paris tended you. You had a fever, but it broke two nights ago."

He looked at her, trying hard to piece together what she was telling him. "I was cut down?"

"Not cut down," Rhoswyn said firmly. "Ye stayed on yer feet until yer grandfather made ye come inside. Ye were strong, Gar, I promise."

He sighed softly, catching snippets of memory from the battle, but what came back to him in general were the words he'd said to his grandfather when Gar had dispatched the big Scotsman who had been trying to kill him.

"I think… I said terrible things to Poppy," he said, lifting a big hand and rubbing at his forehead. "He was fighting when he shouldn't have been and I became angry with him. I must apologize to him."

Jordan heard him. "Whatever ye said was forgiven the moment ye said it," she said. "Ye mustn't concern yerself with that now. Ye must only think of getting well again."

Gar looked at his grandmother, a woman who had been a part of his life as much as his mother had. His earliest memories included Jordan, a genuinely sweet woman who had a soft side for her grandchildren. Reaching out, he took her hand.

"I would not have hurt him for the world, Matha," he murmured, using the name that the de Wolfe grandchildren called her. "I should not have shouted at him. I'm very sorry."

Jordan leaned over and kissed him on the forehead. "Dunna be troubled," she assured him. "Poppy has taken worse abuse from me."

"And me," Paris said as he swept into the chamber. He'd been across the landing, in a smaller chamber, and he'd heard the conversation, including Jordan's last few words. "William will never remember what words you said to him in anger, Gar.

Nor would any grandparent. You are worrying needlessly."

Gar grinned at the sight of his uncle. "Who let you in?" he demanded weakly. "My men have standing orders never to let you into my garrison."

Paris struggled not to grin too as he stood next to Rhoswyn, collecting Gar's wrist to feel for the strength of his pulse. "Then your men are weak and you are a terrible commander," he said, watching Gar chuckle. "It is a good thing they let me in, however. I saved your life. You must name your firstborn after me."

That brought laughter all around, including from Mattie, who also blushed furiously at the mention of a child. In order to have a child, one had to mate, and she still wasn't accustomed to the idea that everyone knew she and Gar were doing naughty, delicious things. When Paris winked at her, she thought she might burst into embarrassed flame, which he thought was quite hilarious.

"I think my grandfather would disown me if I were to name a child after you," Gar said. "Mayhap I will name my next horse after you."

Paris cocked his head as if thinking on that compromise. "It had better be the most beautiful stallion the world has ever seen," he said. "Meanwhile, I do believe you will recover fully, young Gar. I will admit that I had my doubts."

Gar's smile faded. "Is it that bad?"

Paris sat down in the chair next to the bed and began to cut away the bindings around Gar's torso. "It is never a good thing when the stomach has been compromised," he said. "The blade pierced things that should not be pierced, but you are on the mend. I believe that firmly."

Gar was clearly relieved by that statement. He looked at

Mattie, standing toward the end of the bed, and smiled at her. There was joy and hope all around.

"My brave lass," he said to her, as if she were the only person in the room. "I think your marriage to me has taken you from your peaceful life and thrown you into the fire. Thank you for not abandoning me."

Mattie smiled, putting her hand on his foot because it was the part of his body that she was standing closest to. "I had no choice," she said. "If I returned home, my father would only send me back. Moreover, I love you. I could not leave something I love."

He mouthed, *I love you,* in return as Paris pulled away the last of the bindings and began to inspect the wound, which was healing up nicely now. Rhoswyn stepped away from the bed and went to the door, summoning a servant for watered wine and broth, and Mattie had to turn away from the bed because she still couldn't stomach seeing that enormous gash in the right side of Gar's torso.

Gar, however, strained to catch a look at it, but Paris told him not to move too much lest he tear his stitches. As this was going on, Mattie wandered over to the lancet window with a view of the gatehouse. It was the first time in days that she'd been able to look from that window without feeling a sense of angst and grief. But though she had every hope in the world for Gar's recovery, there was someone else on her mind who would never recover.

And Gar didn't know about it yet.

"Gar?" she said.

His head rolled in her direction. "Aye, sweetheart?"

She struggled not to tear up. "Maksim did not survive the battle that saw you injured," she said. "Your father said he died a hero. I... I must take him home."

Gar stared at her a moment before closing his eyes, grief rippling across his face. "My God," he murmured. "What happened?"

"He sounded the alarm when the Scots breached the castle and they killed him for it."

Gar was still trying to remember the details of that night, but some were still evading him. He didn't remember that he'd sent Maksim outside to inspect the castle for the night watch, but that was probably for the best. More than likely, he would have blamed himself and that wouldn't have done him any good. Instead, all he could think of was the loss and his wife's grief.

"I am so sorry, my love," he said quietly. "So very sorry."

Mattie lost the battle against the tears and she wiped them away quickly. "My parents still do not know," she said. "Your grandfather was going to send them word, but he has been in battle. I think that I should tell them myself when I bring Maksim home."

Gar was struggling to sit up. "Of course you should," he said. "And I will go with you."

Paris had to put his hands on Gar to keep him from moving too much. "Easy, lad," he said. "I've warned you against tearing the stitches."

Gar wasn't listening. "Then help me sit up," he said. "Please, Uncle Paris."

Paris wasn't happy about it, but he complied. He pulled Gar into an upright position as Jordan packed pillows behind him. It was enough support that it didn't put any strain on the wound site, but Gar was holding out his hand to Mattie, silently begging her to come to him. In spite of the uncovered injury that made Mattie sick to look at, she did. She crossed the floor and sat down on the bed beside Gar as he pulled her into his powerful embrace.

For her brother, she wept in his arms.

Paris and Jordan stepped away, realizing this was an intensely private moment for Gar and Mattie. As they left the chamber and quietly closed the door, Mattie sobbed for Maksim, this time with Gar's comfort. But she also sobbed because Gar was *able* to give her comfort. Up until the man's fever broke, she wasn't sure that would ever happen again. But it had.

It was a bittersweet moment.

"He just wanted to belong," she wept. "He was so happy at the prospect of serving here, with you."

Gar had his mouth on her forehead. "He was a fine knight and a good friend," he said softly. "I will miss him."

"As will I," Mattie said. But then, she raised her head and looked at him. "He always looked out for me, you know. I think the main reason he came to Gleann na Fola with us was to make sure you treated me well. He was here to protect me."

Gar smoothed the hair away from her face, gently. "And I shall happily continue that duty," he said. "He will be well remembered, Queenie. I promise you."

"I will not name our firstborn after Paris, but I will name him after my brother."

Gar grinned. "I think that is an excellent suggestion."

"Truly?"

"Truly."

Mattie gazed into his eyes, reaching up to caress his stubbled face. "The past several days have shown me something," she said softly.

"What is that?"

"It is difficult to put into words," she said. "Mostly, it has shown me a glimpse of the life I'd always hoped for. I spent years dreaming about our marriage, Gar. Dreaming of what it would be like, what you would be like. That young man who saved me from a bully was the only dream I ever had."

A smile crept across his lips. "Are you sure the last few days haven't been a nightmare instead?" he said. "I can only imagine what you've gone through. I'm so terribly sorry you had to go through it."

But Mattie shook her head. "This will sound strange, but I'm glad I did," she said. "Not for Maksim's death, of course, but for the experience of watching you as a garrison commander. Of watching you as you dealt with your men and your friends and your family. If I knew nothing else about you prior to these moments, the way the people around you respect and honor you would have told me everything I needed to know. The bond you share with them is something not even my dreams could have imagined. *You* are more than I could have imagined, Gar. And I am very thankful that you agreed to marry me. Even if my dog did destroy your breeches."

She turned a beautiful moment into a humorous one and Gar started to laugh, wrapping her up in his embrace once more and hugging her as tightly as he could without compromising his stitches. They pained him when he moved, but he didn't care. He felt weak and drained, but it didn't matter. All of it was a small price to pay for having his wife in his arms.

His wife.

The wife he'd never wanted.

The wife he now couldn't live without.

"Your dog destroying my clothing was the best thing that

could have happened to me," he said. "It introduced me to a woman I am not worthy of, but a woman I love with all my heart. I will strive for the rest of my life to be worthy of you, Queenie. Thank God I was able to marry the most remarkable woman I have ever met."

Mattie smiled at him, her hands on his face as he gently kissed her. It was a deeply intimate moment, one with a depth of emotion that neither one of them had ever experienced. As they reveled in the tenderness, someone knocked swiftly on the door before throwing it open.

"Gar!" It was Caria. "Poppy has returned with the army! Matha has gone to greet him, but she says I must make you stay here. She does not want you getting out of bed and she will bring Poppy to you."

Gar snorted as Caria swept into the chamber and ran right for the lancet window so she could watch the returning army enter the gatehouse.

"I do believe I am hardly able to get out of bed," Gar said. "Even if I could, I have nothing to wear. Where are my breeches, Queenie?"

Mattie chuckled, pointing to the infamous patchwork breeches draped over the back of a chair near the hearth. When Gar saw them, he sighed with satisfaction.

"Ah," he said. "It is good to see my old friend. Thank you for not burning them while I was incapacitated."

Mattie's laughter grew. "I had other things on my mind, Gar," she said. "Burning those terrible breeches was not among them."

"Terrible? *You* made them for me."

"An action I sorely regret, as I've told you."

He scowled at her, but he didn't mean it. "So long as you

did not do anything to them," he said threateningly. But he caught Caria snickering and he frowned at her. "And you—I'm curious to know how you intend to keep me here should I desire to leave."

Caria's answer was to rush over to the bed and lie across his legs. She giggled uncontrollably as the dog jumped on the bed and licked her in the face before moving over to Gar and licking him in the face, too. Gar found himself petting the dog, who was now incredibly friendly, as Caria was repeatedly hit in the face by the wagging tail.

All of it, joyful chaos.

And it was a moment he would remember for the rest of his life.

Eventually, Jordan did bring William to Gar's chamber so that William could see for himself that his grandson was going to recover. Troy wasn't far behind him, as were Andreas, Reed, Corey, and a host of other de Wolfe cousins, uncles, and relatives, all of them crowding into that large chamber, all of them having the opportunity to speak to Gar, shake his hand, or hug him. That young, capable knight who had worked so hard against a common enemy, who had fought the good fight, and who was now on the road to recovery.

In the weeks to follow, Maksim was escorted home by Gar, when he was well enough to move, as well as William and twelve more de Wolfe knights. Mattie was among the escort, too, informing her parents of Maksim's valiant deeds and ultimate sacrifice, and stood beside them as their only son was buried in the family chapel. As difficult as it was for the de Reyne family, they took comfort in Maksim's heroic last actions. They took even more comfort when, eleven months later, Mattie delivered a healthy son.

A son she named Maksim.

Unfortunately, William did not live to see his great-grandson born, but Gar felt his presence that night. He was in Jordan's very existence, in his son's first cries, and in the love that Gar had for his wife. William de Wolfe, a knight of legend, was in every touch, every breath, every word his family spoke, in that moment and every moment thereafter. But when it came down to William's final moments on earth, on a warm August night with his family all around him, Kieran's words came to ring true.

If you want to fight, then fight. But if you want to rest, then rest. You have earned the right to choose. Do not let others do it for you.

In the end, William didn't. He chose for himself.

And that was the way he wanted it.

EPILOGUE

Ten years later
Castle Questing

HE COULDN'T GET them off the crypts.

Gar had offered to take his sons outside into the sunshine, affording his pregnant wife some time to rest, but the boys were much different under their father's control than under their mother's. Five young lads, all of them lively and full of life, and once their father took them outside, they ran straight to the chapel at Castle Questing because it was a place with things to climb on.

And that was what they were doing.

Climbing.

They reminded Gar very much of him and his own brothers when they were younger, and Troy laughed every time he saw Gar trying to control his gang of ruffians—and he especially laughed on this night when he went on the hunt for Gar because no one had seen him in a while. Wandering out into the bailey, he followed the sounds of the shouting children to find Gar sitting on a bench that had been installed in the chapel, watching his children hide from one another.

"There you are," Troy said. "Your wife was wondering where you were."

Gar grinned as he looked up at his father. "Here," he said, gesturing to the boys. "They wanted to visit Poppy and Matha, so here we are."

Troy sat down next to Gar, watching Mak, Keith, Milo, Jasper, and Oliver chase each other around the crypts. They were all dark-haired, all in the image of their father, except for Oliver, who very much favored his mother. Still, they were a wild bunch that had exhausted their mother's old dog so much that Winchester had gone back to Hensingham Castle to live out his elder years in peace with Mattie's parents.

Peace was certainly nothing he'd get at Gleann na Fola these days.

"This is exactly where they need to be," Troy said, eyeing his mother's new crypt. The grief of her recent passing was still fresh for the family. "Matha should see what wild animals her Scots blood has created. They are only like this because of her."

Gar started laughing. "But Mama is Scots, too," he said. "It cannot all be Matha's fault."

Troy shrugged. "I tend to disagree," he said. "Speaking of disagreement, I see you're wearing those patchwork breeches again and I heard that your wife told you not to. Well?"

Gar was still grinning as he looked down at the breeches that had become a legend in his family. "I wear them at every wedding, and proudly so," he said. "Mattie made these for me when we first met and I wore them at our wedding. They bring good fortune. I'll tell you what I told her—I am bringing good fortune to the new couple by wearing them to their celebration."

Troy grunted. "Is that what you think?" he said. "They look terrible, Gar."

"I do not care."

Troy rolled his eyes at his stubborn son and those linen pants that had followed him around through the years. Everyone knew them. Everyone hated them. Everyone but Gar, that was. That being the case, no one could really fault him for being so attached to them.

It *was* rather sweet.

"Have it your own way," Troy said. "But I did come out here for a reason. Evidently, Mattie is having pains and I have been sent to tell you."

That news wiped the smile off Gar's face. "The baby is coming?" he said, sounding concerned. "It is a little early for that."

Troy lifted his big shoulders. "Babies come when they feel like it," he said. "You came almost a month before you were supposed to and you were quite well, so do not be concerned. Mattie is in good hands with Rhos and Avie and a host of other women. Mayhap we will have something more than a de Wolfe wedding to celebrate on this night."

That was why they were at Castle Questing to begin with. Edward de Wolfe's son was marrying none other than Lady de Reyne's former ward, Agnes de Witt, and Edward was adamant that the wedding be held at the de Wolfe seat, so there had been three days of celebration leading up to the marriage mass this morning. The rest of the day had been a feast to end all feasts and Gar's five children were so wound up on sweets and honey that he had gladly taken them off his wife's hands so they could run off their excitement.

Still, he hadn't intended for his sixth child to be born here.

"I did not want her to come, you know," he said, unhappy.

"She is too close to delivering the child and I wanted her to remain at Gleann na Fola, but she would not hear of it. She insisted on coming to the wedding and bringing our coveted goat cheese as a gift. It is expected, you know. We don't go anywhere without that damn cheese."

The Gleann na Fola goat cheese was indeed coveted. He wasn't wrong about that. The idea Mattie had those years ago had blossomed into something that made the castle a good deal of money and she was very proud of it. Truth be told, so was he, and everywhere they went, every event they attended, people expected them to bring that wonderful cheese.

"It *is* rather tasty," Troy said. "You cannot blame her. It is her cousin getting married, after all, and she wanted to celebrate with the family."

"That about sums up the situation," Gar said. "And now, here we are. Her determination to come to the wedding and bring cheese has brought on the birth of our child."

Troy put his hand on his shoulder, struggling not to grin at the nervous father who was evidently blaming cheese for childbirth. "Not to worry," he said. "She is receiving the best of care. You and I will remain out here with the boys while the women do their work."

Gar wasn't so sure about that. He wanted to see his wife now, to find out just how serious the situation was. "Will you mind the lads?" he said, standing up. "I want to see my wife."

It was obvious that no amount of fatherly advice was going to ease him, so Troy waved him on. "Go," he said. "I'll make sure the boys do not kill one another."

"They're not savages, Papa."

"That is up for debate."

Gar frowned for a split second before breaking into a grin.

Troy was honest, if nothing else, and as Gar departed the chapel, he could hear a scream rise up from Jasper. That was his five-year-old. If anyone was going to scream, it was Jasper. He could hear Troy trying to figure out why Jasper was screaming, but he just kept walking.

He had a woman to see.

The keep of Castle Questing was an enormous, multistoried structure with close to fifty chambers. The size of it was legendary. It had belonged to the Dudley family before it became the property of William de Wolfe, and William and Jordan had raised their family here. Most of their grandchildren had been born here as well, and now, great-grandchildren were being born. As Gar headed into the keep, he ran into guests for his cousin's wedding and they all wanted to stop and chat. Given that he wasn't in the mood for idle conversation, Gar tried to be as polite as he could, pushing through the happy, drunk crowds until he spied a familiar face.

His Aunt Bridey.

Brighton de Wolfe was married to Patrick de Wolfe, both of whom were attending this wedding. Gar came up behind his aunt and kissed her on the cheek, capturing her attention.

"Gar!" Brighton gasped. She was a beautiful woman with dark hair and big blue eyes. "What are you doing here?"

"Looking for my wife," he said. "I was outside with my lads, but Papa told me that she is having pains. Do you know where I may find her?"

Brighton nodded quickly. "That's why I asked you what you were doing here, in the midst of this celebration, and not with your wife," she said. Then, she pointed to the ceiling. "She is in Matha's chamber. Your mother is with her."

Gar thanked her and quickly headed up the stairs. The

enormous chamber that William and Jordan had shared was on the top floor, with a brilliant view of the bailey and the verdant countryside beyond. Gar entered the chamber to find his mother, Aunt Avrielle, and two of his sisters standing around as Mattie sat on the end of the bed, speaking to them and seemingly in good spirits. When Gar walked in, looking anxious, the women tittered at his expression.

"She's not going tae explode, Gar," Rhoswyn said. "But it seems as if yer new son is going tae make an appearance soon."

Gar looked straight at Mattie. "How are you feeling?" he said, pushing past his mother to take Mattie's hand and kiss it. "Are you in much pain? Do you need to lie down?"

Mattie grinned and squeezed his hand. "I am quite well," she said. "The pains have started and my waters have broken, so it should not take long."

He looked at her, confused and horrified. "Then why are you not lying down?" he demanded. "You must lie down, sweetheart. Please lie down."

He was beginning to fuss and Mattie squeezed his hand again to calm him. "I am very well," she assured him softly. "I do not need to lie down, I promise. I am content sitting for now."

"But the baby is *coming*."

He wasn't going to let it go and Mattie sighed heavily at her nervous husband. "Very well," she said. "Will you sit next to me and hold my hand if I lie down?"

He nodded. "I will," he said, quickly taking the chair that his mother was pushing at him without releasing Mattie's hand. He sat, looking at her apprehensively. "There. I'm sitting. You must lie down."

Mattie did, but only because she'd told him she would. The

women in the chamber went about preparing for the coming birth by fetching hot water and blankets and rags, for childbirth was a messy business. For the moment, they left Mattie and Gar alone; the pair were only focused on each other.

"Be calm, my love," Mattie said. "There is really nothing to become upset over. I've done this five times before, so I know how to do it."

A strong pain washed over her, but she did nothing more than grunt softly as Gar squeezed her hand and told her how brave she was. Rhoswyn, who had noticed the pain, came alongside the bed and put her hand on Mattie's belly.

"That one was close behind the other," she said softly. "Do ye feel like pushing yet, sweetheart?"

Mattie was quickly growing uncomfortable. The servants had brought out the birthing chair, the one Jordan and several of her daughters and daughters-in-law had used, and Mattie had intended on using it, too, but she was lying on the bed to please Gar, simply to keep him calm. The pains weren't so bad when she was sitting up, but shifting to her back made them come on more swiftly and strongly.

Things were definitely in motion.

"No pushing yet," she said. "I will lie here with my husband for a moment and then he can leave when I move to the chair."

"You want me to leave?" Gar said, hurt. "But I was there for Jasper and Oliver. You let me stay."

"Do you want to stay for this one?"

"I want the first arms to hold my son to be mine."

It was a sweet plea, something he'd said with the last two boys she'd delivered. He hadn't said it with the first three because he'd been terrified of the childbirth process, but Andreas had convinced him that being present with one's wife when she gave birth to your son was a soul-fortifying experience. It had been, except the first time with Jasper, Gar had nearly gagged when he saw his child emerging from his wife. He'd been embarrassed until Mattie reminded how she first reacted to battle wounds those years ago.

Unsurprisingly, that didn't make him feel better.

But being the first one to hold his son did.

"Then you'd better be ready to hold him—because I think he is coming," she said, grunting as another pain washed over her. "Help me to the birthing chair, Gar. This baby is not going to wait."

Trying to keep his nerves under control, Gar gently pulled her up from the bed as he and his mother helped her over to the birthing chair where Avrielle was waiting. Everyone else was busy around them, making sure the water was ready, making sure the rags were ready to clean up the mess. Someone had spread a large towel underneath the chair to help mitigate the blood and fluids that would make the floor very slippery, and Mattie sat down carefully as Rhoswyn pulled up the skirt of her dress. She never even had the chance to change from her wedding finery, which seemed to concern her more than the impending birth of the child at the moment.

"Can we remove the dress?" she asked, feeling another strong pain as she lifted her arms. "Gar, can you help me, please?"

Gar went to work on the laces up the back of the dress, quickly loosening them so he could lift the yellow silk over her head. But just as he pulled it up, Mattie suffered a huge pain and she bore down, groaning.

"The head is here, Mattie!" Avrielle said encouragingly. "Push with your next pain, sweetheart. Your child is ready to be born!"

Gar paused midway in removing the dress, peering down to where his child's head had just emerged into the world. "Is he here?" he said, incredulous and excited. "Is it male?"

"Gar!" Mattie shrieked. "My gown!"

He looked at her, startled, only to realize he'd left the dress over her face and head so she couldn't see a thing. It looked like the top half of her was covered with a big blanket and he yanked it free, greatly remorseful.

"My apologies," he said, kissing her forehead. "I was simply excited to see the child. I am very sorry, truly."

Mattie frowned at him, pushing her hair out of her eyes because the inept removal of the dress had messed her coiffure. Before she could become irate with him, however, another pain rolled over her and she gave a big push—only for the child to come sliding out into Avrielle's waiting hands.

"A lass!" Avrielle said. "Mattie, you have a daughter!"

Mattie crowed happily. "Praise the saints," she said, panting with exertion from the fast delivery. "Gar, did you hear? A lass!"

Gar, who had been momentarily shocked that his wife had actually given birth to a girl-child, quickly put out his hands.

"Give her to me," he said, enraptured by the first glimpse of his daughter. "Please, let me hold her."

With the help of Rhoswyn, Avrielle cut the cord and wrapped the child up in a clean blanket so the eager father could take her.

"Careful, Gar," Avrielle said as she handed over the precious cargo. "Be very careful with your little girl."

Gar was quite competent with infants. Unlike most fathers, he liked being active in their rearing and care. He'd found a good deal of satisfaction and joy in it. He clutched the little one to his chest, bring her over so that Mattie could see her. Together, the parents admired their latest offspring.

"Look how beautiful she is," Gar said, awe in his voice. "She has your hair, Queenie. It's the same color."

Mattie was inspecting the little hands, making sure the infant had all ten fingers. "She's magnificent," she said. "I think she looks like you."

Gar grinned, but there were tears of emotion in his eyes. "She looks like *you*," he said softly, turning to kiss Mattie sweetly. "Thank you, my love. I am so very grateful."

Mattie accepted his kisses. It did her heart good to see how enchanted he was with a daughter. After so many sons, she honestly hadn't been sure she would ever have a girl and was thrilled to know her fears had been for naught. But as Gar kissed her cheek, the pains in her belly started up again and she grunted when a particularly strong one rolled over her.

"God's Bones," she muttered. "That was painful."

"It is the afterbirth," Avrielle said, her hand on Mattie's belly. "It is coming away."

Mattie nodded, but on the tail of the strong pain came another one, even stronger than the first. She gasped at the force of it.

"That does not feel like the afterbirth coming away," she said. "I know what that feels like and that is not it. Something is wrong."

Those words sent terror into Gar's heart and he looked at his wife in panic as both Rhoswyn and Avrielle struggled to see what was happening down below. Mattie's belly was contracting tightly and she was in a good deal of pain, but after a minute of trying to figure out why, it was Rhoswyn who finally realized what was happening.

"A second baby," she said. "There are twins."

"Twins?" Gar gasped. "Two… *two* babies?"

Mattie gripped the chair, grunting as more pain rolled through her. She was giving birth again, so soon after the first one, and the pain had quickly reached a desperate level.

"Can you see it?" she begged. "Please, can you see it? Is it coming?"

It was. Feet-first. Rhoswyn and Avrielle passed concerned glances as Mattie struggled to push the child out. They didn't dare convey their fears to Gar, who was standing beside Mattie, holding the first infant and trying not to become distraught at what was unfolding in front of him. Rhoswyn, who had suffered through a breech birth with her fourth child, knew that this one would be more grueling. She spoke calmly.

"This bairn is a wee bit naughty," she said. "He's coming out with his feet first, Mattie. It just makes it a little more difficult tae push him out, but he will come. With yer next pain, push as hard as ye can, sweetheart."

Terrified, Gar reached down to grasp Mattie's left hand and she squeezed hard enough to break bones as she struggled to push the infant out. Gar didn't even want to see what was happening. He knew it was something terrible and it was all he could do to keep from breaking down. For Mattie, he had to be strong.

He had to be brave.

"Push, Queenie," he said softly. "You're doing so well, my love. You are so brave."

Mattie pushed and pushed. Several minutes later, she was still pushing and Gar looked at his mother to see what her expression was. If he could see fear, he knew he was going to lose his composure, but Rhoswyn was calm, as was Avrielle.

The infant's legs had been delivered and, with a little turning and twisting, a second little girl slid right out into her grandmother's waiting hands.

"Another lass," Rhoswyn announced as Avrielle moved quickly to cut the cord. "A beautiful little lass, Mattie. She's perfect."

But the baby wasn't crying. As exhausted as she was, Mattie realized almost immediately that the child wasn't crying and fear clutched at her.

"Why isn't she making noise?" she asked, frightened. "Why isn't she crying?"

Gar was still holding her hand, but he knelt down next to her and put his free arm around her, hugging her tightly, his lips against her temple.

"All will be well," he whispered. "I swear it, all will be well. She's simply a quiet lass, 'tis all. Give her time."

Rhoswyn was rubbing the child vigorously, trying to force her to breathe, as Avrielle dealt with the afterbirth, which finally came. Just when the tension in the chamber reached a splitting level, the infant let out a weak cry, piercing the warm air.

Mattie began to weep.

"Is she truly well?" she asked. "She is breathing?"

"She is breathing," Rhoswyn assured her calmly, wrapping the infant up. "She's turning pink now. She's well, Mattie, I promise. It just took her a little longer, that's all."

Mattie wanted to hold her, so Avrielle handed the infant over to the desperate mother. With Gar holding the other infant, who was now dozing, the parents doted over their twin girls, one of whom had had a difficult time coming into the world. But she was here now, and seemingly well, and all was right once again.

Gar had never felt so much relief in his entire life.

And gratitude.

"They're beautiful," he murmured, kissing Mattie tenderly. "How do you feel? Are you feeling poorly at all? Do you want to lie down?"

Mattie's tears had calmed sufficiently now that she was holding the second twin, a little girl who was indeed quite pink now that she'd filled her lungs a few times.

"I will be perfect," she said. "I'm simply tired."

"I would believe that," Gar said, his free arm around her as he looked between their infants. "I'm tired simply from watching. But we have two lasses, Queenie. *Two.* I do not think we chose any names for lasses, did we?"

Mattie chuckled wearily. "I did," she said. "But you were convinced it would be a boy. I refuse to name one of my daughters Henry."

He grinned. "Henrietta?"

Mattie shook her head. "Nay," she said, inspecting a tiny, flailing hand and admiring the beautiful shape of the fingers. "I was trying to decide between naming a daughter after your grandmother or my mother. Now, I do not have to choose. They will be called Jordan and Julia."

Gar smiled, looking between his daughters. "Jordan and Julia," he murmured. "Those are perfect names."

Mattie sighed with contentment as he kissed her forehead, hugging her as tightly as he could while the infants mewled and squirmed. Their family had been blessed with two new daughters who, in the weeks to come, would make clear that they were identical. In the years to come, the exploits of Jordan and Julia de Wolfe would become legend.

But that is a story for another time.

As Gar went to inform his family that his wife had given birth to two beautiful daughters, Rhoswyn and Avrielle put Mattie to bed so she could feed the infants and gain some much-needed rest herself. When Gar came back to the chamber later that night, after the boys had been put to bed, he found Mattie lying on her side with Jordan and Julia swaddled tightly next to her. Jordan was suckling on the left breast while Julia was sleeping soundly.

Sliding into bed on the other side, Gar lay down with the new infants between him and his wife, watching the infant feed and marveling at what their love had created. For certain, every child they'd had was conceived in a love that would outlast the sun. Not every child born in the world could claim such a thing, but theirs could.

It was a love story for the ages.

And, yes… Gar wore the patchwork pants to every wedding of his children to remind them what true love looked like.

They looked like an old, stained pair of linen breeches.

And the legend of the Patchwork Pants lived on.

ꟹ THE END ꟹ

Children of Gar and Mattie

Maksim “Mak”

Keith

Milo

Jasper

Oliver

Jordan

Julia

Eleanor

Henry

Douglas

De Wolfe Pack Generations:

WolfeHeart

WolfeStrike

WolfeSword

WolfeBlade

WolfeLord

WolfeShield

Nevermore

WolfeAx

WolfeBorn

WolfeBite

WolfeHound

WolfeBlood

The Parents, Children, and Grandchildren of de Wolfe

(Note: Don't be intimidated by these family trees—skip over them if you wish and then refer back to them if you need clarification on a relationship)

William (deceased 1296 A.D.) and Jordan Scott de Wolfe
Total children: 10
Total grandchildren: 75 (including 4 deceased, 7 adopted, 3 step grandchildren)

Scott (Troy's twin)—(Wife #1 Lady Athena de Norville, has issue. Wife #2 Lady Avrielle Huntley du Rennic, has issue)

With Athena

- William (married Lily de Lohr, has issue.)
- Thomas "Tor"
- Andrew (deceased)
- Beatrice (deceased)

With Avrielle

- Sophia (with Nathaniel du Rennic)
- Stephen (with Nathaniel du Rennic)
- Sorcha (with Nathaniel du Rennic)
- Jeremy
- Nathaniel

- Alexander
- Seraphina
- Jordan

Troy (Scott's twin)—(Wife #1 Lady Helene de Norville, has issue. Wife #2 Lady Rhoswyn Kerr, has issue)

With Helene

- Andreas
- Acacia (deceased)
- Arista (deceased)

With Rhoswyn

- Gareth
- Corey
- Reed
- Tavin
- Tristan
- Elsbeth
- Madeleine

Patrick—(Married to Lady Brighton de Favereux, has issue)

- Markus
- Cassius
- Magnus
- Titus
- Thora
- Kristiana

James—(Wife #1 Lady Rose Hage, has issue. Wife #2 Asmara ap Cader, has issue)

With Rose

- Ronan
- Isabella

With Asmara (as Blayth)

- Maddoc
- Bowen
- Caius
- Garreth (known as Garr and named after Troy's son, Gareth)

Katheryn (James' twin)—(Married to Sir Alec Hage, has issue)

- Edward
- Axel
- Christoph
- Kieran
- Christian

Evelyn—(Married to Sir Hector de Norville, has issue)

- Atreus
- Hermes
- Lisbet
- Adele
- Aline
- Lesander (goes by Zander)

Baby de Wolfe—(Died same day. Christened Madeleine)

Edward—(Married to Lady Cassiopeia de Norville, has issue)

- Helene
- Phoebe
- Hestia
- Asteria
- Leonidas
- Dorian
- Dayne
- Stephan
- Pallas

Thomas—(Married to Lady Maitland "Mae" de Ryes Bowlin, has issue)

- Artus (adopted)
- Nora (adopted)
- Phin (adopted)
- Marybelle (adopted)
- Renard & Roland (adopted)
- Dyana (adopted)
- Alexander
- Cabot
- Matthew
- Wade
- Tacey
- Morgan

Penelope—(Married to Bhrodi de Shera, Earl of Coventry, hereditary King of Anglesey)

- William
- Perri
- Bowen
- Dai
- Catrin
- Morgana
- Maddock
- Anthea
- Talan

Warrick "War" Herringthorpe (William's illegitimate son with Jane de Percy, born before Scott/Troy)

- Liam "Wolfehound"
- Kyle
- Taggart "Tag"
- Logan
- Brody
- Jane
- Mary
- McCall "Mac"
- Edmund "Teddy"

Holdings and Titles of the House of de Wolfe and Close Allies as of 1300 A.D.

Scott de Wolfe—Earl of Warenton (Heir: William "Will" de Wolfe, Lord Killham)

Troy de Wolfe—Lord Braemoor (Heir: Andreas de Wolfe)

Patrick de Wolfe—Earl of Berwick (Heir: Markus de Wolfe, Lord Ravensdowne)

Blayth (James) de Wolfe—Baron Sydenham (Heir: Ronan de Wolfe)

Edward de Wolfe—Baron Kentmere (Heir: Leonidas de Wolfe)

Thomas de Wolfe—Earl of Northumbria (Heir: Alexander de Wolfe, Lord Easington)

Wark Castle (Wolfe's Eye):

Larger outpost for the Earl of Warenton. Literally sits on the border between England and Scotland.

- Titus de Wolfe (son of Patrick de Wolfe), commander
- Ronan de Wolfe (son of Blayth/James de Wolfe)

Berwick Castle (Wolfe's Teeth):

Massive border castle, strategically important, de Wolfe holding and seat of the Earl of Berwick, Patrick de Wolfe.

- Alec Hage, commander
- Edward "Eddie" Hage, commander
- Hermes de Norville, second

Castle Questing (Wolfe's Heart):

Massive fortress, seat of the Earl of Warenton, Scott de Wolfe.

- Apollo de Norville, second
- Nathaniel Hage
- Owen le Mon

Rule Water Castle (Wolfe's Lair):

The largest outpost in the de Wolfe empire, known as The Lair. Seat of William "Will" de Wolfe, Viscount Kilham, heir apparent to the Earldom of Warenton.

- Magnus de Wolfe, second
- Adonis de Norville, second
- Perri de Shera, son of the Earl of Coventry and Penelope de Wolfe de Shera (squire)

Monteviot Tower (Wolfe's Shield):

Smaller outpost in Scotland, strategic. Holding of Troy de Wolfe.

- Andreas de Wolfe, commander

Kale Water Castle (Wolfe's Den):

Larger outpost on the England side of the border, strategic.

- Troy de Wolfe, Lord Braemoor, commander
- Troy also commands Sibbald's Hold, former home of Red Keith Kerr (his wife's father). A minor property commanded by son Garreth de Wolfe.

Gleann na Fola Castle (Wolfe's Blood) Also known as Bloody Castle

- Gar de Wolfe, Commander
- Reed de Wolfe, second

- Linus de Grey
- Atreus de Norville (on loan from Northwood Castle)

Kyloe Castle (Wolfe's Howl):

Seat of the Earl of Northumbria, Thomas de Wolfe.

- Christoph Hage, second

Roxburgh Castle (Wolfe's Claw—unofficially)*

Large royal-held castle near Kelso, formerly manned by knights from Northwood, but awarded to the House of de Wolfe by royal decree for meritorious service to the Crown. Volatile location, often attacked by Scots, and is manned by both royal and de Wolfe troops.

- Blayth (James) de Wolfe, Lord Sydenham, commander
- Axel Hage, second

*Note: Because of the extremely volatile location and nature of this garrison, Blayth (James) de Wolfe was given the title Lord Sydenham and the Sydenham Barony, a small but strategic barony between Wark Castle and the town of Kelso.

Blackpool Castle (acquired by Scott de Wolfe around 1300 A.D.) known as Wolfe's Strike:

- Thomas "Tor" de Wolfe, commander
- Christian Hage, second

Northwood Castle:

Massive border castle, very important and strategic. Belonging to the Earls of Teviot. Not part of the de Wolfe empire, but strongly allied to de Wolfe by marriage and blood. The Earl of Teviot is John Adrian de Longley, Adam de Longley's eldest son. Adrian's mother is Cayetana Fernanda Teresita Silva y Fausto de Longley, Princess of Aragon.

- Hector de Norville, captain of the guard (also Lord Bowmont)
- Atreus de Norville, second
- Tobias de Bocage, second

Edenburn Tower (House of de Norville):

Smaller tower on the southern end of de Wolfe properties belonging to the House of de Norville. Commanded by Alec Hage.

Castle Canaan (Kendal) Wolfe's Bite:

The Earl of Warenton's southernmost holding, not directly related to the Scottish border but a source of additional troops if needed. Inherited the property when he married the widow of Castle Canaan.

- Stephan du Rennic, commander

Seven Gates Castle (Kendal):

- Seat of Edward de Wolfe's Barony—Kentmere in Kendal that adjoins brother Scott's lands at Castle Canaan
- Isleworth House, Surrey

Cheswick Castle (Northumberland) Wolfe's Roar:

- Seat of Markus de Wolfe, Lord Ravensdowne, heir to Berwick earldom
- Also included in this alliance is Trastamara Castle, home of Markus' stepson, Atlas de Abril (formerly Atlas de Sauque) and wife Caria de Wolfe de Abril

Easington Castle (garrison to Bamburgh)

- Liam Herringthorpe, commander

(not genuinely considered a de Wolfe property, but Liam bears the de Wolfe tattoo because of his de Wolfe blood and is accepted by the family as such)

Kathryn Le Veque Novels

Medieval Romance:

De Wolfe Pack Series:
Warwolfe
The Wolfe
Nighthawk
ShadowWolfe
DarkWolfe
A Joyous de Wolfe Christmas
BlackWolfe
Serpent
A Wolfe Among Dragons
Scorpion
StormWolfe
Dark Destroyer
The Lion of the North
Walls of Babylon
The Best Is Yet To Be
BattleWolfe
Castle of Bones

De Wolfe Pack Generations:
WolfeHeart
WolfeStrike
WolfeSword
WolfeBlade
WolfeLord
WolfeShield
Nevermore
WolfeAx
WolfeBorn
WolfeBite
WolfeHound
WolfeBlood

House of de Norville:
The Best Is Yet To Be
Castle of Bones
Nevermore

The Executioner Knights:
By the Unholy Hand
The Mountain Dark
Starless
A Time of End
Winter of Solace
Lord of the Sky
The Splendid Hour
The Whispering Night
Netherworld
Lord of the Shadows
Of Mortal Fury
'Twas the Executioner Knight
Before Christmas
Crimson Shield
The Black Dragon
God of Vengeance

The de Russe Legacy:
The Falls of Erith
Lord of War: Black Angel
The Iron Knight
Beast
The Dark One: Dark Knight
The White Lord of Wellesbourne
Dark Moon
Dark Steel

A de Russe Christmas Miracle
Dark Warrior

The de Lohr Dynasty:
While Angels Slept
Rise of the Defender
Steelheart
Shadowmoor
Silversword
Spectre of the Sword
Unending Love
Archangel
A Blessed de Lohr Christmas

Sons of de Lohr:
Lion of Twilight
Lion of War
Lion of Hearts
Lion of Steel
Lion of Thunder

The Brothers de Lohr:
The Earl in Winter

Lords of East Anglia:
While Angels Slept
Godspeed
Age of Gods and Mortals

Great Lords of le Bec:
Great Protector

House of de Royans:
Lord of Winter
To the Lady Born
The Centurion

Lords of Eire:
Echoes of Ancient Dreams
Lord of Black Castle
The Darkland

Ancient Kings of Anglecynn:
The Whispering Night
Netherworld

Battle Lords of de Velt:
The Dark Lord
Devil's Dominion
Bay of Fear
The Dark Lord's First Christmas
The Dark Spawn
The Dark Conqueror
The Dark Angel

Reign of the House of de Winter:
Lespada
Swords and Shields

De Reyne Domination:
Guardian of Darkness
The Black Storm
A Cold Wynter's Knight
With Dreams
Master of the Dawn
One Wylde Knight

House of d'Vant:
Tender is the Knight (House of d'Vant)
The Red Fury (House of d'Vant)

The Dragonblade Series:
Fragments of Grace
Dragonblade
Island of Glass
The Savage Curtain
The Fallen One

Great Marcher Lords of de Lara
Lord of the Shadows
Dragonblade

House of St. Hever
Fragments of Grace
Island of Glass
Queen of Lost Stars

Lords of Pembury:
The Savage Curtain

Lords of Thunder: The de Shera Brotherhood Trilogy
The Thunder Lord
The Thunder Warrior
The Thunder Knight

The Great Knights of de Moray:
Shield of Kronos
The Gorgon

The House of De Nerra:
The Promise
The Falls of Erith
Vestiges of Valor
Realm of Angels

Highland Legion:
Highland Born
Highland Destroyer
Highland Slayer

Highland Warriors of Munro:
The Red Lion
Deep Into Darkness

The House of de Garr:
Lord of Light
Realm of Angels

Saxon Lords of Hage:
The Crusader
Kingdom Come

High Warriors of Rohan:
High Warrior
High King

The House of Ashbourne:
Upon a Midnight Dream

The House of D'Aurilliac:
Valiant Chaos

The House of De Dere:
Of Love and Legend

St. John and de Gare Clans:
The Warrior Poet

The House of de Bretagne:
The Questing

The House of Summerlin:
The Legend

The Kingdom of Hendocia:
Kingdom by the Sea

The BlackChurch Guild: Shadow Knights:
The Leviathan
The Protector
The Swordsman
The Tempest
The Avenger

Guard of Six:
Absolution
Insurrection
Obliteration

Regency Historical Romance:
Sin Like Flynn: A Regency Historical Romance Duet
The Sin Commandments
Georgina and the Red Charger

Gothic Regency Romance:
Emma

Historical Fiction:
The Girl Made Of Stars

Contemporary Romance:

Kathlyn Trent/Marcus Burton Series:
Valley of the Shadow
The Eden Factor
Canyon of the Sphinx

The Eagle Brotherhood (under the pen name Kat Le Veque):
The Sunset Hour
The Killing Hour
The Secret Hour
The Unholy Hour
The Burning Hour
The Ancient Hour
The Devil's Hour

Sons of Poseidon:
The Immortal Sea

Pirates of Britannia Series (with Eliza Knight):
Savage of the Sea by Eliza Knight
Leader of Titans by Kathryn Le Veque
The Sea Devil by Eliza Knight
Sea Wolfe by Kathryn Le Veque

<u>**Note:**</u> All Kathryn's novels are designed to be read as stand-alones, although many have cross-over characters or cross-over family groups. Novels that are grouped together have related characters or family groups. You will notice that some series have the same books; that is because they are cross-overs. A hero in one book may be the secondary character in another.

There is NO reading order except by chronology, but even in that case, you can still read the books as stand-alones. No novel is connected to another by a cliff hanger, and every book has an HEA.

Series are clearly marked. All series contain the same characters or family groups except the American Heroes Series, which is an anthology with unrelated characters.

For more information, find it in **A Reader's Guide to the Medieval World of Le Veque**.

About Kathryn Le Veque

Bringing the Medieval to Romance

KATHRYN LE VEQUE is a critically acclaimed, multiple USA TODAY Bestselling author, an Indie Reader bestseller, a charter Amazon All-Star author, and a #1 bestselling, award-winning, multi-published author in Medieval Historical Romance with over 100 published novels.

Kathryn is a multiple award nominee and winner, including the winner of Uncaged Book Reviews Magazine 2017 and 2018 "Raven Award" for Favorite Medieval Romance. Kathryn is also a multiple RONE nominee (InD'Tale Magazine), holding a record for the number of nominations. In 2018, her novel WARWOLFE was the winner in the Romance category of the Book Excellence Award and in 2019, her novel A WOLFE AMONG DRAGONS won the prestigious RONE award for best pre-16th century romance.

Kathryn is considered one of the top Indie authors in the world with over 2M copies in circulation, and her novels have been translated into several languages. Kathryn recently signed with Sourcebooks Casablanca for a Medieval Fight Club series, first published in 2020.

In addition to her own published works, Kathryn is also the President/CEO of Dragonblade Publishing, a boutique publishing house specializing in Historical Romance. Dragonblade's success has seen it rise in the ranks to become Amazon's #1 e-book publisher of Historical Romance (K-Lytics report July 2020).

Kathryn loves to hear from her readers. Please find Kathryn on Facebook at Kathryn Le Veque, Author, or join her on Twitter @kathrynleveque. Sign up for Kathryn's blog at www.kathrynleveque.com for the latest news and sales.